SATYA

SATYA

A NOVEL

SIDDHARTH S. SINHA

PARTRIDGE

A Penguin Random House Company

To order additional copies of this book, contact
Partridge India
000 800 10062 62
orders.india@partridgepublishing.com

www.partridgepublishing.com/india

DEDICATION

*It took me over five years to research on the subject of this book.
During this period, my wife, my children, my siblings
and their families were of great moral support.
I dedicate this book to them for their patience, understanding,
support and encouragement, and most importantly for their
love and affection.*

*I thank my PSA and other members of the team of my
Publishers 'Partridge India' for their support.*

Rukhsar Ahmed

Lahore, Pakistan
Present Day

Zubair Ahmed was alive! Her father was alive! Thirty-one year old Rukhsar Ahmed replaced the handset in the receptacle and slumped in the chair; her large light brown eyes crying with joy. She had a lump in her throat.

Twelve years earlier, her father, Major Zubair Ahmed, of the Northern Light Infantry of the Pakistan Army had disappeared suddenly. A week since his disappearance, Rukhsar had run around Rawalpindi offices of the Pakistan military establishment to find out about her father but her every attempt was stone-walled by the authorities. Over the years, Rukhsar had resigned to her fate; her hopes of ever seeing her father had diminished.

An anonymous three minute phone call by a total stranger from India had stirred her suppressed emotions. *He was alive!* Then, a doubt crept into her mind. Was it true? Was the caller real or was it an investigation of some kind? Rukhsar thought hard about the caller. The caller was authoritative and he was convincing in what he had said. The caller sounded credible.

Rukhsar Ahmed, a Lecturer in economics had returned early from college. She was helping her mother, Shabnam Ahmed prepare lunch when she heard the phone ring. She had casually answered the phone but she was surprised to hear a hard male voice ask her, "Miss Rukhsar Ahmed?"

"Yes. Who are you?"

The caller had spoken softly and slowly, "Miss Rukhsar, I can't give you my name for your own safety," the man said and paused, "I am calling from New Delhi. Kindly listen to me... very carefully." The man spoke with precision and clarity but at slower pace than normal. Though the caller was polite and courteous, his tone had an authority. "I am calling to inform you that your father, Major Zubair Ahmed, is alive and presently being held in an Indian prison as a prisoner of war. If you wish to meet your father and take him back to your country, you will have to come to New Delhi with his identity papers. I am not at liberty to disclose anything further."

Rukhsar was confused. Was it a crank call? Who would play such a cruel joke on her? Could it be the secret services who were trying to explore if she had any clue about her father? How could her father end up in an Indian prison - as a prisoner of war? Since nineteen-seventy-one India and Pakistan had not been at war.

"Zubair will be moved to an undisclosed location within a week. I won't be able to help you once he is shifted. Zubair Ahmed doesn't know that I am speaking to you. It is in his interest that he doesn't know of it now. I will call you back." The caller said and the phone was disconnected.

Rukhsar looked at the phone in her hand and put it back. Her mind was racing. She thought about the conversation and the caller. Both seemed genuine from the tone and intensity of the speech. There was a ring of honesty in the tone of the caller, she thought. She had to decide quickly. Rukhsar was desperate. She wanted her father back with her mother who had virtually lost all senses, and Rukhsar was prepared to take any risk for that. In last twelve years she had received first positive information about her father, if it was true. Rukhsar made up her mind. Precisely twenty seconds later, the phone rang again. Rukhsar picked it up in a hurry. "How do I know you are speaking the truth?" She asked doubtfully.

The caller responded in calm and sincere tone, "You are risking your life by prolonging this conversation. Your phone could be tapped. Anyway, when this conversation is over, I suggest you move to a different, safer location for your own safety. As for your doubts, I speak the truth because I have nothing to gain or lose. My only wish is that Zubair Saheb returns home and re-united with his family. That is my only concern because he is a good human being. Beyond this, I have no interest in the matter. It is entirely up to you if you wish to trust or mistrust me."

Rukhsar thought about something else. "How will my presence in Delhi help my father's release?" The phone went dead again.

Precisely twenty seconds later, the phone rang again. Rukhsar picked it up in a hurry, again.

The man once again spoke slowly, and convincingly. "He has no papers to prove that he is a Pakistani citizen. If you bring the documents to the authorities here, it can prove his identity and then he can be sent home under a prisoner exchange programme."

Rukhsar thought hastily. She trusted the caller, so she took her chance. "I will come to New Delhi but please tell me, why and how did my father end up in an Indian prison? And, how can anyone help me free my father from jail?"

"Your father was taken a prisoner on the Indian side of the Line of Control, by Indian soldiers during the Kargil war. I will help you out in having your father released and sent back home." The caller spoke slowly to ensure Rukhsar heard and understood what was being said, "Be present at the reception of Lok Vijay Hospital in New Delhi on Friday, at nine p.m., I will meet you there."

"How can my father be caught during Kargil war? Pakistan wasn't involved in the war." Rukhsar spoke of her doubt.

3

"I speak the truth, Miss Rukhsar. Each word I have said is an absolute truth and I will prove it when we meet. Yet, to believe me or not is your prerogative."

"I don't have a visa. It will take me time to get it and Indian visa is not easily available." Rukhsar said desperately.

"Don't worry about the visa. Dengue is wide-spread in west-Punjab these days. Over a thousand people cross the border for treatment each day. Use this provision. I will meet you at the hospital at nine pm, sharp. Be there! Have a pleasant journey."

"Who are you, please tell me!" Rukhsar begged.

"I am Zubair's friend... I won't call you again. Have a nice trip." The caller spoke with genuine wish.

"How do I know you speak the truth?"

"That is for you to determine."

"Where is my father now? Is he alright?" She asked.

"He is in good health now." The caller paused and spoke rapidly. "Please don't prolong this conversation. It could be dangerous for you."

"How did my father end up in Indian prison?"

"Later," the caller said and line had gone dead again.

Rukhsar was relieved that her father was alive, but worried because she knew that being held as a *'prisoner of war'* in enemy country must have automatically brought in charges of espionage. He could be tortured mentally and physically. She shivered at the thought and made a decision.

She had other worries too. Since childhood, she had learnt through electronic and print media how Muslims in India were ill-treated; how they were deprived of their rights in a *'democratic and secular'* India. She was a Muslim. She had heard that Muslims had no freedom to practice their faith in *'Hindu'* dominated India. There was discrimination against minorities. She fretted but she was determined. She wanted to get her father back and reunite him with her mother. She was willing to go to any extreme for that. This was the first information in twelve years about Zubair and she was determined to follow the lead even if it meant taking huge risks.

She wondered how she would reach New Delhi by Friday. She would have to apply for her leave from University and she knew it won't be easy; it would be next to impossible to convince the obnoxious Dean who controlled the campus like his personal fiefdom. That apart, she would have to make arrangements for someone to take care of her mother who suffered from mental instability ever since Zubair had gone missing. Though Shabnam Ahmed would object to her trip to an enemy country but she knew she can convince her mother. She calculated quickly. She had to reach by Friday, which left her with about eighty hours to reach Lok Vijay Hospital.

Rukhsar's mother was mentally disturbed. Since Zubair's disappearance she had lost interest in life - or so it seemed. She believed that Zubair had left her for another woman. Rukhsar however, had no such illusions; she knew her father was a patriot, a morally upright man, devoted husband and a doting father. Rukhsar had to be cautious how she broke the news to her mother. If Rukhsar as much as hinted about her decision to go to India, Shabnam would create a scene. So, she had to handle it delicately. Nervously, she spoke to her mother. She broke the news of Zubair possibly being alive but spelled her doubts about the authenticity of the caller. To Rukhsar's amazement, when she informed Shabnam of her decision to go to India, Shabnam only asked her to be cautious.

Rukhsar made preparations for her trip but decided against informing any of her colleagues or friends barring two; first, her cousin who would call upon Shabnam in Rukhsar's absence, and a Pakistani diplomat currently stationed in Tehran, Iran - Aman Khan Bux.

Barring her family, Aman Khan Bux was the only person Rukhsar cared for. She was the love in Aman's life. Though it was one sided, Rukhsar always respected Aman's emotions for her and considered Aman Bux as her confidante and best friend. She liked him immensely but she wasn't sure if she loved him; but she did acknowledge Aman as a genuine pearl in her life.

A few months before Zubair's disappearance, Aman had met Rukhsar at a party where she had accompanied her parents. The moment he saw her he was keen to know her, about her. The tall beautiful, slim and elegant, moon faced girl with smiling, large, deep, light brown eyes had smitten him. He gladly learnt that she was as intelligent as she was beautiful. She was a meritorious, first year college student of Economics at the coveted LUMS - Lahore University of Management Studies.

Rukhsar had liked the young, handsome bureaucrat who had just been offered a job by the External Affairs Ministry, for his brilliance. She had especially liked the way he had treated her - like a princess. She had enjoyed his attention and his physical presence. Aman was tall but his slim body and dress code made him appear even taller. Combined with sharp nose and smiling eyes and innocent smile, he had made a decent impression on her. The only factor which went against him was his age. He was twenty-nine years old to her nineteen years. That casual meeting had led to a bonding between them which grew stronger as time passed, and led to marriage proposal by Aman's family, despite initial hesitancy about the different sects the two families belonged to. Rukhsar was a Qadiyani, a sect of Muslims which had been declared 'Non-Muslim' in Pakistan decades ago. This was a major issue with Aman's mother although his father had no qualms. Aman's mother had relented when Aman had declared that he would only marry Rukhsar or he would die a bachelor. The proposal was gladly accepted by Rukhsar's parents. Their wedding was planned for winter of nineteen ninety-nine but it was suspended when Zubair was called to war duty though he was on a four week leave. After

Zubair's disappearance, the couple had agreed to wait till Zubair returned. After twelve years of resistance, a month ago, reluctantly, Rukhsar agreed to a marriage date Aman Khan had proposed. Their wedding date was eight weeks away when this strange phone call had come. Now, suddenly, owing to the information provided during the conversation... based on one telephonic conversation she was setting out on a journey of uncertainties, with no surety of the outcome of her adventure.

- - -

Rukhsar informed Aman of her decision via text message of her India trip. He called her promptly. For an hour he tried convincing her to investigate further before taking a drastic step but he failed. She was desperate to follow the sole lead she had, and he knew he couldn't change her mind. Aman told her to wait till he reached Lahore. He didn't tell her that he would accompany her. He couldn't let her travel to India alone. On Thursday morning he arrived at her house ready for the trip. An hour later the couple were on their way to the Wagah Border. Six hours later they set foot on Indian soil. A journey of past legacies, uncovering of lies, and discoveries of truth and tragedies had begun... a trip which was to cost lives.

* * *

The General's House,

Lahore, Pakistan

The sixty-one year old pre-maturely retired General, who was once in line to become the next Commander-in-Chief of the Pakistan Army held a one page secret report in his hands. He was appalled. This wasn't supposed to happen. If the information was true it could spell disaster for his plans. He had to act fast. The retired General tried to move his electric wheel chair but it wouldn't budge. Not again, he cursed himself. How can he forget to charge the batteries of his wheel chair? He slammed his fist into his motionless and insensitive thighs. If it wasn't for this stupid handicap he would have been the Commander-in-Chief, and won't have to rely on his devoted and trusted nephew for the success of his plan. The General read the report again, folded it and put it in his pocket. He called his nurse who had been instructed to be with him at all times. The crippled ex-General's General nephew had ensured that his uncle got the best treatment and was kept in total comfort. A young, pretty nurse appeared by his side. She saw him struggle to move his wheel chair and wheeled him towards the work desk.

the door. The snake eyed General Wahid Khan came to her room after visiting his uncle in privacy, and made her an offer. She could earn more money if she kept him happy. Mariam was aware of the snake eyed General's intentions and she hated it. She had offered to resign. Four days later it was accepted in general by the doctor who was attending to the crippled General but asked her to continue till they found a suitable nurse as her replacement. She had agreed. Three days later, Wahid Khan had locked his snake eyes into hers and given her an option. She would get twice as much as she made now and do as he said or she would be fired from the job and he would ensure she never got a job anywhere else in the country. He would ensure her passport was impounded and she would never be able to leave the country; just in case if she ever entertained ideas of going abroad to work. Mariam had begged Wahid Khan to spare her but he had no mercy. He had slapped her six times forcing her into submission. Then he had forced himself on her that day and spent the night with her doing as he pleased. Before leaving he had warned that he would make her family disappear if she ever complained to anyone... or if she thought of resigning.

· From that night onwards, General Wahid Khan would come, sit and discuss in privacy with his crippled uncle and then he would come to her and satisfy himself, taking sadistic pleasure in forcing himself on her. He would return every week. If she hated the crippled General in the wheel chair, she found hatred a soft emotion for the snake eyed General. The only factor which helped retain her sanity was that she was indeed very well paid and that helped her to provide for her siblings' studies and look after her retired father and ailing mother.

The other bright spot in her life was a young Lieutenant who would come to deliver and collect sealed envelopes and verbal messages for the crippled General from his nephew. She had liked the dedicated young man and she knew he liked her too; very much. She would offer him snacks and tea as usual and they would talk for as long as time permitted the young soldier. She learnt from him that General Wahid Khan was planning something massive, even audacious. Although the Lieutenant knew very little about the plan yet he refused to tell her the General's plan because he was sworn to secrecy. Though the Lieutenant didn't particularly like the snake eyed General or the cripple, he was devoted to his country which stopped him from speaking of the two Generals' plans. For his country's sake he wanted the two Generals' plans to succeed. If so, it would ensure Pakistan's security for generations.

A few months passed and their fondness grew for each other. One late evening when the crippled General was in severe pain, she had injected a dose of painkillers into his vein and put him to sleep. Before midnight the same evening, the young Lieutenant had come hurriedly wanting to meet the General in wheel chair. When she told him of the General's physical condition, the Lieutenant was upset. He called General Wahid Khan and apprised him of his uncle's condition. Wahid Khan asked the Lieutenant to wait till the cripple woke up. He 'had to' deliver the message and get his advice and return to Rawalpindi to deliver the message in person to Wahid Khan. Frustrated, the Lieutenant waited in the lounge till Mariam invited him for tea. They talked for some time during which she learnt, not to her surprise, that Wahid Khan considered her his personal property and he boasted about it. Wahid Khan had chosen her for her knowledge and efficiency in her work, and for her curves, her stunning good looks, and of her desperate financial situation. Wahid Khan had picked her for himself. Though she had a gut feeling about it, she was infuriated when she heard it from the Lieutenant. She thought, and invited him to her room and confessed her liking for him. She told him she wasn't sure if she loved him but she liked him immensely. Egged by her confession, the Lieutenant confessed his love for her but feared Wahid Khan's wrath if he ever came to learn of it. Mariam and Lieutenant decided to keep it a secret. She wasn't the personal property of that evil man, she told him. She was a woman of intellect and she chose Wahid Khan's assistant as her choice to avenge the snake eyed General, and some day she would get a chance to tell him that she had chosen to offer herself to the Lieutenant because the General was impotent. Mariam Zahir didn't wish for the General's death; that would be easy for him. She wanted him to suffer more than the crippled General; suffer for the rest of his life. She would go to any extent to see Wahid Khan suffer physical and mental ignominy, and hurt his ego.

That night Mariam seduced the young Lieutenant and offered herself to him. The young Lieutenant surrendered himself to her: physically and emotionally. From that day, the Lieutenant took up any assignment from Wahid Khan which got him closer to Mariam. On the other hand, Wahid Khan was delighted to have got a man he could trust immensely.

The crippled General pulled out the single sheet report and fumed again. He sent a message on a secured channel. Wahid Khan called back immediately.

"I have important instructions for you. Send the Lieutenant to fetch it and do exactly as I say or else you could be in trouble. Follow my instructions precisely... to the last letter," the crippled General ordered angrily in one breath and disconnected the call.

The General closed his eyes and cursed his luck. All his plans would come to nought if Zubair Ahmed learns of the dreadful order by Wahid Khan on that ill-fated day during the Kargil war. Rukhsar shouldn't be allowed to meet her father. If she or Zubair learn of Wahid Khan's role they would create a problem which could make his trusted soldiers revolt against him and Wahid Khan. That was not acceptable in any circumstance. The father-daughter duo had to be stopped from learning the truth; if they learn the truth, they had to be eliminated. He wheeled himself to a table three feet away, pulled out his stationary and wrote, *'Rukhsar Ahmed received three calls from untraceable number in India. She is going to India. Is Zubair Ahmed alive? Check. If true, eliminate all. Take no chances.'* The General folded the sheet, put it in an envelope and sealed it. He couldn't send this message over the phone or instruct orally. This instruction was to be hand delivered in person by the young Lieutenant to Wahid Khan.

- - -

The young Lieutenant arrived thirty minutes later. A special order was issued that the message should be guarded with his life. When he was told that the message was of extreme urgency the Lieutenant left promptly.

The Lieutenant returned to the crippled ex-General later that evening. "An assignment has been given to me, Sir," the young man said and told him about the assignment.

The crippled ex-General nodded in appreciation. "Don't be lax on this matter. In no way we can let these people discover about an incident. Wahid trusts you and so do I. Execute it well and you will have a very bright future, I promise you."

The Lieutenant assured the ex-General he won't fail, and left. He closed the door behind him and walked out of the room. Mariam was waiting for him. She grabbed his hand and drew him to her room.

"Why do you look sad?" she asked.

"I am going to India on a mission. It is of utmost urgency. If things don't go according to plan, we may never see each other again," the Lieutenant replied with little clue to his emotional intensity of the moment.

"Is it life threatening?" she asked with an unknown fear in her heart.

"Yes, it is. Either I will live, or those two traitors of the country," he replied.

Mariam Zahir held his face in her palms. A realization struck her. She really loved this man. "Come back to me. I beg you. Please take care of yourself and come back to me."

The Lieutenant saw the love for him in her eyes. He had never seen that before. Today she had confessed her love for him. For the Lieutenant it was a dream come true. He knew she loved him but he wanted her to realize it and then he wanted to hear it from her. He cupped her face in his palms and kissed her, "I promise to do my best. When I return I will get you out of this mess. This assignment is important, my dear. Just hold on till I return. Then I will work out something for our future... this I promise you, my dearest."

"That's a hostile country for Muslims. Please take good care of yourself, Altaf."

"I will," the young Lieutenant Altaf Khos said and kissed her.

* * *

INDIA

Haqeeqat -Reality-

"Whatever sphere of human mind you may select for your special study, Whether it is language or religion, mythology or philosophy, Whether it is law or customs, primitive art or science, you have to come to India, Because some of the most valuable and constructive material of the history of man are treasured up in India, and India only."

~US President Barak Obama, quoting a Western Scholar during his trip to India~

Aman Bux and Rukhsar boarded a cab from Wagah border to Amritsar railway station, and then an overnight train from Amritsar to New Delhi. At dawn on Friday morning the couple reached New Delhi and lodged into a hotel near the hospital where they were to meet a total stranger who would lead them to Zubair Ahmed. Through the day Aman forced Rukhsar to stay in the hotel room and rest. He used his contacts to discreetly find out as much as he could about the whereabouts of Zubair Ahmed. He had got no information though he sought the help of the Pakistan High Commission.

For Rukhsar, this trip was to start with a series of surprises before other major shocks which she was to experience. The first surprise of the trip to this 'hostile' neighbouring country came within an hour. She was truly surprised. She saw no visible hostility or even a hint of it when the couple produced their Pakistani passports at the hotel reception. Instead, to her surprise, she found a warm smile on the face of the receptionist. The courtesy extended to them thereafter was even more surprising when she saw the hotel staff extend the courtesy to their guests from Pakistan. It gave her an impression that they were privileged guests, and throughout the day they received special attention. In the afternoon, when Aman enquired if he could get Punjabi food, the manager quietly asked them to avoid hotel food and go to Jama Masjid area for typical Delhi delights.

When they reached Jama Masjid, they, especially Rukhsar, was jolted by a major shock when she saw a massive congregation of Muslims in hundreds offering customary Friday afternoon *'Namaaz'* at the historical mosque - praying freely and without fear. She reflected on what she had learnt over the years in her country that Muslims were not allowed to freely practice their faith in this country. Within hours this was the second major jolt she had received which belied her earlier perception.

While searching for 'good' restaurant, they found them all over the place and especially the *'Paranthae wali gali'*, which she liked most. Surprised by what she had seen so far, her earlier perceptions were eroding quickly, too quickly for her own sake. Although her mind was pre-occupied by the meeting that evening in the hospital, she wanted to explore more - this was more to do with avoiding her anxiety than to do with exploration on subject of Humanities. As they walked through the food street, they found another surprise awaiting them; they found Hindus, Sikhs, Muslims and surprisingly, numerous foreign tourists, all enjoying the delicacies of the famous North Indian *'Mughlai'* food in the restaurants and on the street-side. They found no discrimination or animosity, nor any negativity or hesitation among people milling in the atmosphere. It was a strange experience; they felt absolutely safe, like they were in their own backyard. They could smell the aroma of life in the air. While Aman was calm about the discoveries, it disturbed Rukhsar. She was seeing exactly the opposite of what she had studied and learnt about India. The series of shocks had confused her. Though she liked what she saw, she was disappointed because somewhere in her heart she hated India for being intolerant and aggressive towards Muslims and especially towards Pakistan. Now that she had seen the contradiction her hatred was subsiding; and it was gradually being replaced by respect for India and its people. She looked at Aman Bux and found him pre-occupied with himself - probably wondering about the meeting later in the evening, or he was probably thinking the same. It occurred to her that they never talked about his work or about what or how he felt about Pakistan's arch enemy - India! When she asked Aman about what he felt about visiting India, Aman had smiled lightly without making a comment. The smile told her something else; he knew the real situation. They felt like they were home. This was like Lahore, Pakistan, of early forties! This was New Delhi, India, of today!

- - -

They reached an hour early as they got off an auto rickshaw and walked towards the main gate of The Lok Vijay Hospital. Enquiries led them towards a special ward of the hospital exclusively for foreign patients. When they entered the lobby, the first scene truly shocked them into silence. The lobby was teeming with people - patients, their relatives and friends; almost all were Pakistani citizen. This was the greatest shock so far. Where was the reality of the stories about anti-Muslim sentiment in India? She didn't find it here. Instead, she found the doctors and hospital staff taking care of each patient, and attending to them professionally, with courtesy, although the sheer volume of patients was phenomenal. She was stunned - fifteen hundred patients arrived at this hospital alone each day, for treatment of Dengue. Though Dengue had reached epidemic proportions in the Punjab province of Pakistan during monsoon, patients were still travelling across the border for treatment. She was wondering why this story wasn't told to the people of Pakistan? Where was the propaganda machine? Where was the media?

- - -

In the hospital lobby a plump burqa clad lady in forties looked at the photographs in her hand and saw them enter the hospital gates. She called the man who had asked her to keep an eye for them. She was told to keep their track till he arrived. In a few minutes and her job would be done. Not a bad thing to get five thousand Rupees for few hours of sitting and observing faces, she thought.

- - -

Rukhsar checked her watch nervously and turned to look at Aman for moral support. He smiled at her without displaying his own anxiety. He sensed her nervousness and gripped her palm firmly. He looked at the crowd in the lobby and tried to pick a pair of eyes which could be watching them. He didn't expect anyone to observe them but didn't see a pair of eyes observing them from the safety of veils. A nurse approached and asked Rukhsar for her name and asked them to follow her. They followed her in the elevator to the fourth floor. They came out of the lift and the nurse turned right, walked to the last room on the floor, knocked on the door and turned the knob to open the door. When the door opened she nodded at the visitors to go in. When the visitors entered the room, the nurse turned around, closed the door and left. The room was a makeshift arrangement for the meeting. It seemed like the room was probably being furbished to make it into a special ward of the hospital.

As they entered the room their nervousness and anxiety evaporated when their eyes fell on the man they were to meet. The tall, well groomed man probably in his late thirties or early forties stood at the far end of the large room. The sheer presence of the man had a calming effect on both the visitors. The man with very fair skin and light grey eyes had a magnetic presence and the hint of a smile on his lips was good enough to restore their confidence. The man greeted them with a 'Namaste', and stepped forward to welcome them. They saw him and instantly their nervousness and anxiety evaporated. They sensed an inherent honesty in the man.

Rukhsar wondered if he was Hindu or Muslim or even a Caucasian going by the texture of his skin. When the man spoke she was sure he was Indian because his pronunciation and dialect in Hindi and Urdu was perfect. The man spoke with a reserved, if not an uncomfortable smile, and greeted Rukhsar with a bow of his head and shook hands with Aman, offered them to sit, and introduced himself. "I am Prakash Rohatgi. At the moment, that's all I can tell you," he said and turned to look at Rukhsar. "I didn't give you my name over the phone because I feared your phone could be tapped. Thank you for coming… and for trusting me." Prakash Rohatgi's smile turned from reserved to a happy one.

"What about Mr. Zubair Ahmed. Where is he?" Aman asked.

"You haven't introduced yourself. Who are you?" Prakash shot back in his clear toned deep throated voice.

"I am Aman Khan Bux, a friend of Rukhsar, and we will be married soon." Aman responded politely.

Prakash Rohatgi looked at the couple and smiled broadly and sat on the chair opposite them, "I'm happy for both of you, Mr. Bux. What do you do for a living?" he asked casually.

Aman hesitated for an instant. He knew that if he spoke the truth, it could lead to a problem in this situation. But if he lied, it could be detrimental to the purpose of their visit to this country. "Mr. Rohatgi, I was a diplomat for the Government of Pakistan until the day before yesterday, stationed in Tehran as a Cultural Attaché. I have resigned, and now I am a civilian."

"What?" Rukhsar screamed in shock.

"What?" Prakash shouted in disbelief and anger.

Aman was silent. He was unsure whom he should first respond to. He looked at his fiancé apologetically, "I will talk to you later on this," he said and turned to Prakash Rohatgi, "Mr. Rohatgi, Rukhsar is my love... She is my life. For her I can travel to hell without a second thought. I understand why you are angry. A diplomat from an unfriendly country in a scenario such as this is unacceptable. Please trust me; I came here because I couldn't let Rukhsar travel alone. She is the only reason for my presence here. Her search for her father is mine as well and having met you, I know that we are on the right track. Please trust me, Mr. Rohatgi," Aman said with a touch of appeasement to ease the tension in the atmosphere which had suddenly crept in.

Prakash quietly observed the man sitting in front of him. He was deciding if he should trust the visitor or not.

Aman assessed the situation correctly. "Mr. Rohatgi, for your confidence I am willing to hand over something which I would never part with," he said and pulled out his diplomatic passport and stretched his hand towards Prakash. "You keep this in your possession till we are in India, and hand it back when I leave."

Rohatgi laughed wryly as he checked the passport. "Who are we kidding, Mr... Aman Khan Bux? You entered India on the side? Your passport doesn't have an entry stamp here," he asked.

"I didn't wish to use my diplomatic passport because it may show my movements. Since I am not a diplomat anymore, I have no reason to use it. I showed my temporary travel papers I have procured especially for this trip."

Prakash nodded his head in understanding, "You see what I mean? You came here on temporary document that you can avail easily in an hour from your mission here. You go to the High Commission and state that your passport was stolen and you get another one in an hour. Mr. Bux, your passport in my hand is of no value, but there is something else which has more value... your word!"

Aman Bux nodded in acceptance. "I want an assurance from you that you will take care of Rukhsar. If so, I will give you her passport too. I think that will instil some confidence in you?" he proposed.

Prakash Rohatgi looked at the smart diplomat for some time and he nodded slightly with a smile, "Okay, Mr. Bux. I will gamble on you. I will trust your word. However," Rohatgi said in earnest with a stern expression, "if you don't keep your part of the deal, I will make you regret it for the rest of your life... I am not threatening you, Mr. Aman Bux. I am stating a brutal truth."

Rukhsar felt a chill in her spine. She had no doubt that Prakash was speaking the truth. She looked at Aman and the two men were staring at each other.

Prakash waited for some comment or response from either Aman Bux or Rukhsar. When neither spoke, he continued, "As for my part, I promise to speak the truth and nothing but the truth... And, some of it is going to be difficult for you and more so for her to accept," Prakash said and pointed his finger at Rukhsar. "If I do not speak or reply to any question it will be my prerogative and you will not press me for it since I don't wish to lie to either of you. Having said that, you will have to understand that what I am about to tell you is strictly between the three of us. Furthermore, I want you to see it from a practical viewpoint."

"I don't understand. Can you please be clearer?" Aman had a good idea that Prakash was about to disclose something more complex than the present situated suggested.

Prakash pulled out an envelope from the desk drawer and pushed it towards the couple. Rukhsar grabbed it hurriedly and opened the enveloped. Another shock awaited Rukhsar and Aman; the biggest one yet. It numbed their nerves. The envelope contained six photographs. Rukhsar saw her father in each of those; at different places with various people. Apart from Zubair, there was another common factor in these photographs. This was the reason why the six photographs had been chosen. Rukhsar tried to keep the photographs away from visual periphery of Aman, but didn't succeed. Aman Bux saw the photographs with a fleecing glance and then focused on them again to be sure what he had seen. Zubair Ahmed was proudly waving the Indian tricolour in each of the six photographs. The shock was visible on both their faces. The expression on their faces was not lost on the host.

It took a few minutes for both the Pakistani visitors to come to terms with what they had just seen. Rukhsar couldn't accept what she had seen. "This is impossible... impossible. My father is a patriotic, diehard Pakistani. He would die before he would defect," she tried to shout but the words were a whisper as she came to terms with reality. Involuntarily, her voice boomed in the room. She shouted angrily, "This isn't true!"

Aman put his arm around her to calm her. It did not work. Rukhsar kept looking at each photograph carefully to see if she could find something which wasn't true. She couldn't find any.

The visitors realized that Prakash Rohatgi had access to Zubair Ahmed, and the other relief they found in their minds and hearts was that Zubair was alive... and well. Aman took the photographs and scanned the photographs slowly to be sure those weren't fake, or morphed. He put them back in the envelope knowing these were original although he knew he wasn't an expert in identifying forgery. He turned to look at Prakash.

Prakash was observing them carefully. He was ready for the reaction to the photographs he had just shown to his visitors. It saved unnecessary explanations and convincing. He knew questions would be coming and he had the answers to each. He wanted the conversations to be prolonged and elaborate. That was the purpose of inviting Rukhsar to India. He changed the topic to surprise his guests. It would give them time to adjust to the reality. "Can I ask both of you to join me for dinner?"

The couple was taken by surprise. They were unsure how to respond. Prakash assumed command and led his guests to his car.

An hour and twenty minutes later, Prakash Rohatgi pulled the car in a large compound of an old, well maintained farmhouse. He opened the gates with a remote control device and drove into a lengthy driveway till the car stopped in front of a modest looking door. He looked at his guests and saw apprehensions on their faces. He smiled, "You have nothing to worry about. You have my word that you are safe here."

Rukhsar and Aman looked at each other; for some reason it was evident that they both trusted Prakash Rohatgi. Aman Bux nodded at Prakash and led Rukhsar out of the car and followed Prakash into the house.

"What area is this?" Aman asked Prakash casually.

"Technically, it is in the National Capital Region, NCR, as it is called, otherwise it is in the district of Ghaziabad in the state of Uttar Pradesh. This is my farmhouse; also my residence and work place."

- - -

A young man in his late twenties had replaced the burqa-clad woman for the nightshift. He had been ordered to keep track of the movements of Aman Khan & Rukhsar, and follow them, and report back. The young man saw the Pakistani couple and a stranger drive away in the car. The tall, well-built man ran to his car and followed them. He could not afford to miss them. Lieutenant Altaf Khos did not wish to fail his General.

- - - -

Prakash unlocked the door and guided the couple into the house. "I have a reason for bringing you people here. There must be many questions in your minds. This is where you will get answers to all your questions," he said and escorted them into a huge lounge, which is called 'hall' or 'drawing room' in India. The lounge was sparsely decorated, with minimum furnishings but it had a strange look because the walls on three sides were lined with books; it looked more like a library than a residence. Prakash Rohatgi did his best to shake Rukhsar out of her disbelief but failed; Aman, however, seemed to have done pretty well.

A totally confused Rukhsar was still holding Aman's hand. She was unwilling to accept Prakash Rohatgi's version that her father, who swore by his country, and followed the legacy of the family of joining the armed forces could ever defect, especially to the arch enemy. She looked at Aman Khan's hands clasping hers, giving her comfort and even solace, if that was possible. "Impossible! My father is not a traitor, or a defector, no matter what the situation," she said loudly more to herself than to the two men in the room.

Both men understood her feelings. Before Aman could speak Prakash Rohatgi intervened, "Miss Rukhsar Ahmed, you should have something to eat before we talk about this. When you hear what I have to say, and why I have invited you, I am sure you won't be as distraught as you are. Instead, you will appreciate his situation. Please bear with me for some time."

Prakash Rohatgi asked his maid to serve dinner. During the meal he shot down any attempt on conversation about Zubair.

After dinner he led his guests to one of the rooms which opened into the lounge. This room was a contrast to the lounge or the rest of the house. It was a big room; forty feet wide, sixteen feet long and twelve feet high. The room was fully equipped with ultramodern devices and lined with books on two sides of the walls, from ceiling to floor, and from wall to wall, except the walls on the other two sides of the room. Next to the door frame, there was a bank of television sets lining the length and breadth of that wall. In the centre of the room was a desk with a large computer monitor, a keyboard and computer peripherals. On the floor there were four chairs and six stools and two tables on either ends of the room. This was Prakash Rohatgi's work-station.

Aman had never seen an intelligence room set-up but he knew it had to be as sophisticated as this or else it would be obsolete if not redundant. Aman Bux realized that Prakash Rohatgi was not an ordinary citizen; he was an extremely powerful man. For him and Rukhsar Prakash was a mystery, and the organization he worked for. "Are you an intelligence officer?" he asked his host.

A loud, roaring laughter came from Prakash and it surprised both his guests. "Not factually! But that isn't important at the moment. You will learn the truth eventually."

"Where is my father?" Rukhsar demanded.

"He isn't here right now but you will meet him soon, I hope. However, there are some pre-conditions which cannot be avoided." Prakash stated clearly.

"Why is he a prisoner? Why does he work for the Indians?" Rukhsar threw the volley of questions which were worrying her from the moment she had seen the photographs.

Prakash observed both his guests as if he was trying to find a clue to something. After a few seconds of silence, he leaned back in his chair and began, "Rukhsar, allow me to call the two of you by your first names. You please call me Prakash. We are in the same age group so it will help if we are not formal. Let me begin by stating this very categorically. I will be speaking only the truth and nothing else. I said that earlier and I re-iterate it. I will be happy if you two can also be as truthful as me. I say this because if we aren't honest with ourselves, we can't find solution to your problems, Rukhsar." Prakash paused to let his words sink into his guests. After a few seconds, he continued, "How did he become an Indian prisoner? Well, he became an Indian prisoner because your country does not accept that he is a Pakistani. They refused to take his dead body from the heights of Kargil."

"Dead Body?" Rukhsar screamed in horror. "You said he was alive. You showed me his recent photographs." Rukhsar rose to her feet in anger. "I don't trust you. You said he was taken from Kargil. My father was not in Kargil. He is not a Kashmiri. Kargil war was fought between the *Kashmiri Mujahids* and the Indian army. I don't believe you."

Prakash began to reply but stopped when Aman raised his arm in his direction asking him to wait and turned to Rukhsar, "Dear, that is not factually correct. We had a…"

Prakash interrupted Aman, "Let me speak, Aman," he said and turned to Rukhsar. "I said your country did not accept the dead body of your father. That is true. It is also true that your father is alive. If this sounds like contradiction, let me explain. Your father was grievously injured when Indian soldiers found him at a hill which they had retaken during the Kargil war. They presumed he was dead, along with dozens others found as the Indian army kept retaking its posts. The fact is, Zubair Ahmed was unconscious and had virtually no pulse. So he was taken to a military hospital where it was discovered that he had slipped into coma. For six weeks he was in that state. Within this span, in our official records, on the front, he was notified as dead. When communication lines opened between the two warring sides, Pakistan army refused to accept any bodies which the Indian army had found. The Pak army couldn't accept them because right from the first day of the war, the Pakistan government and military establishment had maintained that the people occupying the Kargil heights were *Kashmiri Mujahids* and not regular soldiers of Pakistan army. Rukhsar, there wasn't a single *Mujahid* involved in the war. All men were regulars of the Pakistan army," Prakash said and waited for the information to sink into his visitors. "You asked why your father was in Indian prison. He was a prisoner of war. Even in coma, he was in Indian custody. When he came out of coma, he was formally arrested. This leads to the reply to your next question; why is he working with us? Put yourself in his shoes - both of you. What will you do if you have no country to live in? What will you do if you have willingly, almost laid down your life for it and then you find out that your country isn't willing to take back your body, or the bodies of your colleagues? What will you do if you realize that your country has left you to rot in jail of another country as a prisoner of war, fully aware that he is your national? What will you do when your country denies you the right to live in your own country? What will you do when you know that you have no future except a life in jail? You have no right in foreign land, no freedom, more so if you are a prisoner of war. You have no nationality, no rights, no family, no friends, and no future and... No life! What will you do?" Prakash roared angrily.

The ex-diplomat knew it all too well even before Prakash had said it. He looked at Rukhsar, and she was close to tears. Prakash saw the beautiful lady cry out her soul without shedding a tear. He felt sorry for her.

"I don't believe it. Kargil war was not an Indo-Pak war. It was a fight between the Kashmiri freedom fighters and the Indian army. Then how can my father be a participant in that war?" Rukhsar asked angrily.

Prakash shook his head in disappointment. He rose silently and brewed coffee for all three. While they were sipping coffee, Prakash walked to the bank of television monitors and turned on the set on extreme left. He put the screen on 'pause' and turned to Rukhsar. "This is a compilation of stills of newspaper articles, debates, discussions, press conferences, video clippings, press releases, and media briefings by politicians and military men, interviews of soldiers and some other information. These were gathered and compiled from electronic and print media around the world. The one common factor is the Kargil war. After you have seen this I will give you a brief. You may find a lot of information here which will be disturbing, but true, since you do not believe that Kargil was a war between Pakistan and India. Every information in these clippings and press notices or briefs are absolutely true. Kindly watch carefully," he said and pressed the 'play' button.

Rukhsar Ahmed looked at Prakash Rohatgi with disbelief but she knew in her heart that this man wasn't a liar. She glanced at Aman Khan and found him staring at Prakash. The two men seemed to know what was going on.

She turned her attention to the television monitor as the first clipping started to roll.

* * *

OPERATION VIJAY

KARGIL WAR: (May-July, 1999)
Kargil, Batalik and Drass Sector, Jammu & Kashmir, India

The television kept the two Pakistani guests interested for a little over three hours. They were watching news from across the world exclusively on the subject of Kargil conflict. When it was over, a moan escaped Rukhsar's mouth. This was the biggest of all shocks she had experienced in last twenty-four hours; second only to the news of her father working for the Indians.

There was silence in the room. It was past two in the morning but none was willing to move. Each had an agenda.

Prakash served another round of coffee and turned off the monitor. "I want you to learn the truth before you meet your father. I have a vested interest in this. You saw the reports from across the globe. I will tell you the Kargil story in brief. It is vital that you know, because, after you know the truth, and some more of what I have to say, you will have to make a decision which has to be your own. A lot of things depend on your decision, Miss Rukhsar, including... meeting Mr. Zubair Ahmed."

"A lot of things? Like what?" Rukhsar asked curiously.

"Later! Now, the brief! Aman, do you know that the Kargil action plan had been in the files for a long time? It was presented to your ex-Prime Minister Benazir Bhutto, but she and her advisors - military and civilian, turned it down calling it *'impractical'* and *'unviable'*. But some in the ranks never gave up the idea. The Pakistan army had formulated this plan to avenge the loss of Siachen Glaciers, which the Indian army had taken over by launching *'Operation Meghdoot'* in 1984. Ever since, this poor copy of *'Operation Meghdoot'* was formulated as the Kargil plan, some army generals had tried to convince the superiors, civilian, military and religious leaders including General Karamat who preceded Pervez Musharraf. When General Karamat saw the plan, he had junked it. Though the Kargil plan was termed *'strategically unacceptable'* plan a few times, some generals kept re-visiting the plan, but didn't succeed. When Pervez Musharraf was made..."

"Why would India or Pakistan go to war for Siachen? Is it so important? I have read Zia Ul-Haq's statement somewhere that 'not a blade of grass grows in that area'. Why then, have there been people dying for it?" Rukhsar enquired.

"There are various aspects to it. That is true in a way that even a grass doesn't grow because even during summers the temperatures are below freezing and during winters the temperatures plummet to minus fifty degrees Celsius and lower. It is of utmost importance to India because the Siachen glacier overlooks the Aksai Chin area which China annexed from India during the 1962 Indo-Sino war. The other important aspect is that the Siachen glacier feeds the tributaries which run into Indus River. The Indus River feeds the world's largest cultivated farmlands with a water flow of over two hundred billion cubic metres, annually. That alone is a very good reason why both, India and Pakistan want to control the Siachen glaciers."

"So, India did take away Siachen from Pakistan." Rukhsar responded with sarcasm.

Prakash Rohatgi ignored her sarcasm. "Not really! Siachen was a no-man's land until the Indian troops set up their camp. It is true though, that all expedition to peaks like NJ9842, in that region, sought permission from the Pakistan Government because the natural routes to those hills were through Pakistan occupied areas. However, the Siachen glacier itself was a no man's land. When the Pak Government gave permission to Japanese and some other expeditions it worried the Indian Government because if Pakistan gave the expeditions regular permissions, it would lead to Pakistan laying claims, and being acknowledged as having territorial rights to the glacier. The Indian army took a decision and moved to Siachen glacier. The Pakistan military had planned a similar operation to take over Siachen heights but they were late by about a fortnight. It was a matter of who got there first. The Indian army did. Both countries were in armed conflict for many days but Pakistan army was unable to remove the Indians from that glacier. When they were sure they couldn't win, General Zia gave that statement about not a grass growing there. It was a face-saving statement; to save him from embarrassment."

Rukhsar Ahmed nodded her head while Aman Khan Bux looked at Prakash Rohatgi blankly. He knew the importance.

"Anyway," Prakash continued, "let me return to the topic of the Kargil war. When Pervez Musharraf was promoted by PM Nawaz Sharif, he immediately looked at the Kargil plan. The plan had been re-worked by two senior army officers: General Tariq Aziz and Major General Javed Hassan. They presented their plan to Pervez Musharraf who for some weird reason approved their action plan. One more general was taken on board: General Mehmood. These four men planned and executed the entire operation," Prakash said and sipped his coffee. He was waiting for a reaction from his guests. When he didn't get any verbal reaction, he continued, "Going with the plan, army men were sent across the border to check out the Indian posts. They returned and reported that the Indian soldiers, as was the standard norm during winters, had left the posts and descended to the lower hills and plains, and there was no one guarding the posts. During winters, it was a practice by both sides across the 'Line of Control', the LOC. The Pakistani soldiers were told to cross the LOC and occupy the vacant Indian posts, knowing that the Indians won't be back till end June, at the earliest. The Pakistani army had seven months to entrench itself. That is what it did."

His brief was interrupted by a phone call. Prakash picked the cell phone and heard the caller. In the one minute call, he just said two words, "Yes" and "Thanks."

He looked at his visitors. "I have to attend to something important. Kindly wait here and don't touch anything," he said and stormed out of the room without waiting for their reply.

* * *

Rukhsar was surprised at Prakash's abrupt departure. She was a little frightened. What emergency could Prakash have at three in the morning? She turned to Aman again for her confidence. He was looking at her calmly, like it was all normal. "What he has said is all true, isn't it? If it wasn't you would have pounced on him," she asked.

"Yes!"

"Why did Pakistan army and the Government keep shouting that the *Kashmiri Mujahids* were occupying Kargil heights? I saw a television debate on a private channel a few weeks ago about the Kargil war where they were crucifying the Pakistan military and civilian establishment. I didn't watch it thinking it was propaganda by the channel to get better ratings but I realize that it was true. Why have we been silent for so many years? It is a cover-up?"

Aman Khan Bux heard her question but his mind was pre-occupied with some other thoughts. *"I am afraid; we have to hear a lot of things which we, and especially you, may not like. You may think those are lies, but they will be truths. I say so because I know that people have been lied to... for over six decades. We haven't just made mistakes, Rukhsar, we have made blunders and we continue to do so. And as we go on doing it, we are playing it right into the hands of the Indians. Each time we make a mistake, they make us pay for it. Not just Kargil, Pakistan has been the reason for start of each of the three other wars."* He wanted to tell her but he must wait... and avoid it totally if possible. He loved his country too much to talk of treacheries and lies by leaders of his own country - to their own people.

Aman heard her ask him another question. "Why did you resign from your job?"

"I couldn't just take a vacation or leave from my job without giving a plausible reason. I wanted to come with you. Travelling to India without assigning a genuine reason could be viewed with suspicion. If I said that I want to go to India in search of a Pakistan soldier who had gone missing during the Kargil war, some people would have called me a traitor. I couldn't let you travel to India alone, you know that."

Rukhsar wanted to ask another question but stopped when they heard a loud thud in the lounge.

* * *

Prakash stepped out of the gate and turned to the right. Sixty feet away he saw a black sedan among the rows of cars parked on the opposite side of the road. He strolled on his side of the road till he walked past the black sedan parked on the other side, then about thirty feet ahead he turned left and walked on the road further for about hundred feet. He was looking for a taxi or an auto-rickshaw.

The man in the car saw the mysterious man he had seen leave with the Pakistani couple. He saw the man open the gates and walk to the end of the road and turn left. The man kept his eyes on the gates of the house where the couple were still in. He was mainly interested in the couple; the man who accompanied the couple could be a friend or colleague, but was of no interest to him.

Prakash waived down an auto-rickshaw and jumped in, and instructed the driver where he wanted to go. The auto driver was happy with the five hundred rupee note the man had placed in his palm and did as instructed. The three wheeled auto raced down the road after taking a detour and now sped towards the black sedan. When it was ten feet away from the sedan, the auto driver slowed down rapidly. Prakash asked the driver to speed away when Prakash got off the auto, if the driver didn't wish to get into trouble. As the auto slowed, Prakash jumped out of the moving auto and stood next to the driver's seat and tapped the window glass and stepped a foot backwards. The man in the car was stunned to see Prakash holding a gun in his hand. Then he heard a pop and the glass shattered all over the driver. He heard another pop and pain gripped his chest. Prakash smashed the butt of the gun into the man's skull and retreated with the gun still aimed at the heart of the man. The man in the car was still in a state of shock. Prakash dragged the man out of the car and stood him up. "If you don't do as I say, you will be dead," he said into the man's ears and searched him. He found nothing of value except a cell phone. He smashed the phone on the asphalt, removed the SIM card and put it in the gutter. He checked the car for GPS instrument. He found it and destroyed it.

* * *

Rukhsar and Aman rushed into the lounge. They were surprised to see a man severely bruised and bleeding, with his hands and legs tied up, and sprawled in the centre of the lounge and Prakash leaning over him.

"What happened? Who is he?" Aman asked.

"I don't know. He has been following us from the hospital. Let's find out who he is," Prakash said and looked at the man pinned under him. "Who are you? What's your interest in us?"

The man struggled to move in resistance but failed. Prakash waited for a few seconds for the man to respond but the reply wasn't forthcoming. Prakash rammed his boots on the knees of the man. The man screamed. Rukhsar couldn't see the physical torture. She turned her face away in disgust while Aman looked at the captor and the captive with keen interest.

A door opened at the far end of the lounge and the maid servant came running to the spot. She took one look and she disappeared to return with a medical case in her hands. Prakash nodded to the lady and stepped aside. The woman in her mid-thirties turned the man over on his back and attended to his injury with efficient hands. Prakash instructed something to her in a tribal language. The woman looked at him, replied in the same language and concentrated on attending to the man on the floor. The woman produced an X-Stat device and applied it to the open bullet wound of the bleeding man. The device healed the wound in a few seconds as the applicator filled with dozens of sponges soaked the blood. She waited for a minute to view the result. Satisfied with the result, she put a bandage on the chest of the injured man and stood up. She looked at Prakash. He nodded to her and said something again in the woman's native language. The woman smiled, rose and indicated Aman and Rukhsar to follow her.

Aman looked at the woman and then at Prakash. "I want to stay here. I want the answers too."

Prakash asked the woman to leave. The woman eyed the Pakistani couple, nodded to them in respect and left. Prakash saw the woman go to her room and looked at his captive. "The bullet wound will heal quickly. The woman who treated you is a qualified, well trained nurse. She assures me that your life isn't in any danger. But, I have some questions for you. If you give me honest and quick answers, I will make sure that you are alive, or else, I promise you, you will regret it for rest of your mutilated life. It's up to you to choose. You make a choice right now. Are you ready for the questions?"

The man on the floor had no choice. He nodded his head in acceptance.

"What's your name? And who are you?" Prakash asked.

"Altaf Khos. I am a Lieutenant in the Pakistan Army. I have been told to watch the movements of Aman Khan."

Aman Bux was surprised to hear his name from a stranger. He looked down at the tied up man. "Why me? What have I done?" Aman Khan Bux shouted.

"Would a sane man resign as diplomat on flimsy ground like searching for a girlfriend's father in enemy country?" Altaf asked sarcastically. "Zubair Ahmed is a traitor! He is working with the Indians against his own country."

Rukhsar stood over Altaf Khos and kicked him with all her strength. She repeated the dose catching Altaf Khos' face and shouted angrily, "My father is not a traitor!" She yelled. "His people and his country betrayed him. You betrayed him. You lied to us. You said he was missing in action. You lied to your own people. You are the *gaddar*, the traitor, not my father!" Rukhsar screamed through her tears.

A hidden smile appeared on Prakash's lips; his eyes betrayed the success he felt. Rukhsar had said what she truly felt and that was his success.

Aman Bux leaned over Altaf. "What were the orders for you? What were the instructions given to you about us?" Aman had a fear in his mind that even he could be labelled a traitor. That would spell doom not just for him, but also for his relatives and friends in Quetta... and his career would certainly come to an end.

"You were to be taken in and interrogated," Altaf Khos said without blinking.

Aman was suddenly nervous. He knew the real meaning of this term. He was in serious trouble. He knew by experience, consequences in such situations. There were many and he wanted answers. "What about the lady here?" he asked.

"She is irrelevant. So far as she is returns home without making noises, she is free. But if she doesn't return she has to be *removed* from the scene." Altaf replied carelessly.

Rukhsar froze. She stared at Altaf and shouted once again - in horror this time. "You people have destroyed my father's life and now you want to kill him, and me, because you want to maintain your lies as truth? You people want to keep lying to your own people and keep the animosity going for your own petty reasons - you scum. I will ensure that the truth is spoken and it is told to all patriotic Pakistanis to whom you have lied for decades."

Rukhsar was angry and none in the room wanted to stop her. Prakash was glad to see her reaction because it was good for his purpose. Aman was also glad because Rukhsar was venting out her suppressed anger.

Altaf Khos was dragged into Prakash's work-station. Prakash summoned the woman who had attended to Altaf as nurse. He looked at Aman Bux and Rukhsar. "I have to speak to this man alone. It's been quite a day for the two of you. You go with this lady," he pointed towards the tribal woman, and spoke to her in her native language, and turned to the couple, "I will see you both at breakfast. Please go with her and rest. Your bags are already in your room."

- - -

The woman guided the guests to a spacious room on the first floor and left the room. The couple looked at each other and smiled. This was the first time they were alone in a room, spending the night together. Had it not been for the tension and pressures on their minds, it would have been a beautiful romantic moment for them. Aman had made advances a few times in the past but Rukhsar had stopped them always with a smile which betrayed her own wish. On each occasion Aman had respected her and backed away. These had enhanced his respect in Rukhsar's mind.

Rukhsar pressed her face against his chest and suddenly she started to sob. Aman raised her face and looked into her eyes. He hugged her tightly and put his index finger on her lips when she tried to speak. "You are tired, dear. You have had too many shocks for a day. Rest, dear. Whatever it is you wish to talk, we will talk tomorrow."

Rukhsar kissed his finger and asked. "What do you think of Prakash? I am unable to decide if he is a friend or foe." The stress and tension was evident from her tone.

"His intentions seem good. What he has said so far, are facts. He has a reason for helping us and I want to know why he is doing so." He replied honestly. He had another worry on his mind apart from what he had said to Rukhsar. He wasn't sure why Prakash was going out of his way and being courteous to them. Why did Prakash invite Rukhsar to India in the first place? If he wanted Zubair to return to Pakistan, he could have done it himself. The question baffled Aman.

Rukhsar's head was still resting against Aman's chest. She was thinking of too many things; mostly about her father and how it was possible that he was working for India even if what she had heard from Prakash Rohatgi were true. She hadn't said this to Aman but within, she had a fear of sorts regarding Prakash. She had just seen him beat up a man and it frightened her. She tried to mistrust Prakash but her mind told her to trust the man. She asked Aman without raising her head, "Do you trust him, Aman? I am scared of him. He is violent and merciless. If it wasn't for *Abba*, I would have left already but I will stay till I find *Abba* no matter what happens." She expressed her fears and then added, "Aman, whenever I see him, he seems like a friend; like a man who I can trust, but he is still a mystery. We don't know who he is or why is he trying to help us?"

"I have similar feelings. We will find out soon. Now, I want you to sleep," he ordered.

- - -

The following morning, Aman heard a loud rap on the door. He called out loudly, "Wait." He looked at his watch. It was nearly half past nine.

Rukhsar opened her eyes. She found herself snuggled into Aman's chest and her arm spread across his chest. Shyly she split away. Aman smiled and pulled her close and kissed her softly. Another rap on the door made him pull up and walk to the door. He found the tribal woman standing with a fresh pair of toothbrushes in her hands. "Breakfast in ten minutes," she said courteously, turned and left.

At the breakfast table, they found Prakash waiting for them. He rose to greet them. There was no discussion of any kind while they had breakfast. The tribal woman cleaned the table and quietly disappeared into the well-equipped room which was Prakash's work-station. Prakash led his guests again into his work-station. They found Altaf still wound up lying on his back on a make-shift bed. Prakash summoned the maid. She checked Altaf's wounds again. Altaf was fine. Apart from the scar of the gunshot wound, he had no other problems; except that he was a captive.

"What's her story?" Aman asked Prakash Rohatgi about the tribal woman.

Prakash looked at the tribal woman and spoke to his guests softly ensuring the woman didn't hear him. "She hails from a tribal community in Jharkhand. Her name is Purna. She was a nurse in a state hospital where one night the naxals struck and abducted eight women forcing them to become a part of the naxal movement. The naxals are a terror outfit which swears by Mao Tse Tung's ideologies. I met Purna after an operation. She was the best female commando the naxals had in that region. One night, two years ago, she was raped by two of her colleagues. When the local head of the commando group arrived the following morning, she complained to him but when he did not act against the culprits Purna decided to punish them herself. She pulled out her gun and shot the two men who had raped her and then went out and shot the group commander. She and a few of her female colleagues escaped from the camp and went to the local police station and declared their surrender and they demanded that the men in the camp be punished for atrocities they had inflicted on them. The authorities had been waiting for an opportunity like this. The policemen called for help from the local state government and launched a full scale attack on the camp. During that operation the camp was wiped out and all those who survived from the camp were given an option; join the main-stream of Indian democracy or rot in jail for rest of their lives. Purna was the chief instigator so the cops knew she and her family would be targeted by the naxals. So, the authorities contacted us. We brought the families to the neighbouring state of Chhattisgarh and settled them in areas close to the capital, Raipur. Purna opted to stay with me, as my help. I was reluctant but she won't take no for an answer. I needed someone who could work with me and also look after this farmhouse. I knew she was an excellent commando apart from being a good nurse, I happily accepted. Now she is working with me on development of her region on full time basis, and at the same time she is also writing a book on the history of her tribe, in her native *'Kharia'* language."

Aman Bux looked at Purna with new found respect. "I never heard of *Kharia* language. Is it not one of the official languages of India?" he asked keenly. The cultural attaché's inquisitive nature came to fore.

"Officially, there are twenty-two languages, which range from Sanskrit, Hindi and Urdu to Bodo and Assamiya. Then there are at least three hundred widely spoken languages in various dialects. *Kharia* is one of them."

Their conversation stopped when Purna shut the medicine case. She spoke to Prakash in *Kharia* and started to leave. Rukhsar took Purna's hand and shook it in warm gesture. "Thank you," she said sincerely.

Purna smiled coyly and responded, "You are welcome, Ma'am, it's a pleasure."

Rukhsar and Aman were surprised at the clarity and pronunciation of Purna's usage of English language.

Prakash laughed at their expression, "Oh! She speaks four Indian languages apart from her own, which she speaks in three dialects very comfortably," he said in light humour.

Purna smiled at Prakash, nodded at the guests and left the room. Prakash's face suddenly became stern. He walked to Altaf yanked him up and squatted him on a chair next to his, and asked his guests to look at the bank of television sets again. "These are apart from what you saw last night. Watch these carefully and observe the self-contradictions."

All faces turned to the screen to watch interviews of some important people on the screens. Prakash played one where ex-President, General Pervez Musharraf was being interviewed on a private channel. When that was over, Prakash switched to other sets where other interviews were played. In two hours they had seen over twenty clippings of films, un-aired secret documentaries, photographs of original documents and films shot on actual locations.

"What you have just seen, is a continuation of what you saw last night," Prakash said and turned off the screens and leaned back facing his guests. "I will continue from where we left off last night. What we know is that the four Generals, General Pervez Musharraf, Major General Javed Hassan, General Mehmood and General Tariq Aziz did not inform Prime Minister Nawaz Sharif of their plans. Our Prime Minister, Atal Bihari Vajpayee, had accepted your Prime Minister's invite to visit Pakistan. While he was planning this trip the foreign offices on both sides were busy in hectic parleys. They had arrived at mutual agreements on many contentious issues, including Kashmir I know from my very reliable sources in New Delhi and Islamabad. Remember, this was on the backdrop of both countries having tested nuclear bombs less than a year earlier in May - India on the eleventh, and Pakistan on twenty-eighth. Both heads of state had earlier met in New York on twenty-third September, which gave the peace process a major push. Given the scenario, it was a giant stride towards peace. Then in December, Pak troops started moving into territories customarily vacated by Indian soldiers during winters. Initially, they had planned to take a few posts, probably to test the waters, or the hills in this case, but as they kept moving they saw the entire region was there for the taking. This emboldened them to take more positions. By end April, '99 Pakistan soldiers had taken over a hundred and twenty-five posts." Prakash Rohatgi said and saw reactions of his guests, and an unwanted guest, "On February twenty-ninth, PM Vajpayee visited Lahore in the famous Lahore Bus visit. Till then so far as we know your PM was in the dark about this entire operation. We now know that..."

Rukhsar was confused. "How is that possible? Throughout the Kargil incursion we kept ourselves updated about what was happening. Pak army was not on the scene. Kashmiri *'Mujahids'* were fighting the Indian army. If what you are saying is true, how come it has never come to light, never been mentioned by the media? Or is it once again one of the Indian propaganda. For everything that goes wrong in India, the Indian media and the Government starts blaming the Pakistanis for it," she asked.

"Either you are being naive or you too are unwilling to accept the truth like millions of your countrymen because they have been constantly fed lies. I will prove it to you," he said and walked to the bank of screens again. A minute later, a screen lit up. Prakash returned to his chair and punched on the keys of his computer. For the next twelve minutes the people in the room saw some footages and interviews again. When it was over, Prakash turned to Rukhsar, "What you saw just now is not propaganda; it is actual footage of the events as it was aired by Pakistani media. I hope you will trust them at least." Prakash was annoyed and it reflected in his tone. "It is amazing - on three occasions the Pakistan military used the same modus-operandi. Their tactic may have had a chance to succeed in the first instance, in 1947, but on the other two occasions after that, in 1965 and lastly in Kargil it had no chance of success whatsoever. In both instances, Pakistani army infiltrated thousands of Pashtun tribesmen and army men into the valley. They failed because Kashmiri people were not in their favour. Again, in 1965 Ayub Khan and his foreign minister, Zulfiqar Ali Bhutto tried the same trick by launching *'Operation Gibraltar'* in the Kashmir Valley. This time too, the Kashmiri people caught the infiltrators, army men in civilian dress and handed them over to the authorities. In Kargil they tried the same trick of disguising their own army men as Kashmiri rebels, and pushing across the LOC. This time however, these men had a different objective - to occupy Indian posts across the LOC. Lastly, the best proof is your father, Rukhsar. He was injured during the war."

"This is insane!" Altaf shouted from his chair. "Why would the four generals plan this? It is impractical. You are lying to us. This is propaganda."

The three occupants of the room turned to look at Altaf. He was visibly angry; unwilling to accept what Prakash had just stated about the involvement of Pakistani army.

"You are right about one thing. It was impractical. This was not just impractical; it was as audacious an attempt as it was stupid to embarrass your own civilian, democratically elected government. It isn't a secret anymore. The whole world knew even as the war was raging on, that there wasn't a single man from Kashmir on those hills. It was thoroughly a military operation by Pak army." Prakash responded calmly. "Here are some irrefutable evidences which even the government of Pakistan can't deny. First, this is the function where Hawaldar Lalak Jan was posthumously awarded the *'Nishan-e Haider'*, the *'Highest Military Honour for bravery'* in the Kargil war, in 1999. He died fighting the Indian army on Tiger Hill, in Kargil, and tell me if this is an Indian propaganda," Prakash said and played a two minute video recording of the event. When it was over, he turned to Altaf Khos and Aman, "Now, let's listen to these recordings of conversations between General Pervez Musharraf and General Tariq Aziz. General Musharraf was on an official visit to China from where he had some long conversations with General Aziz who was at the GHQ, the General Head Quarters in Rawalpindi. These conversations were recorded by a Chinese agency. This will prove how these men conspired and executed the plan without any information to Prime Minister Nawaz Sharif."

Prakash punched the keyboard again and played the audios of the recordings. Over an hour later, the audio stopped and there was an uneasy silence in the room. Aman knew Prakash was accurate and precise in his presentation. There wasn't a single point to which he or Altaf could refute or counter.

Rukhsar was shaken; all her perceptions about Indian and Pakistan relations were being continuously decimated. Her pride that her country never infringed into Indian Territory was turned upside down. The general perception in Pakistan was that India was the aggressor in all wars and that India had thrust these wars on Pakistan. Community leaders, opinion makers, Government authorities and the media were silent on this. A perception was created that India and its belligerent forces wanted war to destabilize and destroy Pakistan. She looked at Aman hoping he would counter Prakash's charges. Aman glanced at her and remained silent. She shook her head in disbelief. She was aware now that Aman knew Prakash had spoken the truth. "Why has our Government lied to us? We have a right to know the truth. We have lost our family members in these operations. Why was this covered up?"

Aman patted Rukhsar's hand. "It's complicated, dear. The electronic media was under government control till recently, you know. It is only after the arrival of the private channels that truth is starting to emerge. Recently some books were published which throw light on reality. And... If General Musharraf hadn't staged the coup d'état, there would have been a judicial enquiry. Bear in mind that Kargil war ended in July and in October Government was toppled. Till recently we didn't accept that Pak army was involved in Kargil, or that Musharraf was one of the culprits. We never had an enquiry because Musharraf was in power and he couldn't set up a commission to investigate his own blunder, could he?"

"We heard Musharraf claim that Kargil operation was a great success - a 'tactical operation' undermined by the civilian government. If that was so, why didn't he set up a commission of enquiry? He says it was a successful operation," Rukhsar countered a defence.

Prakash laughed loudly. Rukhsar and the two other men in the room were surprised. They stared at him with bewildered looks. Prakash Rohatgi raised his hands to apologize. "That is the contradiction. Do you realize that Pakistan on one hand calls it a *Kashmiri Mujahid* operation against the Indian army and then you have the likes of Pervez Musharraf who says it was a 'successful, tactical operation'? What other proof do you want?" Prakash said and looked at his guests and his captive. They were thinking the same.

Prakash smiled, "General Musharraf would never set up an enquiry. How can he explain why he physically spent a night across the LOC, on the Indian side at Zakaria Mustakar with Brigadier Masood Aslam of the eighteenth Brigade?" Prakash said and paused, "By the way, do you know that the Brigadier who violated the LOC is now a General?" Prakash said and moved to the subject of earlier discussion, "It was Musharraf, who according to my sources gave the go-ahead to Captain Nadeem, Captain Ali and Hawaldar Lalak Jan to cross the border on 18th December, 1998 and do a survey of the area. As for the success of the operation, or Musharraf's claims of it being a tactical operation, any person with scantiest knowledge of modern warfare would know it was doomed from the start. It was a disaster in making the moment one analyses how Kargil operation was planned and executed. Apart from an element of surprise, there was nothing good about the misadventure. Before mounting of Kargil operation the Pakistan army had not done any analysis, or so it seems. Kargil operation had no strategic thinking or logic behind it. It was an absurd... weird operation. The army kept the civilian government in dark and had the audacity, or you can call it stupidity if you wish, of not informing even the Air Force or Navy. Do you call this tactical?"

"We took the Kargil, Drass and Batalic heights. The Kargil was a successful operation. We had control over it for over six months." Altaf shouted from the back.

Prakash laughed again, "Sneaking up and occupying the heights for over six months when the enemy is not present makes it a successful operation? When Pak army launched this operation, it had no enemy to fight... no one to confront. So, to that extent you can claim it to be successful. But what happened when the Indian army responded? Within four weeks the whole plan collapsed. Though Pak soldiers were on higher ground... higher hills actually, they couldn't defend the posts they had occupied because the planning was so poor, so unprofessional. Yes, there was an element of surprise, but nothing more. This operation would have failed miserably if Indian intelligence was better," Prakash stressed on the last sentence.

Now Rukhsar was sure how Kargil operation was mounted; she had seen proves of it. But she was confused why it had no strategy behind it, "Why did they launch an audacious operation if they couldn't have achieved any strategic gains?"

"It was an embarrassment for all parties involved here," Aman replied, "The Indian army was embarrassed because it had under-read the situation after the Lahore summit, and embarrassed due to their intelligence failure. Pakistan military establishment was embarrassed because its misadventure cost it hundreds of lives and severe loss of credibility with the International community. Moreover, they couldn't help their own men when the Indian army started to pound them with heavy artillery and their heavy guns, like the Bofors - these, they had not factored in their calculations when they had assessed Indian response to the attack. Lastly, and most importantly, Pakistan Foreign office had panicked. They had successfully negotiated many mutual agreements with their Indian counterparts on a whole range of issues - from commerce and trade, to sports, Siachen and even Kashmir. The foreign office knew that their efforts would lay waste if Kargil situation was not contained. Pakistan would face universal condemnation for its immoral act." Aman paused and looked at Prakash. Aman held Rukhsar's hand and patted it gently, "PM Nawaz Sharif was embarrassed because on one hand he was hosting the Indian Prime Minister at the Lahore summit a few weeks earlier and here was a situation where his actions would be termed as chicanery of the highest order. It was a no win situation for Pakistan."

Rukhsar looked at them blankly, "What did Pakistan, or its overzealous Generals wish to achieve with this operation?"

"We can only speculate... only four people can provide us real answers - the four Generals." Aman replied, "I have my own theory based on my conversations with many foreign office people and other diplomats. The first theory is that the army wanted to derail the peace process. It's ..."

Rukhsar was surprised. "Why would the army derail the peace process? It is in their interest that there is peace with India. Then army can concentrate on FATA, Baluchistan, Khyber Pakhtunkhwa and other areas like Waziristan where Pakistan's sovereignty is being challenged...."

Aman laughed sarcastically and replied with sadness, "Look at our political map. Barring India, there is no country which can challenge our military might. If there is sustained peace with India, the military loses its influence and very reason for existence. It would lose its importance. To retain it the army has been doing a lot of misadventures. That's one theory. The second theory is that the military wanted to topple the Nawaz Sharif government."

"Why?" she asked.

"Because, as I said earlier, if peace process was successful the military wouldn't just lose its importance there would be huge budget cuts in defence. Good reason, don't you think?"

"Why did the operation fail so miserably?" she asked.

"Part of the answer is in your earlier query. You asked why the strategy was flawed. The generals hadn't thought out their plan in detail. There was no proper analysis of the operation, no war gaming; post-operation scenario wasn't discussed... There are theories abound. They had not expected the way India responded - with full force. Our soldiers had no chance of success once the Indians introduced their heavy guns, and when the Indian Air Force arrived on the scene our soldiers were sitting ducks. The planners hadn't thought of it. The Indians rolled in over a hundred thousand armed men to the war scene. Being massively outnumbered, apart, the Pakistani military couldn't send re-enforcements openly because they were claiming that the men in Kargil were *Kashmiri Mujahids* whereas the Indians used all the resources at their disposal. When IAF and the Bofors began to bombard, casualties started to mount. Within two weeks Pakistani army knew the operation had failed. Our soldiers were in bunkers without food or re-enforcement. If they tried to retreat, the Indian guns were ready to blow them away and the IAF had them pinned. It was a bad scene." Aman Bux paused again, his eyes boring into hers. The disappointment was written large on his face. "We have made blunders, Rukhsar."

Altaf was angry that the information he had on Kargil was poor in comparison with what he was hearing. He wanted to convince himself that the information he was fed by his army superiors was true. "How can you say that Nawaz Sharif was not aware of the military plan when we know that he famously asked, *'when are you going to hand over Kashmir?* doesn't that say that he was in the know of the plan? Wasn't he in Skardu on January 17th, where he was given a brief by the army?" Altaf asked, challenging Prakash and Aman.

Aman had no answer to Altaf's question. He and Rukhsar turned to Prakash who was listening to the conversation and appreciating what Aman had said. It was more than he had expected. This was the final piece of puzzle which would convince his guests of what he knew was true, and he wanted them to be fully convinced about the facts. Then he would take them on board for a mission for which he was working. He smiled at Altaf Khos and replied, "On 17th January your PM did have a meeting at Skardu but it wasn't about Kargil. It was about a bypass road being constructed by the army along the Neelum Valley. Your

PM was given another brief sometime in early May where he was told that the Kargil heights were occupied by *Mujahids*, not by their army regulars and that the army was giving them moral and 'some' logistical support. But, around eighteenth May he was given another briefing when he was given the full picture. Your PM couldn't help in the situation because the crime was already committed. He could only go along and hope that things worked out in their favour. You should know that your system is so heavily tilted towards the army in your country that even if he wanted, your PM couldn't have done anything."

"Didn't Nawaz Sharif betray his country by going to the US to ask them to broker peace?" Altaf asked.

Prakash laughed. "You can draw your own conclusions and make your own deductions. By asking this question you just confirmed to us that you knew that it was the Pak army not Kashmiri separatists on those hills. PM Nawaz Sharif had no options left to him. Casualties were mounting by the hour; rations had run out as had the bullets, and no re-enforcement was going through because the Indian army had cut off the supply lines, and the Pak army was helpless. It could do nothing. According to some on my reliable sources General Musharraf met your PM and asked him to allow the Pak army to send re-enforcements openly to help the Pak soldiers retain the Indian posts. There was another fear, a factor which they had not considered. This was end June and the monsoon was due to set in. If the rains came down in full, it could add to their woes and any chance of retrieval of their men would be impossible. They still had over a thousand men holding the posts and the Indian army was pushing them with all its might. Nawaz Sharif, apparently, declined to send re-enforcements because that would mean open declaration of war; a war which neither the Pak PM nor your General thought they could win. So, the General asked his PM to help them evacuate their men. They knew Indian army or the Government would not relent, so what other option did your PM really have?

The war was unsustainable for Pakistan. He contacted the US President but he was told in no uncertain terms by President Clinton that US considered Pakistan as an aggressor, and it did not agree with the Pakistani version of Kargil. The Americans knew that it was the Pak army which had crossed the LOC and not the *Mujahids*, as Pakistan had been telling the International community. By twelfth June whole world knew it was a conspiracy by Pakistan army when the conversation between Tariq Aziz and Pervez Musharraf... which we just heard, become public. Every newspaper of that day in India and around the world had published the entire transcript of the conversation on the front pages, with headlines. It was a disaster for Pakistani Diplomacy. President Clinton told PM Nawaz Sharif that if Pakistan expected any mediation by the US, Nawaz Sharif had to order its army to withdraw *'immediately and unconditionally'*. PM Nawaz Sharif turned to China, hoping to get some leverage or assistance but got nothing. By now, Pakistan establishment... both civilian and military were desperate to salvage themselves and emerge unscathed from the mess. Once again, Nawaz Sharif contacted the US, and though uninvited, he decided to go to Washington DC and arrived on the fourth of July, the US Independence Day, a US holiday. Here I can confirm what transpired thanks to a book written by former Deputy Secretary of State, Strobe Talbott. Aman, you! And especially you, Rukhsar, let it be etched in your memory what I am about to say now. In his book, Strobe Talbott writes a chapter on the events of fourth July and the days leading up to it." Prakash stopped and looked at three people in the room. His eyes were cold and face expressing the tension of what he was to say. "After Hiroshima and Nagasaki, it is commonly believed that the world came closest to a nuclear war during the Cuban missile crisis. Isn't it? Well, not entirely. The closest the world came to a nuclear war after Nagasaki, was during the Kargil war."

The other three occupants of the room were staring at him in disbelief. Prakash Rohatgi noticed their expressions. He saw the fear in their eyes; they were probably wondering if this was true or not. Prakash paused and punched the keyboard. A large television screen lit up on the top right of the wall of screens. It had the pages of the book, with the paragraphs highlighted in bold. The guests, including Altaf, read the contents and they felt a chill in their spines. Rukhsar rested her elbows on the table with shivering hands cupping her face. She was truly shaken. She knew she had to control herself or else she would lose her sanity. She found solace in presence of Aman by her side. She grabbed his hand, brought it to her face and cried in his palms. Aman was staring blankly at the television screen which was still flashing the last line of the paragraph on it. *'US President Bill Clinton and his advisers gathered in the Oval office before the President's meeting with Nawaz Sharif, it was learnt through an overnight report that Pakistan had taken steps with its nuclear arsenal. The world was saved from a catastrophic war which could have engulfed the entire region. President Bill Clinton's pro-active step and negotiation had averted a possible nuclear war in the sub-continent.'*

Prakash Rohatgi understood the reactions of the people in the room. This was exactly what he wanted to see. He turned to Altaf and he was surprised to see the captive's reaction. Altaf was in a state of shock; he was staring at the screen, imagining of the consequences of an incident which was averted.

"How did the President Clinton convince Nawaz Sharif to retreat?" Aman Khan asked.

"The President gave him an ultimatum to either withdraw his forces *immediately and unconditionally*, in which case, the US won't block $100 million IMF fund that Pakistan desperately sought because its forex reserves had depleted to dangerously low levels. If Nawaz Sharif did not agree to the President's terms, US would block the IMF funds and issue a press statement stating that Pakistan was supporting terrorism in Afghanistan directly, and in Kashmir through assistance to separatists, and that would in effect officially categorize Pakistan as a Terror sponsoring state.

If that was done, all aids and assistance provided to Pakistan would have stopped and Pakistan would have plummeted into economic oblivion and chaos. Given the limited options your PM had, he could do nothing but submit to the wishes of the US President."

The gloomy atmosphere of the room became tense when they heard the knob turn and saw Purna enter with a worried look on her face. She spoke to Prakash in *Kharia*.

"Let's go," Prakash told Aman and Rukhsar.

"What happened?" Aman asked worriedly.

"I will tell you on the way."

"What about him?" Aman asked, pointed towards Altaf.

"He will be here. Purna will guard him."

Aman looked at Prakash doubtfully. "Can she?"

Prakash laughed. "I will advise him to do exactly as she says or else he will learn that she can take on a couple of people like him and still emerge a victor easily."

While Prakash was preparing for what seemed a long trip, he was pestered by Rukhsar. "Please tell me how you met my father?" Rukhsar asked.

Prakash nodded and told her. *Three years ago, Zubair Ahmed wrote a letter to the Home Ministry with request that he be allowed to have access to books for his research. At the time the Governments of India and Pakistan were negotiating on exchange of prisoners. It is quite common that people from both sides, by accident walk past the border because the borders are not clearly defined, and porous, and fishermen, farmers and civilians on both sides often venture into territory of the other country.*

Among the list of prisoners to be exchanged, the Indian Government had added the prisoners of war taken during Kargil war. The Pakistani Government had acknowledged virtually all prisoners as their citizen or soldier. However, suddenly, the Pakistan Home Ministry told their Indian counterparts that Zubair Ahmed was not their Military officer as claimed by the man or by the Indian Government. This surprised the Indians because Pakistan Government had earlier acknowledged Zubair as their soldier. This sudden turn around had come as a big surprise. Home Ministry asked the Intelligence network to investigate the matter.

An intelligence officer investigated Zubair's claims and found that he was speaking the truth. The mystery deepened when Zubair had asked for access to books. Nitin Tyagi was deputed to speak to this Pakistan Major and see if he could be used to India's advantage. When Nitin Tyagi met Zubair Ahmed, he pitied the man's living condition. Over a period of three months the men met a few times and became good friends. Zubair Ahmed was shown the official documents which disclaimed him as a Pakistani. Zubair was angry. He swore to Tyagi that he spoke the truth. Tyagi believed him mainly because he was found in army uniform on the hills of Kargil almost dead. Four months later Nitin Tyagi had made Zubair an offer. Zubair had not trusted Tyagi's intentions at first but the more he thought about it, the more he was convinced that Tyagi was sincere in his intent. Zubair Ahmed agreed to work with Nitin Tyagi for the mission jointly with the Indians.

It took Nitin Tyagi over a week to have Zubair Ahmed evicted from the prison. On the day of his release, Zubair Ahmed was escorted by a man with whom he was to work. That was when Zubair met Prakash Rohatgi for the first time and ever since, Zubair had been staying with Prakash Rohatgi, as a guest, as a friend, and as a guide.

Rukhsar heard the unbelievable story but believed it probably because she trusted Prakash. Many emotions came to the fore and stayed. Whether right or not, she felt eternally in debt of Prakash Rohatgi for taking care of her father... she hoped he did. Another severe emotion was gripping her; her rage for her government and military establishment for disclaiming her father as Pakistan's citizen.

Aman put his hands across Rukhsar's shoulder but Rukhsar brushed it aside; he too was a part of the government which had committed the sin. She cried silently without letting the two men see her tears. Few minutes later, she calmed down and looked at the man who had resigned from his job for her sake. She felt guilty of her behaviour. She pulled his hands in hers and kissed it. As she did, she swore to herself that she will make the people who did this to her father, pay for it heavily. She won't stop till she got justice for her father.

- - -

* * *

Zubair Ahmed

ASTITVA - Identity

Prakash stopped at a *dhaba* on the outskirts of Ghaziabad in Uttar Pradesh. The two hundred kilometre drive from this place to Agra would take at least another two and a half hours despite the modern expressway. He was anxious about Zubair Ahmed's persistence. It bothered him. Zubair's request was unexpected though understandable. Prakash had to handle it delicately. He wondered how Zubair would react when he saw his daughter who he missed so much, despite Prakash's promise to Zubair that the latter's family would not be involved under any circumstance. In any case, Prakash could not let Zubair be upset. The former Major in Pakistan Army, disclaimed by his own army, was probably the most vital cog in the plan Prakash and his people were working on; a plan which would change the socio-political situation between the two countries, especially in Pakistan.

Rukhsar looked tired and worried. When they were seated she asked Prakash nervously, "Where are we going?"

"To Agra... to meet your father." Prakash replied, with a little smile.

Rukhsar's eyes lit up; her fatigued face lit up with a gorgeous smile and radiance erased the tiredness she had a minute ago. Her eyes moist with tears holding on the edges, she grabbed Prakash's hand and held her in his, and rested her forehead on it not letting the men see her tears roll down. Then, a moment later a glum expression replaced the smile. "Is he in a prison in Agra?"

"No, he is not. I told you he is staying with me. He is living in a safe-house in Agra right now. Normally he stays with me at my farmhouse. He is a free man," Prakash replied, trying to ease Rukhsar's anxiety.

Rukhsar and Aman were surprised. "I thought you said he was held as a POW. That's why you wanted me to come to India. What happened?"

"Let's eat and reach Agra. Zubair Saheb will explain to you. At the moment it is important that you relax. A tension free mind is best when it comes to making decisions." Prakash said with a mysterious look in his eyes.

"To make a decision? For what?" Rukhsar asked.

"Later." This wasn't the right time to tell her. He had to wait till she was ready, and meeting her father would be the second step in his plan.

- - -

Three hours later, when their SUV entered the compound of an old, dilapidated, run-down bungalow on the outskirts of Agra, Rukhsar was taken by surprise. The compound was lined with numerous massive trees which were quite old but stood proudly, guarding the visibility of the compound from the outside. The bungalow appeared to have seen better days. The ground was littered with thick dried leaves which hadn't been swept for months, and the fountain in the middle of the ground was certainly remnant of the old semi-royal days of the British

Raj. How could this be a place where her father could be staying, or being held? Rukhsar thought when she saw the house.

Aman didn't seem to care so far as Rukhsar's purpose was met. Prakash stopped the vehicle. He got off and wrapped on a large wooden door. A few seconds later a guard opened the door slightly, saw Prakash and swung the door ajar. Prakash gestured to his guests to follow him and went inside. Rukhsar slowly got off the vehicle and walked towards the door hesitantly; her anxiety of meeting her father and bit of fear had mixed up her emotions. She waited for Aman to alight and she momentarily stood still. Aman put his arm around her shoulder confidently and led her into the house.

Rukhsar stepped inside and the first look of the interiors of the bungalow left her amazed. She saw a huge, thousand square feet lounge which over shadowed any private library she had ever seen in her life. The lounge was lined with book shelves from floor to ceiling, from wall to wall, except three wide openings for the doors which led to the rooms of the house, and a staircase which opened to a roof-top garden. In the centre was a large twenty-five feet wide oval wooden table with two computer monitors and keyboards. It seemed like a replica of the Prakash's farmhouse. A few chairs and stools were neatly set alongside the table. On one corner there was a sofa for six people, with an antique granite slab in the centre. This wasn't just any ordinary library; this was a research place where history, geography, politics and economics was studied and researched.

Rukhsar's pulse rate rose as seconds ticked by. She held Aman's wrist tightly, sinking her nails into his skin in anxiety.

"All will be fine, *Insha-Allah*," Aman comforted Rukhsar though he had fears of his own. Were they being led into a trap? But he had confidence in himself and... And strangely, trust in the man who was leading them.

"Where is Prakash?" she asked nervously.

"Here," she heard Prakash's voice behind her.

Rukhsar and Aman turned around to see Prakash standing next to the main door. He walked up to them and stood facing them.

"Where is *Abbu*?" Rukhsar asked.

"He is in that room. He is upset about something so I have to talk to him." Prakash pointed to the door behind him from where he had emerged. He paused for a moment, hesitant, he added, "He doesn't know you are here, and he didn't expect to ever see you again so this might come as a shock to him. Please bear with me. I will call you in a little while after I have spoken to him." Prakash turned and left without waiting for a reply from them.

The man dressed in a guard's dress appeared and stood smiling before the confused couple. He led them to the sofa and disappeared again to return a minute later with snacks and juices. "Akash Pradhan," the man introduced himself courteously, "I am in charge here. This is an exclusive library for people who become members - strictly by invitation. No one is expected to come here today except for you. So please relax. If there is anything you need, just ask me," he said and returned to his room.

Prakash saw Zubair Ahmed reading a book with his back to the door when he entered Zubair's study room which was an extension of his three room apartment that had been provided to him the day after Prakash had ejected him from the darkness of the prisons. This was one of the two places where Zubair liked to spend his time. Mostly he stayed with Prakash at his house in New Delhi but he was surprised when Akash Pradhan was asked to move him here for a couple of days although Prakash knew Zubair liked to spend his weekends with a young girl who spent her weekends with them at the farmhouse and she would be upset if she missed a weekend.

This bungalow belonged to an aristocratic family whose last heir had no children. He had donated it to Prakash Rohatgi on a promise that this bungalow would be turned into a library for research in honour of the aristocrat's ancestors. Prakash had kept his promise and used it for special purposes. He had temporarily moved Zubair Ahmed to Agra when Rukhsar was to arrive in New Delhi. He had another guest who stayed at the weekends in New Delhi. And normally, he liked to spend his time with her without being disturbed. She demanded all his attention and she always got it from him. Prakash shrugged his shoulder at the thought of the young girl. God! He missed her.

Zubair heard the door open and turned to see Prakash enter the room. "Am I a prisoner? If not, why am I stopped from visiting Lucknow? It is important for me, Prakash. I have to trace my family roots." Over two years the two men had grown fond of each other with developed mutual respect. Though Zubair was complaining, his tone didn't imply it.

"Don't blame Akash for it. He had asked me if he should escort you, I told him to ask you to wait..."

"...if he should escort me? Am I a child, Prakash?" Zubair humoured.

Prakash laughed softly. "You know better. You know your life could be in danger if your whereabouts is known. We had agreed that if you venture out, it has to be after sunset when this area is deserted. Going out of town is not much of a problem so far as your identity is protected. I am not ready to take any chances with your life. You are extremely important for our mission." Prakash spoke normally, as he did always with Zubair; like he was speaking to his dearest friend. "I had one more reason to keep you here till I reached, even if that meant holding you at point of a gun," Prakash said and sat in the chair facing Zubair with smile belying the last part of his sentence.

"Really? What's so important?" Zubair asked with raised eyebrows.

"I have two people in the lounge who I want you to meet. You will be delighted to meet them, and also upset. But since you were already upset with Akash, I thought of speaking with you before I brought the two people here. I will bring them in now."

"Who are they, Prakash? Why are they so important that you should bring them 'here'? I wanted to be with my angel," Zubair quizzed.

Prakash's face broke into a warm smile. "In a minute you will know," he said and walked out.

Zubair didn't make much of Prakash's talk of two guests. He wasn't much interested in meeting anyone except Prakash and that young girl in New Delhi, and occasionally when her mother visited them. Zubair Ahmed shook his head and returned to the book he was reading.

Prakash briskly paced the length of the lounge and stood next to the sofa, "Let's go. You have travelled far for this moment, Rukhsar. I request you both not to derive any hasty conclusions about him. I know you will talk to him. I request you to listen and understand him before you arrive at your decisions. Please come," he said and led the couple to the room and stood at the door. He turned the knob and walked in.

Rukhsar and Aman followed him anxiously, excitedly.

Zubair was still engrossed in the book he was reading. He didn't bother to turn to look. He hated disturbance when he was reading, and he didn't want any distraction especially when he was researching on a very important subject.

Rukhsar walked up to her father and stood behind him. She was nervous, anxious. *"Abbu..."* she said softly.

Zubair was stunned. He hadn't expected to hear this voice in his life time again. His eyes were still fixed on the book he was reading, but unable to believe what he had heard. A silent yearning filled his heart with a soul desire... he wished he was to see what he wanted to see most... He turned with emotions gaining control over his senses. He saw her standing behind him; beautiful as ever.

"Rukhsar...?" he said and saw Aman standing formally next to her. He rose slowly, *"Aman...? How did you..."* he said and a lump in his throat choked his voice. He stared at the two faces in front of him and froze for a moment. Then the tears rolled down.

Rukhsar hugged her father and she couldn't hold back her tears either. Zubair tried to control his emotions but he failed. He rapped his daughter with his arms and let her cry. Aman came forward and bowed his head in respect to his would be father-in-law. Zubair thrust his arm out and enveloped Aman Khan Bux, patting him like a son.

A few minutes later, having overcome the emotions they came to the lounge. Rukhsar was unable to control her emotions. For over twelve years she had been searching for her father. And now, here in a country with which her country had fought four wars... her father and grand-father had fought on the battlefields, she had found her father. He was healthy and he was with her now. She was staring at Zubair Ahmed without blinking. Her father's handsome looks were still there with those sharp, intelligent, dark brown eyes, but his hairline had receded. The signs of being under constant pressure and strain had taken its toll and deep lines on his forehead were the evidences. The broad, firm jaw still held the crooked smile her father was known for.

Aman Bux was quiet. He was observing Zubair, looking for clues why the former soldier was working for, and with the enemy. Then he was surprised at a question which came to his mind. India is an enemy? Was it true? He couldn't decide. He wanted to be sure of the answer in his own mind.

Zubair had too many questions but those will have to wait. For now he wanted to be with his daughter. He was wondering if Rukhsar and Aman were married. He wanted to ask his daughter but he waited to talk to her when they were alone.

When did she get married? Did they have any children, his grand-children? His thoughts were disrupted by Rukhsar. She took over the role of the host from Prakash Rohatgi and Akash and served happily.

Zubair Ahmed looked at Prakash Rohatgi. Till a little over two years ago, he wouldn't have believed if anyone had told him that his only and best friend would be an Indian and that too, a Hindu. He was fifty-eight years old and he never had a friend in real sense. It all changed that evening when Prakash came to meet him in jail. From that day Zubair's life changed and there was a new mission in his life. For that mission he had voluntarily sacrificed his family - that was until he saw Rukhsar again.

"How did you find them?" Zubair asked Prakash.

"You know our contacts. One of them told me about Rukhsar and about your family, and I followed it up."

"Thank you, Prakash. However, you have put their lives in peril. I had accepted to help so far as my family was kept out of this. Why did you get them involved?"

"I didn't wish to deprive you or your family of each other. I have taken precautions. Rukhsar has come here as a medical tourist. I didn't know about Aman so I hadn't counted on his presence. Until this moment I don't think there is any issue about him being in India. Because he has resigned, his visit to India could raise some eyebrows. So far I think its well under control. We found a man who was tracking his movements but we have him in our custody." Prakash replied and turned to Aman. "When you return, you could face serious and some really tough questions. If you mention about Zubair Saheb, it will not be taken kindly. I hope you understand the gravity of the situation."

"When I decided to accompany Rukhsar I knew exactly what I was doing and I am ready for whatever I have to face. I have no regrets." Aman replied honestly, confidently.

Zubair and Prakash nodded their heads but both knew that situation was going to get worse if he didn't return to Pakistan with plausible explanation. They suspected even Rukhsar was aware of that.

- - -

Prakash and Aman decided to take a walk after dinner. This would allow them to talk and get better acquainted with each other while letting Zubair and Rukhsar to catch up. As they walked through the trees, Aman realized that the compound wasn't just a small bungalow. It was an estate - a large one. They walked past three little cottages situated far from the main bungalow towards the countryside. Aman was pleasantly surprised to see a large area covered with a canopy of pristine forest trees.

Aman stopped abruptly. "What's your story?" he asked.

Prakash was a few feet ahead when Aman posed the question. He turned around and replied with sadness, "I hope I can tell you my story, but now is not the right time for it. My work and my oath stops me from telling you. Maybe, if..." Prakash paused, weighing his words carefully, "if someday situations permit me to tell you the story, I will be glad to share it with you. Right now, I have a question for you. We are walking through a forest in a country which you consider as enemy. Do you have that feeling at this moment?"

Aman was surprised by the question. He had no immediate reply but he did know what he felt. "No, I don't. Oddly, when I heard stories from people who travelled to India and said that they didn't find any animosity among the general population, I didn't completely believe it, or at best, I thought they were exaggerating or being generous towards India or... even being biased. I have had interactions with my counterparts from India and I admit those have been quite good. But when you talk of this moment, I feel I am in my own country. It seems surreal that I am saying this but it's true. I haven't seen or experienced any animosity towards Pakistanis or Muslims. I have to accept what I have seen."

Prakash nodded his head with a little inward smile, *'another candidate possibly?'* he thought and his eyes glittered in the dark.

- - -

Rukhsar and Zubair were slowly catching up on lost twelve years. Initially, it was about Shabnam and about Rukhsar's career, which later drifted to her marriage. Zubair was sad when Rukhsar told him the reason why she wasn't married. He felt guilty and responsible for delay in her marriage. Then came the issue both knew was going to be contentious. When Rukhsar asked him about his capture, Zubair avoided the topic and smiled wryly.

"Why are you working for the Indians, *Abbu*? Why have you turned?" Rukhsar asked her father.

"I haven't turned, my dear, I have returned."

Rukhsar was taken aback by her father's strange reply. "What does that mean?"

Zubair's eyes bore into his daughter's with such intensity on his face that Rukhsar held her breath. Zubair took her hands in his, "It means that I haven't turned against my country but I have returned to my roots. I have returned to the place where the history of our family's migration started over sixty years ago with my grand-parents. The continuous state of our family's migration has ended. I have returned home. I..." he stopped and looked at his daughter. "How I wish..."

"What, *Abbu*? What do you wish?"

"I wish you and Shabnam could come and live with me." Zubair expressed his desire and looked at his daughter with expectation.

Rukhsar was shocked. How could her father who had fought for his country and nearly died in an army operation, willingly live in a country he had fought with? Even more surprising was his wish that his family migrate with him. How could he? What could have led him to take such extreme step? What did her father go through? She was upset and she was disappointed. When Prakash had said that her father was working with him, she hadn't believed it. It was inconceivable then, it was still improbable for her even though her father had stated it quite clearly, and gone ahead to wish that his family join him.

"*Abbu*, why?" Rukhsar pleaded to her father. "You always said India was our enemy. What has made you change sides?"

"People mature, my dear. Truth has its way of convincing people to act in accordance. In last two years I have learnt the truth. I know of lies propagated by our civilian and military rulers. For over six decades I have... we have been fed lies. We are still being told lies. I was fighting on the hills of Kargil and I was ready to die for my country. I almost did... When I was given up as dead, my country... no, the rulers of the country, my own establishment decided to deny my existence, my rights. What was the crime of those brave soldiers who were fought on those hills? They had no food for days but they kept fighting. When, on rare occasions we were able to make contact, our soldiers asked for bullets not food, though they were near starvation but they kept fighting... only to be disowned by its own army? And left to die? Those were very young men on that hill, my child - men in early twenties! They kept on fighting till they died... some from injuries, others of starvation and then came the ultimate humiliation. Our country disowned the dead bodies of those brave men. I would have died on that hill and you would never have known if I got a proper burial or not. Is that fair? We are soldiers, and we expect to be respected. We were not given respect. The Indian soldiers, whom we call our enemies, gave them proper burials. Which army should I be obliged to? Which country should I respect; the one which disowns its own men or the one which respects even the enemy's dead soldier?" Zubair Ahmed stopped and looked at his daughter. "Yet, I am not working against Pakistan; I am working for a greater future of Pakistan and for the people of Pakistan."

"But you said you have returned. It makes no sense to me." Rukhsar was confused.

"You know that your great-grand parents migrated from India to Pakistan during partition. I have returned to the soil of my forefathers. Here lye the roots of my ancestors who have walked and lived on this land. It's mine... and yours!"

Their conversation stopped abruptly when Prakash and Aman returned. When the two men entered, they sensed that there was a certain amount of tension in the air. Prakash guessed the reason for the tension correctly and changed the subject. "Why do you want to go to Lucknow?" he asked Zubair.

"My forefathers hail from a village near Lucknow. I want to visit my ancestral place. I have a personal reason... I want to pay my respects to my ancestors. I hope you will respect my wish."

Prakash nodded, "We will start tomorrow morning."

* * *

Prakash Rohatgi's Residence

New Delhi, India

Altaf lay on a cot with his hands and feet spread apart, tied to the posts. He was desperate; he thought his bowels would explode. He tried shouting but feared the strain it would cause on his bowels. He called out to Purna. A few seconds later Purna stood in front of him.

"I have to go to the bathroom," Altaf said.

Purna looked at him suspiciously. She knew he hadn't been to the bathroom since morning. She approached the cot slowly and warned Altaf, "Don't try any stunts. You will regret it."

Altaf nodded. Purna untied him and showed him towards the bathroom in a different room. Altaf locked the bathroom from the inside and looked around as he relieved himself. There was no window or opening in the walls except a five inch circular cavity for an exhaust fan which turned on automatically once the light switch was turned on in the otherwise dark bathroom. He was thinking of a plan to escape but he couldn't find a way. He stepped out of the bathroom. Purna was waiting in her military fatigues she had used in naxal camps two years ago. She directed him towards the room where he was tied up earlier. Altaf nodded and headed in the direction and Purna followed him. Altaf turned around and lunged at her. He realized his mistake a fraction too late. Purna, anticipating a move had side-stepped and twisted in the air like a cat, slammed Altaf on the mouth with surprising force, and landed on her feet ready to strike again. Altaf's mouth exploded in pain as Purna's shoes smashed flush on his mouth again. Blood filled his mouth as he landed on the granite floor. The fall hurt his knees as he crashed. Coinciding with his fall, he felt another jolt as he landed. He realised that Purna had leapt and landed the heels of her shoes on the small of his back. A loud moan escaped his mouth and he spewed blood when he screamed in pain.

"I told you... no stunts... you will regret it... Do what I say if you don't want pain." Purna warned.

Altaf looked up and saw the five feet two inch fragile frame of Purna looming over him. Her strength and skills defied her physique. He nodded. Purna helped him stand and pushed him on the cot, tied him up and left the room to call Prakash.

*   *   *

The Family Roots

Akbarpur, Lucknow
Uttar Pradesh, India

For Aman and Rukhsar the eight hour drive to Lucknow was a chance to explore the Indian countryside. For Zubair it was a journey of pilgrimage to the land of his ancestry. For Prakash it was simply to concentrate on the road. Even on the expressway traffic indiscipline was everywhere. The three hundred and fifty kilometre drive was tedious and exhausting. The only saving grace was the onset of winter. The lush green farmlands mixed with yellow mustard fields were pleasing to the eyes and it was a glorious day with winter sun providing some warmth to the chilly weather.

The group had to overcome a problem. Zubair knew the name of his ancestral village but he had no idea where it was. All he knew was that it was in the district of Lucknow. Quite often villages had similar names located hundreds of miles apart.

Prakash swerved off the expressway towards the city centre. He stopped near a post-office and enquired about the village - Akbarpur. When they reached the *bazaar* of Akbarpur Zubair was surprised. The *bazaar* was teeming with people. He could see

71

shops and temporary stalls of virtually every commodity he could think of. Prakash invited them to indulge in some local snacks and delicacies. They learnt the reason for the crowded bazaar. Each day of the week, every village from the surrounding area had an allocated day when the main village road was packed with traders who set up their temporary stalls and wheel carts. Today was Sunday. It was Akbarpur's 'bazaar' day. The group had more surprises waiting. They learnt that the village with a population of about three hundred people had a community centre, a health centre, a school up to Higher Secondary and a twelve feet wide canal that fed the village farms.

The group decided to have early lunch and then search for the ancestral house of Ahmed family. Driving through the crowd was difficult, so Prakash found a spot to park his SUV and the group set about on foot to the village centre. On the way, to Rukhsar and Aman's amazement they learnt that the village had an elected committee called *'Panchayat'*. The head of the village was a *'Sarpanch'*, duly elected by the members of *Panchayat,* which assembled once a week to discuss matters relating to the village. While Prakash and Aman set off to find Sheikh Rashid Haji, the *Sarpanch*, Rukhsar and Zubair enquired about the location of their ancestral house. When the group re-assembled a few minutes later, they had no good news to share. Zubair wasn't able to trace his ancestral house and the locals had no idea what he was talking about, and Prakash couldn't find the *Sarpanch*. They enquired with the locals and to their relief they learnt that the *Sarpanch* had gone to a nearby village to attend a meeting of the heads of villages and would return by dusk. Until then they were invited by the locals to rest in the village *'Chaupal'*, the village central square where *Panchayat* assembled each week, or on special meetings, if required.

- - -

While they waited for the *Sarpanch,* Rukhsar decided to explore the village and learn more about the situation of a rare village with a predominantly Muslim population. Aman offered to walk with her and Rukhsar was glad. She was comfortable with him which she could never be with anyone outside her family, gender notwithstanding. She could speak on any subject with him without inhibition or hesitation. His wisdom always tended to overshadow his soft and polished nature.

As they walked through the village, talking to locals, trying to understand locals' psyche and thought process they were surprised to see a sight which contradicted what they had heard and seen all their lives. They found a temple on the side of the road with a large permanent stage, which according to villagers was especially set up for the annual performances of the *Ram-Leela*, a traditional opera performed by local actors stretched over a period of ten days during the festival of *Nav-Ratri*. The opera portrayed the life of *Lord Rama*, one of the most revered Gods. More amazingly, they learnt that most costumes worn during the opera, or items required, were provided by the Muslim community who were in two-thirds majority. To her utter amazement again, she found that many characters were played by some of the most gifted men in the village, some of them Muslims. The village opera was famous in the area and had an eighty year history of uninterrupted performances.

"Why don't we hear these stories across the border, Aman? We only hear negative stories in Pakistan. In last two days what I have seen seems like a dream to me." Rukhsar asked.

"Since independence India has been painted as an enemy. We have gone to war with India on various occasions for varied reasons, but none judicious. Pakistan was created for a purpose: to create a state where Muslims of the sub-continent could live peacefully, without the fear of domination by the Hindu majority. Since then, our leaders and military men have made strenuous efforts to ensure that India remains our arch enemy.

We have gone out of our way to make it our enemy. If you look at our policies - any policy; education, commerce or defence… all are Indian centric. In our school history texts it is clearly written that Hindus are our enemies, and India is Pakistan's enemy. With such mind-set and consistent brain-washing since childhood, do you expect good stories from India to be told? That would amount to treason according to some sections of our society." Aman said and paused, his eyes looking at the distance, his mind thoughtful, he turned to Rukhsar with a slight frown on his face, "Rukhsar, I have experienced something quite strange. I have travelled to over thirty countries in various capacities, mostly in the Asian region. What truly amazes me is that I never felt at home or even in relative comfort as I have felt here ever since we have arrived. You must have also noticed that culturally Pakistanis, especially *Punjabis* and *Muhajirs,* have more in common with India than they have with Sindh, Baluchistan, the Northern areas or Khyber Pakhtunkhwa. Vast majority in Pakistan people speak two languages, Punjabi and Urdu. Both these languages are common in India too and they originated here. Look at the life-styles, the dresses, the food habits, and even the folk music and dance forms; they all are common. The movie stars and musicians from across the borders are loved by one and all but we don't express our sentiments openly. Indian good stories are shared and admired and even praised privately but never openly. I say this though I am a *Pashtun* myself. I remember listening to interviews of two Pakistani cricketers of the day India won the 1983 cricket world cup in London. As the story goes, the whole Pakistan contingent celebrated the Indian victory in the Indian dressing room; dancing and singing all night. That bonhomie and liking for each other has eroded with time and it has been replaced by jealousy, dislike, mistrust and hatred."

"But I don't see any jealousy or hatred among Indians. I am sure it's there but I still have to experience it, but I really doubt if I will see it."

What would India be jealous of?" Aman asked bluntly and honestly, "They have gone miles ahead of Pakistan in virtually any field you can think of. We don't have a single thing which would make Indians jealous of us. Can you tell me one?"

Rukhsar stared at him in surprise. She had felt exactly the same a few moments ago. "Then why do we have so much anti-India propaganda? Here in India, barring accusations of Pakistani links to terrorism and its support to terrorists who strike in India, I hear nothing about Pakistan. There is an army operation by Pak against the militants in the FATA and Baluchistan areas. But I see no mention of these. They don't mention about the Pakistan problems or achievements at all. For them Pakistan news it like news from any other country in the foreign news segment. That's the difference I have found between the two countries. Why so?"

"There is a fundamental reason for it," Aman said, thinking hard, "I don't remember who said it, but it's true, 'Pakistan is obsessed with India, and India is obsessed with itself'."

Rukhsar was silent for a few moments. The last sentence of Aman gave her the all-encompassing reason for reactions in India and back in her own country. She looked at Aman as he walked beside her. He was thinking deeply about something. She took his hand in hers and clasped it firmly. He turned and looked at her, smiled and clasped her hand firmly.

"Aman, people here are so much like us. When they learn we are from across the border, I have seen special efforts on their part to make us comfortable. I saw that with the hotel staff in New Delhi, and again, here. It is the same in Pakistan. When we have guests from India they are treated as royalty. When this is true why is there so much hatred in the media and from our leaders?" Rukhsar asked helplessly.

"In Pakistan, nothing sells like anti-India sentiment and the media uses it to the fullest. In the Indian media I haven't found that intensity of anti-Pakistan sentiment, but there are some who do use it for their ratings. As for the rulers; civilian or military, they have created hype against India since Pakistan was created, and now that they have created an enemy, they use the sentiments of the people... they exploit it. It's come to a state where they can't simply change their stance overnight, though every government of the day knows that India has to be an important part of their plan if they want to see Pakistan progress. And yet, they use India to stir up emotions and exploit it to the fullest. It is not restricted to Pakistan alone. Politicians in India do the same from time to time when it suits them, especially during their election times. It's a pity!"

- - -

The late afternoon winter chill of the plains of North India was beginning to take effect. Rukhsar and Aman returned to the *Chaupal* to find a gathering around the visitors. Zubair and Prakash sat under a large tree on a platform which was the seat of the *Panchayat*. Some elders were keenly conversing with the two *Mehmaans* - the guests. When they saw the couple approach, two chairs were promptly placed in front of the seat of the *Sarpanch*. Zubair sadly informed them that they couldn't locate their ancestral house because of the sixty-five year gap in the family history; villagers were unable to recall which off the many houses belonged to his grandfather. However, there was an elderly man in the village who may have some knowledge about his ancestry and they were waiting for his arrival.

"Did you like our village?" the *Sarpanch* asked the couple casually.

"Yes, we did. It's self-sufficient. I see an efficient irrigation system and decent roads. You have schools and medical centre. What do you lack?" Rukhsar asked first.

The sixty-two year old *Sarpanch*, Hussein Inayatullah with long grey beard and wrinkles which were beginning to appear on his otherwise likeable face and smiling eyes, laughed, "Over the years things have changed. The villages around here have prospered. Government has set up *'Mandis'* where we sell our agro produce with a minimum support price. That helps in getting a decent return for our efforts. Government takes care of these things, but we do have issues and *'Insha-Allah'*, it will be done soon... things like uninterrupted power. Currently, we get eighteen to twenty hours of electricity, but it is better than many other villages which have sixteen to twenty hours, but things are improving. In few years we will have ample power. We are also expecting a medical college in this area in two-three years. Otherwise, we are doing well. Conditions are good although we are still not in a perfect situation."

"Then you are far better off than most people in this country. Why do you complain?" Rukhsar asked in humour.

The *Sarpanch* smiled and turned to Aman, who he felt, was hesitating. "You wish to ask something? Feel free."

Prakash Rohatgi laughed. "He's a career diplomat. He can't overcome his tactfulness in a week."

Hussein Inayatullah's face turned serious. "What do you hesitate to ask, Mr. Bux?"

Aman thought if he should ask, then he posed the question, "Do you ever regret not having migrated to Pakistan when you had a chance?" The moment he had asked, he realized his mistake and the next moment he hoped he hadn't spoiled the rapport Zubair and Prakash had created for themselves.

There was an uneasy silence in the dimming natural evening light. There were over thirty-five people excluding the visitors and all were silent. A sensitive issue had been raised. Aman Bux was disappointed with himself. As a diplomat he had hundreds of meetings on sensitive issues but he always came out trumps with his articulation. But at this instance he had failed himself momentarily - with his choice of words.

Hussein Inayatullah observed Aman. "You ask because you come from Pakistan? What is your intent, Aman?" *Sarpanch* asked without attempting to hide suspicion in his tone.

Aman looked at the *Sarpanch* apologetically. "I am sorry if I have hurt your sentiment. My intention is to understand what you think of the partition and it's after effects?"

The *Sarpanch* nodded his head but stayed silent for a while before replying, "I was born after partition. Till a few years after Independence this was a common topic for discussion but now it has become irrelevant. My father used to say that his financial situation did not allow him to migrate, though, till '63 people used to travel to and fro normally because it didn't need a passport, and train travel was free. However, over a period of time he said that he and others in the village and the Muslims here in general considered it to be a blessing in disguise. Today, we are happy to be in India and proud to be Indians. We don't call ourselves as Muslims of India, we call ourselves Indians first. We are *'Indian Muslims'*. I am a very proud Indian, Mr. Aman Khan Bux. I request you not to demean us because our forefathers didn't migrate to Pakistan. We are happy to be part of a country which gives us more freedom than any country in the world... or have you missed observing that?" The *Sarpanch* taunted.

Aman ignored the *Sarpanch's* tone and nodded his head in acceptance. "Sir, I apologize again for my poor choice of words. I did not mean to offend. We arrived in India two days ago and we hadn't expected what we have seen. The general Muslim population in India is better off than the general population in my own country - in many respects. That is in contrast to what we keep hearing from our media and leaders. Having seen the difference, I want to understand the feelings you have for Pakistan and for people who had migrated. I am curious to know what people who couldn't migrate felt about it."

Before the *Sarpanch* could speak, a man in his early twenties spoke. "Do you feel there is discrimination against Muslims?"

"I am given to understand so. Yes!" Aman replied honestly.

The young man looked at Aman and the other three guests. "I will tell you the difference between the peoples of Pakistan and India. But before that, let me introduce myself. I am Imran Ali Zaidi. Originally, my forefathers hail from Iran. My great grand-father came to India as a trader almost a century ago. He fell in love with this country, married a local girl and stayed back. I am an Engineering student who couldn't afford to pay the fees. The government provides us special facilities. I got an education loan through the scheme which allows people of poor financial background and other backward communities for higher studies. Is that discrimination? The sovereign of the country is the President. India has had three Muslim Presidents. Is that discrimination? There was a strange situation recently, where we had a Sikh Prime Minister from a ruling party headed by a Christian woman, under a Muslim President; an Attorney General who belongs to probably the world's smallest minority, the Parsis. And the leader of the opposition was a Hindu. Is that discrimination? Remember, Sir! These are elected leaders of a predominantly Hindu country which chose to elect its leaders through a free and fair electoral process. Where do you see discrimination?"

"What you say is true but there are stories about communal clashes. Isn't that a fact too?" Aman Khan asked.

"That is true. There are religious clashes but not to the extent as it is propagated. In a country of over one billion with two hundred million Muslims and nearly nine hundred million Hindus you will expect to get some rogue elements and zealots in both communities. But if you see the track record, we are faring far better than most countries, including your own." The young Zaidi said defiantly, angrily.

Prakash Rohatgi was keenly observing the conversation. He knew Aman's intentions were noble. Aman was keen to know how the people whose forefathers hadn't migrated felt about living in India, a Hindu majority country. Having heard Ali's response, Prakash wanted his guests to have a clearer picture. He raised his hand to add his comment. "There are negatives which do exist. Illiteracy, poverty, lack of countrywide modern infrastructure, etc., But these are areas where we are working hard. Illiteracy was over seventy-four present at the time of independence which is below twenty present today. Among the illiterate, most are people over the age of fifty. Among the younger generation, the illiteracy rate is below six per cent, but it is there and we can't ignore that fact. Poverty has gone down to below thirty per cent, but it's there. The central and state governments provide grains at very cheap rates to the population which is below poverty line; in twenty years this will be below ten per cent. We do have problems but we are working towards it, Aman. We have major issues like providing continuous power to entire population. All these are problems but there are some which in my opinion are graver than illiteracy and infrastructure or depravity. We have serious challenges like crimes against women, sectarianism; class divides etc., No, Aman! We are far from being a satisfied community. But... we are working, and we shall get there. We are not a country which is depressed or dejected. We are people of a nation which knows it is working hard and it will go places. It is a beginning and we will reach the top. Wait and watch!"

There was an uncomfortable silence for a few moments. Prakash thought of something and smiled, "Aman... Rukhsar... let me tell you something strange about ancient, medieval and modern India. These are facts which are not spoken of as often or as clearly as they should be. Do you know that the oldest built mosque in the world after the Mosque in Medina is in India; and contrary to your teachers, Islam didn't arrive in India through Mohammed bin-Qasim, it came through a Kerelite, Cheraman Perumal, who was a contemporary of Prophet Mohammad. On his visit to Arabia Perumal embraced Islam and he sent an emissary to Kerela, and through his letter requested that the emissary Malik Ibn-Dinar be given land to build a mosque. The King gifted a 'Buddha-Vihar' to Malik Ibn-Dinar and in 629 this mosque was completed. That was built in the life time of the Prophet. It still exists in pristine condition and you can still see the grandeur of it. It is called the Cheraman Juma Masjid. This mosque was renovated in the 11th and 18th century, expanded in 1974 and re-expanded in 1984. To this day, it is revered by people of many sects and religions. You will be surprised that many non-Muslims come to this place for the Hindu ceremony of 'Vidya-arambham', which means 'initiation of education', for their children." Prakash Rohatgi paused and continued, "Not just Islam, you can find historical evidences of other religions which came to India lot before people generally know about them. Judaism also arrived in Cochin and the King there, who by the way was a devout Hindu, gifted a land to the Jews to build a synagogue. This was also the area where the first Christian church was built. Incidentally, all these are in Kerela. Kerela means '*God's own country*', and it isn't just for namesake. These religions came to Indian shores from this area and thrived. Also one of the most revered Hindu seers '*Adi Shankarcharya*' also hailed from Kerela and He is credited with re-writing and translation of Vedas in simple language for all to understand." Prakash looked at Zubair and Rukhsar, and continued, "The Parsis, The Zoroastrians, are probably the smallest minority in the world. When they were being persecuted in Iran, they sought refuge in Gujarat, where the King gave them land and facilities. Today, the Parsis are the most prosperous community in the world in terms wealth-population ratio. You name the religion or sects and you will find them in abundance in India. You will find people from virtually any country you can think of, living in India and thriving, with level-playing field for all. I say this to tell you that we may have odd Hindu-Muslim clashes but you will also find that India is a world in microcosm; with people from Afro-origins in various parts of India, Europeans who stayed back after the independence, be it British, Dutch, French or Portuguese. India is said to be the land of religions, I add to it. I say India is more a land of spirituality than religion."

Aman was thinking of questioning about a sensitive matter but he thought otherwise and decided to wait. Surprisingly, Rukhsar asked that question, "Why is the general Muslim population relatively poorer than its Hindu brethren?"

Prakash's face turned grim. He thought for a while, looked at her and replied. "The reason isn't discrimination as you are trying to say. The major problem here is basic: education. It is a tragedy that the ratio of school and college dropouts among Muslims is as high as most backward communities here. That is a big problem. Without higher education we can't expect people to have a decent life in modern times. Otherwise, there is no discrimination when it comes to Government or private jobs. If you see in the corporate or private jobs, you will find people from all communities working together. And, you will find one thing common among all; they are all well-educated and they get jobs on merit, not on the religion they belong to." Prakash clarified, and added as an afterthought to clear another point, "What Zaidi said a little while ago. I am adding to it. In India, four or more people pelting stones, is technically called a riot. When these are between two groups of different sects, classes or religions, it is termed as sectarian or communal riots. There have been such riots between religious groups especially during festivals, but as the days go by, the numbers have fallen. Then again, once or twice in a decade, there are large scale riots in some city or other; it is a fact that it happens but happily, the numbers there too have come down drastically. With progress and better livelihood, riots will be less. Riots are mostly related to two factors: religion and socio-economic situation. The first is not a big issue in India. India is a truly secular state; every religion has equal rights, without bias. The second, socio-economic conditions are a major issue..."

Prakash stopped mid-way when he saw Hussein Inayatullah rise to greet an elderly person. The old man probably in his late eighties or early nineties walked slowly to the centre and acknowledged respectful greetings from every person. He sat next to the *Sarpanch* and humorously enquired, "What's so important to drag this old man from his quiet rest?"

The *Sarpanch* introduced the visitors and told him the reason why they had sought the help of the eldest man in the village. The old man, Haji Mohammed Bari, observed Zubair keenly. "You are Gulzar Ahmed's son?" the old man asked.

Zubair was surprised at the casualness of the tone when the old man mentioned his father's name, "Yes," he said eagerly.

"Why have you come here?" Haji asked with annoyance closely bordering on anger.

Zubair was surprised at Haji's tone. He had no idea why Haji Bari was angry. "I want to visit my ancestral house, Haji Sa'ab," he replied respectfully.

"You must seek the permission of Thakur Pukhraj *Saheb* if you wish to see your house. He owns that *'haveli'* now. Your grandfather sold it to him before he migrated to Pakistan." The old man said without mellow in his tone.

"You are upset with me. Can you please tell me why, Haji Sa'ab?" Zubair asked politely.

The freckled old man didn't reply. He kept staring at Zubair with contempt. Prakash Rohatgi sensed it too and he diverted the topic and asked the Haji if they could meet Thakur Pukhraj Singh. Haji told him that they could meet him any time they wished but advised him not to tell Thakur about Zubair's ancestry. Once again the visitors were surprised. Haji Mohammed Bari, for some reason was extremely upset with Zubair. Rukhsar took over from her father and Prakash, and pressed Haji to know why he was upset. Haji couldn't be rude to the beautiful, cultured lady. He politely asked her to discuss it with Thakur Pukhraj Singh, and he fell silent. The visitors knew the conversation with the grand old man was over. The visitors took the permission of the *Panchayat* and decided to leave. When they asked for the directions to the *'haveli'* - the palatial house, Imran Ali Zaidi offered to escort them to the Thakur residence.

-    -   -

Fifteen minutes later the group stood outside the gates of Thakur's residence. Ali had informed that Thakur Pukhraj Singh was the motivator of the village. He didn't involve himself in local politics but when guidance was sought, Thakur was approached. Thakur's advice was always followed. The eighty-nine year old Thakur was the man the entire village looked up to. He had single-handedly worked to turn the fortunes of a backward Akbarpur into self-sufficient modern village. He had two sons; one had migrated with his family to Kolkata where he had a flourishing business and occasionally visited the village, while the other son looked after the farm and he was the advisor to the *'Panchayat'* in Thakur's absence. The younger son's family had grown to set up small cottage industries where virtually all villagers were employed which added to the earnings of the villagers.

Imran Ali asked the guests to wait while he went in to speak to the Thakur.

Zubair couldn't help but admire the opulent and large estate which belonged to his ancestors. An excitement grew in his heart as he looked around the estate. The weather was cold now, almost freezing and they were not aptly dressed. They waited outside the gate for a few minutes till Ali came running to them, smiling from ear to ear.

The group entered the gates happily, but when they would return to the gates, their plans would have turned upside down.

*   *   *

The Ahmed Ancestry

1947-1971

At the gates, the visitors were welcomed by Thakur Pukhraj Singh's younger son, Sumer Singh. He led them through the courtyard into a large open sitting room which had a look of antiquity about it. The royal lounge was huge. It had a seating capacity for over thirty people, lined with divans and chairs, and three large tables decorated in a classical *Rajputana* style with satin drapes lining the sitting area without doors. The guests were led to the divans. As they occupied their seats a distinguished looking man in his late eighties entered with a regal gait. The man had an aura the visitors had rarely seen. Thakur Pukhraj Singh was a true giant; stretching over six feet, broad shouldered with a face that oozed royalty and elegance. His magnetic presence nearly numbed his visitors into submission. Thakur walked up to each of them shaking their hands and greeting Rukhsar with a '*Namaste*' and putting his hands on her head to bless her.

Prakash started to speak but stopped when he saw Thakur's hand rise. "You have come here at dinner time. So, kindly join us. We can talk after dinner," Thakur said and produced a magnetic smile which charmed the visitors again. He took Rukhsar's hand authoritatively and led the group to the diner. Rukhsar was shocked at the affection which emanated from the way Thakur Pukhraj Singh held her. She walked beside him and the rest followed.

In contrast to the exotic, palatial house, the food was simple but delightfully tasty though prepared at short notice.

After dinner the group re-assembled in the lounge - the *Divan*. Thakur Sumer Singh also joined the group. Alerted already by Haji Mohammed Bari, Zubair Ahmed did not dare to initiate the conversation. He hoped Prakash would do that for him; instead Aman Bux touched the topic after Rukhsar had drifted towards it. Thakur Pukhraj Singh was a good listener and a prolific speaker. His intelligent eyes and saintly posture still had a mesmerising effect on the guests.

Aman started diplomatically. "Thakur Sa'ab, this is a fantastic house. How long have you owned it?"

Thakur had a wide smile on his lips. He was silent for a while before smiling, "My late father bought this house from her great-grandfather, Mukhtar Ahmed," he said and put his hand on Rukhsar's head affectionately.

Zubair gathered his courage and spoke after a few moments of silence. "I thank you for maintaining the house so well. I did not have an idea that our house was so grand."

"Your father, Gulzar, and I were good friends. When your grand-father sold it to my father, for a phenomenal sum of two thousand in that era, Gulzar had asked me to maintain it. I have kept my promise but he didn't. He had promised to return and live with us for a few days but he didn't return."

"You are sad," Rukhsar said.

"Yes, I am. His father and mine were friends. Then Gulzar and I were friends. At the time of independence, your great grandfather had already migrated to Lahore. The week before independence, he returned, sold this house and the estate and went back to Lahore. I was hoping to meet Gulzar but..." the sadness on that saintly face was obvious.

Rukhsar felt the vibes of sincere love and affection from her grand-father's friend. She had a strange feeling; it was like her own great grandfather was sitting next to her and caring for her. She thought for a moment and asked the Thakur hesitantly, "Why are you and Haji Saheb upset with Abbu?"

"What do you know about your family history, Rukhsar?" Thakur asked her.

"I don't know much about it. *Abbu* doesn't talk about it. All I know is that my great grand-father migrated to Pakistan after the partition. He lived with my great grand-mother till they died in the fifties. My grand-father was an army officer in Pakistan army and he was married to his first cousin on his mother's side. He was martyred on the Eastern front during the 1971 Indo-Pak war and my grand-mother passed away in 1984. My father was a Major in Pakistan Armed Forces and my mother is a home-maker in Lahore. That's it. Why do you ask, *Baba*?" She took the reference of *Baba*, meaning grand-father, from Sumer's twenty year old son, Avdhesh Singh.

Thakur Pukhraj Singh smiled when Rukhsar referred to him as *Baba*. He put his hand on her head to bless her again. Then he turned to Zubair and asked him, "Can you add to that?" His tone did not have the same affection as it did when he had spoken to Rukhsar, but not in anger either.

"No, Thakur Sa'ab, nothing that I can add... nothing which could be of any consequence." Zubair replied honestly.

Thakur nodded his head, "What happened to Gulzar?" This time his tone was softer, more mellowed.

Zubair wondered what the Thakur meant or implied by that question. "What do you mean, Thakur Sa'ab?"

"How and where did he die? What were the circumstances of his death?" Thakur enquired bluntly.

"He died in Dhaka on 4th December in 1971, fighting the Indian Army and the Mukti Bahini." Zubair replied eagerly. He had a suspicious feeling about the conversation. He had a sinking feeling that there was bad news to come during this conversation.

While Prakash and Aman were intrigued by the line and tone of the conversation, Rukhsar felt numbness in her spine. She too had a feeling that the conversation was leading to some information.

Thakur stared at Zubair half in disbelief, half in suspicion. He was trying to convince himself that Zubair was speaking the truth. The atmosphere in the *divan* was tensed. Pukhraj Singh's stare had made it palpable. Sumer Singh walked out and returned a minute later with a set of photographs which he handed to Zubair. Zubair took the photographs, looked at Sumer Singh doubtfully and looked at the photographs.

"Do you recognize the people in these photographs?" Sumer Singh asked Zubair.

One by one Zubair sifted through the photographs slowly; looking at each photograph, trying to recognize the people in them. He recognized some faces in the faded old black and white photographs, others he didn't, but those who he didn't know had striking resemblance to the members of his family. A sudden thought occurred to him. These were members of his family but he didn't recognise most of them. Then he saw some photographs at the end which brought a lump in his throat. He placed the photographs on the table, bowed his head, closed his eyes and tried his best not to cry; emotions were overpowering and feelings uncontrollable. He steeled his lips stopping himself from crying.

The other guests were surprised to see a strong man like Zubair moved to tears. Rukhsar and Aman took the photos and scanned them. Rukhsar found a young Thakur Pukhraj Singh standing with a group of people: her great grand-father and his family. She saw a photograph of her grand-father looking very boyish, posing with his parents and some other people she didn't recognise. There were people whom she could identify and some she could not. Then there were eight coloured photographs which were quite recent. In these, she could identify an aged Gulzar Ahmed, her grand-father. She was shocked. Was this true?

Rukhsar turned to Pukhraj Singh, *"Baba,* is this true?" she asked the revered old man, and the next moment she realized the futility of the question. It had to be true.

Pukhraj Singh patted her hand affectionately and turned to Zubair. "Zubair, I thought you knew. I learn now that you don't."

Zubair looked at Thakur and nodded his head. "I don't know what to say. What is the story behind these? Those girls in the picture with my father, they resemble my grandparents. They... who are they?"

Thakur's face was grim. It was not for the reasons the guests thought but for the fact he realized that Zubair was actually un-aware of his family history and legacy. He asked Rukhsar, "Who christened your name Rukhsar, dear?"

The out of the context question again surprised Rukhsar, "My grandmother, I think."

Pukhraj Singh nodded his head, "I thought so..." he said and put his finger tip on a girl who stood happily holding her sister's hand in a faded black and white photograph. "That, my dear, is Rukhsar. You have been named after her. The girl whose hands she holds is her younger sister, Shazia. They were Gulzar's younger sisters."

The room fell into silence. Rukhsar was looking at her grand-aunts' picture and staring at others in the photograph. They were part of her family, ancestry. Slowly, Thakur introduced her to each person in the photograph. Zubair did not know them by name or face but he was starting to predict each one of them by the time Thakur had reached half way. They saw Mukhtar Ahmed with his wife, Amina Begum, with their three children: Gulzar, Rukhsar and Shazia. Then there were pictures of Mukhtar Ahmed's relatives on his father's and mother's side, and there were some pictures of young people: Gulzar, Thakur Pukhraj, Shazia, Rukhsar and two other young men whom Thakur identified as Rama Shankar, a family friend, and a young Haji Mohammed Bari. When he came to the coloured photographs, Thakur paused, thinking if he should let the guests know who these people were; and more importantly, if he should tell them how those people were related to the Ahmed family.

By now Zubair was desperate to learn about the people in the coloured photographs. He knew he was about to get some news he didn't want to. But, he had to be certain. "Who are these people? What is the story about my aunts? What happened? Please tell me," he pleaded.

Thakur looked at the photos and back at Zubair. "Do you have to know this? If you do, it is not easy to live with it."

"I... have... to know," Zubair said softly, desperately.

Thakur started to speak but he was interrupted by his son. "He wakes up at four in the morning and normally retires to sleep by nine pm. It's already too late for him. Can we continue tomorrow?" he asked the guests.

"It's ok. I will manage." Thakur dismissed his son's request to the guests. This was too important to be postponed. When Zubair had expressed his wish to know, he had the right to know the history. Thakur turned to Zubair Ahmed, "There is some information which I have gathered but I am afraid I don't have the minute details, so I will tell you what I know. I don't know where to begin so I begin with the time of partition from where our families drifted apart," Thakur stood upright and paced the large sitting area. "Before partition, your grand-father, Mukhtar Ahmed approached my father one morning and offered to sell his estate. My father had a large estate himself, and he was well respected as a *Zamindar* and a philanthropist; that was a weird combination in those days. My father was his best friend so when he was asked why he wanted to sell his property, Mukhtar Sa'ab expressed his fear that after partition, it would be difficult for

Muslims to live in India and so he was migrating to Pakistan. My father tried to persuade him to re-consider his decision but he didn't succeed. He agreed to purchase the estate at approximately the prevalent market price at the time. When he had sold his property, your grandfather went to Lahore to buy properties there. He didn't find any to his liking there so he went to Lyallpur, which is Faisalabad now, I believe. He met a Sikh *Zamindar* who had farmland in Cholistan. Mukhtar Sa'ab bought the farmland and a house in Lahore. After purchasing the properties he returned to India to take his family but by then the carnage has begun on both sides. Sikhs and Hindus coming to India and Muslims going to Pakistan were being massacred. Mukhtar Sa'ab didn't risk taking chance and drove to Lahore from Amritsar. Just then news arrived of a train loaded with Hindus and Sikhs migrating to India had been attacked and set ablaze. In that carnage very few people survived. Then stories of brutality began to filter through: women and young girls were being abducted, raped and killed or forcibly taken away. We knew there would be repercussions. The following week another train was attacked. This time the train was travelling in the other direction. Similar atrocities were committed again by the other side. Meanwhile, here we had many villages with Muslim majority, while there were other villages where Muslims were in a minority. The surrounding villages of this area like Malihabad, Chinhut, and Utratiyaa etc. were in real danger of being attacked. Sardar Vallabhbhai Patel, the then Home Minister ordered the police to keep strict vigil in these areas. We formed groups that helped the police to prevent attacks. But massacres and insanity had unnerved Mukhtar Sa'ab. He was beginning to have second thoughts about going to Pakistan but since he had already invested virtually all his wealth in Pakistan, he had to go. He waited for situation to calm down but when the carnage continued for weeks, he made a decision; a decision which was opposed by everyone in this village. He decided to take his wife and Gulzar with him and leave his daughters with us till it was safe to take them to Lahore. He left in May, '48. We were hoping he would return to take his daughters but he never did. As the years passed by, we expected Gulzar to return but he didn't come either. In the meantime, here, Rukhsar went into a depression; she felt that the sisters were abandoned because they were girls. Shazia went on to become a teacher in a local school and our dear Haji Mohammed Bari Sa'ab fell in love with her. We received a telegram, a wired message, from Gulzar about six years after they had migrated. He was coming to take back his sisters. In '54 he arrived one night and met us, his sisters, Haji Sa'ab whom Shazia had married just a few months earlier, and then abruptly he left the same night with a promise to return soon. To this day he hasn't returned. In the hope of seeing their family again, both sisters went into depression. From what I have gathered, there was a reason…"

Thakur's grandson, Avdhesh Singh entered with snacks and tea for the guests. In the cold winter night it was a welcome drink. It helped in settling the emotionally charged atmosphere in the room. When the plates were cleared, Zubair hesitantly asked Thakur, "What happened to my aunts? Where are they now?"

Thakur raised his hand asking him to wait. "I will come to that later. I don't want to miss out on anything that I know. It may help you, once I finish what I have to say. I was talking about Gulzar's sudden departure and then not returning. My theory is that Gulzar wanted to return to India for good. Maybe that was the other reason why he came to visit us that night. From what I understood, he was fearful of sectarian violence against the *Qadiyanis*. In '53, there was mass persecution of the *Ahmediya* community across Pakistan, and specifically in your Punjab province. You people belong to that sect and so, his life and yours was in peril. His fears came true years later when in '74 *Ahmediya* community was declared non-Muslims by government of Pakistan headed by Prime Minister Zulfiqar Ali Bhutto. Gulzar had assessed correctly. I learnt recently that Gulzar, a decorated, commissioned army officer, requested his superiors in '55 to be transferred to East-Pakistan. He was transferred to an army base near Chittagong and later to Dhaka. I understand his situation but people in this village can't forgive him or Mukhtar Sa'ab. We hold them responsible for the depression and loneliness of your aunts. Now you know why Haji Sa'ab is upset?"

"Where are my aunts, Thakur Saheb?" Zubair asked again in sheer desperation.

Thakur Pukhraj Singh looked at Zubair with sadness, "India's partition cost millions of lives. But these were people who were physically killed in the insanity by zealots who had no love or respect for humanity. There were greater casualties in the list of people who weren't killed but affected because of the partition," Thakur turned to Rukhsar, "Your grand-aunts were in that category, my dear child," he said and turned to Zubair. "I will take you where Rukhsar rests in peace."

Gloom descended in the large sitting area. Prakash and Aman seemed unaffected but no one knew the agony they felt. Their history was no different. There was a silent prayer for the departed soul on every lip. Thakur rose and stood in front of Zubair's divan and patted him on the shoulder in empathy. "Shazia and Rukhsar were like members of my family. We and the villagers did all we could but we couldn't replace the affection and love they desired from their family. Throughout their lives, those poor girls kept shunting between depression and sadness, between hope and despair, and virtually between life and death. I wish you had come a year earlier. It would have given Rukhsar some solace, some redemption for the pain, suffering and agony those poor souls went through."

Zubair Ahmed gathered his strength and controlled his emotions to ask Thakur about his other aunt, Shazia. Thakur did not reply, instead he asked Zubair to wait until the next morning.

- - -

Zubair heard a rap on the door. He opened his eyes and noticed it was still dark. He wondered why they were woken up so early. His watch showed 5am. He opened the door and saw the giant figure of Avdhesh Singh standing studiously. "Is everything all right?" Zubair asked.

Avdhesh smiled courteously, "*Baba* is ready. He is waiting for you and others in the *divan*. He says we should leave early and return before breakfast time. Can you be ready in twenty minutes?"

Zubair replied in the affirmative.

A half hour later the guests assembled in the *divan*. The three generation of the Thakur family were waiting for them. "I know you must be inconvenienced but we are early risers and we have a tradition. If we go to a cemetery we must leave and return early before we take our baths or do *Pujas*." Sumer Singh explained.

Zubair Ahmed acknowledged. "You said, 'cemetery'? Where are we going?"

"Come with me," Thakur ordered.

Eighty-nine year old Pukhraj Singh briskly walked through unpaved paths and through vast fields, leading the group. Although all were aptly dressed, the visitors were surprised to see Thakur with just a shawl thrown over a thick *Kurta and dhoti*. A few minutes later they stood in front of the gates of a Muslim cemetery. Thakur led the group through the gates to a large tombstone in a corner. Around it was neatly carpeted area with a lawn where the tombstone stood defiantly to the life the remains of whose lay beneath. The black tombstone with golden script etched in Urdu with Rukhsar's name and dates of her birth and death. The group read the inscription on the epitaph and sadness was writ large on their faces. The epitaph read: *'Here lie the remains of a great soul which got no love in return for hers. God bless her with peace! ~ Haji Mohammed Bari!*

The group stood in front of the tombstone and paid respects in their own way. Zubair, his daughter Rukhsar and Aman read the *'Fateha'* for Rukhsar senior. It was strange that in all her life she never got love and respects she yearned for, but sadly, she got her wishes only a year after her death.

- - -

Before returning, Thakur led the group to the rear of his *haveli*, to a small, beautiful four room house. He asked Sumer to unlock the house and lead the team inside. Zubair had one look inside and he knew this was the house where his aunts had lived. He was surprised how well it was maintained; in its pristine condition. Throughout the house he sensed the love and longing for family by the Ahmed sisters. He was stunned to find a beautiful portrait of the family picture in vibrant colours; it was a coloured version of the black and white family photo they had seen the previous night.

Zubair had an expression of longing, Thakur Pukhraj Singh guessed correctly. He patted Zubair on his shoulder. "Shazia and Rukhsar lived here. Shazia stayed in this house to take care of her sister even after marriage. She used to shunt between Haji Saheb's house and this. It was her daily routine. To Haji's credit, he never objected or intervened in Shazia's affairs. The younger sister would start the day by tending to her sister, go to school, and return by lunch time to cook if Rukhsar was not in mood to do so. Then she would go to Haji Saheb's house and return in the evening. Most of the times, Shazia would take her sister with her." Thakur paused, thought and said softly, "They were angels, Zubair. They deserved a better life!"

Zubair couldn't speak. He wandered around the house with a strange feeling; a sense of Déjà vu. He felt as if he had been to this place. The sense of belonging and ownership was overwhelming. He knew now why he had been desperate to come here. This place belonged to him, to his ancestors, and to his children. The place had beckoned him to his roots. He was home!

As if Thakur was reading his mind, he informed Zubair, "If you wish to live here, it is yours. After the sisters, only Haji Bari Sa'ab has claim on this property. Though I had this built for the sisters, I have no moral claim over it. I had transferred this house to the sisters when they had matured. So, if Haji Bari doesn't object, you can claim this property because Shazia and Haji Sa'ab didn't have any children. If the villagers have any objections I will overrule it through the *'Panchayat'*."

Zubair looked at the saintly figure of his father's friend and bowed in respect and silently observed the glowing face of the village's most powerful man and knew why the villagers revered him. Thakur Pukhraj Singh was the man who ruled the surrounding villages not through *Panchayat* or official authority, but through his sheer stature and wisdom. Zubair bowed to Thakur in gratitude again, but said nothing - his face said it all… And he cried.

- - -

As day broke, the group walked back silently. No one had the courage or wish to speak, though the visitors still wanted to learn about Shazia, and they thought of other photographs and the people in them with family resemblance. It was heart wrenching to see resembling faces and that of Gulzar Ahmed. Was he alive? If so, where was he? If he wasn't home, why did he abandon the family he loved so much?

After breakfast, they reassembled in the divan. In three days since landing their feet in India, Rukhsar Ahmed's mind had been in turmoil. A determination to take her father back to Pakistan had turned into a journey into family history and now she had learnt that she had grandaunts; one of whom had existed and died in loneliness. And, she had no information earlier that they ever existed. Now she feared there were still more pages of her family album to be turned.

—   —   —

Pukhraj Singh asked Sumer to fetch the photographs again. He turned to his guests and addressed them in general, "You have many questions in your minds. It was not the time to answer them yesterday. There are some things you may learn today which may shock you."

Aman hesitantly asked Thakur, "Thakur *Baba*, how did you get these photographs?"

"We found some from the almirahs Mukhtar Sa'ab had left behind. The coloured ones have come from someone whom you do not know, but I suspect… you will meet soon."

Sumer put the photographs on the table and left the room to attend to his farm. Thakur saw Avdhesh and Sumer Singh drive away before returning to the sensitive matter. He knew this would emotionally hurt his guests. "You must wonder how I know a lot about your family's post partition history. I will start by asking you. Look at these pictures once again and tell me if you recognize anyone here," he asked Zubair.

Zubair picked up two photographs and brought them close to Thakur's hands. "The old, frail looking man resembles my father," he said hesitantly. He wasn't sure if he would be happy to know if his guess was right or wrong; either way he would be at a loss. If the man in the picture was indeed his father, why had he abandoned them? If not, then he would wish that the man would be his father whom he had missed for over forty years.

Thakur Pukhraj Singh took a deep breath, looked at Zubair and Rukhsar and declared, "That *is* your father."

Zubair closed his eyes in relief; in prayer and in thanking to God. "He… What happened? Who are the others in the picture?"

Thakur looked at Zubair thoughtfully. He stayed quiet for a few moments, then waived at Rukhsar to sit next to him. Rukhsar sat next to Thakur on his luxurious royal divan. Thakur put his hand around Rukhsar's shoulder affectionately and replied to Zubair's questions, "The elderly woman is your step-mother and the kids are your half-siblings: two sisters and a brother."

Zubair stared at Thakur blankly unwilling to believe what he had heard. His father was neither a traitor nor a deserter of his family or country. He knew his father was a hero in more ways than one. There must be a profound reason for his father to have done what he did. Zubair had to find answers, and his father. He had to know how and why his father decided to have another family. The questions were too many and he had no answers.

For Rukhsar it was a repeat of the history. She had come to fetch her father and now it was she and her father seeking to learn about her grand-father. It was ironic. What could be the circumstances under which Gulzar Ahmed had to abandon his family? They did not wish to judge without knowing the situations in which Gulzar was, because they had experienced it with Zubair and it could have happened with Gulzar too.

Thakur stretched his hand out at Rukhsar. She held it and smiled nervously. Thakur beamed wryly and turned to Zubair, "I have the papers of your aunts' house. I will transfer them to you. If Haji Sa'ab objects, I will convince him that you deserve it because the property in the absence of the sisters is morally mine and I know Haji Sa'ab is a man of high morality so he will not oppose. But, I have a strict condition attached to it." He looked at Zubair with an amusing smile on his lips.

"Whatever you say, Thakur Sa'ab," Zubair replied happily.

"You should know my 'strict condition' before you agree. You must also know why I put that condition." Thakur said to Zubair and looked at Rukhsar, "My dear, our family seems to be cursed. For six generations we haven't had a girl child born in our family. Amongst us it is not considered good. We have been blessed with a large family but no female child. So, my condition is - that I will hand over the papers if you let Rukhsar be the owner. She will have to retain and maintain that house."

Zubair nodded and smiled despite the situation. Rukhsar looked at her father and Thakur. She noticed that her host's face was smiling but his eyes were sad; longing somewhere deep inside. She knew how deeply Thakur meant about his yearning for a girl child. It occurred to her why he was showing extra affection to her.

Thakur hugged her, "Whether you are in Lahore, Lucknow or London you must maintain that house. You will always be happy and you will flourish further if you own and maintain this house. Blessings of the ancestors never go waste, child."

"I will, *Baba*. I promise you." Rukhsar promised solemnly.

Zubair was silent. He was engrossed in his thoughts and Thakur was waiting for him to ask his questions, answers to most of which he did not have.

"What else should I know, Thakur Sa'ab?" Zubair asked in a soft, mellowed tone.

"I have almost nothing to add here, only little bits which aren't so relevant. You can get more information from your extended family."

"How do I get in touch with them?" Zubair asked eagerly.

"I will give you contact details of your step-brother," Thakur pulled out a writing pad and looked up the details in his old styled telephone diary, jotted down the details and handed it to Zubair.

Zubair looked at the note and again he was surprised. He looked at Thakur, "Dhaka? My father is in Dhaka? What about my aunt Shazia?"

Thakur nodded. With a sad note he replied, "Shadab gave me his contact details when he came here a year ago and took Shazia along with him. This was a few months after Rukhsar had passed away. Shazia was distraught after her sister's death so she decided to visit Dhaka to meet her brother. Shadab called Haji a month later to inform him that his wife had died in an accident."

- - -

When the guests sought Thakur's permission to leave, he summoned Rukhsar and Aman to his room. There, Sumer Singh presented a gift to Rukhsar and a packet to Aman Bux. Rukhsar opened her gift and her jaws dropped when she saw an exquisite wedding dress. Made from crimson Banaras silk, the traditional wedding dress was intricately embroidered with golden *'zari'*, threads. Thakur didn't tell her that it was the dress Shazia had worn at her wedding nearly half century ago.

Aman opened his packet to find a hand written, *'Quran-e-Majid'* which dated back to early seventeenth century. It was owned by the Ahmed family for generations. Thakur family had found it in one of the almirahs in Gulzar Ahmed's bedroom.

"I hope you will invite me to your wedding. In any case, this is our wedding gift for the two of you in advance," Thakur said and blessed the couple.

Aman was overcome with affection. They hugged Thakur Pukhraj Singh and promised to invite him to their wedding.

"There is one more thing. It's important," Thakur said to Rukhsar, "Your father probably doesn't know of it. My dear, the Ahmed family has a regal history of two centuries. You come from a lineage of a semi-royal family. Your forefathers were trusted ministers of the Nawabs of Lucknow before the British took over."

Thakur Pukhraj Singh's guests gathered in the room where Zubair had slept the previous night.

"I am going to Dhaka." Zubair declared to all in general, but meant it specifically for Prakash Rohatgi.

Prakash nodded. "I will make arrangements for the trip to Kolkata this evening and from there to Dhaka probably tomorrow morning. What about Rukhsar and Aman?"

"They will return to Lahore." Zubair stated.

Rukhsar screamed, "No!" She looked at her father and stated clearly, "I am going with you. That is final."

"If she goes, I go too," Aman said firmly.

"I can't use my passport. I could get into trouble," Zubair tried reasoning his daughter, "Aman can't use his passport because he is still officially, a diplomat and if you use your passport, people may be looking out for you and Aman. Don't forget what happened in New Delhi. That man was following Aman. This is a risky trip and I can't let you take risks."

"Can you stop me from going, *Abbu*?" she asked defiantly.

"Yes, I can, by not going to Dhaka."

"No! You must go to Dhaka. You must meet *Dadaji*. You can't miss this chance. Let me come with you, please. I am sure Prakash can manage something. He is resourceful. I want to be with you, *Abbu*."

Zubair and Rukhsar stared at each other; neither willing to back down. Zubair gave in first, and turned to Prakash, and shrugged helplessly. Prakash was hoping Aman would be able to change Rukhsar's decision. Aman clasped his hands and drew a deep breath. "I wish she didn't make the trip but if her mind is made up we can't change it."

- - -

Two hours later, the visitors were ready to leave. They went to bid farewell to Thakur Pukhraj Singh. Thakur was quiet. He smiled wryly. "When you meet Gulzar tell him that I have kept my promise, he hasn't. He had my contact number but he didn't bother to call me though I had called him thrice, and he did not take my call."

Zubair and others understood why Thakur Pukhraj Singh was upset. He had every reason to be. Zubair bowed to him and offered his sincere apologies but he knew it wasn't accepted. Rukhsar's hand touched Thakur's wrists and she apologized too. Thakur melted instantly. He put his hands on her head and blessed her happily.

The group offered their respects and departed.

Thakur Pukhraj Singh stood at the edge of his terrace and watched Avdhesh Singh drive away the visitors to the airport. His heart ached - Partition of India hadn't just created a great divide between the peoples of two religions with common languages and cultures; the partition had divided the hearts and minds of peoples into two nations along religious lines. The greatest tragedy was that the partition had replaced love, respect, brotherhood and sharing with intolerance, animosity, jealousy and hatred. In this, the sub-continent lost over two million people directly and multiples later. Thakur Pukhraj Singh thought sadly - this tragedy could have been averted.

* * *

GULZAR AHMED

Tragedy of Partition

The flight from Lucknow to Kolkata was short. Prakash booked a hotel near Netaji Subhash Airport for convenience to board the flight to Dhaka the following morning. Zubair called Shadab Ahmed in Dhaka from his hotel room and he was relieved to get a warm response from his step brother. When Zubair asked if he could speak to their father, he was informed that Gulzar Ahmed was feeling a little weak so he had gone to sleep after medication.

Zubair decided to have an early dinner and sleep. Previous night he hadn't slept well because of the odd circumstances. All night he had been thinking about the *haveli* of Thakur Pukhraj Singh, which formerly belonged to his ancestors and now he was a 'guest' in his own ancestral house. Strangely, he hadn't felt he was a guest. He still had a sense of ownership about the *haveli*. The thought of having aunts he didn't know about, and then to learn about his father being alive, had taken its toll on his sleep. He was disturbed. Now that he was just a few hours away from meeting his father, he felt as ease.

- - -

Rukhsar was alone in her room. Aman had gone to his room to freshen up. Rukhsar was momentarily contented to be alone for some time. Since she had arrived in India she had encountered surprises and learnt truths. She hadn't expected the reception she had received in *Hindu* India; misconceptions about India and Indians, especially Hindus were washed out within two days. She was surprised by the warmth and love she got from the locals against whom there was such hatred that it had driven a wedge between the peoples of the two countries - yet, she hadn't felt the animosity. So far she had unforgettable, fond memories of this place which would last a life time. She also knew now that Aman knew the truth even before they had come to India but he had kept it within him. That too said a story; maybe there were too many people who believed that the stories of hatred being spread in her country were lies but they did not challenge it for various reasons. Aman had the courage to speak about it, and he did when he had a chance but that wasn't sufficient. General public should know the truth. The people back in her country were no less affectionate, generous and loving as people on this side of the border. If people of both countries were so beautiful why was there so much mutual hatred? Aman had told her the reasons but that still didn't make sense, at least not completely.

A question started to tease her with every experience she had. What was the logic of dividing India? It did not make sense. If India wasn't divided, the combined strength of both nations, now three nations, could have made India an even greater power than it was now.

Another aspect struck Rukhsar; with the division of India, based on the 'two nation theory' - the Muslims of India were divided into two countries initially, India and Pakistan, and into three parts, in 1971. What if India wasn't divided? What if the Muslims of the sub-continent were united and part of a greater India? With over fifty million Muslims, a third of the world's Muslim population, Indian Muslims would be a major force to reckon with. She was a devout, proud Muslim, and she was pragmatic. She wondered how India would have looked if it was undivided. The sheer numbers of Muslims within India would have been fantastic; they would be united and... And she had a feeling that the infighting would not be as severe as it was presently, especially in Pakistan.

Since arriving in India, she had seen a contrast. She had seen a highly developed India with modern infrastructure and happy people. She also knew there were people living in extreme poverty in this country. She had seen glimpses of it in Delhi and Agra but those were fragments of the real problem. She felt an excitement in the way India was growing and surging forward. And then, another question surprised her. Why was she happy to see an enemy country progress? Why wasn't she jealous of India? Instead, she felt pride, and a sense of belonging. She looked at Thakur Pukhraj Singh's gift and the answer came to her. This was the country of her forefathers. This was India! This was her country too.

- - -

Aman Bux cared about Rukhsar and her family; he was glad to see her re-united with her father, whom he too respected immensely but his excitement had a different dimension to it. Now, Rukhsar too would be as excited as he to get married. He had waited for twelve years. He only hoped that his boss would keep his promise and wait for a few days. If he did, Aman would return to his job and his life would be a dream come true.

When he had tendered his resignation, it had been kept aside by his boss, the Ambassador. Aman was an asset in the Pakistan Foreign office establishment and he knew his worth so when the Ambassador hadn't granted him the leave, Aman had gone back to his desk, drafted his letter of resignation and emailed it to his boss - with a hard copy delivered by hand.

Ambassador Jaffer Sharif had come to Aman's chamber, slammed the letter on the desk and demanded an explanation. "What is this? We have a month long Pakistan fest in a week and you want to resign? What's more important than your career?"

The *'Pakistan Fest'*, an exhibition of Pakistani products in Iran was Aman's brainchild. Six months ago he had proposed organizing the fest for benefit of the artisans of traditional handicrafts in Pakistan. It would also help in exports of traditional items of Pakistan. The morning he had received Rukhsar's text message he had called her intending to talk her into re-thinking about her trip to India but he knew it was not possible. Rukhsar would follow the lead without bothering to verify the authenticity of the call or the caller. Rukhsar was intelligent but emotional, and weak when it came to the latter. When he failed in his attempt he knew he had to go with her for her sake. He spoke to her for an hour but that was fruitless. Rukhsar was adamant. She didn't budge from her decision; she would go to India and bring her father back home. He had to make a decision - he made it promptly without any second thoughts. He decided to resign and accompany her to India.

"My life is more important to me than my career, Sir. Rukhsar is my life," Aman said and explained the situation, "I can't let her travel alone. She needs me and I can't forego my responsibility." Aman justified his action.

The man who had struggled his way up to become a respected Ambassador, Jaffer Sharif looked down at one of his brightest men, "I will hold this letter for a week. I hope you can sort out your problems with Rukhsar and return by then. After a week, if you don't return I will take a call. When do you have to reach Lahore?"

"On Thursday, Sir."

"Ok," the Ambassador smiled and left the room. He had met Rukhsar once in Islamabad when she had come to meet her beau. He had liked her immensely. He had a special liking for Aman Bux and he was happy for him that he had found Rukhsar.

- - -

Aman Bux walked towards Rukhsar's room. It was shut. He raised his fingers to rap on the door and withdrew. He knew she needed some privacy to mull over the events of last three days. He returned to his room and opened the closet and his eyes caught the packet gifted by to him by the Thakur's family. His mind drifted to the events as they had unfolded since his arrival in India. He hadn't anticipated nor expected what he had experienced. Earlier he was like an ordinary man in the street who considered India as an enemy which wanted to destroy Pakistan. Over the years he had many good and some not so good stories about India and he had found them true. The only thing he found more endearing was the attitude of the locals, especially towards Pakistanis. He was reminded of an incident when he had attended a *'Mushayara'* in Karachi. The local poets got into an argument with one of the guest poet who was invited to participate in the event from India. When a local poet asked his Indian guest if he, as a Muslim felt safe living in India, the Indian poet had proudly declared that Muslims were safest in India. The local poets had pounced on him for stating that. The Indian poet had stuck to his statement and defended it unflinchingly. Though Aman had thought that the Indian *'shayar'* was being unnecessarily boastful about his claims, he knew now that the poet was right. Last three days had proved that; he felt safer here than he had felt in any other country though he had been stationed in many countries including various Islamic countries. He felt lot safer than he felt in any Pakistani city. But he was worried. Although his trip had been memorable, there were serious concerns. He was worried about Prakash and his motives. The mysterious man had been cooperative but his intentions were doubtful. Aman tried his best to guess Prakash's motive but so far he was unsuccessful, and swore to find out. But, there was something else; whenever he spoke to Prakash, he felt the man was a thorough gentleman. Was Prakash Rohatgi devious? Why was he going 'out of the way' to help? Why had he helped Zubair Ahmed? What was the motive behind uniting Zubair and Rukhsar? And, who was Prakash Rohatgi? Was he an intelligence officer or a man working for an NGO? It was all too mysterious. Whatever it was, Aman was sure he can protect Rukhsar and he will take her and Zubair back to Pakistan. And, what was Zubair's purpose? Why was he working with Prakash?

- - -

Prakash disconnected the call to Purna and smiled. Altaf had been a naughty boy. He had tried to overpower Purna but failed twice; each time he had tried he was punished by Purna who treated him like a strict mother. Prakash laughed to himself when he thought about it. Then, the next moment his smile disappeared - a personal tragedy of gigantic proportions clogged his mind and sadness filled his heart. The loneliness was back. He shrugged his head and concentrated on resolving an urgent matter. He was unable to connect with his Dhaka contact. He and his guests were scheduled to board an early morning flight the next morning but without proper documents the trip might be postponed. He stepped out and knocked on Aman's door.

Aman Bux opened the door. Prakash looked behind Aman to ensure he was alone. He didn't find Rukhsar in the room, so he invited himself into the room and occupied a chair next to the bed. Aman was amused. "All okay?" he asked.

"I have a problem. I thought I will let you know. I couldn't reach my Dhaka contact. Till we don't get an okay from him I may have to postpone our trip. I hope I am able to manage it before we start for the airport."

Aman started to speak when he heard a knock on the door and saw the knob turn. Rukhsar opened the door and stopped when she saw Prakash in the room. Aman escorted her to the chair, "He has a problem. We were discussing something. You should also ask *Abbu* to join us." Aman explained.

"What's so serious?" she asked worriedly.

"Nothing to worry about," Prakash said and explained the little problem he was facing.

"I checked on *Abbu*. He is resting. We shouldn't bother him with trivialities," she said and occupied the chair next to Prakash, avoiding her temptation to sit beside Aman. "We shouldn't have any problems, Prakash. We have our passports and we do not need visas. We will get it on arrival there."

"It isn't easy," Aman explained. *"Abbu* doesn't have a valid passport. If I use my passport, it will send alarm bells ringing in unwanted quarters and right now we must avoid attracting unnecessary attention. You can't use your passport because it will also attract attention because you are Zubair Ahmed's daughter… but in your case I am guessing. Anyway, *Abbu* and I certainly can't use our passports." Aman clarified the situation. Rukhsar understood the problem now.

"How are you managing it?" Rukhsar asked Prakash.

"I have travel documents for all of us from my sources in the Home Office which gives you all Indian identities for this trip and it's valid for a fortnight. I am worried about the entry point in Dhaka. That may delay our trip. I am not worried, just irritated because we could waste a day," Prakash clarified.

- - -

The group decided to go out for dinner and try the local food and the famous sweets of Bengal. When they requested Zubair to join them he asked them to carry on. He wanted to rest. Aman, Rukhsar and Prakash decided to explore the city. A cab dropped them in central Kolkata and they decided to walk through the vast open spaces of Kolkata greens and feel the pulse of the city made famous worldwide by Dominique Lapierre's 'The City of Joy'. Was it the atmosphere or was it the magic of the city which really made them feel that the title of the book justified it. The couple sensed a feeling of joy within. What amazed them was the simplicity of the city. Until few years ago, it was the world's most populous city; yet, they found the life to be easy and laid back. People seemed to be at peace with themselves. The city had a considerable number of people who lived in poverty but there was no depression in the eyes of the people. They saw life and the willingness to survive, struggle and improve the quality of their lives.

When Prakash told the couple that this was the capital of India for a major part of British rule in India, Aman nodded his head while Rukhsar looked at him with surprise. She was more surprised to see sadness in his eyes. It was a pleasant evening. There wasn't any reason for Prakash to be sad. It made no sense. Rukhsar asked him the reason.

Prakash's expression didn't change when he replied. "Kolkata... Calcutta, as it was then known, was at the centre of the bloodbath that took place on Mr. Jinnah's call of *'Direct Action Day'*. It is now notoriously called *'The Great Calcutta Killing'*. In four days of madness nearly ten thousand people were killed and many more injured, mainly Hindus because they did not have a militant leader in this part of India. We talk about the millions who died after the partition of India, but we forget that it all started here exactly a year earlier on August 19. Muslim League leaders led a large mob massacring thousands of Hindus to prove that if Indian National Congress did not agree to the creation of a Muslim state, this would happen throughout India. There would be a civil war the likes of which the world had never seen. Today we see the result of the actions of a few people of that era. Two peoples with identical cultures and everything in common except religion were split apart on religious grounds, on both sides of the border; Bengal and Punjab. It's sad to see the situation we find ourselves in today."

"Didn't Suhrawardy do anything about it? He was the Chief Minister of Bengal." Rukhsar asked curiously.

Huseyn Suhrawardy was a follower of a well-known freedom fighter of India, Chitranjan Das, and the leader of 'Swaraj Party'. Suhrawardy joined his party to follow Chitranjan Das but when Das died in 1925 or thereabouts Suhrawardy joined Awami Muslim League and became a prominent leader for Bengalis: Hindus and Muslims. Indian National Congress was against division of India while Jinnah wanted a separate nation for Muslims carved out of India. When it was clear that the Congress won't accept the division, Jinnah called for *'Direct Action Day'*. Jinnah had threatened all, especially Gandhi and Nehru that if Congress rejected his *'Two nation Theory'*, there would be civil war. He gave an ultimatum to Congress to choose between division of India and civil war. The response was massive and there was violence across Calcutta. Suhrawardy was accused of instigating crowds. However, immediately after partition there was another crowd violence. This time however, Muslims were at the receiving end. Suhrawardy invited Gandhiji to come and stay at his house and help in stopping the communal violence. Gandhi*ji* accepted Suhrawardy's request against the wishes of other Congress leaders. When Gandhi*ji* saw the carnage, he appealed to people and called for cession of hostilities. Hindus were upset that Gandhi*ji* had accepted Suhrawardy's invitation to stay at his house because they held Suhrawardy responsible for the massacre of Hindus a year earlier. Gandhi*ji*'s appeal didn't work initially. So, Gandhi*ji* went on *'Satyagrah'* - fast unto death. It had the desired effect. Violence ceased in a week. Leaders from both communities surrendered their arms and swore to Gandhiji to stop all fighting, Prakash narrated the tragic story. He had slowed his pace while narrating the tragedy which was never talked about. "The irony is that Suhrawardy was banned from entering East-Pakistan because of his actions, but I feel there was a more sinister reason behind it. Suhrawardy should have become the Prime Minister of Pakistan. With him gone, path was clear for Liaqat Ali Khan to become the PM."

They were walking through the beautifully lit up Park Street in the centre of Kolkata. Prakash led his two guests into a dimly lit restaurant and chose a table at the far end for privacy. They ordered food and relaxed into a casual conversation about Prakash and his life.

Hesitantly, Rukhsar asked Prakash a question which also bothered Aman, "Prakash, why is Dad working with you and the Indian Government? What is he working on?" She hadn't come to terms with her father's decision and she couldn't accept that her patriotic father could work for an enemy. It was inconceivable.

Prakash smiled mildly, "Your father isn't working for Indian Government; nor am I. We are working for a greater cause, Rukhsar. Before you leave, you will know the truth. Then you won't blame your father for what he is doing. Trust me! It is just a matter of a couple of days before you return."

Aman started to ask a question but stopped when he heard Prakash's cell phone ring. Prakash saw the name of the caller and conversed in Bengali which neither Aman nor Rukhsar understood. After four minutes Prakash disconnected the call and beamed at the couple sitting opposite him.

Aman guessed, "That was your contact man in Dhaka?"

Prakash nodded his head. "Yes."

- - -

Back in the hotel Rukhsar stopped in front of Zubair's room, tapped on the door and entered the room to find him bent over and deeply engrossed in a thick book. She stood behind him and looked down. "What's so interesting, *Abbu*?"

Zubair turned around to her and smiled. He had forgotten there was someone in the room. Zubair held Rukhsar by her wrist and gestured her to sit opposite him. "I am reading a fascinating book about ancient Indian culture dating back to almost 3000 years BC. Anyway, how was your evening?"

"It was nice," she replied and looked at her father with pleading eyes.

"What's the matter?" Zubair asked with concern.

"Is it possible for me to give you any motive to return home, *Abbu*?"

Zubair didn't know if Rukhsar had pleaded or cried softly in desperation. He thrust his hand out and patted her. "You have asked that a few times and I truly wish I could. You know my situation at present. It is nearly impossible for me to return."

"How can you work for India, *Abbu?* They can't work for our benefit," Rukhsar yelled, "You will be branded as *'gaddar'*. You are not a traitor but you know what could happen to us? People will kill us too." Rukhsar cried out in desperation.

"That is why I want you and Shabnam to come to India. You will be safe here." Zubair replied calmly, convincingly.

Rukhsar was quiet.

Zubair patted his daughter's back, "You will be surprised how safe you will be here. Yes, there are fanatics here too, but they still believe in their country. There is a good chance that you will change your perception before you return home."

Rukhsar spoke softly, *"Abbu*, Pakistan is our country."

"True, it is... was, for me too. I am not against my country. But I am working for the benefit of my countries - Pakistan and India."

"Who are you working for?" Rukhsar asked angrily, "Why would they work for the good of Pakistan? Why do you feel so much for India now?"

"I can't answer your first two questions. Prakash can. As for your third question; India is country of our ancestors. If India wasn't divided, it would still be my country. The country my ancestors adopted was part of India, Rukhsar," Zubair tried to explain, "I have learnt one thing in last two years - if I, or children of other generations of my family have any problem, I am sure of one thing; this country of my ancestors will give them refuge because this is where our roots are."

Rukhsar looked at her father helplessly, with moist eyes.

Zubair cupped his daughter's hands. He wanted her to stay in India. She didn't know how much he missed her and Shabnam. They were the only people he cared for earlier... and now he had few others whom he loved just as much: Prakash, Aman and the charming, beautiful girl who stayed each weekend with Prakash at the farmhouse in New Delhi.

Rukhsar understood his reasons for his love of India but her own love for Pakistan was far greater than India's. She couldn't speak because sadness in Zubair's eyes discouraged her.

"Rukhsar, people in Pakistan must acknowledge that before '47 a country called Pakistan didn't exist. Pakistan was a poor creation of few selfish men who rightly or wrongly thought that the Muslims of the Indian sub-continent would be better off living in a country where they weren't in minority. They carved out two parts from India to create a state for Muslims; a country where Muslims would have democratic rights and where they would thrive and have freedom to practice their religion. That young country was split into two because of its inherent contradiction. The worst thing you can do is when you contradict yourself; when you heroes out of villains. When the descendants of Imam Hasan and Imam Hussain were being killed by the Umayyad rulers, they sought, and got refuge in the Hindu kingdoms of Sind. To kill them Hajjaj bin Yusuf sent Mohammad bin Qasim. Those Hindu kings and their families paid for it with their lives but they did not betray their guests. That bin-Qasim is our hero and the King Dahir who saved my Prophet's descendants is our villain. Why? Because the idiots falsely believe that Bib-Qasim brought Islam to India, and because King Dahir was a Hindu and Bin-Qasim was a Muslim. We revere our Prophet but we also glorify bin-Qasim as our hero. That is contradiction. The zealots have named missiles after invaders like Ahmed Shah Abdali who massacred the population of Lahore and burnt the city for good measure, but we shy away from accepting that Bhagat Singh was our hero, a freedom fighter who was illegally hung by the British. Contradiction! Ghori is our other missile who too has nothing to do with Pakistan but the local heroes like Ashoka and Chandragupta are not taught. That is the contradiction! It is also a contradiction when the country's and Islamic world's only Nobel laureate for Physics is chased out of the country because he was a Qadiyani, and our hero is a man who didn't have the ability to make an atom bomb but is credited with it."

Rukhsar was suddenly upset. She knew her father had made a mistake this time. "How can you say that about our most respected scientist, *Abbu*?"

Zubair looked at his daughter strangely, "my child, you shouldn't expect a mechanical engineer to perform surgeries on a medical patient," he said with disappointment.

"What do you mean?"

"Dr. A. Q. Khan is a metallurgist not a nuclear physicist, you should know the difference between the two," Zubair said, shook his head in disappointment, and caressed his daughter's hand, "A country devoid of its identity can't succeed, and we are trying to create an artificial identity which we can't have. That is a contradiction. How can a country survive when its two parts are separated by thousand miles of a country which it considers as enemy? Muslims of the sub-continent are now split in three equal parts. You have been in India for last three days. Where do you find Muslims having better scope to thrive; is it India or Pakistan? Has the plan worked or failed? What could have Muslims achieved if they were still a part of a united India with their strength in numbers? You have to be fair minded and then decide."

Rukhsar's eyes grew wide. Hearing her thoughts from her father was a confirmation for her; thoughts which turned into belief.

Zubair understood his daughter's dilemma. She desperately wanted to take him to Lahore while he wanted her to live in India but her patriotism stopped her. He looked at the door when he heard a knock. Aman opened the door and he and Prakash walked in. Aman's arrival inspired Rukhsar to press Zubair to change his mind. She looked at Aman with pleading eyes for help.

"What's wrong?" Aman asked innocently.

Before Rukhsar could reply Zubair replied, "She has asked me again to return. Please tell her why it is impossible for me to return; instead you must try to convince her that it is better that she and Shabnam come to India. They will have serious problems if people back home learn that I am working with the Indians. People in Pakistan will not accept my explanation that I am in a way, working for Pakistan; the whole media and the Government establishment will be after their blood. She is an emotional fool. She does not understand the gravity of my situation." Zubair pleaded to his would-be son-in-law. He paused, thought for a while and added, softly, "I love them, Aman. I can't see them suffer for my actions. When Prakash asked me to work for him, I had put a condition; that he will never involve or inform my family about me." Zubair turned to Prakash, "You have transgressed on your word to me." Zubair said and looked away in desperation and sadness.

There was silence in the room. Every occupant of the room was thoughtful in an emotionally charged atmosphere.

Prakash looked at Zubair with sympathy. "I would never go back on my word, Sir. But, in last one month I saw that you have been searching for Rukhsar on the internet and social media. You never gave us your home address so I used my contacts in

Lahore and Rawalpindi to trace them. Rukhsar had also been searching for you all these years. It would be unfair that members of a family should be kept away from each other. There is too much love to be lost. I lied to her to get her here," he defended his decision.

Zubair nodded his headed in agreement. "I understand... and I thank you for that but you know that you have put their lives in danger. Now you have a responsibility; to convince her to stay back in India. I remember what you said when we first met, *'we may have been working on opposite sides earlier but now we will work together.'* That statement is still etched in my memory but what now, Prakash? The situation I find my family in, isn't what I had asked for. It is your responsibility to solve the matter."

"I will do my best. We are discussing if your family should move to India or if you should return to Pakistan. I think we should also think about Aman. He has put his career on line for Rukhsar. If Rukhsar decides to stay here what will Aman do? Will he also come to India? If so, how? We will have serious problems in getting them Indian citizenship. Anyway, we are jumping the gun here. First, you have to decide who stays where, and then we should give real consideration to Aman's situation as well."

Aman stared at Prakash with obligation and great affection. Neither the father nor his daughter had thought of it but the man whom he had met three days ago had thought of it. Prakash had mentioned the problem which had occupied Aman's mind from the moment Zubair had expressed his wish to see Rukhsar stay in India. If she did, he was in trouble; he couldn't be happy if she stayed in India. He knew Zubair's fears about Rukhsar and her mother were justified so ideally they should be with him in India; although he didn't fancy the idea. It would mean that he would have to travel to India with Rukhsar each time she wanted to meet her parents.

Rukhsar and Zubair looked at Aman with certain guilt. Both knew his situation but their own wishes were overriding it.

Zubair patted Aman on the back. "What you have done for her cannot be stated in words, Aman. You are a diplomat, so you understand my situation better than any of us. You have to make a decision too. I have been selfishly thinking about Rukhsar and myself. Prakash is right. Rukhsar will be married to you soon and then the problems will arise. I can't return to Pakistan and Rukhsar can't stay there. What then, Aman? How are you going to protect her? How will you manage?"

"Ideally I would like to stay in Pakistan with Rukhsar, but I understand the situation. You are right. She and... even my life could be in danger if your story breaks out. I have been thinking of various options but nothing is apt as yet. Let me think. There has to be a way out," Aman assured Zubair.

"I have an idea. Let me check if it's viable," Prakash intervened unexpectedly. "Let me work on it."

"What is your idea, Prakash?" Aman asked enthusiastically.

Prakash had a glitter in his eyes. "Altaf Khos! Isn't it strange that he turns up just when you and Rukhsar land in India? Why did he follow you? I think Altaf lied to us. During interrogation he made a mistake in his replies; he mentioned Zubair Saheb. That was out of context."

Aman's eyes grew in surprise. Prakash was right. Altaf had lied to them. "Yet, what do you have in mind?"

"Later," Prakash said, turned and left the room.

— — —

An hour later Aman heard a knock on the door and found Rukhsar standing nervously. He escorted her to the chair, "You are nervous. What's the matter?"

"I am jittery, Aman. *Abbu's* statement has made me nervous," Rukhsar replied.

"I have been thinking of how I can convince *Abbu* to return to Lahore. But he is right. He can't return without risk," Aman tried explaining her father's situation again.

"I understand that but I want to see him back home." Rukhsar cried out desperately.

Aman leaned back against the pillow and pulled her next to him to let her head rest on his chest and wrapped his arm around her. It had the desired effect. Rukhsar felt protected and relaxed. "*Abba* has more experience and knowledge than both of us put together. His analyses are accurate. We must empathise with him. Put yourself in his shoes and see if he is doing the right thing or not."

Rukhsar knew the risks. If he returned to Lahore Zubair's enemies won't let him live. For his own sake, it was better he lived in India till circumstances permitted him to return. She looked at Aman and his presence gave her confidence; she knew he will do his best to get her father back to Lahore if it was possible. She rested her head on his chest, closed her eyes and she day-dreamt of her father living with them in Lahore.

A few minutes later Rukhsar asked, "How can I leave *Abba* alone in a foreign land without someone to look after him? He will be sixty soon. He and *Ammi* need each other."

"I want to ask you a question. Tell me honestly. Don't you think there is a solid bond between *Abba* and Prakash?"

Rukhsar raised her face and looked at Aman. She had felt it too. Zubair treated Prakash like a son and in return he got the respect from Prakash like a father would. She had observed it but not thought of it until Aman Bux had mentioned it.

*   *   *

The General Head-Quarters,

Pakistan Army, Rawalpindi

On the first floor in the vast labyrinth of the General Head Quarters of Pakistan Army, General Imran Saddiq Pathan put his phone down worriedly. The fifty-three year old General was among rare breed of Generals in the army establishment; he came from a poor family and risen through the ranks by virtues of their performances and merit; and one of the few truly respected men in the military establishment.

General Pathan had called his source in JCIB, the 'Joint Counter-Intelligence Bureau' department of ISI, the Inter-Services Intelligence, headquartered in Islamabad. What happened, he wondered. Who was Altaf Khos? What was his mission in New Delhi? His source in HQ of ISI had informed him that he or no one he knew had any idea why Khos was in India. Whether Altaf was on a personal visit or on covert mission couldn't be established. The source had said that Altaf's last communication was after midnight two nights ago. General Pathan was worried about Aman Bux's safety. Aman had no reason to go to India as far as he knew. It was a bad decision on

Aman's part to accompany Rukhsar. It would be ideal if Aman had stopped Rukhsar from visiting India. Had Rukhsar met Zubair Ahmed?

General Pathan knew Prakash Rohatgi's immense potential to get what he wanted; he had the power, contacts and ability to achieve what he wished. Aman's contact with Prakash Rohatgi could spell trouble if things went out of hand. If the ISI or any authority which had sent Altaf Khos to New Delhi knew what Imran Pathan had learnt, Aman will be forced to return to Pakistan. If that wasn't possible, they would not hesitate to eliminate the brilliant young diplomat. Rukhsar was not General Imran's concern. She won't stay in India, he was certain. She would return, and if she did, he could convert her into an asset for his plans. But he was concerned about Aman. He had to get Aman Bux safely back to Pakistan.

General Pathan decided to wait before taking a call on the options he had. In the meantime he wanted to know why a former Major in Pakistan army had become so dangerous that a Lieutenant was sent on a mission to kill him; a Major who had almost died fighting for his country during Kargil war. He had to solve the mystery.

General Pathan rose to his feet and strode briskly towards the man who had been his guide since Pathan had joined the army. On the second floor of the complex he turned right and walked to the third door on the left side. He tapped softly and opened the door without permission.

Seeing General Pathan enter worriedly, General Basheer Qureishi sat cautiously. "What happened? You look worried," he asked.

General Pathan laid out the situation and asked, "What should I do with Aman Khan Bux and Rukhsar Ahmed?" General Pathan replied with questions, "What's going on?"

General Qureishi nodded. That was the problem, he thought. If he could extract Aman Khan Bux, it would be a miracle. What does he do about Zubair and his daughter?

*   *   *

GULZAR AHMED

Dhaka, Bangladesh

As expected there wasn't any problem at the immigration desk of Dhaka's Hazrat Shahjalal International Airport. The group found Shadab Ahmed waiting for them eagerly in the arrival lounge. The greetings were hesitant but formal. Small conversations were attempts to break the ice. While Prakash asked them to wait for a few minutes, Zubair's half-brother led them to coffee shop where conversations were bit more open.

Shadab Ahmed was a likable man. The five feet eight inches man had an innocent face with an ever present smile which made him more likable. Shadab had an affable nature and amiable persona. He started his career as a merchandiser in a garment factory on the outskirts of Dhaka and in a few years he was a successful garments exporter and his was among the fastest growing exporting house in Bangladesh. His wife was a banker and his son was preparing for college.

Before starting, Shadab cautioned his guests about Gulzar's poor health. Gulzar had suffered a heart stroke eighteen years ago and since then his movements had been severely restricted. Gulzar was stable but his family was advised against any emotional or physical strain to Gulzar.

- - -

As the car cruised on Dhaka-MymenSingh Highway towards Rabindra Sarani the sight of a rapidly developing city caught the attention of the passengers. While Zubair was thinking with mixed feelings of nervousness and excitement about meeting his father and the extended family, he was a little circumspect how they would be received by the family.

Aman was observing the sight of a city which was young in modern identity; capital city of a young country, just over four decades old - earlier the prime city of East Pakistan, and even earlier, a part of an undivided India. Having broken away from Pakistan, the new country had started to grow faster than Pakistan despite facing numerous challenges like the annual natural disasters. Bangladesh was successful to quite an extent in controlling two major problems which its mother country was still grappling with - population and poverty. The young nation was beginning to assert itself. A thought stirred Aman. Wouldn't it have been fantastic if the Governments of United Pakistan had treated its eastern section at par with its western section? If so, today the two parts would have been a force to contend with. The united country would have had buoyant economy and greater influence in the region, not to speak of being militarily much stronger and thereby, challenging even India. His thoughts were disrupted when Shadab turned his car into the parking lot of a large mansion off Rabindra Avenue and stopped in front of a Victorian gate. There were a few moments of absolute silence and nervous excitement in the air as the group emerged from the car.

- - -

Shadab led them to a large drawing room in the house. The group walked in slowly behind Shadab. As they entered they saw a frail looking man in mid-eighties rise as he saw them. All stood silently as Gulzar Ahmed walked to them cautiously moving a step at a time with the help of a walking cane. Zubair was shocked to see his once handsome father look so weak. He stepped a few paces and stood before Gulzar. The frail octogenarian stood silently looking into his son's eyes for some time, scanning his eldest son longingly and wrapped his arms around Zubair and hugged him tightly. Zubair hugged his father and his eyes welled up. Zubair introduced Rukhsar, Aman Bux to his father, and introduced Prakash as the man who had arranged the trip. Gulzar Ahmed opened his arms for them and embraced Aman and Prakash, then looked at Rukhsar and his smile brought tears in his eyes. Rukhsar bowed her head in *'salaam'*.

A strikingly attractive elderly, but younger looking middle-aged woman entered the room and greeted the guests with a happy smile as she was introduced to each guest. Her olive skin glowed in the dim winter afternoon light. She had an air of authority about herself. Her large eyes surveyed the room as she sat beside her ailing husband, who looked at least thirty years elder to her. Their conversations were restricted to formalities and getting to know each other. This was intentionally done to keep Gulzar away from any strenuous subject. The important queries would come but casually the guests, Shadab and his mother agreed.

Shahida Rahman-Ahmed, Shadab's mother was cultured, highly educated, blessed with high intellect and maturity since an early age. Coupled with her stunning looks, highlighted by her large doe like eyes and a ravishing smile, Shahida had an aura about her. Though she was six years older than Zubair, she appeared much younger. As the hosts introduced the guests to Shadab's wife Rehana and son Wasim, two families entered the house. Shahida introduced the new guests individually as Raeesa Idris, her elder daughter and her husband Mohammed Qadeer Idris and their daughters Ramola and Rhea, and then introduced the family of her younger daughter Kaneez, her husband Iqbal and their children Irfan and Saeeda.

The guests from India knew that the conversation about what happened, and how and why Gulzar Ahmed ended up living in erstwhile East Pakistan instead of returning to West Pakistan and how and why he married Shahida without caring about his first marriage would have to wait for later.

- - -

As the guests mingled Prakash felt like an intruder who had gate-crashed a private function. Although Aman and Shadab kept him company, Prakash was uncomfortable. He sought permission of his hosts and stepped out of the house to catch up on other matters which were left pending due to this trip. The afternoon Dhaka sun was warm and biting but Prakash sighed in relief as he stepped out. He was later caught up by Aman and Shadab.

"I am sorry about the chaos in the house. You can imagine the excitement and curiosity," Aman stated apologetically.

Prakash nodded his head with a mild smile, "I understand."

"I think our stay here will be extended by a day. You will be inconvenienced by this change of plans."

"I thought it would take a couple of days for Rukhsar and Zubair Saheb to meet and catch up for the years they have missed. At weekends I have a special guest in New Delhi, but this is important." Prakash replied and smiled lightly, "I am happy for both families. This trip has brought two families together which, by the look of things, will be a bonding of sorts. Gulzar Saheb and Zubair Saheb are decent men caught in weird circumstances yet they have retained their sanity. Those men deserve the best." Prakash replied.

Aman Looked at Prakash and questions flooded his mind again. Why was this man spending his time, money and effort to help them? What was his motive? What was his story? Who was he? Prakash was still a mystery for Rukhsar and him. Zubair knew but he refused to talk about Prakash.

Shadab escorted Aman back into the house and left Prakash to himself. Prakash switched on his cell phone and made three calls. Then he called to update himself and promised to return in two days and disconnected the phone.

- - -

Late afternoon, Shadab's sisters departed with their families insisting that the guests visit them before leaving Dhaka. The guests from India accepted their invites but wondered if they will have the time to visit. As the sun started it's descend, Shahida Ahmed asked the guests if they would like to go for a walk and the guests agreed.

Zubair and Rukhsar walked alongside Shahida and Shadab while Aman kept Prakash company. They walked for twenty minutes along the Uttara Lake and found a quiet, isolated space to sit on grass and marvel at the view.

"If you people have any complains with Gulzar Saheb, I am responsible, and the tragic circumstances under which Gulzar Saheb and I met. It was a life and death situation for us when Gulzar Saheb came like a knight to rescue me from a life of indignity, or certain death." Shahida said to Zubair.

"What happened? I was twelve when he left for East Pakistan and then I... we... never heard from him. I remember him as a devoted family man with immense dignity and pride. It would be against his nature to abandon his family. We were told of his bravado during the war and then we learnt he had deserted the army and disappeared and later we learnt that he was killed during army operation in East Pakistan when he was on the front fighting the Indian army." Zubair asked.

"Your father *is* a devoted family man, Zubair, but those were extraordinary circumstances which forced him to..." Shahida spoke slowly but with typical authority, "Your father did the bravest thing he could do and saved me."

"What happened?" Rukhsar asked her step-grandmother.

They could feel Shahida going back to the circumstances or incident she had been through. Rukhsar could see moisture at the corners of her eyes. She knew there had to be a tragedy of huge proportions for such a strong woman to cry. Zubair didn't wish to scrape Shahida's scars but he had to know what had happened. What situation could have been so great that it kept his father away from family?

Shahida struggled to keep her emotions in check and after a while she started softly, "My father was a renowned Bangla writer and a Professor at Dhaka University. Few days before the Indo-Pak war broke out the *Razakars* came one morning and took him away at gun point because he was an active member of the Awami League. He..."

"*Razakars* means volunteers. Why would volunteers kidnap a Professor?" Rukhsar interrupted Shahida with her query.

"*Razakars* were volunteers, but not in the social sense of the word," Zubair answered his daughter, "these volunteers were auxiliary forces of the Pak army. These volunteers split into many forces, like '*Al Badr*' and '*Al Shams*' although there were other smaller groups with similar mission."

Rukhsar looked at her father in near disbelief and then at her step-grandmother.

Shahida nodded and continued, "My father was a member of the Muslim League who had fought alongside Suhrawardy and Sheikh Mujib for creation of Pakistan but after Pakistan was created he was disillusioned with what he saw, and how people of East Pakistan were treated; like second rate citizens. He joined the Awami League and worked with Sheikh Mujib. When Awami League won a landslide victory in '70 elections, he was sure Sheikh Mujib would be Prime Minister but when leaders of West Pakistan, especially President Yahya Khan did not transfer power, my father was angry." Shahida pressed a handkerchief against her eyes to stop her tears.

For a few seconds there was silence. Rukhsar tried to speak to her but Shahida held her hand up asking them to wait. Despite the emotions, Shahida was handling it well, and with dignity. Shahida was a strong woman but deep scars made even the strongest go emotionally weak. That was happening with her. As seconds passed, there was an awkward silence. Shadab put his arm around his mother, "Let's go home," he said to the others, "its dark. We can talk later... after *Abba* is asleep. I will try and provide you with information which you seek, and if need be *Maa* can fill you in."

- - -

Gulzar seemed a little more energetic and happier than he was earlier in the day. Zubair's arrival had infused fresh life into the fragile body. When he tried to speak about past the family asked him not to. Shahida told him that she will take care of the guests and put Gulzar at ease. Gulzar resisted his family's attempts to send him to his room; he wanted to spend time with Zubair and Rukhsar. For years he had held guilt in his heart. Despite his ultimate wish to meet his wife and son, whom he had to abandon when he was just twelve, he couldn't dare to try and meet them for sake of their safety. The adverse circumstances prohibited him to think of daring. He had tried a few covert attempts but he had to pull back when he thought the danger would be greater than the joy he would get of seeing his family. He wanted to explain that to his son but his wife and younger son won't permit him to strain himself.

Sometime after Gulzar Ahmed was forced to retire to his room Shahida led the visitors to the living room, a large hall with furniture settings reminiscent of classical Bengali style. The relaxing atmosphere and Gulzar Ahmed's absence made it comfortable for everyone to talk freely. Shahida smiled with a little wryness, "I am sorry about this evening," she said, "I will continue from where I had left off because in a way I am responsible for Gulzar Saheb's action which deprived him of his family, and you of him," Shahida spoke to Zubair. "My father was among those who planned *Operation Jackpot* in August, 1971." Shahida resumed her tale, "So he was..."

"Pardon me for interrupting. What was *Operation Jackpot*?" The question surprisingly came from Aman Khan Bux.

"You don't know the details of the war?" Shadab asked curtly. A moment later he realised he was rude and retracted. "Sorry! I know some business colleagues in Pakistan who don't know the facts. They are misinformed."

The visitors were initially taken aback by Shadab's response but his immediate apology eased them. "We only know what we have been told and what we have read. I have learned in last few days that a lot of information we have been fed aren't true but we are here to learn why my grand-father abandoned his family," Rukhsar replied with equal curtness.

"I will try to answer your question in brief. *Maa's* father was taken away by one of the two groups of *Razakars*; we believe it was the *Al Shams* faction. A few days after he was gone, some men entered their house and killed Maa's brother and a sister; they were fourteen and thirteen," Shadab said softly, "my mother was in college at the time. When they learnt about her, they went to the college and she was identified by one of the accomplices who were feeding information to the group about the family. Three men from the group barged into her classroom and pulled her out of the class and..."

"Shahida, it is time to tell your son the truth," Gulzar's soft voice suddenly interrupted Shadab and ordered his mother.

Shadab turned to look at his father standing at the door and looked at his *Maa*. It was a shock. He thought he knew the tragedy of his mother's family, but apparently, judging by his father's tone it was not complete.

"What are you doing here, Saheb?" Shahida asked Gulzar, "You shouldn't be here."

Gulzar ignored her question, "For years you have kept it in your heart. It's time our children learnt the truth. After us the story will die, so you must tell them what we went through, especially you. If you don't tell them, I will." Gulzar said firmly.

Shahida looked at her husband with pleading eyes. She wasn't sure if telling the gory details was a good idea but since Gulzar had given an ultimatum and she knew he would tell if she didn't. Shahida lowered her head and wanted to cry; memories of the past were too painful to bear. For years she had blanked out those memories. She knew Gulzar was right; children had a right to know. Why a man such as Gulzar had to stay away from his family which had the first right on him. Shahida tried to speak but choked at the start. The images of past started to play in her mind. Gulzar pushed Shadab aside and sat next to Shahida and held her palms giving her strength. He knew she was reluctant to speak on the tragedy she and her family had suffered.

Prakash sought permission from Gulzar and Zubair to go to his room.

Gulzar ordered him to sit. "You are a part of family now. I am eternally grateful to you for bringing them here. Shahida is uncomfortable because the incidents were unbearable for me though I was a soldier."

Prakash acknowledged Gulzar's gesture and returned to his seat. He still felt uneasy but accepted the elderly man's order.

Gulzar Ahmed sat upright next to his wife and looked at his older son, "The *Razakars* drove away when they saw our jeep stop. I drove Shahida to her house where a small group of people were agitating. In those days Pak soldiers and officials were very unpopular. When people saw me in the jeep with my soldiers the group turned towards us. I asked Shahida to step out of the jeep and I escorted her through the crowd protected by three soldiers guarding us. When we entered the house, the sight was gruesome." Gulzar paused and looked at his wife, "She was extremely brave to have survived the scene which confronted us. When she opened the door we saw blood all over. Shahida froze at the sight. It was a bloodbath. Her mother lay in a pool of blood with a broken skull. She was brutally tortured before she died. Shahida was frigid. She stood next to her mother's body and suddenly ran upstairs. I followed her and stopped half way when I heard her scream. I ran up the steps and saw the horror mankind was capable of. Her fourteen year old brother, Azam's body had numerous slashes from a sharp weapon... bayonets were used, I suspect. He was lying naked on the floor. Shahida couldn't move. I asked her if there was anyone else in the house and she pointed towards the adjacent room. I asked the soldiers to guard her and went to the other room and the sight I saw there was even worse. Her thirteen year old sister, Zubeida was lying naked covered in blood. Her body was slashed like her brother but worse, she had been raped. I saw her lips move and I ran to her. Her body had numerous deep gashes but she was alive. I picked her in my arms. She opened her eyes saw me and her head fell back. She was unconscious. I covered her body and put her in the jeep. Shahida jumped into the jeep and held her sister till we reached the hospital. At the hospital, I picked her up and her body went limp. I knew she was dead. Doctors tried their best to revive her but all exercise proved futile. That evening, I asked my men to return to the camp while I attended to the family funeral. We buried the bodies of all three but when we reached home, I knew if I left Shahida alone it could be dangerous. I talked to her but she wouldn't leave her house. She wanted to stay in her house.

I knew better. The atrocities were committed by one of the two wings of the *Razakars*; either *Al Badr* or *Al Shams*. I knew they would return for Shahida because she had told me that her father was working for the independence of Bangladesh."

Gulzar Ahmed paused, reliving the incident. He looked at his wife. She was silent. He knew the gory scene was playing on her mind too. Gulzar looked at his younger son, "Your mother was determined but she was frightened. She had only me for company. Her relatives had abandoned her and the little group which had gathered earlier in the day had vanished leaving her alone to face the wrath of the *Razakars*. I stayed with her that evening. In those days, Bengalis of East Pakistan lived in fear psychosis. They were being massacred by their own countrymen. When we returned after cremating her family members, she gathered herself enough to clean the house but she cried all evening till she saw a small truck screech to a halt at the gates. She ran to her father's room upstairs and pulled out his gun and stood at the door. I pushed her behind the wall and stood facing the gate. Three men jumped out of the truck and demanded Shahida be turned over to them. I refused and threatened to shoot if they did not retreat. When they came close and the first one tried to push me, I shot him in the heart from two inches away and fired at the other two. Almost on cue, I saw an army jeep stop at the gate. Two army men ran towards me, one of them was my senior. I was surprised when they fired at me and a bullet hit me in the stomach. I shot three rounds and caught both men but the fatal bullets came from Shahida. She had waited till the two men neared me and then she had stepped out of the shadows of the wall and shot them. They were dead. Your mother and I, we had no place to go from that moment on. I knew we would be hunted by the *Razakars* and the army. I asked her to take all her valuables and go to any place where she could be safe. She declined to leave my side. She went into her parents' room and returned with all the valuables she could carry. She supported me and took me to the local mosque.

The *Qazi* of the mosque was a friend of her father's so he hid us in a room. A few minutes later a doctor arrived and attended to my injury. The doctor also made arrangements for our transport to a safe area. At night we were covertly driven to Narayanganj and from there we were escorted by two men to a hamlet just out of city. For a week we were in that hamlet where a doctor visited each morning and evening to check my injury." Gulzar said and stopped momentarily.

Shadab was looking at his parents with disbelief. He stretched his arm across his father's lap to his mother's wrist and held it to console her. He wanted to say something but before he could speak Zubair asked.

"Why didn't you contact us, *Abba*?" Zubair asked Gulzar.

"I was a hunted man. I had killed two soldiers and three *Razakars*. I was declared a deserter. The army and *Razakars* were after me for what I had done; I suppose they didn't know that Shahida had shot the fatal bullets at the soldiers. A fortnight after the incident I called a colleague in Rawalpindi, explaining what had happened. He informed me that our house was being watched. Though you and your mother were safe it wasn't advisable for me to return. For two years, I kept in touch with my colleague in Rawalpindi but situation for my return kept going from bad to worse. In a court martial, I was convicted of treason in absentia. In the newly created state of Bangladesh however, destiny had other plans for me. I was appointed as a Colonel in the Bangladesh Rifles. Now I had a new country." Gulzar Ahmed had a sarcastic smile, "This was the third country of which I become a citizen. Anyway... after two years of best efforts I realised I would be only harming my family if I returned, or contacted you. So, I resigned to my fate and accepted what destiny had designed for me. In those two years Shahida was my best help and despite the disparity in our ages... I mean I was forty-one to her twenty-one. We fell in love and got married. That is the truth. I did the best I could do in the given situation and I am proud of what I did. Yes, I am guilty of abandoning my family and I will accept any punishment God wishes me to endure."

"I remember you as a devoutly religious man. What you did was the only right thing you could have, *Abba*. According to the law of the land, you may have committed crime but you did not commit any sin... on the contrary, you acted virtuously. Don't hold any guilt in your heart, *Abba*. I am proud of what you have done." Zubair stated proudly.

Off all people Rukhsar was affected the most by the tragic story. She stared at her step-grandmother with a dazed look. She was looking at the intelligent, graceful woman who had suffered great losses. Rukhsar had heard of 'some' atrocities committed by the 'Punjabi' Pakistan army in erstwhile East Pakistan but she had no idea about the scale or the gravity of it. She had been told that the atrocities or crimes perpetrated by Pak army were lies spread by propaganda machine from India and Bangladesh. This was her first-hand experience about the authenticity of the stories. It had directly affected her family and she knew there would be many similar stories. Why had it happened? She wanted answers, so she asked in general, "Do you know why the Pakistan army carried out these operations?"

Aman nodded but didn't speak. He wanted to reply but he knew this wasn't the right time to go into minute details. To Rukhsar's surprise, Gulzar Ahmed replied, "Such operations are not planned or executed at a moment's whim. There is a series of events and circumstances which lead to it. Situations went wrong right from the day Pakistan was created. A series of poor political decisions, misadventures, administrative failures, lackadaisical attitude, and a disconnect between the rulers and people led to events which ultimately resulted in breakup of a country which couldn't stay untied for twenty-five years. That is food for thought, don't you think?"

"You said it started from the day of the creation. What do you mean by that?" she asked respectfully.

"The rift between the eastern and western units of Pakistan began immediately after its creation when Jinnah Sa'ab declared that the national language of Pakistan, including its eastern part should be Urdu. This enraged the people of East Pakistan. I thought *Qaid-e-Azam* had the right idea but at the time I was thinking as a Pakistani whose mother tongue was Urdu. When I think of it from the perspective of the Bengalis who were in majority, I realise the mistake. Bangla language has a thousand year history while Urdu is a young language; an amalgamation of various languages like Sanskrit, Hindi, Arabic and Persian, with brief history whereas Bengali culture is millennia old. Bengalis consider Nobel Laureate Gurudev Rabindranath Tagore and Kazi Nazrul Islam far greater than Urdu writers and poets, including Alama Iqbal. We may contend that but the fact remains that they believe it and it is their right to do so."

"Every country has an official language. Urdu is the official language of Pakistan. Why was it a problem?" Rukhsar asked.

"One official language in a country is common but there are countries which have more than one official language. Singapore, a tiny country with tiny population has four official languages: Malay, Mandarin, Tamil and English. Switzerland, again a small country has four official languages: German, French, Italian and Romansh. Belgium has Dutch, French and German, and India which has eighteen official languages. These countries have numerous official languages because they respect the culture and the people who speak those languages. People say it doesn't matter much if a language is imposed on users of another language but it isn't true. You take out a language and you destroy the entire culture of the people who speak those languages. Imposition of Urdu in East Pakistan was the first in a series of blunders. Bengali people kept agitating till 1954 when government had to accede to their demands and Bangla remained the first official language of East Pakistan."

"If the language issue was settled then why did the country break up?" she asked Gulzar.

Shahida raised her hand stopping any further conversation in the hall. She asked Shadab to escort Gulzar to his room. When he left, Shahida ordered others to retire. "We can talk tomorrow if there is anything else you wish to talk to him about."

- - -

Prakash and Aman Bux volunteered to stay at a hotel nearby which was promptly dismissed by Shahida and ordered to share a spare room together and she would share a room with Rukhsar while Zubair would share the room with his father. When all were settled, Prakash and Aman thought to themselves, instead of this shifting and re-shifting, a hotel room was a better idea. Before retiring, Zubair alerted his daughter not to disclose their whereabouts or mention about Gulzar in any way when she spoke to her mother.

Shahida's reasons for allocating rooms had a specific purpose. Father and son would want to catch up on matters they couldn't have discussed in the open. She and Rukhsar had to do some talking about the half families on both side; getting to know more about the families. And the two men, Prakash Rohatgi and Aman Khan Bux could do with some rest because they would have nothing to talk about, mutually or otherwise.

- - -

Aman was disturbed by the sounds he heard. He opened his eyes in the darkness and sat up guessing if Prakash was still there in the bed. He heard sound of running water again and he guessed Prakash was in the bath and tried to go back to sleep but the sound of falling water distracted his sleep. He sat up and groped in the dark to find the light switch. He turned on the lights and looked at his watch. It was quite early. 5:14 Am. Then he saw Prakash emerge from the bath and go about his daily routine. He had seen Hindu prayers being offered only in Indian films. Now he saw his roommate do it in real. It was intriguing to see how strikingly similar the essence of prayers were - devotion, faith and surrender to the Almighty. Aman never understood why people fought about religion. He observed Prakash closely as the latter went about his yogic and breathing exercises. He liked to learn about cultures and respected all cultures and religions which he knew was also the case with the man who was his roommate. Then, Aman had an odd feeling. The feeling came to him as he closely observed Prakash's expressions. Prakash sat on the floor cross legged practicing *'Pranayama'* which was getting quite a recognition and popularity. The perfect calmness on Prakash Rohatgi's face told Aman another story; Prakash had experienced great suffering and he was quite sad within and by controlling his emotions through exercises he was able to calm his mind. Aman hoped his presumptions were wrong. Prakash was a fantastic human being and Aman hoped he had established a lifelong friendship. And, again, questions propped in his mind: Who was this man? He shook his head when he didn't find answers, closed his eyes and slid back in the bed. Barely two minutes later he heard the door open and saw Prakash leaving the room.

"You going somewhere," Aman asked.

Prakash turned and held the door latch, "Yes. I have to sort a few things. My plans have been turned upside down by this trip." Prakash smiled and left.

* * *

General Head Quarters,

Rawalpindi, Pakistan

General Pathan was seriously worried. The man from JCIB was able to get some information. If that 'some' information, as the agent had mentioned, was what he had, then General Pathan wondered what the 'complete' information would be like. This was a disaster in the making in many ways. Aman Bux was not reachable, nor was Rukhsar. Altaf Khos had not reported in three days and he wasn't reachable either. General Pathan had a gut feeling that Prakash Rohatgi was involved in this. When he approached General Qureishi, the senior asked him to wait for another day.

General Pathan worried that if Rukhsar and Aman had met Zubair Ahmed and learn what had happened, they would go to any extreme to bring Zubair back to Lahore, and that could open cans of worms on which the army establishment had kept a tight lid so far. It would be a catastrophe. Pakistan army's reputation would be severely dented. There could be serious repercussions for Pak army if Zubair Ahmed returned to Lahore, or if he was to discover what had happened on 'Tiger Hill' during the Kargil war. There would be an outcry in media. Even the powerful Pakistan

Army establishment won't be able to contain the backlash for the actions of a Lieutenant General. He couldn't let that happen. Pakistan military establishment was the most respected institution of Pakistan. This pious institution had been misused, raped and plundered by many from within but people still had absolute faith in it and trusted its army to defend the country from its arch enemy; the rapidly growing powerful enemy - India!

Rukhsar, Zubair and Aman could create a lot of trouble if they decided to take on the military establishment. Knowing Rukhsar's determination and her integrity for truth, she won't stop. Zubair too would ensure truth prevailed.

In Kargil war Pakistan was fortunate to emerge unscathed, barring the irretrievable loss of lives of over sixteen hundred brave men. They can't afford more losses. Rukhsar and her father had to be stopped and Aman too if it came to that.

General Imran Pathan had four options. The first was to eject Aman Bux out of India through diplomatic channels and force him to bring Rukhsar back, minus Zubair.

The second option was to contact his undercover agents in New Delhi to know what was happening but that would mean providing sensitive information; work on which he had spent a decade working on. This was a risky proposition.

Third option was to contact Prakash Rohatgi directly, and work out a mutual settlement whereby Zubair stays in India but Rukhsar and Aman are forced to return to Pakistan. This would be tricky. If Prakash Rohatgi had made it possible for Rukhsar and Aman to meet Zubair Ahmed and if Zubair knew about the Tiger Hill orders, then it would be impossible to stop his daughter from creating a storm.

The fourth option was certainly distasteful. If Zubair was to return to Pakistan with Aman and Rukhsar, he had to be stopped! At all cost!

General Pathan felt sickness in his guts. For two decades he had known Zubair as one of the best brains in the Pakistan army; a soldier whose intellect and grasp of situations outweighed most seniors. That man was a soldier with absolute integrity. He wouldn't take orders from his seniors without knowing exactly what the plan was and what the strategic importance of an operation was. If Zubair returned to Pakistan he would investigate the incident on Tiger Hill where he was injured and his twelve men had died. And *'if'* he learnt the truth, all hell would break loose. Zubair had to be stopped from discovering the truth. This was a secret he shouldn't discover, come what may.

General Pathan remembered Zubair's rage when he learnt of the orders issued for Zubair. Zubair was on leave for four weeks to make arrangements for Rukhsar's wedding when he was informed of the Pakistan army incursion in Jammu & Kashmir. Zubair Ahmed had stormed into General Pathan's office demanding to know the aims and objectives of the Kargil operation. When General Pathan showed the plans to Zubair, the latter had roared in anger. Their long association notwithstanding, Zubair had called General Pathan a coward for not stopping the incursion. General Pathan remembered distinctly what Zubair had said. *"These fools don't realize that this operation is doomed to fail. These aren't the times of General Ayub when he could launch Operation 'Gibraltar' and hope to get away with it. These are modern times where communications are intercepted and informations are leaked. It will be a catastrophe if we don't stop this. Our whole Kashmir objective will be lost for good and we will gain nothing except loss of lives and loss of faith, General."*

General Pathan learnt in a fortnight how true Zubair was in his analyses. Pakistan stood isolated; even the staunchest of Pakistan's allies had turned their backs on her. Then he heard of the news which came through: Zubair had gone to the hills to evacuate the soldiers from his battalion who were stuck in a hopeless situation. In two weeks of fighting, soldiers were out of ammunition and the supply lines had been cut off by the Indian Air Force and ground forces. Soldiers were dying of starvation and Pakistan establishment couldn't do anything except to look on helplessly. Zubair had gone with few brave soldiers and made arrangements for the men he could find, to retreat to safer zone but then a zealous Lieutenant General had stopped the men from retreating and ordered them back to the hills. When confronted him, the Lieutenant General promised Zubair full supply of arms and food. When Zubair asked how, the Lieutenant General had no answers. Zubair didn't trust him so he returned to the hills. The Lieutenant General was angry at Zubair for insubordination and lack of respect for his senior. He wanted Zubair to pay for not obeying his orders. He issued an order to his troops to bomb the location stating that he had information that the Indian soldiers had retaken that post. The troops had launched an attack from three kilometres away and wiped out the post. Only, there were no Indian soldiers there except Zubair Ahmed and his dozen men. There were no survivors. Zubair was presumed dead; that was until Zubair Ahmed had been miraculously saved by Indian doctors. When news of Zubair's survival arrived through the list sent by the Indian army to its Pakistani counterparts, the Lieutenant General was stumped. When Pakistan government and army refuted Indian claims that the men on the hills were Pakistan army regulars, Lt. Gen. had breathed easy but kept tabs on the matter. He knew some day Zubair would return and when he would learn of the order, it would be the end of that Lt. Gen's career; the Lieutenant General was now a full-fledged General. For over a decade General Pathan had worked covertly with the most powerful people in Pakistan and Indian bureaucracy and army on a plan which would save Pakistan from Indian aggression. Zubair or his family's intervention at the wrong time could jeopardise that. So, Zubair had to be stopped from returning to Pakistan, and stop him from discovering the truth.

General Pathan thought of contacting that sweet, petit lady of the Chinese Assembly to seek her assistance. Her contacts were better and more reliable than his. But if he asked her for help he will have to give explanations. That was not advisable at the present moment. There was another factor: She liked the man who was in the middle of all this, and if the last option was to be taken even the life of Prakash Rohatgi could be at risk and that would not be acceptable to her.

What then, Pathan asked himself. The fourth option looked like the best option. A dead Zubair Ahmed couldn't discover the truth. General Pathan decided to wait and see if Zubair was returning to Pakistan; if he did, he will have to die.

'Damn you, Wahid Khan! Damn you for sending Altaf Khos to kill Aman and Zubair. I hope he is not able to find Zubair. Damn you, Wahid Khan, for giving orders to kill your own men in the battlefield. God damn you! You sent a mercenary to kill Zubair and Rukhsar and get them out of the way because you want be the next Commander in Chief of Army staff.' General Pathan cursed Wahid Khan mutedly. *'I will wait for a day and maybe I will inform Prakash Rohatgi'.*

* * *

Ahmed Residence

Dhaka, Bangladesh

Prakash Rohatgi had an idea. He suggested it to Shahida and Gulzar, and Gulzar spoke to Zubair and told him what Prakash had suggested. Zubair happily agreed. Shahida called Rukhsar to her room and discussed it. Rukhsar Ahmed stared at her step-grandmother with mixed feelings of disbelief and joy. She was overwhelmed by affection and love she was receiving from Shahida. She thanked her grandma for thinking about it. Shahida candidly told her that it was the idea spawned by Prakash. Rukhsar Ahmed smiled mildly. She felt a surge of affection for Prakash. Though she trusted the man from the beginning she knew this was beyond affection. Prakash had more to him than she had thought until now.

Rukhsar had a concern though. She couldn't accept Shahida's plan unless Aman agreed to it. Aman would like the presence of his colleagues and friends at his wedding. She asked Shahida to speak to Aman about it.

After lunch, the elders assembled in the hall where they had met the previous night. Gulzar took the onus upon himself to speak to Aman. "Aman, you have been very supportive of

Rukhsar. We think you deserve much more than you have got so far. Since all members of her family are here except for Shabnam we wish that the two of you get married tomorrow, here in Dhaka, in our presence."

Aman looked at Gulzar with wide eyes and then at others. They were smiling and he knew it was a serious proposal. He choked for a moment in joy. He looked at Rukhsar sitting next to Shahida and her smile told him instantly that she knew about it. He leaned back in his chair and thought for a moment without commenting. He liked the idea and wanted it immediately but he wished... Rukhsar knew the reason of his silence. "I wish we could have people close to you here too. If you wish, I will wait till they are here with us."

Aman nodded in agreement, and then he sat up straight and looked at her, "For thirteen years I have waited for this moment. We should get married tomorrow and I will inform my relatives and friends. When we return, we can throw a party for them in Lahore and Quetta."

The hall was suddenly abuzz with excitement; everyone trying to provide their opinion in preparations for the hastily arranged wedding.

Prakash stood silently leaning against the sill, observing everyone. But he had a worried look. Zubair noticed it and asked for the reason.

"When I proposed the wedding it skipped my mind. Aman's a diplomat who has just gone off the radar for people who are looking for him. I purposely asked everyone not to contact their family members in Pakistan. One mistake and they could be in serious trouble. In my opinion, if the wedding ceremony has to be performed we should keep it very private - family only. Rukhsar and Aman do not want any additional attraction especially from authorities looking out for them." Prakash stated clearly.

People in the hall knew what that meant. In the celebratory mood they hadn't thought of it. Aman knew the situation best.

He knew Prakash was right. They were in Bangladesh where they weren't supposed to be. If the authorities had picked up their arrival in India, they had a story to tell but their presence in Bangladesh without prior notice could land Aman in serious trouble. Though Aman had resigned, his resignation wasn't formally accepted so officially he was still a diplomat. If his trip was picked up, there would be serious questions asked and he won't have convincing answers unless he opened up the stinking tales of what he had witnessed in his short trip so far. And, he and Rukhsar were travelling on fake papers.

Aman Bux was sullen for a while. Rukhsar was upset as well but she kept up her spirits. Aman rose from his chair, walked slowly to the window and looked out. Many opinions came forth but none were apt. He asked Shadab if he could arrange for a Qazi who could solemnize the wedding without asking questions. Shadab nodded and left the room. He returned an hour later with a broad smile on his lips and informed that the Qazi of their mosque was told about the situation and he had agreed to solemnize the wedding.

Shadab put forth another little issue they had to contend with, "There are two small issues to sort. Though Rukhsar is represented by her family, there's no one from Aman's side. Also, the *Qazi* has advised us to tell Aman that the *Qazi Saheb* belongs to the *Qadiyani* sect while Aman is a Pathan. Would he have a problem if a *Qadiyani* solemnized the wedding?"

"He is a believer and that is what matters to me. I don't have an issue with that." Aman Khan Bux replied in protest.

- - -

Ahmed family made arrangements hastily but methodically. While members of the family were busy, Gulzar and Zubair were in their room talking casually about unimportant issues and Zubair's Lucknow experience. Abruptly, Gulzar looked at his son and wondered why he was working for the Indians - Rukhsar had told him about it the previous evening. Gulzar had soft corner for India and even loved the country. He had a good reason for it. He was born and brought up in India and had fondest memories of that village. But he wasn't sure if Zubair was doing the right thing. After all, Pakistan was his country and his faith did not permit working against one's own country. If Zubair was doing it, he was working against his own faith. He asked Zubair about it.

Zubair shook his head, "I am not working against any country. I am working for the good of both countries, *Abba*."

Gulzar couldn't understand how that was possible. Knowing the long history of animosity between the two countries it was difficult to understand how Zubair could work with the Indians and not harm Pakistan in the process. "I have seen enough in life to know that we can't hope to see a day when India and Pakistan could have a relationship like United States and Canada, like *Qaid-e-Azam* had envisioned. We have created so much angst against India that mind-sets of people on both sides of the border are poisoned. Yes, the Indians had a big role in breaking Pakistan but we have to realize that it was our mistakes which allowed the Indians to take advantage of the situation."

Zubair nodded, "If we had given East Pakistan its due we wouldn't have lost half our country. Indians took advantage because we gave them the opportunity on a platter and gift wrapped it with our misadventures." Zubair paused and looked at his father with great pride. "Was it really as bad as the stories about the atrocities are said to be?"

"It was worse. People don't realize that bad blood between the Eastern and Western units of the country was flowing deep." Gulzar suddenly went quiet. He was in deep thought.

"What happened?" Zubair asked his father.

"I am amazed. People don't relate a tragic event to the great divide between the two units. When I was stationed here in

'70, East Pakistan suffered probably the greatest natural disaster mankind has witnessed in recent times. A calamity which cost lives of over half a million…" Gulzar said and stopped when he heard a knock on the door.

The door opened and Rukhsar entered with a trey in her hands. The trey had a set of glasses of *sherbets*. Aman followed her. They greeted the elders and sat next to Zubair.

"I heard you talk about a natural disaster when I was at the door. What were you talking about?" Rukhsar asked Gulzar.

Gulzar Ahmed took a sip and looked at Rukhsar and put down the glass slowly on the trey, "It was called *cyclone 'Bhola'* and it was the probably the worst natural disaster of the last century in terms of lives lost. Well over half a million people lost their lives. The apathy of the Government of the time widened the existing crevice between the East and West. The locals of this part of the country were convinced that they were the step children of the country…"

"What about the cyclone? Why blame a Government for a natural calamity like cyclone?" Rukhsar asked.

"The cyclone hit East Pakistan around mid-November if I recollect well. It had come after the annual destruction caused by monsoon. It was disastrous but it wasn't the cyclone itself but the apathy of the authorities which caused the pain in the hearts of people. The Yahya Khan government didn't care. It was a time when the country was facing severe problems and the best effort by Yahya Khan was a helicopter fly by, an aerial survey to see the scale of disaster. If the Government had given some consideration towards the people here, we probably could have still been united but that wasn't destined to happen. Over half a million people died in that disaster and there was virtually no Government help. This turned out to be another big reason why people of East Pakistan voted overwhelmingly for Sheikh Mujibur Rahman and his Awami League during the election just a few weeks later."

Rukhsar had never heard about this disaster. "How did that election influence breakup of the Pakistan?"

"The election results clearly marked out huge differences: Zulfiqar Ali Bhutto and his Pakistan People's Party won quite comfortably in the Western unit but here in the East, Awami League swept the polls. According to democratic norms Awami League with clear majority should have been invited to form the Government but Yahya Khan did not transfer power to Awami League. Instead..." Gulzar replied but he was again interrupted by Rukhsar.

"*Baba*, I am sorry to interrupt you but it is all so confusing. I am unable to get the proper sequence. I have read in school text books and followed some events in print and electronic media. Many important facts have been misrepresented and distorted by successive Governments and the media as well. I remember some television programmes on these subjects but they were dismissed as distortions of facts by the agencies and ministries. Now it seems that the truth is far from what I have read, but before you start, can somebody please tell me who won the war in 1965? India and Pakistan both claim that they won the war. What is the truth?"

Gulzar and Zubair looked at each other with surprise; they were surprised by the question. "Your history text books say that Pakistan won the war of '65?" Gulzar asked Rukhsar.

The conversation was interrupted when Shahida entered the room with a wide smile. Rukhsar rose to make space for Shahida to sit next to Gulzar on the bed but Shahida waived her back and she sat at the foot of the bed.

"What's the good news?" Gulzar asked Shahida.

"Shadab met Qazi *Saheb* again and explained the situation and asked for his advice. *Qazi* Saheb said that we will be witness to the *'Nikaah'* from Rukhsar's' side but as an exception he had agreed to accept Prakash as witness from Aman's side because the wedding will be solemnized here."

"Have you asked Prakash about it?" Zubair asked.

"It was his idea," Shahida replied happily.

*   *   *

Prakash walked two kilometres towards the lake front and looked for a dark blue sedan. He spotted the car, walked to the driver's side and tapped on the window. The burly figure in the car invited him to sit in the car. Prakash sat on the passenger's seat. The burly man smiled and shook hands.

"What is the emergency? I said I was not to be disturbed," Prakash asked.

The driver replied respectfully, "I don't know who you are or what your name is. Our respected mutual friend asked me to meet you and tell you what he couldn't say on the phone."

Prakash nodded his head, "Ok. And?"

The burly man's face turned serious. "You requested him to extend your stay with your guests in Dhaka for three or four days. Our friend will do as requested but tells me to alert you about information he has received from his sources. Questions from unexpected quarters are being asked about your friends who have crossed the border with you."

"What unexpected quarters?"

"Our friend says question have come from Pakistan GHQ. This was not expected. They are trying to find out if you and three others, one of them a diplomat, have crossed border on this side. Our friend, Sir, is worried. He wants to meet you in person but not when you travel with your friends carry fake identities and travel covertly. Our friend suggests you leave as early as possible. He may not be able to hide your arrival for long. He also requests you to distance yourself from them. If people who ask questions can't achieve what they want, your companions will be 'taken care of'. Our friend doesn't want you involved in any covert operation which may jeopardize his mission."

"Thank our friend and tell him these are my own people, my guests, and if any of them is harmed, the once responsible will pay with their lives," Prakash said angrily, "Tell our friend that I am working on an important mission. If I succeed our group will be stronger and more effective. And, tell him that I want that extension of stay without any questions asked."

"Sir, I am just a messenger. I will convey your message but I suggest you think about his suggestion. He doesn't want to see you harmed in any way, and he doesn't know who your guests are but he wants you to return safely back home for the sake of the mission."

Prakash bore into the burly man's eyes, "Tell our friend to do as I say," he said, got off the car and banged the door behind him, and walked away. The burly man called out but he did not turn. Prakash kept walking till he saw the car turn left. For another kilometre he kept walking in the opposite direction and sat on a wooden bench, and called Purna.

She informed him that his SUV had arrived from Akbarpur. Prakash instructed Purna to perform a delicate task. She had to take care of Altaf Khos. Prakash asked her to wait for his call again. He disconnected and called a number in New Delhi's North Block and instructed the bureaucrat what was to be done. The bureaucrat hesitated initially but had to do what Prakash asked; circumstances were such. Prakash called Purna and told her to blindfold and tie Altaf. When she was done she put the cell phone on his ear for Prakash to speak.

Prakash was straightforward in his conditions to his captive. "Altaf, we are letting you go because we don't believe in killing people unless it is absolutely necessary. However, if I learn that you are in India, I will come for you and personally carve you up. You will be left in an alley and found by cops. If you can manage to return to Pakistan, good luck. I must warn you that if the cops learn that you are a Pakistani who has come here on any mission, you could have a miserable time for the rest of his life."

Prakash said and told Purna to call him after 'dropping' Altaf. He didn't have to tell her to be cautious either; she was too much of a professional for that.

The lights were brightly lit as he walked through the market on main Rabindra Sarani Road. He saw something he liked in one of the showroom displays. He walked into the store and six minutes later he walked out with a heavy packet in hand.

A few meters away he walked inside a large electronics store and spoke to the owner of the store and inquired where he could find the gadgets he was looking for. The owner looked at Prakash suspiciously asking why he wanted sophisticated, expensive surveillance and communication gadgets. Prakash dug into his wallet and produced a Bangla identity card which identified him as an intelligence officer with fictitious name, working on Indo-Bangla joint operation. Prakash lied to the owner that he had been accosted earlier in the day by anti-social elements and lost his gadgets. A little conversation convinced the owner of the store about Prakash's credentials. The owner agreed to source the gadgets for him but it won't be available before the following morning. Prakash paid half the amount in cash as advance and made the owner promise that the items will be there the next morning. Having received the large amount in cash, the owner smiled and promised him timely delivery and confidentiality. Prakash walked out of the store wondering how easy it always was to get things done by simply showing the colour of money. He was also surprised how easily such items were available.

As he walked towards the house Prakash began worrying about the threat from GHQ, Rawalpindi. He understood why it wanted Aman Bux and Zubair out of Pakistan. There were too many skeletons in one cupboard in this case. If story of the soldiers' family of tragedies and betrayals by its own country was known to the public it would be a disaster for the military and for the state of Pakistan. General Pathan was a decent man, he knew, but under these circumstances even a decent, sane mind such as General Pathan wouldn't hesitate to take extreme measures. His trust in Military establishment in Rawalpindi was very low but he trusted General Pathan for his integrity. General Pathan wouldn't be inhibited in taking any action to stop Zubair, Rukhsar and Aman individually or collectively, if they became a threat to the reputation of his establishment. Public embarrassment of his establishment was unacceptable.

Prakash knew that if the authorities in Pakistan were to learn his co-travellers were in Bangladesh and that they were travelling on fake papers the three could be arrested. Prakash knew he would be able to extract Zubair but to help Rukhsar and Aman would be virtually impossible because travelling on fake documents would invite charges of espionage because Aman was a diplomat and Rukhsar his companion. Prakash had to ensure that the couple were safe. He had taken utmost precaution including minor things like asking them not to use their cell phones and not calling their homes or friends till they returned home. Rukhsar had made that error once when she had called her mother from India. Prakash couldn't cover it up because the calls had already been traced.

- - -

Prakash sensed the joyous atmosphere when he entered the house. He had presumed that his suggestion to be a witness for Aman during the wedding was accepted by the *Qazi*. Prakash led Aman to a quiet corner and spoke to him. "We have trouble. I have learnt from my very reliable source..." he alerted Aman, "Rawalpindi and Islamabad are looking out for you and Rukhsar."

Aman nodded his head slowly. "It's ok. I expected it when Rukhsar used her phone to speak to *Ammi*. I'd warned her against it but she didn't heed. What's the situation now?"

"Ask Rukhsar not to use any phone. I will get an untraceable phone which you both can use."

"How did you manage that?" Aman asked humorously.

"Later," Prakash replied nonchalantly, "that isn't important right now. After the wedding I want you, Rukhsar and Zubair Saheb to return with me. I can't take chances."

Aman was cautious, "Why tomorrow? Is it so serious?"

"I can extend it by a day but why take chances? I don't think they are concerned about Rukhsar but she may become a threat to them. They want to see you all back in Pakistan, or in your case back in Tehran."

"Can we at least spend one extra day here?"

"I can manage one day but the following day I must be back in India for personal reasons."

"I must tell Rukhsar," Aman said and rose to leave.

The door flew open and Rukhsar entered the room with a wide smile on her face. A childlike enthusiasm has replaced the decade old sadness and scepticism. She side stepped Aman and walked to Prakash and hugged him, "Where have you been? We have been looking for you," she said with fake anger, and then smiled again, "I thank you for this day. There are many things I have to thank you for; for asking me to come to India and bringing *Abbu* back into my life and then for helping in uniting the two families and lastly, for making the wedding possible. Thank you!" She said solemnly.

Prakash forced a smile but the usual calmness on his face was absent.

"What's the matter?" She asked.

Aman told her. Rukhsar's enthusiasm receded. She slumped in the chair, looking at both men helplessly. Prakash held her wrist and clasped her hands, "I promise you two that I won't let any harm come to anyone. Those who threaten us know I am with you. If they try any misadventure it will backfire. They know me so they won't try stunts while I am with you. Though Rawalpindi and Islamabad want you two back, they will be extra cautious to take any action. But why instigate? Our job here is done. You have met your family and you can come back later when you travel with original documents. I suggest we leave after your wedding tomorrow," he said and added as an afterthought, "After returning to India you will go on a perfect honeymoon trip," he said with a mysterious smile and a wink.

Rukhsar withdrew her hand from the men's grasp, smiled shyly and left the room hurriedly. Aman looked at her as she left and turned to Prakash, his hand still in Prakash's. He turned the clasp into hand shake and spoke to him as solemnly as Rukhsar had, "She is absolutely right. You should get the credit for everything. Thank you!"

Prakash smiled widely and gripped Aman's hand firmly as a confirmation of friendship. Aman hugged his new friend and slapped his back. "I owe you now... but there is something which has bothered me very much. I want you to clarify it for me, to erase some doubts I have."

"What is it?"

"Who are you? You must be a powerful man to dare the authorities in Islamabad and Rawalpindi without hesitation. I had a doubt that you were working for India against Pakistan but that can't be true because I have observed how you have acted. I ask again. Who are you? Who do you work for? What is your interest in us? These questions are a mystery to me and as a friend I would like to know."

Prakash's expression turned hard. Aman could read nothing from his face except the eyes which he felt were experiencing or reliving a torture. For a few moments Aman saw deathlike sadness in his eyes and extreme loneliness. He felt he had tread into a past which had opened old wounds and scraped the scars of tragedy which was his history perhaps. He saw Prakash gulp and turn his face away.

Prakash turned around again a few moments later to face his friend. "For the time being you need to know is that I am your friend. You asked about my history earlier. I promise you I will tell you later," Prakash replied honestly, "Tonight and tomorrow will be the two finest days of your life. This is no time for sad sops. Let's celebrate the event, Aman."

Aman wanted to prod further. Prakash was emotionally weak at the moment and if prodded he could tell Aman about the things he wanted to know but he decided to respect his friend's privacy and trust him to keep his promise. He nodded his head and turned to leave. Prakash held him back and asked him to wait and stepped out of the room, and returned a minute later with a large packet in his hand. He gave it to Aman.

Aman looked at Prakash quizzically. Prakash pointed in the direction of the packet. Aman spread the packet carefully on the bed and opened it. A little gasp escaped his mouth when he saw an exotic, intricately embroidered silk *Shervani* in classic beige with a red *Sarrafa*. This was his wedding dress. Aman hadn't thought about his wedding dress; it had totally skipped his mind. He also saw a blue velvet box and he knew what that contained. He opened it to find a small diamond studded platinum ring sitting royally at the bottom of the box.

"If it doesn't fit Rukhsar you can have it mended," Prakash said with a tone of humour in his voice.

Aman was temporarily lost in a world of his own till he heard Prakash. He turned and smiled. He wanted to thank Prakash for the gesture but that would have reduced the value of the gesture. He took Prakash's hand and shook it again. Both men understood the value of that hand shake.

Aman knocked on Gulzar's door and entered the room, followed by Prakash. They were glad to find Rukhsar, Zubair and Shahida there. The two men knew the topic of discussion was their departure to India. It was a mixed expression of joy and sadness on the faces in the room. When they saw Aman, automatically their faces turned to smile. The room was cramped for space so the group moved to the hall downstairs.

- - -

"Can we stay for a couple of days, Prakash?" Zubair asked.

"Yes, you can, for a day, but why antagonize anyone? Other than that there isn't a problem except that I have a personal reason to be in Delhi the day after. It can't be avoided."

Aman looked at Zubair and Prakash, and declared his intent. "I would love to stay here for a week because I wanted to learn a bit about the history first hand but I understand what Prakash says. He told me that he spoke to some people to see if we can stay further but it could be trouble if we are found travelling with fake documents. I trust his judgement and I believe that we should follow his suggestion. After the wedding and celebrations, it is wise to leave."

Prakash saw sad faces and thought hard about altering his plan. He walked up to the window and leaned against the sill watching the evening lights flow in the distance. He did a quick mental calculation and when he was sure he had found an alternative, he turned to the people and interrupted their conversation without caring to know what they were talking about. "We can stay another night, but leave at dawn the day after tomorrow, latest. It is the best I can safely manage."

The faces lit up. They looked at Prakash and waited for him to continue but Prakash waited for them to respond.

Zubair replied, "That should be fine, I suppose."

Prakash nodded and returned to his chair. It was decided. They would leave at dawn after the evening reception which was to be held at the Ahmed residence. Family members finalized plans for ceremony the next day and chatted about nothing in particular. The group knew that they were together just because the guests would leave, and they wanted to spend time together. The bonding was becoming stronger.

Rukhsar suddenly returned to previous evening's topic. She put her hand on her grandfather's wrist, "*Baba*, we will leave soon. Can you please tell me about the seventy-one war?" she pleaded, "I have learnt so much on this trip but I can't go back with half information. I want to know the truth."

"It is a story of lies and betrayals, of apathy and torture, my child. Why do you want to get into it? Let the past be buried. Each war has given our family heartburns and separation. Is there any point in discussing about it?" Gulzar asked.

"Yes, it's important for me. *Abba* was a brave soldier who nearly got himself killed while fighting for his country and he is in a situation where he is working for a country whose army he fought. You, a brave soldier but you had to let go of your army and country. You were punished for your virtues... And we are told lies about the war in our history text books."

Gulzar and Zubair were truly surprised. The Octogenarian looked at his grand-daughter and commented. "That is a very strong statement to make."

Rukhsar nodded, "But it's true, you agree. Since I arrived in India, I have learnt truths from my father and I am starting to believe that we are a nation of disillusioned people who have been fed lies for decades. Our history books are written by liars who want to hide their blunders and let the countrymen believe that they were pious in what they say to them; by design, and with purpose. They do not want people to know about their mistakes. I am not willing to live with lies. I want the truth and I will know it from you people who were on the 'scene of the crime' as it were. I want the truth because I am marrying a diplomat... And I don't want to raise my children on lies. I want them to know the truth... be it about war or about real life. If I have children I want them to be their own selves not some misinformed children raised on lies."

Gulzar was taken aback by the intensity of Rukhsar's last sentence. Her reason to seek truth and the logic behind it was indisputable. He stared into her beautiful large eyes, nodded his head and asked Shadab to ask his wife to join them.

Shahida objected, "I don't want her to hear of tragedies of the family. I don't want her children to hear gory stories. I have kept them away from such conversations." Shahida objected.

"I have just learnt from my granddaughter that we should not raise our children on lies. I also say we should not deprive our children of truth. It is their right to know the truth. Any truth hidden is as good as a lie. Shadab's children are young today but I want the parents to know the truth and tell their children about it when they grow up. I agree with Rukhsar. Our children should not be raised on lies." Gulzar said and it was an order which Shahida could not ride over.

Rehana, Shadab's wife was bewildered why she was asked to be present. Her mother-in-law had protected her from strain, physical or mental. She protested mildly but when Shadab stressed she reluctantly joined the group.

When Rehana entered, Gulzar smiled affectionately to ease her anxiety. Then he spoke to all and to Rukhsar and Rehana in particular. "I think I should begin with the greatest of all lies. It is stated in general that Sheikh Mujib and the Hindu '*baniyas*' broke up Pakistan. That is a lie! They hide their own sins. Indians broke up East Pakistan and helped the Awami League and Sheikh Mujib create Bangladesh because we gave them the opportunity. If a country is united no enemy can break it up no matter how hard we try. It was..."

"I have a question because I have no information on it." Shadab interrupted unexpectedly, "Pakistan and India started at the same point. When and how did the two drift away from each other? Both countries started with same issues they faced: illiteracy, backwardness, poverty. Why has India grown so fast in comparison with Pakistan?" Shadab asked.

People waited for Gulzar to reply but Gulzar did not have an answer to that. To every one's surprise Rukhsar replied. "I have studied a little about it as one of my projects. I did some research on the economies of the two countries and how the policies determined the future of both countries."

"Really? How?" Shadab asked.

Rukhsar raise her hands in air in defence of her statement, "I only talk about economic decisions and how it determined the future... nothing else."

"Okay. Tell me," Shadab said.

"After independence Indian political leaders had an agenda, a road map for India's future. Pundit Nehru's Government decided at the beginning that India would follow a 'socialist' path where concern of the citizens of the country was the priority. The Government agenda was based on thrusts in key, vitally important areas: Science & Technology, Industry, Education and Agriculture. Pundit Nehru was a visionary and his Government worked on these. Here in Pakistan however, we were unfortunate to lose our two great leaders right at the start who could have matched Pakistan with India's progress; *Qaid-e-Azam* Mohammed Ali Jinnah died within a year of independence and Prime Minister Liaqat Ali Khan was shot dead. While India started to grow under Pandit Nehru, in Pakistan, the leaders after Liaqat Ali Khan weren't visionaries; and they were quite petty. Industrial growth was non-existent because there were no industries to speak of in East or West Pakistan. All the major industries were in the present day India. That too was a major disadvantage. It is important to note here there was another major factor which played a vital role in the development of India and stagnation of Pakistan. Within a few years of gaining independence, India ended the rule of feudal landlords. The *Zamindars* were out and new farmers came into existence in India, whereas in Pakistan, to this day we have landlords who own stretches of land that can be seen for tens of miles. From economic viewpoint the biggest mistake in my view, was the dependency we created on US arms for our military power and US aid to take care of our economy. India, on the other hand did not rely on either superpower of the time for economy or arms. Pandit Nehru remained neutral and created the 'Non-Aligned Movement' by bringing in Nasser of Egypt, Sukarno of Indonesia and Tito of Yugoslavia. 'NAM' became a mass movement; over a hundred countries became part of NAM." Rukhsar paused to look at her elders to see if there was any comment. She saw respectful eyes staring at her and continued, "The decision to be self-dependant and remain neutral, in my opinion, was the first of two major differences between India and Pakistan. Then the second was India's stress on education. We are seeing the results of those decisions today."

Gulzar nodded in appreciation. "You are right. I am not an economist like you but I understand what you say."

There was silence in the room. All were waiting for Gulzar to resume from where he had left off. Gulzar's eyes turned stone-like. He tilted backwards and rested his back on a cushion and closed his eyes. "I wish India wasn't divided. It has only brought misery and animosity not just between the Hindus and Muslims, but between peoples of three nations now. When we migrated to Pakistan we thought we would help create the greatest Muslim nation on Earth. Within a few years my father was disillusioned and prayed for a chance to return to India but that chance was gone. He had invested too much in Pakistan and we had lost our foothold in India."

Gulzar looked at Shadab and said, "We had the greatest chance in history to really create a modern state for Muslims but it failed... it turned into a disaster. For our every failure the politicians blamed India. Since teenage I have heard lies that India interfered in Pakistan's domestic issues. And I learn from you," Gulzar said to Rukhsar, "that they are still doing it. Lies! India was never interested in our affairs. They have lied since the day Pakistan came into existence, and we shall pay a very heavy price for it one day - mark my words!"

Gulzar stopped to control his anger and he spoke again, "Rukhsar said about the acquiring of arms from the US. She is right. We took arms from US and allocated a major chunk of our budget for the military citing Kashmir issue, and India as the enemy. Once that first decision was made, Pakistan became a 'security state', a concept which doesn't make any sense to me to this day. Then our leaders portrayed India as an existential threat to Pakistan which created such hype that to this day every policy has become India-centric. Pakistan started pinpricking India from the year both countries became independent; it started by sending marauders and butchers across the border into Kashmir in 1947 to keep the scars of partition bleeding. It gave Pak army the legitimacy to acquire arms it couldn't afford. In 1965 they ran up the Indian posts like they did again during the Kargil war. On each occasion it was ill-planned and poorly executed. The worst was the '71 war where the army didn't just brutalize the locals; it created proxy armies to massacre its own people."

"Why?" Rukhsar asked. She wanted to know the reasons which led to the separation of Pakistan.

"...because Yahya Khan did not want to relinquish power, at least not to the 'Bengalis'. In the elections of December,'70 and January '71, Awami League had a clear majority but Yahya Khan, the Martial Law Administrator who was also the President did not wish to relinquish power to a political party from East Pakistan. Foreign Minister Zulfiqar Ali Bhutto had won handsomely in West Pakistan but Sheikh Mujib' Awami League had won 160 seats out of 313, but the leaders including Bhutto did not want to see Sheikh Mujib in power. The power struggle continued but the transfer of power never happened."

"Why was there so much disparity between the voters of East and West?" Rukhsar asked.

"I should remind you of *cyclone 'Bhola'* and the devastation it caused in November of 1970. People of East Pakistan didn't forgive the administration. The country paid for the apathy of its leaders." Gulzar replied with obvious pain in his speech.

"How could it lead to separation?" Rukhsar asked.

"There was a needle between the popular leaders of East and West Pakistan. In '68, the Government of Pakistan filed a sedition case against Sheikh Mujibur Rahman. Sheikh Mujib was accused of conspiring with India to destabilise Pakistan. It is famously called the *'Agartala Conspiracy Case'*. It was to be a court Martial but switched to civilian law suit under sedition charges. There were thirty-four people who had travelled to meet some people in the Eastern Indian state of Tripura, on the eastern border of East Pakistan and Agartala is its capital. During the trial some witnesses renegade on their earlier statement stating they were coerced into making statements under duress. These accusations of forcing people to make false statements further estranged delicate relations between people of East Pakistan and Islamabad Government. The case was withdrawn in '69 when there was a massive uprising. Some attempts were made to control the situation but failed. Later there was a three way dialogue between Bhutto, Sheikh Mujib, and overseen by Yahya Khan. During the meeting Mujibur Rahman wanted agreement on his six basic demands. These six conditions by Mujib were mainly a demand to have more political autonomy and say of the people of East in running of the government. Bhutto and Yahya Khan did not accede to Mujib's demands and the talks failed. A few days later the final nail in the coffin was hammered when Bhutto, during a speech proposed the 'two Prime Ministers' theory and then made a cardinal blunder of saying to Bengalis, *'You on that side and we on this side'*. That statement clearly spelt the discrimination."

Gulzar paused and sipped water. He was straining his heart. Shahida tried to stop him but Gulzar patted her hand to comfort her. He wanted to tell Rukhsar, Shadab and Rehana the truth as it was. He leaned back in his chair and resumed, "After the meeting with Sheikh Mujib failed, Yahya Khan and Bhutto returned to Islamabad. They met Lt. Gen. Sahebzada Yakub Ali Khan who was the Chief of General Staff and confided in him that they couldn't transfer power to Sheikh Mujib so the government had to arrest him and his supporters. Yakub Khan wanted a political settlement instead of military action as was suggested by Yahya Khan. When Yahya Khan insisted, Yakub Khan resigned in protest. Within a few days Yahya Khan deputed General Mohammad Tikka Khan as the Martial Law Administrator and Governor of East Pakistan. General Tikka Khan became all powerful in East Pakistan because he was in charge of the army's Eastern Command."

"As I said earlier, the leaders in the West did not want to give up power to the Bengalis whom they used to refer to as *'short, dark skinned and Hindu agents'*. Although they had declared in January that Sheikh Mujib would be the Prime Minister and that the first elected assembly would be called in Dhaka, it never happened. It was declared that a constitution would be drafted in four months before transfer of power to Awami League. The Awami League declared an all-out strike in Bengal. On March 25th, Tikka Khan launched the nefarious *'Operation Searchlight'*. He brought in *'Biharis'* who hated the Bengalis, and like the west wing of the country, considered Bengali locals as *'Hindu agents'* who were working for the separation of East Pakistan at India's behest. Tikka Khan organized and planned the *'Operation Searchlight'* in which over three hundred thousand to half a million people were killed according to conservative estimate. The figure goes up to three million dead according to Bangladesh Government's official assessments. During this operation, as I and Shahida experienced first-hand, there was no morality or ethics, no sense of decency or mercy. I am not sure how true it is, but I heard that Tikka Khan had said, *"I don't want the people. I only want the land.'* Tikka

Khan was called the *'Butcher of Baluchistan'* for his actions in Baluchistan just a year before he was made the Governor of East Pakistan. His suppressive and brutal action to quell the uprising in Baluchistan was the reason why he was deputed to East - to suppress the uprising of Bengalis with any methods he could use. With absolute power, Tikka Khan set about his work in the most brutal way possible. Any person who was found to be member or sympathiser of the Awami League was executed. Mostly these atrocities were carried out by the *Razakars* and they did it with gay abandon because they were not accountable to any one... and they had the blessings of the supreme authority: Tikka Khan. As Major General Rao Farman Ali wrote in his diary, *'Green land of East Pakistan will be painted red. It was painted red with Bengali blood'.*"

Gulzar Ahmed paused again. He was beginning to shiver. Others could see his wet eyes. Gulzar put his hand on Shahida's shoulder for emotional support - to give and gain. Shahida looked at her husband with pleading eyes. She was reliving those days of terror and fright just like Gulzar was.

As Gulzar Ahmed started to speak again, he saw Prakash walk to him and hold his hand and nod his head in empathy. "If you permit me, I will continue... the facts of how events actually occurred. If there is any gap to be filled I am sure you and Zubair Saheb can do it. We know of your personal losses, especially of Shahida Ma'am. It would be cruel to open those scars again. Since it is only the incidents of the war which are to be told in proper chronology, I can do it."

Gulzar looked at Prakash and nodded his head slowly.

Rukhsar asked a question in general, to all. "If such atrocities were being committed why didn't the international community take notice of it? Why didn't it intervene?"

Prakash replied, "International community did intervene but when it did, Yahya Khan and Bhutto lost that chance to save East Pakistan. Before Tikka Khan launched *'Operation*

Searchlight' on March 25th, all foreign journalists were told to leave the Eastern wing. These journalists had their sources, and the information they got, was dispatched worldwide. They were stationed in Calcutta in West Bengal so their only sources of information were the refugees. Western journalists were showing footages and interviews of the millions who were fleeing East Pakistan from the *ethnic cleansing* of *'Bengalis'* and *'Hindus'*. East Pakistan had about twenty per cent Hindu, Bangla speaking people. The Hindus and followers of Awami League were targeted by the army and *Razakars*. Pakistan Government was taking a hammering but these informations were being kept a secret from citizens of West Pakistan. However, the Government knew that the truth was beginning to trickle in. To counter it they invited ten Pakistan journalists to witness how the army was controlling the uprising of *'anti-Pakistanis'* in the east. It was a guided tour and the journalists were dictated to write what script they were provided. Among these there was one journalist who did some investigation of his own. When he saw what was truly happening, he was appalled. He returned to Karachi, and overnight he moved his family to London leaving behind all his belongings, giving up his house and all his assets. When this Goa born, Karachi based journalist, Anthony Mascarenhas' news article titled *'Genocide'* hit the international headlines published by Sunday Times, with gory, graphic details and heart wrenching stories, the world was stunned at the scale of atrocities perpetrated by the army and its proxy militia, the *'Razakars',* the *'Al Badr'* and *'Al Shams'* militia. As Anthony Mascarenhas' wrote, he was witness to a *'systematic killing spree'* in the *'kill and burn'* mission across towns and villages, which the Pakistan army called *'the final solution'*. Overnight, the world media turned its attention to East Pakistan and Time magazine ran at least two cover stories on it. Pakistan army and Government denied all reports and called it an Indian propaganda, and called Mascarenhas a betrayer and an Indian agent."

"Why didn't the International community act against Pakistan then?" Rukhsar asked, yet unable to believe that her country's army had committed such heinous atrocities.

"It did! Poland, after condemning the acts on floor of the United Nations, presented a proposal to bring secession in hostilities, with a political solution. That, in my opinion, was the best possible chance for Zulfiqar Ali Bhutto to seize the initiative of the UN and settle the matter and save Pakistan from breaking up but Mr. Bhutto, contrary to expectations of the UN, tore up the proposal on the floor of the Assembly and walked out. With him walking out, the neutral countries opted to side with India and East Pakistan. This action by Mr. Bhutto changed world opinion decisively against Pakistan and the UN member countries encouraged India to play a more 'decisive role', meaning that India must intervene and settle the matter in one way or the other."

"Why didn't Mrs. Gandhi take an initiative early in the war? Why did she wait to attack till December?" Rukhsar asked.

"Firstly, India did not attack Pakistan. I will come to that later. That is the irony. Officially, India and Pakistan were not at war. What was happening in East Pakistan was a domestic problem of Pakistan. Indian army was not directly involved in any action." Prakash clarified, and continued, "Mrs. Gandhi took this opportunity and travelled to numerous countries, mainly the western powers, and Russia. Her trips influenced those Governments to side with India on diplomacy. Having said that, there is an incident which took place on April 27 when Mrs. Gandhi invited General Sam Maneckshaw to discuss the issue of refugees who were coming in tens of thousands a day. By mid-April the numbers of refugees had swelled to over half a million. India wasn't financially sound or equipped with the logistics or means to cater to such large numbers of refugees in short span. When they saw that the influx of refugees could not be contained, Mrs. Gandhi asked Maneckshaw to go into East Pakistan and help *'Mukti Bahini'*. Sam Maneckshaw categorically told his Prime Minister that it was not possible immediately because the army wasn't ready for a large scale operation. Moreover, monsoon was a few weeks away. The army could not ignore the elements and so the military intervention was stalled till after monsoon."

"So India was not the reason for the breakup of Pakistan?" she asked, knowing well that India in some way or the other was responsible for it.

"That happened much later and Pakistan provided India with the opportunity... as Gulzar Saheb said, 'offered on a platter'" Prakash replied honestly.

"How were the East Pakistanis able to respond to the attacks on their brethren?"

"When *'Operation Searchlight'* was launched, it killed many local Bengalis. Soldiers from two Pakistan military regiments, *'East Pakistan Rifles'* and *'Bengal Regiment'* revolted and formed the core of *'Mukti Bahini'*, supporting Sheikh Mujib in his fight to create Bangladesh. It is notable that before the Dhaka talks had failed, Sheikh Mujib was seeking autonomy for the East wing, not independence. When *'Operation Searchlight',* was launched, Awami League declared that it wanted to secede from Pakistan and that they were fighting for the creation of Bangladesh; struggle for autonomy turned into fight for freedom struggle. Also, Zia Ur-Rehman, who later became Bangladesh's dictator, was a major in Pakistan army. When Sheikh Mujib was arrested and put in a jail in western unit of Pakistan, Zia-Ur Rehman revolted and captured Dhaka Radio Station and declared that East Pakistan was now a separate country: Bangladesh. He also set up a government in exile in India."

"And still, the Pakistan army was not able to beat *Mukti Bahini*?"

Prakash shook his head, "It was a no win situation once the whole province of Bangla people joined the freedom struggle. There was only so much the Pakistan army could do. Though the Indian army did not send its troops across the border, it trained men of *Mukti Bahini* on Indian soil and armed them. International community was now firmly against Pakistan and so as far as India did not send in its troops across the border, the world community appreciated what India was doing. The East Pakistan army and establishment spread information that it was acting against supporters of so-called *'Bangladesh Movement'*. It declared that people fighting against the Pakistan army were *'enemies of Pakistan, Islam and Muslims'*. This silenced the critics in West Pakistan. However, conditions in the east were deteriorating rapidly."

"When did India officially go to war with Pakistan?" Rukhsar asked.

"Officially, on 3rd December! It was not India which sent its army. Situation in East Pakistan was so precarious, Pakistan establishment and military decided to open a front with India and Pakistan Air Force planes struck six Indian airbases on that day. India was waiting for an opportunity like this. India officially declared it was at war on that day. Within thirteen days the war was over."

"How come the war ended so quickly?" she asked.

"Pakistan army was ambushed throughout the Eastern wing. *'Mukti Bahini'*, through open attacks or guerrilla tactics kept harassing, and pushing Pakistan soldiers back. Pakistan army had very few sympathizers in the East barring the Urdu speaking Muslims who had migrated from the Indian states of UP and Bihar, at the time of partition. These people were called *'Biharis'* and considered outsiders by the majority Bengali speaking Muslims of the East. As Gulzar Saheb said, these were the *'Razakars'*, the volunteers who did the dirty job for Pak army. On the other hand, once Pak forces attacked India on the western front, they brought India into open warfare. Though Pakistan had more sophisticated and superior arms, air and naval power, Indian army was far more disciplined and more professional in its planning and execution. Remember, in April Mrs. Indira Gandhi had asked General Maneckshaw to go into East Pakistan. Then the army wasn't ready but by December they were well prepared and they had their plans ready. When the war started, within three days the Indian naval ships were off Karachi port and bombing the city. The Indian army, according to their carefully planned course of action, executed it professionally. The Indian army had four strategic thrust areas in East Pakistan, from the west through west Bengal, from the North through Assam and from the east through Tripura. The locals welcomed them with open arms and with intelligence reports. Both, the Pakistani and the Indian army were fighting on two fronts, the east and the west but while the Indian army was fresh and executing the well laid plans, the Pakistan army was being punished on both fronts: on the west by the Indian army and Indian Air force and in the east it was severely embarrassed by *'Mukti Bahini'* and the small number of Indian soldiers. The Pakistan army was in total disarray."

"Tikka Khan had obviously failed. Why wasn't he replaced?" Shadab asked curiously.

"He was shifted out but quite late. He was replaced by Amir Abdullah Khan Niazi - *'Tiger Niazi'* as he was called. But why wasn't Tikka Khan stopped earlier, I have no answer to that. Maybe, replacing Tikka Khan within seven months could have embarrassed the Yahya Khan government. Tikka Khan was brought in to control the situation. Instead, he put the situation totally out of control. The *'Butcher of Bengal'* tried his best to eliminate the anti-Pakistani supporters and in the process he created more enemies and became the reason for breakup of Pakistan. He used the same tactics in Baluchistan again two years later and his operations were successful in military terms. The *'Butcher of Bengal'* had become the *'Butcher of Baluchistan'* for the second time."

Rukhsar looked at Aman. "You knew about the history?" she asked him.

Aman was a reluctant participant in this assembly. He had his reasons for being silent. He looked at his bride to be and nodded his head. "I knew most of it but not the little details. What I am hearing is a confirmation of what I already knew." He turned to Gulzar Ahmed, "As diplomat I fail to understand one thing. When India had not officially entered the war, what did Pakistan want to achieve by attacking India's western front, especially when it was struggling to save its reputation in the east?"

"I have thought about it a lot but to this day I don't see any logic behind the action. Pakistan should have been grateful that India hadn't sent in its army although it was helping the '*Mukti Bahini*' directly." Gulzar shrugged his frail shoulders. "I wish I know why the western front was opened. That is what Mrs. Gandhi was waiting for; an opportunity to hit Pakistan," Gulzar sarcastically said as he lowered his head in disgust.

"Are you saying that Mrs. Indira Gandhi had personal grudge against Pakistan?" Rukhsar asked.

"Not against Pakistan. She had a personal grudge against Yahya Khan because during a radio broadcast Yahya Khan had used abusive language while referring to her." Gulzar Ahmed said.

"Wasn't anyone punished for these misadventures or for the atrocities?" Rukhsar asked.

Zubair coughed a sarcastic laugh. "Yes, '*Tiger Niazi*' was punished, but without trial. After the war, he was held responsible for the surrender and charged with human rights violations in East Pakistan. He was dismissed from the army and stripped of his military decorations. Though he was part of the nefarious '*Operation Searchlight*', and also guilty of massacre, Tiger Niazi was not the only culprit. Tikka Khan, the main culprit in the East Pakistan massacres, got away scot free. I was to learn later that he was not only sent to take care of another uprising in the tribal areas of Baluchistan, he was promoted and made the Chief of Army Staff the following year, and more appallingly, he was Pakistan's Defence Minister in Bhutto's Government."

Everyone in the hall was silent. The tragic sequence of events was bearing down on their minds. Few unfortunate, poor administrative decisions had led to country's breakup. Though Shadab and Shahida were Bangladesh patriots they could feel the loss in the hearts of the two ex-soldiers.

Rukhsar stared at her father and grandfather blankly with the sense of loss. "Why weren't earlier governments able to rectify the situation? Why did they let it come to this stage?" Rukhsar asked in anger and sadness.

Zubair shook his head with a wry smile, "There are many issues which don't get the mention they deserve in the context of Pakistan's division. One such decision by PM Mohammed Ali Bogra was the seed to many problems Pakistan faces today. In '54 he drafted a plan which spawned these problems. The country will continue to pay the price for it unless matters are politically settled soon. In a rash move he seized all powers of the provinces and came up with a theory of 'Two Units'; East and West Pakistan! After independence, the provinces and princely states like Kalat and Bahawalpur had joined Pakistan with promises that their provincial autonomies would be maintained. With Bogra's 'two unit' theory, all privileges and autonomies were withdrawn, and that created a vast fissure between the Federal and local provincial Governments which kept widening as days went on. The provinces of North West Frontier Province, Sindh and the princely states opposed it vehemently but they were stamped down promptly and ruthlessly. The mistrust in Federal Government finds its roots to that era. See what is happening in Baluchistan and Sindh or in Khyber Pakhtunkhwa. This will go on spreading unless the trust is reinstated in the hearts of these people."

Zubair looked at his daughter and continued, "There were blunders after blunders by successive governments. Look at

Baluchistan. It should have been handled delicately," Zubair said and asked Rukhsar, "Do you know that Kalat was an independent country, born three days before Pakistan? Apparently, the Khan wanted to join India and not Pakistan, but according to a press release VP Menon, secretary in the Ministry of States, during a press conference said that the Khan was pressing India to accept Kalat's accession but India was not keen on it. Mir Ahmadyar Khan was the sovereign of Kalat and Jinnah was his lawyer who helped the Khan deal with the British. After independence Jinnah Saheb asked the Khan of Kalat, to join Pakistan. The Khan of Kalat put some pre-conditions which were rejected by the Government of the day. The Khan was still hoping that India would accept his wishes but nothing came through. In the meantime, after talks between Pakistan and the Khan failed, in March '48 the Pak army invaded Kalat and forced the Khan of Kalat to sign the accession treaty…"

This was new information for Aman and Prakash. Both men looked at Zubair with keen interest. "Why would the Khan want to be a part of India rather than Pakistan?" Aman asked.

Zubair laughed sarcastically, "He probably saw what would become of Baluchistan. What do you see today?"

"Why didn't India accept the Khan's proposal?" Rukhsar asked.

"Indians probably saw the same problems Pakistan faced in the '71 war. Two parts of a country separated by a hostile country would be nothing but trouble. But that is just guess work. I don't know the real reason." Zubair clarified, and he continued from where he had diverted on the topic, "All the rights of Kalat were withdrawn in accordance with the two-unit theory of Mr. Bogra. From that day onward the Baloch have been fighting for their rights and autonomy. If we don't learn lessons from history there will be further breakups of country. Oppression of people will never get us anything except greater animosity towards the Government. Various Baloch tribes are up in arms because we did not respect their provincial and cultural rights. *'Bugti'* and *'Marri'* tribes have gone to the extent of stating that they will even take arms from devil if it helps them to gain freedom from Pakistan. This was avoidable if Baloch people were given their rights as they had been promised before annexation. There are vast stretches of lands where the Pakistan federal government has lost control. Thousands of miles of 'FATA', Waziristan, and many parts of Baluchistan are no go areas for Government officials. Pak army is reluctant to conduct operation in those areas because of hostility and fear of mass casualties on both sides. The oppression of people in those areas will result in another breakup if we don't learn our lessons. Each passing day body counts are mounting and Baloch are getting angrier. Unless we give them their legitimate rights, we can bid goodbye to those parts of the country."

No one except Rukhsar noticed something strange in the manner Zubair Ahmed was saying 'we' whenever he referred to Pakistan or its people. The old soldier was still a patriot and it reflected in his speech; the flame was still brightly lit. And men like him were forced to live in exile? She saw her grandfather, another martyr for his country now living and working with a country he had fought.

Aman was silent. He wanted to speak about his own people but he decided against it. For him it was too sensitive an issue to speak here. He only talked of it in right atmosphere and to the right people because he wanted results, not just talks. He wanted results because his family had paid for it... with their lives.

Prakash keenly observed the serious faces in the hall. He had to be sure that he chose the right people for the job which was going to be ultra-sensitive and certainly dangerous for anyone who was associated with it. There were zealots in powerful positions and to irk them wasn't a good idea. So far he was happy with the responses he had seen, especially from Aman. Aman's silence spoke a lot and Rukhsar's questions to Gulzar and Zubair

Ahmed were interesting. It was giving him an insight into her mind - into her character.

Rukhsar was glum. She had many questions racing through her mind but she was unsure if those were reasonable. "When we had better arms and bigger force in East Pakistan, why did we lose? Why did the Pakistan army surrender so quickly?" She asked Prakash Rohatgi.

Prakash looked at Gulzar Ahmed to see if he wanted to reply. Gulzar Ahmed nodded at him to reply. "There is a confluence of reasons. Though Pak army was better armed, it was having a tough time against *Mukti Bahini*. Pak soldiers were unable to counter the guerrillas of *Mukti Bahini*. The intelligence network of *Mukti Bahini* and the Indian army was excellent while Pak army was being fed false information even by reliable sources at times. Awami League and *Mukti Bahini* supporters were too many and pro-unionists too few. The supply lines were severely disrupted and as a result, even before the Pakistan forces opened the western front and India got involved directly in the war, body count of Pakistan soldiers had crossed twenty thousand. Situation was so critical that even the Indian army could not save the Pak soldiers from the *Mukti Bahini*." Prakash Rohatgi was replying to her, "One incident amplifies it quite well. Though the Pak army agreed to unconditional surrender, the Indian army asked Pak soldiers to retain their arms for their own safety from *Mukti Bahini* until formal surrender. Only after General Niazi signed the surrender document, Pak soldiers laid down their arms and the Indian army ensured the safety of Pak soldiers."

"General Niazi had over twenty-six thousand armed soldiers to about three thousand armed Indian soldiers and some '*Mukti Bahini*' men in Dhaka. Why did he surrender?" Rukhsar asked.

Gulzar Ahmed patted his wife's wrist to tell her he was fine and turned to Rukhsar, "I have a theory. General Niazi was as guilty as Tikka Khan because he too was responsible for '*Operation Searchlight*'," Gulzar said sarcastically, "He oversaw the operation after arming and training the *Razakars*. When Niazi was sure that the loss was inevitable, he consulted his superiors. Having weighed the situation on the eastern and western fronts he got instructions to surrender and cut the losses the army was incurring on both fronts. Tikka Khan was transferred from East Pakistan and asked to command the western front. I am not sure, but it was probably his idea to open the western front and take on India. The operation was once again, a great misadventure which led to massive human casualties. Coupled with millions of refugees that the war created, the world wanted an end to this war. Pakistan ran out of excuses and ideas. So, it had to surrender."

"There is another aspect which is never spoken about. This tells us the true intent of the rulers. In his book, 'From Jinnah to Zia', the author, a Chief Justice of Pakistan quotes an incident where a Bengali Minister Ramizzuddin was asked if there was a way whereby the eastern unit separates itself from the western unit. This question was asked with the blessings of Ayub Khan. The minister replied by stating that they, the Bengalis were in majority and the people of west were a minority, so if they wanted to separate, they would have to leave the Federation. Another confirmation comes from an interview of Ayub Khan by Herbert Feldman published in 'The Telegraph' where he accepted that he had decided to break away from East Pakistan and detach from the Bengalis but the conditions weren't favourable. The two reports come to the fore when we speak about the thought process of the rulers of that time. Yahya Khan's secretary said on record that when he approached Yahya Khan to do something to save East Pakistan, Yahya Khan had venomously stated that he wasn't willing to risk west Pakistan for the sake of *'short, black Bengalis'*... such despise for one's countrymen? And we all know what Bhutto famously meant when he said 'you on that side', to the Bengalis, and 'we on this side'. Don't these prove that these men didn't intend to keep Pakistan united?" Prakash asked, and continued, "What do you expect the end to be of a country which has such rulers?"

There was pin drop silence.

"Why did it have to be such a humiliation? Why a theatrical show of surrender?" Zubair asked his father to divert his mind from what he had just heard from Prakash.

Gulzar thought for a while before replying. He was trying to figure out the mystery himself. He didn't find adequate reply so he asked Prakash Rohatgi if he had any ideas.

Prakash nodded, "I am not sure. The surrender proposal was prepared, and sent to the Pakistan army by Lt. General JFR Jacob of the Indian army on General Maneckshaw's orders. What were the reasons, I do not know, but I do know that the Pak army could have fought or at least a month. The situation on the western front was as poor as it was in the east. Karachi was pounded by the Indian navy and the Indian Air Force was wreaking havoc throughout. It was a no win situation, so, surrender was the only way to salvage whatever they could. Pakistan was ruled by a man who didn't care. Justice Hamoodur Rahman in his commission report states that Yahya Khan was an alcoholic, a womanizer and hardly ever visited the war room even though the war was raging on two fronts. I have recordings of his appalling radio speech on National Radio on December 16; that evening *'after'* Tiger Niazi had signed the surrender document, and in his address he lied to the people of Pakistan and swore to keep fighting till the war was won by Pakistan. These tell us about the willingness, or the lack of it, of those who were in power."

Gulzar added to Prakash's statement, "Till 1971, it was over twenty-four years since Pakistan had been independent but it did not see a single day of democracy. A country was born to become a *'Republic'* and broke into two without a day of rule by a democratically elected government; without witnessing a day under constitutionally held general elections. Doesn't that tell you something? The present constitution of Pakistan was introduced by Bhutto Government after it had lost its eastern wing. There was no accountability and so whoever came to power was autocratic and brutal. They didn't care about people. Such nations are humiliated and the public surrender was the ultimate humiliation... but for the shameless who didn't care, it didn't matter. Hamoodur Rahman Commission directly implicates the army generals and people in power and especially Yahya Khan for his lackadaisical approach towards his responsibilities as the President, as Commander in Chief and as the Martial Law Administrator. Won't such people face humiliation by law of nature?" Gulzar shouted angrily.

"What happened after the surrender? What about the people who were taken as prisoners of war?" Rukhsar asked, "Why weren't you there?" she asked Gulzar.

Gulzar replied calmly, but with sadness in his eyes and his tone. "Do you know that there were two surrenders: First in Dhaka on 16th December, as it is well documented... there was another surrender in Chittagong the following day when Brigadier Takseenudin surrendered to his Indian counterpart, Brigadier Sindhu... Ironically, Takseenudin was Sindhu's instructor at the Indian Military Academy before Partition. After the surrender by the General Niazi on the sixteenth, Indian army held over ninety-three thousand POWs including civilians and officials, and thirty-six thousand Pak soldiers. Here again the Pakistani Government showed its casual approach towards these POWs. In July the following year, the two Prime Ministers, Bhutto and Mrs. Indira Gandhi signed first of the two '*Simla Agreements*' which became the base for return and exchange of the POWs. But the newly formed Bangladesh Government had another problem. It wanted to punish the thousands of suspected *Razakars* it had rounded up as POWs but it had to reluctantly release them in exchange for over 200,000 Bengali speaking Military men and civilians who were stranded in West Pakistan."

"So no one was prosecuted for the atrocities of the war?" she asked, looking at her father and grandfather.

"No. Not one," Zubair replied.

"Was the situation really as bad as that, Aman?" Rukhsar asked in frustration.

Aman shook his head in dejection, "The crimes... the sins perpetrated by our forces and its proxies can be summed up by a few statics: according to Bangladesh Government, nearly three million civilians died. If that isn't enough, let me tell you a more horrible fact; United Nations had to set up abortion camps where over a hundred thousand women, young girls included, aborted their pregnancy. Neither before nor since, has the UN had to do that. And remember, these are official abortions under UN supervision - how many abortions went unrecorded and how many more women gave birth to illegitimate children, we can only guess."

There was silence in the room. The sheer numbers numbed Rukhsar. She felt uneasy so after a while, to get her mind away from the line of thought, she asked, "Why do they say India was responsible for Pakistan's breakup?" she asked.

"History is written by its rulers. The government couldn't blame itself or the powerful military for East Pakistan debacle so someone had to be blamed. So, three people were held responsible: Yahya Khan for his ineptitude, Bhutto for his lust for power and Sheikh Mujib for being an *'Indian agent'*. Since they couldn't take the blame... remember, Zulfiqar Ali Bhutto was the Foreign Minister under Yahya Khan, his government blamed India. In twenty-five years it had created so much hatred in the hearts of its people against India that it was easy for them to blame India for the breakup and it had the war to show for it."

"But India did help the separatists by arming and training them. It was responsible for the breakup." Rukhsar defended the history she had learnt.

"What could India do, Rukhsar?" Aman asked, "Pakistan army and the *Razakars* had pushed its people in the East so such extent that people thought they will be safer in 'enemy country' than in their own. There were millions of refugees. We had similar situation in Pakistan during the Afghan war. Didn't we turn our guns at the enemy? The same happened during '71 war. Yes, India was 'also' responsible for the breakup, but like always, we keep overlooking our own mistakes. If we were united could India have broken up the country? We have an old habit; whenever things go wrong, blame India!" People in the hall were seeing a different side of Aman. He was angry. They were silent. Aman's intensity prohibited them from interrupting. "Since independence our rulers, ignoring the sentiments of the population, created an enemy out of India. They went out of their way to create an enemy. For personal, vested interests, these rulers created unnecessary hostility towards India. What happened to the Bhutto slogan of *'Bleeding India with a Thousand cuts'* and waging *'Thousand year war'* with India? Why did he create that slogan? No reason! Within two years of that slogan he was forced to sign the *'Simla Agreement'*. This is how they stir up emotions for their mileage. Every politician and dictator who came to power started with similar slogans and in a short while, changed the stance and took a 'U' turn to have better relations with India. Before we can have some benefits of having some kind of truce, a new government is in power and the process starts all over again. This happened with successive governments under Bhutto, Zia-Ul Haq, Benazir, Nawaz Sharif and Pervez Musharraf. India as an enemy has been used as tool to divert attention of general population from basic issues like unemployment, poverty, illiteracy, lack of basic necessities like water, sanitation and infrastructure etcetera, but no... India! It sells! Two sentiments have ready takers: Anti-India slogan and Islam!"

While others were pondering over Aman's statement, Prakash smiled inwardly congratulating himself. Aman Bux was perfect for what Prakash had in mind.

Aman looked at his would-be-bride and tried to control his rage; he was angry about something, people felt and Aman was venting it out, "Instead of making an enemy out of India, if they had been an ally and worked as partners, the people of Pakistan, east and west, would have a totally different story to tell today. Immediately after gaining independence, India had not taken off like it did since the 1990s, but it created a base, a platform for the lift-off. While India worked its way out of extreme poverty with the world's second largest population, lack of foresight and vision amongst our rulers after Liaqat Ali Khan, stagnated a country which could have become a great nation. Instead of trying to out-match a much stronger nation, it could have developed a healthy, peaceful rivalry in terms of growth and achievement and competed with it on the world stage. But that was past; and now it has already split into two and while the breakaway portion is growing faster, Pakistan is in turmoil; with violence in the streets of Karachi and all along its north-western and western boundaries, from Waziristan to Pakhtunkhwa. Islamic extremists from near and far away nations infiltrate Pakistan and use it to launch strikes within and outside Pakistan. This isn't only ruining Pakistan's reputation; Pakistan has become a hub for extremists from around the world. Large sections of these areas have become havens for these extremists and government has no control in these areas. Any attempt by the government or military to bring these areas under control would result in an open war with its own people and the supporters of these extremists. The country will plunge into a bloody civil war. Situation is precarious and more delicate than most people realise. Even politicians are not being realistically aware of how dangerous the situation in this area had become. Presence of extremist organisations is an existential threat but it isn't being seriously considered. If due attention it deserves isn't given and issues are not sorted out in the near future, Pakistan will cease to exist in its present form. It will splinter into small areas which will become outposts for terrorists worldwide. The same goes for Baluchistan. Baloch problem can be settled but we have to be pragmatic and settle the disputes with Baloch leaders, especially the Marri and Bugti tribes. If the Baloch are given their honest share the Baloch would still be willing partners in the Federal Union of Pakistan; if not, the Baloch as they ask now, will want to be independent. Assassination of leaders of Baloch tribes like Nawab Bugti, and false imprisonments of leaders of the Marri tribes is beginning to hurt Pakistan. The leaders of Pakistan must understand the culture and the history of these tribes to know that these are martial tribes who take to guns at slightest provocation. If these tribes are to be managed, an honest, sincere dialogue is needed. These tribes won't give up arms if they keep finding bullet ridden, tortured bodies of their people - killed by the Pakistan army."

People in the lounge were being given a dreadful scenario by the man who knew the scenario as well as anyone in the room. Aman Khan Bux was agitated. There was something which was hurting him a lot, and that came out in his speech.

Aman Bux was close to tears, "These problems aside, the country and its leaders must overcome their obsession with India and forge a permanent, peaceful partnership with it. It needs major change in the mind-set of the military and the politicians. There must be paradigm shift in policies and thought process. If we achieve it, our dependence on foreign aid for economic survival will cease and Pakistan can grow economically and democratically. Pakistan has an enviable position where it has no natural enemy, barring India; an enemy which in real terms did not exist but it was created specifically for the purpose of emotional exploitation of the masses of Pakistan using the most pious of all entities; religion!"

Rukhsar saw her agitated fiancé deeply engrossed in thought, as were others, and to her surprise, even Prakash. "It would be beneficial for us if we can have meaningful friendly relations with India," she said softly.

There was a chorus of sarcastic chuckles from Gulzar, Zubair and Aman. Aman shook his head in disgust, "That was required at the time of partition. After *Qaid*... and Liaqat Ali Khan we had visionless leaders who had no idea what was to be done." Aman Bux replied, "We should have made India our spring board to progress; instead, we created an enemy - an enemy which is far too stronger than us in every respect; technology or economy, population and nationalism, and in infrastructure, education and military strength. When we had a chance to forge an alliance, we sent armed tribesmen into Kashmir in 1947 who looted, raped and killed the locals. When we should have had a dialogue on regional peace in the region after the Indo-Sino war, we foolishly sent in armed men in Kashmir again in 1965 and in response we lost a war. When we should have handled a situation in East Pakistan, instead of empathising with local population we started to massacre them and broke the nation in two. When we should have talked with India we armed and trained Kashmiri and Sikh militants to weaken India by creating *Khalistan* and *Kashmir* movements, and in response we lose Siachen. When should discuss collaboration, we sponsor militants who attack the Indian Parliament. When we should have controlled our militants and extremist jihadis, our people are involved in the Mumbai massacre and the serial train blasts in Mumbai. When we had a golden opportunity to establish long-term peace after the Lahore summit in 1999 our military Generals launched an insane attack on Indian positions across the 'LOC' and we don't just lose that war, we attract International community's attention to 'State Sponsored terrorism'. While earlier we were shouting that we morally support *Kashmiri separatists*, we were arming and training them. Kargil war has hurt our claims on Kashmir like none other. With that single, stupid, rash action we lost our already fragile stance on Kashmir. You want friendly relations with India? Good! So do I. But how do we explain it to the Indians? Why should they trust us? I am a diplomat... or... I was, for two decades. I know how things work on the ground. Has anyone noticed the recent statements of our foreign office? We have removed Kashmir from our statements as the 'core issue' and we have been forced to have a 'composite dialogue' with India, 'which includes' Kashmir. Do you understand the dramatic policy shift between the two statements? It means that Kashmir is not our 'core issue'. Do our politicians or military Generals realise what has happened because of our thoughtless actions? Until Kargil war India and the United States had a somewhat shaky relationship. Since the war, US and India have become strategic allies in defence, economy and in any other way you can think of. Their bonding is so good that even the biggest issues are promptly sorted out. On the other hand we have our foreign policies. There is a total disconnect between our statements and actions. We created a potent force with the help of CIA to fight the Russians in Afghanistan: the *Taliban*. When the Russians left, we did not bother to disarm them or other *Jihadi* groups we had created. We pushed them in Kashmir to fight our proxy war and then, after 9/11 we disown them under International pressure. It has come to a stage where we are forced to realise the enemy is within - the Jihadi forces we had created! Why? Because they have turned their guns on us and we are unable to control the monster we created. We created militant organisations to infiltrate India and now they are fighting against the state. Has our policy worked? It is high time we revisit our policies and acknowledge our mistakes, and rectify them. But, is it possible? I don't think so, because the war mongers in power won't let it happen. If Pakistan has been put twelfth in the list of failed or failing states don't you think there is a reason for it?" Aman asked in desperation.

Aman was also speaking what Zubair and Gulzar had in mind. Prakash, leaning against the window sill was wondering if Aman was reading his mind and speaking the words Prakash would have spoken. He was sure he had made a good decision against a small risk he had taken. The plan to get Aman to work for the cause was brighter than he had earlier thought.

Aman Bux shrugged his shoulders in dejection. He looked at Rukhsar helplessly. There was something amiss about Aman people thought correctly. Aman was not naming what was hurting him so much. Aman stood up to his full height and walked to the edge of the hall, receded into a corner to control his emotions. He did not wish to cry in front of these people. Rukhsar knew what was hurting Aman. She knew the reason for his sudden explosion. She wanted to talk to him and hug and console him but couldn't do it in the presence of her elders. Nevertheless, she walked and stood next to him and put her hand on his forearm in sympathy. "You want to talk to me about it?" She asked but the tone came out like she was pleading.

Aman clutched her fingers and shut his eyes to control his emotions. He felt another hand on his shoulder. He knew the firm hands belonged to Prakash Rohatgi.

Prakash leaned over and whispered in Aman Khan's ears. "I want to talk to you."

Aman shook his head, "There are many tragedies and many stories. I hope I can tell you about it someday," he said softly. "But that isn't my concern right now. I am worried about my country... I don't want to see it disintegrate." Aman paused and looked into his fiancé's eyes with sadness. His voice was low when he spoke again, "Last month I went to southern Iran to catch the *Hazara* tribesmen who migrate to Iran daily for work. Six men I had spoken to the previous evening were missing," Aman said and paused to control his weakening emotions. "When I enquired, I learnt from their colleagues that the bus in which they were travelling the previous evening was stopped by armed men who asked for identities of each individual, dragged them down from the bus and killed them in cold blood. These *Hazara* tribesmen were killed because their appearance was Central Asian; different from regular Pakistanis: because these were *Shiites*. Rukhsar..." Aman put his face in his hands and broke down.

Rukhsar was close to tears herself. She didn't know how to console him. Then she saw Prakash grip Aman's shoulders and pat him. Aman shivered at the sight he was visualising in his mind. A scene from the past had struck his softest chords and stirred his emotions. He gripped Prakash's hand and held it firmly to control himself. A minute later he was calm and in control but the anger was still there. Then he saw the fragile figure of Gulzar standing next to him. "Such stories are far too many for us to cry on. For how long can we cry, and for many can we cry, my son? We all have our stories to tell. We have all been victims and witness to such atrocities. You have had your share, we have had ours. We have to work to stop these. I wish I was fifty years younger. But you people have an opportunity to do something. You are a diplomat and Rukhsar an economist. You both have a chance to work for the country unlike us who were army officers and had no say in such matters." The tone in which Gulzar spoke made it abundantly clear that his love for his country was still well lit in his heart though he was now a Bangladeshi. "Rukhsar can work on the economy and you can work on better diplomacy. You two can make a difference." Gulzar pleaded.

"Our economy is in shambles," Rukhsar replied softly, "We can do only so much. Real power lies with the policy makers and the military establishment. Our best bet is to have healthy relations with India because that country is economically powerful. It has the financial capacity to put Pakistan back on the tracks. India will be in the top three economies in two decades. If we don't use its potential and continue behaving like enemy we are doomed. We will lose out unless we make a dramatic change in our policies. India has the world's largest middle-class but due to our foreign policy we are unable to benefit from it. There are hundreds of items of daily use and edibles which we can't import from India directly because they are banned. Pakistani traders import these products channelled through the UAE. If we remove the trade barriers we can bring these items from across the border in trucks. Instead, due to our stupid policies these are transported to Indian ports, which are a greater distance than transporting it across the border. Then these products are shipped to the UAE and reshipped to Pakistan with false documents stating that these products are of 'non-Indian' origin. If we just remove the barriers on essential items at least, Pakistan will save over five billion dollars in foreign exchange and it will prod India to relax its rules. Though India has accorded us the MFN - Most Favoured Nation status, we are unable to use it because we have our own barriers. If we can do that we can create a win-win situation for both. But no sir! The anti-India sentiment and bias won't permit us. There is a greater barrier. The India specific policy, be it defence, economic or strategic - is military's domain. Civilian government has no say there. Knowing the thought process of our Generals and their rigid anti-India stance it is not going to be an easy task to have healthy trade relations with India." Rukhsar paused and seemed to look beyond the room, her eyes focused in the distance, "When I was in New Delhi four days ago the sight of hundreds of Pakistanis in a hospital for basic treatment was a major shock. If we open up our borders for trade and tourism, especially medical tourism our people will benefit. The most important part is that if we openly trade with India, though Indian items may flood our markets, we will have a greater advantage because it will open the doors to over five-hundred million Indian middle class. We have the ability so we will be able to compete with our Indian counterparts. But that isn't possible in the near future unless our rulers and our military establishment change their mind-set towards India. That is the tragic part."

"You can still work towards it with some like-minded people. I am sure there are thousands of them." Zubair said, "If few people get together and make a pressure group, can't you influence the people who really matter? I am sure they will see the logic behind it. After all, it is to benefit of the general population and economy of the country."

"How can we influence the military Generals who make the important decisions about India? It is their domain, not of the civilian government." She retorted sharply.

Zubair and Gulzar looked at her with disappointment.

"And... our foreign policy is in a mess," Aman replied to the other point Gulzar had raised. "I have worked hard to improve our International relations with every country but no government had any clear policy. We have no clear vision in our foreign policy. At best, our policies are a paradox. It lacks direction. Every country's foreign policy is heavily influenced by its domestic necessity, ideology and philosophy. Jinnah Saheb had a vision of a secular Pakistan. So the first Constitution of Pakistan was drafted and constituted in '56 making Pakistan a Republic, a Parliamentary Democracy. Two years later, General Ayub Khan who had sworn by that constitution, and was appointed by Iskander Mirza as Chief Martial Law Administrator, deposes Iskander Mirza in *Coup d'état* and he declares himself the President and abolishes the Constitution. He presents a new Constitution in 1962 with a Presidential form of Democracy. After Ayub Khan lost the 1965 war, he was forced to leave and Yahya Khan was now the new President. After the '71 debacle, Yahya Khan goes out and Zulfiqar Ali Bhutto became the Prime Minister and gave us the present Constitution. Though this Constitution still holds, it's been raped by successive Dictators, from Zia-Ul-Haq to Pervez Musharraf. It is strange how the rulers who replaced the earlier one were appointed by the predecessor. Ayub Khan, in a coup d'état, kicks out Iskander Mirza and becomes the President. After the loss of 1965 war with India, Yahya Khan replaces Ayub Khan and brings in Zulfiqar Ali Bhutto to form the Pakistan People's Party to counter Sheikh Mujib's Awami League in East Pakistan. After the debacle of '71, Bhutto takes control and brings in Zia-Ul-Haq whom he elevates to the post of Lieutenant General and then makes him the Chief of Army staff in '76. The following year, Zia seizes power and becomes the Martial Law Administrator and executes Bhutto. Zia dies in a mysterious air crash. When Nawaz Sharif appoints Pervez Musharraf, as Chairman of Chief of Army Staff, he is imprisoned by his nominee. After elections were declared by Musharraf, when Bhutto's daughter, Benazir was sure of winning the election, she was assassinated. When the PPP comes to power Musharraf goes into exile. We never had any democratically elected government for a reasonable length of time to form any consistent foreign policy. When our domestic situation is unclear, and without a powerful government at the helm, we could never determine a clear foreign policy. We started with secular philosophy and turned into an Islamic Republic."

"Pakistan was created as an Islamic state. How can you refute that?" Rukhsar asked Aman with resentment.

Aman Bux laughed, "When we return, I will hand you a transcript of Jinnah Saheb's speech to the first Constituent Assembly on August 11; four days before independence. In that speech he said, and I quote, *'You are free; you are free to go to your temples, you are free to go to your mosques or to any other place or worship in this State of Pakistan. You may belong to any religion or caste or creed -- that has nothing to do with the business of the State.'* To emphasise on this he later said in his speech, *'you will find that in course of time Hindus would cease to be Hindus, and Muslims would cease to be Muslims, not in the religious sense, because that is the personal faith of each individual, but in the political sense as citizens of the State.'* Do you think that was the statement of the creator of a Muslim nation… certainly not an Islamic state? *Qaid* wanted a secular Pakistan. During one of his meetings with Liaqat Ali Khan, Qaid had said categorically to the Prime

Minister that he didn't create Pakistan to be run on whims of the Mullahs; he had a vision of a truly secular country."

"If *Qaid* wanted a secular country he wouldn't have created Pakistan," Rukhsar countered Aman's statement.

"That is a misconception. Jinnah Saheb wanted a country where Muslims were not in a minority; but he also wanted a country where people of all religions could co-exist. Pakistan was created in the interest of Muslims of the sub-continent, not for Islam; there is a difference." Aman presented his view which was contrary to the common belief. He waited for Rukhsar to reply but she was thinking about something, "We were supposed to be a democratic country but for major part we were ruled by military dictators. Every ruler had his own foreign policy; nothing to do with what the nation needed. We are in a situation where we don't have a single country which would unwaveringly stand by us. Our foreign offices and diplomats, me included, are running in all direction to eke something out from nothing. Our reputation is at its lowest ebb. When the Americans call us 'pathological liars', the world accepts it not because our intentions are poor; it's because we have several foreign policies - some are handled by the military and others by bureaucrats and some others by civilian governments. We aren't sure which direction we want to go. What is our foreign policy, we don't know. What are the main objectives which our foreign policies should reflect? We have no idea. Our policies change on weekly basis to overcome the existing emergency or catastrophe we face. We call China as our best friend but they don't trust us because Pakistan arms, trains and funds the Uyghur separatists. How do you expect the Chinese to trust us?" Aman asked, "Do you remember what Prakash said about the telephone conversation between Musharraf and Tariq Aziz during the Kargil war? Think! Who apart from the Chinese could have listened into that conversation and recorded it? Somehow, that conversation was fed to the media, or leaked. Who could have done it? Certainly not the CIA agents sitting in

Langley could have done that nor could the Indian agents tuned into those conversations. I believe that the Chinese did it, but they didn't cover it up. Instead they leaked it to the Indians or the US and made sure it was given the importance it deserved. That transcript was printed on the front pages of Indian newspapers. If Chinese are our friends why did it reach the Indians?"

Rukhsar looked at the man she was marrying in a few hours. She had a gut feeling that he was right. Standing by the window, Prakash was staring at Aman. He was surprised at what Aman had just said. He was pin point accurate. Prakash had a mysterious smile; he knew he had made the right decision.

"Our other close ally is Saudi Arabia which sends us hundreds of millions of dollars each year in aid but look at its voting pattern at the UN. It either refrains from voting or votes against us on critical issues. Look at other Islamic nations. Whenever, there was a vote on Kashmir, these nations have voted against Pakistan, and in favour of India. Don't you think our foreign policy is flawed? In last ten years since the 'war on terror', the US has given us over eighteen billion dollars in aid in numerous ways but it does not apologise for the *Salala* check-post drone attack or for the thousands of Pakistani civilians who have died in drone attacks. On the other hand, when India's ex-President APJ Abdul Kalam is asked to remove his shoes for security check or a film star is detained for casual questioning at the US airports, US government promptly tenders a formal apology though if you look how India votes on various issues at the UN, you will find that India and China are two nations who consistently vote against US resolutions. Look how the US and Indian diplomats work in tandem if there is a contentious issue which could hamper mutual relations, and then look at us. Has our diplomacy worked?" Aman asked sarcastically.

The room was silent. The gravity of the situation coming from the mouth of a diplomat was worrisome. Ground realities were appalling and Aman had painted a bleak picture.

Aman suddenly burst with sarcastic chuckle that surprised all in the room. "Let me give you a few classic examples of our foreign policy. Pervez Musharraf was totally against any use of Pakistan land or air for armed action in Afghanistan but he had to relent under pressure or else, as he said, *'the US would bomb us into stone age'*. We created the *Taliban* to fight the Russians in Afghanistan but we did 'U turn' and we were *forced* to declare that we are going to be allies of NATO, and *Taliban* and the *Al Qaeda* are our enemies. Have we succeeded with our present foreign policy, if we have any? Here is another one; a real classic; the only neighbouring country after India which has any economic standing, is Iran. In last few months we messed that up too with the way we acted on the gas pipeline issue. As agreed, Iran has constructed its part of the pipeline to our borders. When we said that we don't have money to build our part of the pipeline, Iran agreed to fund the project. At crucial juncture when he was supposed to go to Tehran to sign the agreement, our President quietly takes off for London with no intimation to the Iranians. What do you think should be the reaction of the Iranians? I was there and our Embassy was embarrassed by the questions we were asked. Then we speak to the Chinese to help us to fund the project. A consortium of banks in China agrees to help us but under US pressure, they tell us one day that they are sorry for being unable to fund us for the time being. That is the state of our foreign policy and policy makers. Can anyone name one country which is our true ally? Our foreign policy is in such a mess that we are unable to untangle simple equations. We had leased out Shamsi airbase to the UAE. When UAE gave it to US and NATO forces to use the base were we able to question UAE? We didn't have the courage. There is an incident which even seasoned diplomats like my own boss feels ashamed at, especially when our Minister for Foreign affairs tells a US Under-Secretary of State *'we will do whatever you ask us to do'*. What is our Foreign policy, I wonder. When Benazir Bhutto was asked why she supported

Pervez Musharraf, she said candidly '*because US asked us to do so*'. That is the state we have come to. What foreign policy, *Baba*? It changes faster than Chicago weather. What do you expect us to do?"

Shahida Ahmed saw Gulzar's desperation and she changed the topic. "Tell us about your life story, Aman."

The question from Shahida caught Aman unprepared. He felt hollowness in his heart. He did not want to talk about it at this moment. As it is, the topic they were discussing was not to his liking either. It had tapped his frustration which had been building up over the years. He shook his head in response to Shahida's question. "With all due respects to you, I will talk of it some other time. Not now please, I request."

Aman rose and went to the bathroom and returned five minutes later looking fresh. He was glad Rukhsar had changed her seat and she was sitting next to his chair. He smiled when he saw Prakash sitting on the other side of his chair. He sat in the middle calmly and looked at Rukhsar. She smiled and came closer to his chair without being too obvious. Aman returned her smile. He looked at the others and took a deep breath. He couldn't totally ignore Shahida's request. She had been a fantastic host; almost taking over the role of a mother for him and Rukhsar. The past scars were haunting him. He couldn't tell his story but he decided to relate it somehow. "History is merciless and cruel. It has a habit of repeating itself. Unless we rectify our mistakes we will continue to commit blunders after blunders till Pakistan ceases to exist. I say this sadly… because… I have witnessed these blunders over and over again, through decades. We have already lost half our country and we haven't learnt our lesson. Every day, we see militant extremists killing people in the northern areas, in Karachi, in rural Sindh, in Baluchistan and now it has started to affect the Punjab province. In Quetta, I had heard of daily sectarian killings. I happened to visit it one day about a year ago, and trust me; it's an ugly and pitiful sight! I visited the house of an MNA and he took me to a graveyard. If you stand at the centre and look as far as your eyes can see you will see newly dug graves of young men... and kids as young as five years old... That is ethnic cleansing in its crudest form. I saw women sitting on graves of their loved ones because they had no family members to go home to. They had no one else and so these women spent their entire day sitting by the graves and crying out their hearts. It is a heart wrenching scene if you have a heart. These people are being killed because they are *Shiites*; they are being killed because they don't look like the rest of the Pakistanis, because they are of Central Asian origins. They are killed because the killers say they aren't Pakistanis. The *Hazaras* will bear till they can, and some day they will do what people in Baluchistan and North Waziristan have done: they will take to arms and the retaliation will be swift and it will be brutal. As the counts of 'missing persons' rises by each passing day, as people keep finding dead bodies with '*Pakistan Zindabad*' carved on their bodies with knives... as bodies keep dropping from choppers, the threat of breakup grows. What's happening in Ziarat and in Mastung, in Quetta or Khuzdar, in tribal areas of Dera Bugti or Marri, in Gwadar or Mekran, in Turbat or Mashke, in Dera Ghazi Khan or any such incident of brutal massacres, we are getting closer to utter chaos and total disintegration of the country. This is East Pakistan all over again. Think what the end result will be. It is..."

Rukhsar interrupted him, "The *Sardars* of Baluchistan are no angels. They are brutal, and they were sharing power in Baluchistan with Pakistan establishment. Most of them like Nawab Akbar Bugti and Ghaus Bizenjo were Governors of Baluchistan but they did precious little for their people. Don't hold the Government or military establishment responsible for the situation."

"Quite correct! During a media interview Bizenjo was put the same question. When the anchor asked Bizenjo about Nawab Akbar Khan Bugti's brutal and authoritarian rule and, why now he had become a hero for his tribesmen, Bizenjo had replied by countering a question. He asked the anchor to imagine the kind of atrocities the military was committing that it made even Nawab Akbar Bugti a hero in eyes of their tribesmen. Today the *Sardars*, be it Ataullah Mengal, Nawab Akbar Khan Bugti or Ghaus Bakhsh Bizenjo or any of the eighteen tribal *Sardars,* are heroes for their tribesmen. Bizenjo was severely opposed to the state of Kalat joining Pakistan. He had asked that if Islam was the reason for Kalat to join Pakistan why Afghans and Iranians weren't asked to join in. For this, Bizenjo was jailed in Quli camp in Quetta Cantonment for weeks… and he was tortured. Ataullah Mengal said that after weeks of torture when soldiers brought Bizenjo back to the cell, the clean shaven Bizenjo had beard and looked old… On the other side of Baluchistan we have the situation in Gwadar where we don't acknowledge the rights of the people of Afro-origin brought in as slaves centuries ago. They are rightful citizens of Pakistan. You are right! The *Sardars* of the Baloch tribes are no angels but for these tribesmen, their *Sardars* are the only hope; to save them from army's tyranny. What else can they do? Memories of these martial tribes last for generations, Rukhsar. They don't forget! It takes ages to create an environment of trust. This trust cannot be created if our Generals keep making threats like Musharraf issued when he said that *'this is not the 70s. They won't know what hit them'.* Musharraf was talking of Baluchistan situation and relating it to Bangladesh. Such ridiculous statements only widen the rift between people and its rulers. When Prime Minister Raja Rental dismisses an elected local government in Baluchistan and imposes Governor's rule, which is followed by massacre of the *Hazara Shiites* by *Lashkar-e-Jhangvi*, or when Nawab Akbar Bugti is killed in a shelling in the caves, be rest assured that history will take a call and then it will be difficult to even manage the uprising - when it comes with vengeance."

Shadab was wondering why Baluchistan was so big an issue. It was a land with barren hills and hardly any vegetation in the area. "Why does Pakistan establishment keep Baluchistan under its thumb? What is so important?" he asked innocently.

Rukhsar responded to this one. "Baluchistan is extremely rich with natural resources. Most of Pakistan's gas and oil comes from this area and now it has discovered large deposits of gold in that area. It's believed to have world's fifth largest reserves of copper and gold in *Reko Diq* near Baluchistan's border with Iran and Afghanistan. It is literally a gold mine."

There was a silence of reckoning. A missing piece was put together in one statement. Reason behind forceful occupation was clear.

"That is good for Baluchistan, isn't it? The government must be paying healthy sum in royalty to the province. Then why is there so much poverty and illiteracy?" Shadab asked.

"The royalty that Baluchistan gets is miniscule compared to Punjab and Sindh. Move out of capital Quetta and try finding a decent civil hospital or school in all of Baluchistan and you will be surprised if you found any," Aman replied, "Area wise, it is over forty three per cent of Pakistan and richest in mineral and natural resources, with population under five per cent but it has the poorest infrastructure in all of Pakistan. Rukhsar mentioned about gas, oil reserves and gold deposits, she didn't mention vast iron ore and zinc, marble and semi-precious metal deposits Baluchistan has to offer but it has been poorly managed. The port of Gwadar is among the best natural ports of the world with strategic positioning but it was poorly used. If Pakistan Government, the army establishment and the *Sardars* put their heads together, Baluchistan alone can give the people of Pakistan finest quality of life. But... but..." Aman shook his head in frustration.

"India and USA won't let it happen." Rukhsar commented.

Gulzar coughed a laugh. "How can foreign countries, no matter how powerful they are, influence people if there is cohesion and they work together? We shouldn't blame the enemy for our negligence and mismanagement. US and India did not forcefully occupy Baluchistan, we did. We created a situation which forced the Baloch to invite these people to interfere in our domestic affairs; if they are interfering."

"Indian made guns was discovered in raids. How can we overlook that?" Rukhsar countered.

"So were Russian, Chinese, European and South African cache of arms found," Zubair defended Gulzar, "Why don't we blame other countries? We pick India and US because the sentiments are against them. We must consider carefully. If countries like the US or India supply arms to the Baloch, believe me dear, there would be full scale war between the Baloch nationalists and Pakistan army. It would be carnage of the scale we haven't seen yet. The Baloch want freedom at any cost now. *Sardars* of three major tribes, Ghaus Bizenjo especially, have already said that had India supplied arms they could have achieved success already. Those statements are important. If we wish to retain Baluchistan as a province, it is imperative that we settle the issues peacefully without being sceptical. We must be pragmatic when we deal with a serious situation. The guns are freely available in the International market. Where do you think ammunitions come from? There is a powerful black market for illegal arms. You can buy any sophisticated arms in the streets of Peshawar. What else do you want?"

Rukhsar had a fear in her heart. The scale of the problem was dawning on her. In last two hours she had heard stories and incidents which had heightened her earlier notion that her beloved country was plunging into an abyss of war and bloodshed. If the situation wasn't contained Pakistan would disintegrate very soon. She recalled a statement she had read in an editorials which had said categorically that Pakistan did not need any foreign enemy to destroy it; the enemies within were fully capable of destroying it. She realised the mammoth scale of the tragedy which was ready to descend on her country; if it hadn't already.

"Lies and deceit!" She cried out in desperation.

"That isn't new. Let me tell you the true scale of deceit if you aren't aware of it." Gulzar looked at his granddaughter and son. His expression was grim. "In September 1960, in Karachi... the Ayub Khan led Pakistan Government signed an agreement with India. According to this agreement Pakistan forfeited virtually all rights to three rivers that flowed from India into Pakistan: Sutlej, Ravi and Beas, for a compensation of a little over a hundred and six million Pound Sterling. I don't know in the history of the world where a nation had sold its rivers to another country. Is there any incident more deceitful as this?" Gulzar asked angrily.

"What?" Rukhsar shouted in disbelief.

"It's true! My father had invested all his money he had got from sale of his property in Punjab province. In 1953, when there was large scale massacre of our community, he quickly sold off the farmland and invested his money in Cholistan. In few years the entire fertile green belt of Cholistan was dry because the Indians had blocked the run of the river flow by constructing dams on those rivers. Only during monsoon we got some water which was not even sufficient for regular usage, let alone farming. We were financially wiped out. You think it's a joke?" Gulzar asked her angrily.

Zubair looked at his father in shock. "We had farmlands near Lahore when I grew up. We still own them, *Abba*. We don't have any lands in Cholistan." Zubair Ahmed stopped suddenly and turned to his daughter. "We still own it, Dear?"

Rukhsar smiled at him, "Yes, *Abbu*, we do. I go there once in three-four months when I get time."

Gulzar looked at his granddaughter with pride and nodded his head, "I sold it at the best price I could and bought the farms near Lahore because I was confident that rivers in this part of

Punjab will always be taken care of. This was the best stretch of farmland in all of Pakistan. I sold out a hundred and twelve acres of land in Cholistan to buy eighteen acres near Haji Kot, outside of Lahore because if the water beds run dry here then we can say goodbye to agriculture in Punjab. It was a safe bet so I bought it though I had to pay extra." Gulzar replied sadly.

Suddenly, Aman Bux looked at Prakash leaning against the window sill patiently listening to the discussion. He hadn't spoken much for some time. Aman was keen to know what he had to say. "You are the only Indian citizen here. Don't you have to put some light on this?" Aman asked Prakash.

Prakash stood straight and looked at Gulzar and Zubair in the eyes. "What has been discussed here has provided me some information apart from what I already knew. However, there is one aspect which has been omitted." He looked at Aman and asked pointedly, "As a diplomat, do you know how delicate the scenario was at the time of '71 war?"

Aman looked at him blankly, "What do you mean?"

Prakash returned to his chair and sat between Zubair and Aman. "All great military world powers of the time, excluding China, had taken their stance. The west condemned Pak army actions in East Pakistan yet it sided with Pakistan, and against India. Their reason was simply ideological. India was closer to 'communist' Russia, and Pakistan was the only 'non-communist' country in the region. There is history behind this. For years India had vehemently opposed US actions in Vietnam, and just as importantly, a year earlier, India had signed a security treaty with Russians, USSR as it was then. This angered Richard Nixon and Henry Kissinger. These two made no bones about their hatred for India and especially for Mrs. Gandhi. They had foul mouthed about her at times. Anyway, they did not want to see India, a Russian ally to win the war because it would establish India as the undisputed power in the sub-continent. If India emerged as the regional power, Russians would have considerable influence in the region," Prakash paused to align his thoughts and spoke again a few seconds later. "I will give you the scenario as it was a week into the war. The day after Pakistan struck India, Indian Navy launched *'Operation Trident'* and within four hours of the operation, it sank and destroyed four Pak Navy vessels without any casualty on its side. Within a week, ten Pak Naval Ships were at the bottom of the Arabian Sea. Karachi is the Headquarters of the Pak Navy. It was so rattled that when it sent co-ordinates to Pakistan Air Force, in utter confusion and lack of cohesion, PAF struck a vessel in the Arabian Sea off the coast of Karachi and destroyed its own *PNS Zulfiqar*. And there was an incident which irked the US. One of the PNS carriers destroyed was *PNS Shah Jahan*. It was escorting a merchant vessel *'MV Venus Challenger'* which was also sunk by the Indian Navy. This merchant vessel according to Indian intelligence was carrying US ammunition from Saigon, for Pak forces in Karachi. This further enraged the duo of Nixon and Kissinger. US promptly despatched its seventh fleet from Gulf of Tonkin in South China Sea, near Vietnam, to the Indian Ocean. This fleet was led by USS Enterprise and it included heavy duty vessels like USS King, USS Tripoli, USS Decatur which were guided missile carriers and destroyers, and other vessels supporting the fleet. US had three battalions of Marines on standby just in case. With the US taking sides, the British sent in their warships led by HMS *'Eagle'* to bolster Pak Navy. Indonesians had sent their naval ship to join the British and US fleet. The Jordanians had despatched fighter aircrafts to bolster the PAF. A week into the war and PAF was in ruins, Pakistan navy was in shambles and the land forces were incurring irreversible losses. When the fighter planes sent by Jordan were inadequate, twenty more aircrafts were ready for delivery to Pakistan, and UAE sent half a squadron of fighter aircrafts. French negotiated sales of aircrafts to Pakistan. The Iranians and Turks also sent their aircrafts to help Pakistan. The plan was that the British would engage Indians in the Arabian

Sea while the Americans would push through the Bay of Bengal to thwart the Indians. The Indian Navy stood in their way led by the aircraft carrier INS Vikrant. For three days situation was so tense that it was leading to a flashpoint. Then, the British intelligence intercepted a communiqué from the Soviets that their flotilla of ships was sailing into the Indian Ocean and just to confirm that, a Soviet nuclear submarine showed itself and that settled the issue. The US and British led navies moved out of the area fearing the worst."

"What about the Chinese?" Aman asked.

"China sent some military hardware but we aren't sure what but nothing beyond that. US made several attempts to ask the Chinese to make a move or to at least say that they would, but despite that, and Pakistan Government's desperate calls for help the Chinese didn't move," Prakash said.

"All these major powers couldn't handle India and Russia at the same time?" Aman asked.

"The important question was, did they want to? To what end? Pakistan had lost everything it could fight with."

"What is your point here?" Aman Khan asked Prakash.

Prakash looked at Aman Khan and smiled, "To irk USSR at that time could have ignited a situation when cold war was at its peak. With all world powers taking sides one wrong move by any of them... could have...."

"... potentially led to another world war." Zubair completed the sentence.

There was pin drop silence in the room. Aman Bux looked at Prakash and he knew there was something else Prakash wanted to say or point at, but all had missed it. "What did you want to point out, Prakash?"

"I draw your attention to the incident where Nawaz Sharif had to submit to President Clinton. I hoped you would relate it to what I just said." Prakash Rohatgi asked Aman.

Aman Khan Bux was still confused. "What are you trying to say?"

Prakash took a deep breath, "During the '71war the world was a shot away from another world war. During the Kargil war the world came close to a nuclear war. What if there is a time where just one mad man on either side decides to exhibit his madness? The region will go up in flames. What are we doing to stop it?"

People in the room looked at Prakash for an answer to his own question. Prakash was staring at Aman and Rukhsar.

Rukhsar asked Prakash, "What should be done?"

Prakash looked at them solemnly, "Later", he said and went back to the window sill. Zubair Ahmed was the only man who knew what Prakash was talking about. But why did he speak of it now, Zubair wondered.

Shahida asked everyone to get some rest before the big day.

As others started to leave, Prakash walked up to Shahida, "I am sorry about your father. I learnt it from Shadab in the evening. Please accept my condolences."

Shahida closed her eyes and nodded in acceptance. Aman and Rukhsar heard Prakash's condolence message. Rukhsar started to ask but stopped when Prakash waved his hand at her. Prakash informed them later that two days before Tiger Niazi surrendered, her father's body was found floating in a ravine with sixteen other people. These were the intellectuals of East Pakistan who had dared to support Sheikh Mujib.

* * *

General Head-Quarters,

Rawalpindi, Pakistan

General Wahid Khan was furious. He was woken up at five in the morning by his wife to be informed that he had to reach GHQ at the earliest. The caller had given no name. He only told her that he had come from New Delhi. Wahid Khan woke up in disgust. He expected good news after three days of silence from his trusted man. Instead, the man was back in Rawalpindi and demanding to meet the man who was many ranks his senior. Wahid Khan wanted the information Altaf Khos had gathered and meeting privately in his office was the best place to talk.

An hour and a half later, when his car reached GHQ gates, security guards were disappointed when the normally jovial General Wahid Khan had retorted angrily to their salutes and barked at them to open the gates. Three minutes later Wahid Khan found Altaf Khos sitting outside the chamber. Altaf saluted his senior while Wahid Khan saw the bandages on his trusted man's hands and asked, "What happened to you?", and opened the door to his chamber and waived Altaf in.

With embarrassment Altaf Khos narrated his misadventure during the New Delhi trip and how he was held captive but let off for no reason by the tribal woman who had dumped him on the road for the police to pick him up.

When Altaf was finished, Wahid Khan burst in laughter. He was disappointed that Altaf had failed to provide him the most important information he was seeking but the story was quite humorous. "You were beaten up by a tribal woman?" Wahid said and laughed loudly, again.

Altaf Khos lowered his gaze. His hatred for Wahid Khan was growing. The more he learnt about Wahid Khan, his hatred grew for the General. Altaf had arrived an hour ago from Lahore where Mariam told him that the General had raped her again. *'When this is over, I will get even with you,'* Altaf Khos looked at the General and swore to himself.

Altaf's eyes gazed at the floor wondering if this despicable man really deserved any respect. He must be punished for his sins. Altaf heard the General roar loudly again, mocking him. He sat with his bowed head awaiting instructions. He wished the General would ask him to deliver a message to that scum - the crippled General.

"How did you manage to get away from the police?" Wahid Khan asked.

"I told the New Delhi police that I was a Pakistani diplomat and I was accosted by thugs the previous night. I called up the military attaché at our mission and asked for help. He came an hour later to align our stories. That evening police let me go."

"You didn't tell them about your purpose of visit?"

"I told Majid Khan, the military attaché that I was given an assignment to follow Aman Bux because he had resigned but was travelling in India without informing his superiors. We wonder what he was doing there unless it was a Government related assignment." Altaf clarified.

Wahid Khan knew Altaf was an intelligent man, but he could make mistakes, especially of dropping or propping names when he shouldn't be, "You didn't utter about Zubair Ahmed or his daughter to anyone?"

"No, Sir. I restricted my story to Aman Bux. The reason was plausible so no one asked me anything else."

General Wahid Khan nodded in appreciation. '*Smart man*', he thought. "Did you try to use Majid's influence to find out about Zubair or his daughter?"

"You strictly instructed me to avoid using official channels, Sir. I tried to use his sources to track Aman's location." Altaf said confidently, "Majid Khan tracked Aman's cell phone and learnt that he and Rukhsar were driven away by Prakash Rohatgi to a village in UP. I found out that Zubair's ancestry hails from that village near Lucknow. I asked him to allow me to travel to Akbarpur but Majid Khan adamantly refused to help me and asked me to leave India promptly."

Though Altaf had begged Majid Khan to help find out what Aman Bux was up to, Majid had refused to let him travel lest Altaf was in trouble again. Majid won't be able to help him and he didn't want an International incident either. It was a risk Majid was unwilling to take. After great persuasion, Majid had agreed to try and track Aman's whereabouts and let him know when he gets any information. Altaf told General Wahid Khan.

"So we have no idea where Rukhsar is, or if she met Zubair?" Wahid Khan asked.

"No, Sir."

Wahid Khan thought hard. His uncle, the retired General had clear orders. '*Get them!*' "Are you sure this Prakash Rohatgi... he's as influential and powerful as he claims to be?"

"General, I assure you he is influential but claims nothing. That's his asset. I have seen his place. He could be working for RAW or Indian Military Intelligence, or... I fear he could be working for... maybe... CIA or Mosad. He is well informed, highly trained, intelligent... and quite capable, Sir."

"Hmm... And so, we ought to believe him when he promised Rukhsar that she can meet her father?"

"Yes Sir."

Wahid Khan was quiet for a while. He trusted Altaf's ability and judgement. His uncle did not make mistakes and his analysis was always precise. If he wanted the threat removed, he meant it. Wahid Khan knew he had to take immediate steps to stop Zubair from discovering a dark secret. If Zubair discovered it, Wahid Khan could be prosecuted for treason and murder of a dozen Pakistani soldiers. If he can stop Zubair and his daughter from learning the truth he would become the youngest Commander in-Chief of the Army, the most powerful man in the country.

After a few minutes of silence, Altaf asked, "You have instructions for me, General?"

General Wahid leaned forward and bore his snake eyes into Altaf's, with a stern look, "I have an assignment for you. Don't fail me, and no matter what happens, you must finish this task. I want you to get to that '*Qadiyani*' Zubair... and call me when you find him. I will tell you what questions to ask. If he knows the answer, kill him. If he doesn't know, kill him anyway. If any of the others know about it, kill them too," Wahid said coldly. "This is extremely important. If Zubair, Aman Bux or Rukhsar... or any person learns what he or she shouldn't know, I want them dead. If either of them as much as proves a point, our plan will be in jeopardy."

Altaf sat obediently without emoting his feelings. He wasn't going to show the shock he felt at the orders he had received. The sheer evilness of the order has shocked him into silence. His eyes were fixed on the General whom he wished he could kill right then.

Wahid Khan leaned back and looked at Altaf, "You will get all the assistance you need. Track them down. But I warn you, Altaf... You can get killed but you can't get caught. If you are caught, or if you fail, you better be dead."

- - -

The General Wahid saw Altaf walk out of the chamber and cursed himself for the blunder he had committed. A dozen brave men died in that 'friendly fire' but the man who was the real target had somehow survived. He stared at his desk as sunlight filtered through the glass panes. *"These feeble, weak men did not know how to rule a country. Let me take charge and I will be the ruler of this country and then the country will know how its greatest son will take all measures to re-integrate the country under one umbrella. The soft kneed politicians and coward Generals did not know how to use power to rule. I will show you how it is done. Three more months..."*

– – –

Altaf walked out of the gates, a confused man. Wahid Khan had chosen Altaf from lower ranks because he was a good and dedicated soldier. He knew Wahid Khan had great plans for Pakistan but why did he want that beautiful woman or her beau dead? Why would he want to kill a retired soldier when he was not a threat? There were too unanswered questions and he wanted answers. *'I love my country too much to blindly follow your instructions, General. If there was a plausible reason why you wanted those good people dead, you would have told me. You want me to track them down and then interrogate them about an incident which you hide from me and tell me only when I have taken them. But before I take them I want your reason. I will find out.'*

*   *   *

General Head-Quarters

Rawalpindi, Pakistan

This could lead to disaster if the events were left to run their course. General Imran Pathan had to rethink about his decision of two days ago. Situation had changed since then. The information he had was too dangerous for Pakistan than he earlier thought. An ambitious General had devious intent; his plans were being privately echoed in whispers. A Brigadier provided the information to General Pathan confidentially. Many young soldiers were being recruited to join a secret organization within the army with promises of promotions and power. Men from all departments were carefully chosen. There was a disturbing trend; young men had volunteered to join the group, and the list was growing rapidly - to work under a tough command centre with a strong leader at the helm. General Pathan had spent two days trying to find out if the rumours were true. This morning he got the information he was dreading. These weren't rumours. A devious plan had been devised but kept a secret. When General Pathan learnt of the plan he shuddered at its implications. Young soldiers were being recruited to become part of a dream plan which would elevate Pakistan to world power, and bring India to its knees. Sacrifices were to be made and soldiers were ready to do it - with their lives.

A General and his men didn't care for human life. They knew well that young minds wee susceptible to two emotions which never failed: Country and Religion! Both were being used to evoke hatred for Jewish Israel for Palestinian occupation, Christian west for exploiting the Islamic world, and arch enemy of Pakistan and Muslims - Hindu India! The General and his men had prepared a deadly cocktail to encash on the recruits' emotions by stirring up religious and national fervour. These two sentiments had been propagated for six decades through school text books for the younger minds, and through media for adults. It couldn't fail!

If General Pathan interfered he would be swiftly eliminated. He had to find a way to get to the man who was at the helm of this plan. If maniacs succeeded, it would destroy Pakistan. They had to be stopped. Leaning back the General rocked his chair back and forth thinking of ways to combat this insane plan but none came close to what he would consider feasible. He spent the day concentrating on what he could do. He had to work without arousing suspicion in minds of the scheming Generals, or their subordinates. An idea started to form. He jotted some points and put the notes in his waist pocket. He had to wait for now - wait, because he had to find the real mastermind of the plan and then find the precise plan they had. He knew he had time in hand to uncover the plot because, for a plan of such magnitude to succeed it had to be executed with precision; it needed time, probably months. Now he had to identify a man who could acquire information by being a part of the group. He called and asked for Captain Nazeer to come 'Urgently'.

*   *   *

The Ahmed Residence

Dhaka, Bangladesh

Aman found electronic gadgets which he didn't understand and a futuristic looking phone, from the box Prakash gave him. Prakash explained how they worked and handed them to Rukhsar and Aman advising them to use the phone 'only' to inform important people and strictly prohibiting them from using local phone. The phone wasn't traceable he told them.

Rukhsar called her mother and spoke to her for over thirty minutes trying her best to calm her upset mother. Shabnam was upset that her daughter was getting married and she won't be attending it. Then Zubair spoke to her for a long time. Shabnam Ahmed was near tears when she spoke to her husband again. After they were finished, Aman spoke to her for some time promising to return to Lahore soon.

To Prakash's surprise, Aman only spoke to one friend in Quetta and Shabnam Ahmed and no one else. What about family, he wondered.

Gulzar moved around with vigour. He looked younger and healthier than he had in a decade. He and Shahida went over last minute details. Their daughters arrived early, taking over bridal decorations while Shadab ran around arranging for the event. Rehana took charge of culinary arrangements for the feast which was to follow the wedding ceremony later in the evening. Only selected guests were invited to the reception. Zubair decided to go and buy gifts for the couple. He was guided through the market by his step brother's eleven year old son, Wasim.

On Rukhsar's persistence Gulzar Ahmed called Thakur Pukhraj Singh. Rukhsar learnt that her grandfather felt guilty of renegading on his promise and so he didn't have courage to call his only dear friend whose number Shadab had given to him. After Gulzar, Aman and Rukhsar spoke to Thakur and apologized for the rushed up wedding which didn't allow them time to invite him. Thakur Pukhraj Singh blessed the couple and promised them that documents of the house in Akbarpur will reach New Delhi at Prakash's address. It was their wedding gift.

Aman was alone in the room and sad. He wished he had a family member present at the most joyful event of his life but he had none. He sighed and diverted his mind to the traditional wedding dress bought by Prakash; a gift he hadn't expected to find in Bangladesh but Prakash had managed it somehow. Though the dress was not the typical dress worn by grooms during Pashtun weddings, it was at least a North Indian dress mostly worn by the Punjabis. Another thought made him realize the ironies of life. He had waited for over a decade and now, when he least expected it, in a foreign land among people he hadn't known until three days ago, he was getting married. And then there was one man whom he owed all this to; his dear, mysterious friend - Prakash Rohatgi, whom he had met just four days earlier.

When he first met Prakash Rohatgi he had an instant liking and trust for the man. That trust however, was overpowered by his mind which told him not to trust Prakash because Prakash was a Hindu. Suddenly, Aman's mind started to ask questions about his pre-judgement. He didn't understand why an educated, well informed man like him could have a myopic view, given his experience and broad mindedness. If he could fall prey to such perception, how could he expect lay men to override the hatred grained into their minds for generations? Aman Bux shook his head in disbelief at his own shortfall at a time when he should have trusted his own instincts and experience. He opened the wardrobe and his eyes caught the dress Prakash had bought the previous evening. He put out his hand and touched the exquisite *'Shervani'*. *"Thank you, Prakash."* He stepped out of the room to find Prakash but to everyone's surprise no one knew where he was. They hadn't noticed him quietly slip out.

- - -

On the eastern side of the lake the burly man waited for the man he had met the previous evening. The man was confused why the ultra-nationalist bureaucrat was secretly receiving and sending messages to a man who had smuggled Pakistanis into Bangladesh. He saw the mysterious Indian man walk towards him at brisk pace, open the door and sit in the car.

"You have enemies," the burly man said with humour.

"I always had. Which new enemy have I created in few hours?" Prakash asked with complimenting humour.

"Our friend says that your captive has reached his master and he has been ordered to eliminate your senior co-traveller and kill the two other companions too, if necessary. He asks you to be careful. Your request to extend the stay for an extra day is dangerous; our friend says and asks you to reconsider. After today he will not be able to provide information. He will be on trip to the Middle-East. He wishes you the best," the burly man said and waited for Prakash to reply.

"Thank him and tell him I will be careful. We will leave in the morning so nothing to worry," Prakash said and walked out of the car in the opposite direction.

As Prakash walked towards Ahmed residence, he thought about the brief conversation he just had. If his contact was out of the country, situation could be slightly dangerous. He sent a one line email to his Dacca contact from his cell. A minute before he reached the Ahmed residence, he got the reply. He smiled but he knew he had to get his companions back in India at the earliest. He wished he could manage an extra day for the newly wedded couple to celebrate with the family but he couldn't. It wasn't the threat to Zubair or his family's lives; he could handle that. It was a personal reason that did not permit him to stay away from his home on that specific day. He also missed the angel who should have spent her weekend with him. She made him home sick!

-   -   -

Aman Khan Bux was ready to curse, when he saw Prakash walk through the door. An involuntary smile appeared on his face as he skipped down the stairs and pulled Prakash aside, "Where have you been?"

"My contact called me," Prakash replied, "He has asked me to leave soon because he is on a trip from tomorrow. I asked him to arrange our stay for one extra day but that may not be possible. Ideally we should leave now, but... I leave it to you to decide. The longer we stay the bigger the trouble for you people." Prakash avoided mentioning about Altaf reaching Pakistan or about the threat. He patted Aman, "Let's get you married first," he said and laughed.

Aman smiled and turned when he heard footsteps. Shahida entered the room. Prakash told her about the conversation and it disappointed her. They agreed to decide what to do after the wedding.

- - -

The *'Nikaah'* ceremony was short and sweet. The *Qazi* read the terms of wedding, asking Rukhsar if she agreed to marry Aman Khan Bux, son of Bakhtyar Khan, of Navshera of Khyber Pakhtunkhwa, with a sum of Pakistani Rupees Five Hundred Thousand as her *'Meher'* money. Rukhsar sitting behind a translucent satin fabric, wearing a gorgeous red classical, traditional wear, gifted to her by Thakur, accepted by terms by thrice uttering, *'Qabool hai'*. The Qazi smiled happily and shook hands with Prakash Rohatgi who stood witness on behalf of the groom.

Qazi went to the groom's room and repeated the question asking him if he agreed to marry Rukhsar, daughter of Zubair Ahmed from Lahore, Punjab. Aman smiled broadly and repeated *'Qabool hai'* thrice. As witness, Shadab congratulated the groom and embraced him. *Qazi* Saheb with the blessings and grace of *'Allah'*, and by the powers vested in him by the *'Almighty'*, declared Aman Khan Bux and Rukhsar Ahmed as husband and wife and presented the *'Nikaah-nama'* - marriage certificate, to the couple and congratulated them again. Gulzar attended to the *Qazi* because he had special affection for him because his father had helped Gulzar when he and Shahida were trying to hide from the *Razakars* during the war of 1971.

While the guests feasted, Shahida summoned the elders and mentioned about Prakash's advice to return to India. Gulzar and Zubair were silent but their eyes showed desperation. After forty years they had met for barely two days and now it was time for them to part again. Shahida was sad too. She liked Rukhsar and

Aman and wanted them to stay a little longer but they had to leave. The tragic part for all concerned was that they didn't know when they will meet again - or if they ever will.

After some time, it was agreed that the group would depart after midnight to avoid problems. Gulzar whispered to his wife and she left the hall to return a minute later. Gulzar took a large packet and put it in Prakash's hands. "This is for my friend Thakur Pukhraj Singh. Tell him that he is dear to me as a friend. Thank him for taking care of my sisters. I wanted to visit the village but my health prohibits me to travel, so I had sent Shadab instead. Ask him to visit us if possible. I will be obliged if he will be my guest." Gulzar said with a lingering sadness in his tone.

- - -

Zubair Ahmed with his daughter, son-in-law, and Prakash went to Gulzar Ahmed's room to seek his permission before leaving. Gulzar was sitting on a chair looking outside the window with his back to the door. They entered and waited for him to turn. For a while when he didn't turn, Shahida tapped on Gulzar's shoulders. Gulzar still didn't turn. Shahida sat on the chair next to him to notice that Gulzar was crying though there were no tear.

Shahida held his hands tenderly, "They have promised to return next year."

Zubair and Rukhsar stood quietly next to Gulzar. Then Zubair kneeled and hugged his father. "I am leaving because I can't stay here too long. I promise to return soon and stay for a few days."

Gulzar looked at Rukhsar, "You are going home?"

"Yes, *Dadaji*. I will go to Delhi and then to Lahore."

"Have you missed your home?"

"Yes, *Dadaji*."

216

"How does it feel when you are returning home?"

"It's indescribable. I am elated but that is not the complete truth. It is..." Rukhsar couldn't describe the real feeling. "Yes, I am happy that I am going home but I am sad because I will miss you people."

Gulzar raised his hand asking her to bend down. Rukhsar kneeled next to his chair. Gulzar, with the tears suspended in his eyes, caressed her head, "Did it inconvenience you when you had to suddenly leave home and go to India?"

"Yes, I had to pack and arrange everything for *Ammi* before I left," she said and coughed laugh to lighten the atmosphere, "but it will be a mess when I return; to reset things as it was when I left," Rukhsar said, but her humour had an adverse effect.

"Some people are not so fortunate. A little inconvenience in life, for minor things which upset people's routine irritates them," Gulzar said, "I was uprooted from my soil and moved to foreign soil first, and then I was forced by my adopted country to live in exile in an alien land. Who understands the feelings of people who crave for their motherland? I am condemned to live... and die in exile. I can't return to my motherland where I wish to die. You will be upset when you return home because you will have to get used to your earlier routine of a few days ago. What about people like us who can't return to their soil to offer their prayers at the graveyards of my sister in one country, or at the graveyards of my parents..." and he broke down, "I haven't offered my respects to the woman who was my wife... I am an unblessed soul who is forbidden to return to house and offer his prayers to his wife. Why is it so? We, who left behind their ancestors' graves, left behind our culture and roots to create a country of dreams, have been declared heretics. Who gave them the rights to call us non-Muslims? Why am I forced to live a life in exile; for my virtues? What about people like us, Rukhsar? Don't we have a right to live? Why am I forced to live in faraway land away from my home and motherland? Why am I condemned to live with only my memories? What about me, Rukhsar?"

"We are in the same boat, *Abba*." Zubair responded in vain, to comfort his father; he felt the same in his heart. "I couldn't say goodbye to my family either," Zubair choked. He turned to look at his daughter, held her hand and kissed it. "I would have given anything for these few days with her. I understand what you mean, *Abba*. No one can understand... how people like you and me suffer from being displaced from our soils."

Everyone saw the tears suspended around the eyes of father and son. Gulzar didn't care if people saw him cry. "I want to go back home and... die there."

Aman knew of the plight of displaced people from Pakistan and India since partition but he never grasped the deep scars of those affected. He had seen mass emigrations from war zones around the world but the International community had overlooked the psychological aspect of such situations. Aman swore that if he was reinstated he would concentrate on this aspect of humanity's tragedy. And then, there was his family history. Aman Khan Bux felt his heart torn apart by the scene which played in his mind.

Rukhsar put her arms around her grandfather and hugged him. Two men empathized with Gulzar Ahmed because they knew what it was to be forced out of their homelands: Zubair Ahmed and Prakash Rohatgi.

- - -

Two hours later while Gulzar, Rukhsar and Aman rested in a private lounge at the airport, Prakash excused himself and left, promising them to be back in an hour.

Prakash walked hurriedly to the VIP lounge of the Airport to catch his Bangladesh contact in time. He found the man sitting separately and tapped his shoulders. The man turned around and smiled nervously, pulled Prakash aside, leading him to another room. The man locked the room and turned to Prakash. "You fool! You took a risk by bringing those people here. What happened to the cautious person I know? You are compromising arrangements," the man said with disappointment.

"I am careful. I took some risk because I think I have two fabulously talented people who will be part of our group; people who will work gladly with us. I wasn't sure earlier but I am, now." Prakash replied with a brimming smile.

"It may be so... be careful." The man said with lesser frown.

"What's irked Islamabad and Rawalpindi? I haven't heard anything from them in a week. Why is Aman targeted?"

The bureaucrat leaned forward and whispered, "I have a feeling about this. Aman may not be the real target. It could be Zubair. I do not know why. I am on my way to Dubai where I may meet our Rawalpindi colleague. He was upset when he called me this morning. His questions tell me that your guest, Zubair is of the interest to whoever sent that man to your house."

"Altaf, you mean?" Prakash asked.

"If that is the man who was dumped in the street of Delhi. You should have had disposed of him in a more efficient way. He has reached Rawalpindi."

Prakash nodded, "I couldn't get information I wanted from him. Zubair Saheb was adamant about visiting his ancestral house so I had to let go of Altaf."

The bureaucrat nodded, "I understand that but you should have handled Altaf better. Our colleague in Pindi is nervous about something he learnt today. I will speak to him in a day or two and I will call you."

"It sounds quite serious." Prakash asked.

"He will tell me when he digs deeper into the matter. When can you get on network again? It has been five days."

"Tomorrow perhaps," Prakash replied casually.

The man patted Prakash's back. "I couldn't manage more time for the couple. I am sorry but it is necessary to be cautious and I am not going to take chances like you. I am not young like you." The man said and smiled.

*   *   *

Prakash Rohatgi's Residence,

New Delhi, India

The group returned to Prakash Rohatgi's residence at dawn. Though Zubair, Rukhsar and Aman felt comfortable being in the house they had not seen Prakash since their return. He stayed away from his guests until lunch time. When Purna asked them to come to the dining hall, the guests were surprised to find Prakash missing again. When pushed, Purna only said that Prakash was busy with something and he had asked her not to let anyone disturb him.

After lunch Rukhsar and Zubair retreated to their room but Aman was disturbed. He went to Prakash's room but Prakash was not in his room. Then Aman heard sounds from the adjacent room. He went to the door and knocked lightly. He knocked a few times but got no reply. He pressed his ears against the door and heard faint sounds. The sounds seemed familiar. He tried to recall where he had heard them before. Before he could determine or recollect his wife appeared next to him.

Aman looked at her worriedly, "I can hear sounds from the room but Prakash is not responding."

Rukhsar looked at her husband first and then at the door. A tensed look appeared on her face. She pressed her ear against the door and heard the sounds, banged her fist against the door and shouted angrily, "Prakash, please open the door. We want to talk to you."

She rapped the door thrice before Prakash opened the door; he stood bare-chested except a thin white cotton cloth thrown over his shoulder and a white traditional Indian dhoti below the waist. Vermillion powder applied as a *teeka* graced his forehead. He stood blocking the entrance of the door with no expression, and looked at them with aloofness. The couple saw deep sadness in his eyes. A realization struck Aman; he was embarrassed at himself and sad for Prakash. He recalled the sounds as ritual chants; *Shlokas* in *Sanskrit* he knew by the perfection of the recitations, and by precision of pronunciation. Prakash's dress code gave him a clue to the occasion and his eyes confirmed his fears.

Aman lowered his head in embarrassment, "I am sorry. I... we didn't know."

Rukhsar looked at her husband with surprise and then at her host, "What happened?"

"Come..." Aman ordered Rukhsar and turned to Prakash, "I am sorry for disturbing you."

Prakash looked at the couple, closed his eyes momentarily and waived them into the room. When they tried to enter, he stopped them and pointed at their foot wears. The couple removed the foot wears and entered the room. Rukhsar was surprised by what she saw, and Aman was stunned by the gravity of the occasion. Rukhsar had no clue but Aman knew that this was traditional honouring, an annual ritual to honour the souls of the dead.

Rukhsar saw an unfurnished room with a row of mattresses on the floor and a ritual being performed, with fruits, flowers, incense sticks, garlands, purified butter and lamps against a row of eighteen photographs. Prakash waived them to sit on the mattress and he disappeared into the adjacent room.

Aman whispered softly, telling Rukhsar what the occasion was. Suddenly, Rukhsar's glowing face had a shade of sadness and unknown fear in her. She looked at the rows of garlanded photographs but she couldn't identify any of them although the facial features matched Prakash's with one person in the row; a saintly looking female, second from the left.

Prakash returned a few minutes later. He was calm but the calmness also exhibited the turmoil in the man. "I heard your knocks on the door but I couldn't have stopped my ritual in the middle of it. I am sorry I had to keep you waiting."

"We are sorry, Prakash. We intruded in your private affair. I know this... is a ritual for honouring... departed souls." Aman Khan replied choosing his words carefully as he and Rukhsar sat facing the row of framed photographs.

Prakash nodded and looked at the photographs like he was still praying, "I am the only surviving member from either family; my father's and my mother's, so I have to perform the rites for all of them." Prakash paused and looked at them. "I could have extended your stay by a day in Dacca but I had to perform these rites today. It is the only day of the year when I can perform these rituals for all if I am not aware of the exact dates of death of my elders or dear ones. According to *'Vikram-Samvat'* calendar, today is the only day so I had to return."

Aman and Rukhsar nodded their heads. Now they had many questions, especially about people for whom Prakash was performing the rites, but didn't ask, sensing the gravity of the moment. Both were quiet but sought answers. This man had gone beyond extending normal courtesies and been their best friend. Aman hinted with his eyes to Rukhsar to let it be for the time being. Abruptly, Prakash rose to his feet and asked them to meet him in Zubair's study room and left with a promise to join them shortly.

- - -

Zubair opened the door and the newlywed couple entered his room with sullen looks on their faces. They sat on the chairs next to his desk. Aman wanted to ask Zubair about Prakash's family history but he was surprised by Zubair's topic of research: 'The history of Ancient India'. He asked his father-in-law why he was studying about India and not about Pakistan's ancient history.

Zubair's looked at him thoughtfully, "Pakistan didn't exist before '47 - it was a part of a very large India. I am studying about ancient history of present day Pakistan. Over the last two years I have learnt to my dismay that a lot of our problems are because of our erred history books and by our reluctance to acknowledge the truth as it is."

"What do you mean?" Rukhsar asked.

"Our history texts don't mention the glorious past of the region because our historians and rulers are obsessed with anti-Hindu sentiments, so they won't talk about the great era of the *Mauryan Empire* or about the great universities we had in the past before the arrival of 'their' hero - *Mohammed Bin-Qasim*. We must tell our children truth; that our region has the most revered ancient history than any in mankind."

Rukhsar looked at her father with surprise, "Is it so?"

Zubair shook his head with dismay, but chuckled, "That's what I mean. You can imagine that if an educated person like you has no idea about it, what should we expect our lesser educated children or illiterates to know?"

Rukhsar wasn't sure what her father meant. She turned to her husband. He was nodding at Zubair. Aman knew history texts were biased and littered with lies but not to the extent that even an educated woman like his wife had no idea what was they were talking about.

Zubair flipped the pages and put his finger on a map and asked Rukhsar to look. Rukhsar and Aman leaned forward to look at the small map of 'Bharat' - India, as it was in the reign of Emperor Ashoka.

Rukhsar was amazed to see the vastness of Ashoka's empire; it was far bigger than present day India - stretching from parts of Myanmar in the east to the western borders of Afghanistan. The only part he didn't rule was the southern Indian peninsula. "Pakistan, India, Afghanistan, Bangladesh, parts of Nepal and Myanmar under one kingdom? Why don't we read about it, Aman? What era was this?" Rukhsar asked.

"The Mauryan Empire was established by Ashoka's grand-father, the great Chandragupta Maurya. This was in early part of the third century bce., We don't learn about it because our historians were, and still are, obsessed with anti-India, anti-Hindu sentiment. How can they talk of the greatest era of the region, or of the world, was during that period? What that era achieved in its time is unparalleled in modern history, or I dare say, in the history of mankind. India was rich, had very high standard of education; law and order was fantastic primarily because Chandragupta was taught by *Chanakya*. Very few people know that Chanakya has written treatise on various subjects. He wrote *'Kautilya'* on politics, *'Arth-Shastra'* on economics, and various books on whole range of subjects from diplomacy, administration, military warfare and state craft. Vishnugupta, which was his real name or *Kautilya*, as he was also called, *Chanakya*, was a product of the world's first ever university which was situated in present day Pakistan but you have not read about it in your text books. For centuries it was the only university in the world till *Nalanda* and other universities were built in North India. Even these latter universities came centuries before the Moroccan university was set up which the west considers as the oldest university. Shouldn't I be proud of my ancient heritage? Sure, but that is possible only if we acknowledge that it was millennia before *Mohammed Bin-Qasim* arrived in India. When we accept that the era which went by was greater than any we have seen only then can we accept our history as fact otherwise we can continue to believe that Pakistan was 'created' by *Mohammed Bin-Qasim*. For anti-India, and especially anti-Hindu zealots it won't be acceptable. So, it is not taught or spoken about. *Taksha-Shila* was established before 500bce. It had over ten thousand students from as far as Greece, Syria, and China. The ancient culture hasn't vanished. It thrives, but not where it originated. The great students of *Taksha-Shila*... Taxila as we call it in Pakistan created the greatest literary works in literature, performing arts, sciences, medicines and any field you can think of. The most perfect grammar was written by one of the students of *Taksha-Shila: Panini*. He originally hailed from an area in present day Afghanistan. Panini wrote volumes in *Sanskrit* grammar with such perfection that it still remains unparalleled, unrivalled by any language ever spoken or written by mankind, before or since. It is so precise that it is considered the best language, in fact, the only language for computer programming nearly three millennia later. That's why Sanskrit is considered the perfect language; because the grammar is unrivalled till date. Sanskrit was the first language to have loads of scriptures and treatise, yet we deprive our children of it. We can learn from the rich heritage and culture of our ancestors to further our knowledge. It is weird that the greatest language ever known to mankind comes from our region and we, instead of being proud of it, have obliterated it from our minds and deny our children the right to know of our ancestors' achievements. Isn't that blasphemy? Prophet Mohammed, peace be upon Him, urged His followers to go to China, if need be, to acquire knowledge… but we deny ourselves?" Zubair shouted in anger.

Rukhsar and Aman were silent. They didn't dare to counter Zubair with lesser logic or knowledge.

"I am a proud Muslim, an ardent follower of Islam. I dare say that I have not witnessed the true spirit of the *Holy Quran* in my life. A vast majority of us swear by the Holy book but how many follow it in spirit? Does it state that we should forego our knowledge by following words of some misguided clergy who in his zeal forgets the basic tenets? It is sacrilege to override these tenets." Zubair said with frustration. He was silent for a few moments and virtually pleaded, 'My children, I have discovered that the greatest era of knowledge was in our region. From east of Indus to the banks of the Holy Ganges, knowledge flowed like their crystal clear waters used to. It reminds me of the Lord Thomas Babington Macaulay speech he made in the British Parliament in 1835, and I quote him: *'I have travelled the length and breadth of India and I have not seen a beggar, who is a thief. I have seen such wealth and moral values and people of such high calibre that I don't think we would ever conquer this country, which is her spiritual and cultural heritage and therefore I propose that we replace her old and ancient education system, her culture, for if the Indians think that all that is foreign and English, is good and greater than their own, they will lose their self-esteem, their native culture. They will become what we want them, a truly dominated nation.'* Lord Macaulay's speech may sound rude but look at us. Haven't the British succeeded?" Zubair asked.

The content of Zubair's speech made Rukhsar and Aman speechless. Aman Bux had some clue of it, but for his wife it was an absolute shock. She knew though, that if her father had said it and her husband had not countered it, it must be true, but it was still unbelievable.

Zubair resumed, "If you see what I read these days you may think I am reading Hindu scriptures. That is the problem with people who don't understand that to acquire knowledge we must read: read what is relevant and understand the contents. For example, I read a treatise on old Indian medical practices. You will be surprised at what I learned. For millennia our ancestors had fantastic knowledge of medical sciences. I have read the *'Sushrut'* and *'Charak' Samhitas*, which were written a few centuries before the Christian era. In them I find a wealth of sciences which are practiced to this day in forms of *'Ayurveda'*, especially in India. It's amazing that even in that era these sages performed surgeries, including complex ones like brain surgery and they were performed with instruments which, by the descriptions, are contemporary instruments used today. When I read these, I was excited to learn more. I began to research and read more and more and I was blessed by God to have read these books. These are not scriptures of Hinduism but treatise on various subjects. I have read books on economics and sciences, including space sciences where they talk about parallel and multiple universes and the various theories on the creation and destruction, or end of universes; these have already been discussed in these books. These are not holy books," he told Rukhsar, "these are books on sciences; aeronautics, chemistry, spirituality, politics, medicine and surgery, human anatomy and from biology to ..." Zubair stopped abruptly. He suddenly realized he was speaking to his daughter and son-in-law and the next word would have been and embarrassment for both and to himself.

Aman completed the sentence rather plainly, "... to *Kama Sutra* on erotology."

Zubair looked at Aman with surprise. His son-in-law had said it in a subtle manner instead of saying the book on sex.

"True!" Zubair nodded.

Rukhsar looked at both men with disbelief. Aman's half sentence had endorsed Zubair's statement. "Have you read any of these books, Aman?"

"No. But we learn about many things during cultural fests. The latest craze which the west... in fact the whole world is crazy about is the physical exercises of the '*Yoga*'. These aren't religious practices; it is an ancient Indian system of exercises for mental health and physical fitness."

"What a shame!" Zubair said sadly, "The marvel of that era is amazing when you learn that the Mathematician *Bhaskara* calculated the time taken by Earth to orbit around the Sun or rotation on its axis is disputed by modern scientists by decimals of a second. Can you imagine that we had mathematician of that calibre living in our region two and half millennia ago?

Modern mathematics is a gift of those sages who gave the world modern numeral system which we use today? They were the one to give mankind the concept of '*zero*' and its decimal places and mathematician greats like Pythagoras went to the banks of Ganga to learn maths. It was India which gave the world the binary system a few millennia ago. Can you imagine what modern world would do without Indian numeric, decimal or binary systems? How could you make a computer work without the binary system?" Zubair asked and observed the reactions of Rukhsar in particular.

Rukhsar was silent. The information was coming too fast for her to grasp readily. As Zubair stopped speaking, her mind analysed the importance of what her father was saying.

"We don't tell our children that the qualities of metallurgy our ancestors mastered in many fields are unmatched to this day. Why?" Zubair waived at them to lean forward, opened a book and sifted through the bookmarks. He stopped at a page and asked them to look at the photographs and read the captions against them.

Rukhsar gasped, "Is this true?"

"The one in New Delhi is world famous but the other three aren't so famous. The best metallurgists of modern era have failed to replicate these 'rust free' iron columns forged and erected by ancient Indians. Among these the most remarkable 'rust-free' iron pillar is the one in '*Kollar*' in southern Indian state of Karnataka. It is remarkable because this column was forged not by metallurgists but by tribals to honour the visit of the great Hindu Seer, Adi Shankaracharya in eighth century. The pillar still stands as a sample of achievements of our ancestors of that era." Zubair leaned back in frustration. He wanted to convince his daughter that he was doing the right thing. Zubair opened another bookmark and put his finger on a word. '*Ukku*'. "Do you know what it means?" he asked Aman.

Aman Khan shook his head in negative.

"*Ukku* is original word in Telugu and Kannada for 'wootz steel', which is an anglicised name. This fantastic metal was exported by Indians for three millennia to Europeans and Arabs. It is the finest example of metallurgical expertise of that era. Wootz steel was used to manufacture the finest products, especially swords. This art is dead except for small pockets in Rajasthan where it's still made in crucibles like it was done for millennia. Even Alexander, Romans and Greeks used it. Do you know that for four Millennia, India alone had the technology to distil Zinc? But... do we teach our children about it? No! Why? Because, it is considered unpatriotic, even heresy, to sing praises of pre-Islamic era of the region. Isn't it a shame that knowledge is restricted because some idiots don't want to think beyond religion? Isn't it true that we lie to our children? This is blasphemy!"

Zubair folded the books and kept them gently aside. "If I want to tell you of the achievements and the brilliance of our ancestors, it will take me months just to provide you with details. I wish our children learn that the region where we live today was the most educated, civilized place that ever existed. Pakistan has a goldmine in its past but we deprive them of our identity. It is a fallacy to think that we are children of invaders who invaded India a thousand years ago. The history texts lie that our forefathers were Arabs, not Indians. This blasphemy had led us to loss of identity amongst our people. It was propagated falsely by those who were ashamed to call themselves Indians. They wanted to create a separate identity; instead they have created a nation which has lost its identity."

"How can we justify that statement, *Abbu*?" Rukhsar asked.

"Look at yourself, dear. Look at your language and culture. Does it have anything to do with the Arabs? Invaders impose their language and culture upon occupied lands and people but our forefathers were able to retain their language and culture, even surnames. They accepted Islam but they did not lose their culture. To this day we celebrate Hindu festivals like *'Basant'*. For your information *Basant* is a month in a Hindu calendar and it is celebrated on the first day of the month, which is the end of the summer season and it is related to farming, not religion," Zubair said and looked at his daughter. "*Sanskrit* is the fountain-head of every language we speak. Punjabi, Sindhi or Hindko do not come from Arabia but from the sister languages of which, once again, Sanskrit is the mother. Get your DNA checked and you will know with which people it matches, the Indians or Arabs. These are scientific proofs that we are Indians, my dear."

"If you say that in Lahore, you could invite the wrath of lots or people." Aman said bluntly.

"That is true. By the way, do you know that the Hindu God Rama had two sons, twins: Lahore was called *'Loh-Awar'* and it was named after Lav, the elder son of Rama? And, Kasur was called *Kushapur*, and named after Kush, the younger twin of Lava? Similarly Rama's younger brother was Bharat, whose son was *Taksha*, the ruler of *Taksh-Khand*, a kingdom which was bigger than present day Pakistan. The University of *Taksha-Shila* was named after Taksha. Our greatest mountain range is the *'Hindu-Kush'*. It was named after Rama's younger of twin-sons. We alienate ourselves from our Buddhist and Hindu past so some zealots have linked the name *'Kush'* to Persian *'Koh'* which means *'kill'*. There lies the zealotic sentiment of people with sick mentality. The word *'koh'* comes from Prussian language but they did not stop to think that Prussian came many millennia after the advent of Rama or His sons. In the great Indian epic *Maha-Bharata*, the blind prince *Dhritrashtra* married *Draupadi*, the sister of Shakuni. Shakuni was the prince of *'Gaandhaar'*, which we today know as Kandahar, in Afghanistan. Strange, isn't it? We have the greatest heritage in our backyard and we struggle for identity. Why can't we simply acknowledge that we are Indians though we may be Muslims? Our self-denial will lead to greater crises of identity. Unless we acknowledge truth, we will never have an identity. Pakistan has lost its identity because it isn't sure where to look for its past. We don't accept our history so we look at the Arabs with whom we have no connect whatsoever except that they were invaders who conquered our lands only to destroy what was beautiful and enlightened. Today, they don't consider us as real Muslims. So, what is our identity? Present day Pakistan is land of geniuses who were born there, and created a near perfect society in ancient times. It is a shame that we are disconnected from our past. I fail to understand why we are teaching lies to our children when we can proudly say that though we are Muslims, we are proud of our heritage and ancestry? This was the land where the great *Vedas* were written after thousands of years of oral recitation. This was the land where mankind sent children for education and enlightenment, to Universities in eras of Chandragupta and Ashoka, and centuries after that." Zubair paused and suddenly his eyes had a brilliance of a saint, "Ashoka was the greatest king mankind has ever known. He was a king who ruled over a population four times the size of any Roman Emperor and larger area than the Romans had at their peak. He was a brutal ruler who renounced violence when he won the *Kalinga* war. He spread the message of peace throughout the world by spreading Buddha's preaching. It was our land which spread Buddhism throughout East, to as far as Japan and to the west up to Mediterranean. If it wasn't for Ashoka, Buddhism would have been lost to the world within two centuries after Buddha." Zubair smiled wryly. "What is the proud heritage of our people is lost to whims of zealots who won't accept their origins, and deny children the true history of their ancestors. I am a man who proudly says that I am a proud Muslim of the *Aryan* race, not a Muslim of some invading *Arab* tribe." Zubair roared in exultation.

Aman and Rukhsar watched Zubair silently wondered how a former soldier was professing peace and knowledge through his little speech. In the next few minutes Zubair showed the couple the books he had read and a thesis he was writing on the subject. Rukhsar was engrossed in the book as Aman rose and walked around looking at the small library, apart from the great collection of books lined along the walls in the lounge. Aman was stunned by the rare books and artefacts he saw in Zubair's collection. This was the wealth he was looking for. His appetite for knowledge urged him to pull out books and glance through the pages, especially those which were page-marked. He picked two books and asked if he could borrow them. Zubair readily agreed on condition that Aman won't take them out of that house. When Rukhsar asked the reason, Zubair stated that those were rare books he had borrowed from a library and because the pages were fragile.

Rukhsar wanted to talk to Zubair on his decision to return to Pakistan. Having heard his passionate speech she knew he won't be too keen. But she promised herself to keep trying till he succumbed.

* * *

Islamabad

Pakistan

Altaf Khos spent the day searching for facts on Kargil war. To his disappointment all the facts he learnt corroborated with what he had learnt during his captivity in New Delhi. Altaf had to find out more. He wanted to know why Wahid Khan wanted Zubair Ahmed dead. Altaf had an idea. He had to learn where Wahid Khan was stationed during Kargil war. That could provide a link to how Wahid Khan and Zubair Ahmed had come in direct contact with each other.

- - -

Altaf stood a few yards away from the gates of the Records Office in the Military compound, for his colleague from military training days. He saw the man he was waiting for and walked a few paces to the entrance of the gate and flashed his badge and identity card. The sentry allowed him in with a long salute.

Altaf stepped up his pace and caught up with the man, and greeted him, "*Salaam-Walequm*,"

"*Walequm-as-Salaam*", the man in late twenties replied and turned to look at his wisher and laughed loudly, "Altaf, my friend, how are you?"

Altaf Khos roared in laughter, "You are still working for that ugly man who was our trainer, Junaid?"

"No, I chopped his hands on the last day of the training as I had promised, remember?"

The two men laughed at their wishful joke and walked to the gates of the building. They flashed their Ids again and walked into the building.

"What brings you here?"

Altaf produced an identity card which General Wahid Khan had made available for him to get his work done promptly.

"Aah! A Major? Working for the Inter Services? Wow! We always knew you would go places. You always dared to take chances. What are you doing here?"

"I have been given a task, a secret task, Junaid. I am seeking some information about a General." Altaf asked.

"Which General?" Junaid asked suspiciously.

Altaf bore his eye in to his ex-colleague's as they reached the latter's desk. "What I am about to tell you is confidential. If you wish to work with us you must first commit yourself. I advise you to be honest because once you commit yourself you can't go back. If you wish to withdraw, do it now. If you work with us, however, there will be great benefits in the near future. We are friends so I ask you to weigh your decision. If you have any doubts, I will respect your decision and I won't ask for favours." Altaf Khos tempted Junaid.

The rank always works in any field. More so if the person at the opposite end is not powerful in stature.

Junaid bore into Altaf's eyes and replied in earnest. "I will keep my part of the deal, Altaf. What do you want to know about this General?"

Altaf Khos took a deep breath without letting Junaid notice it. He smiled, "I want to know about his whereabouts at the time of Kargil war. I remind you, this is strictly confidential."

"I understand! Tell me what you want to know."

"We suspect this General is up to something which could be detrimental to nation's interest. He may have issued orders which resulted in loss of a few posts during the Kargil war." Altaf fired a shot in the dark, "We are investigating the role of General Wahid Khan who was a Lieutenant General at the time. Find out where he was stationed during the war and what was he doing at the time?"

"Give me a day to find out."

"While you are on it, try and get me as much details as you can on this Lieutenant General but keep the information only to yourself. I will catch you up in a day or two." Altaf said.

"I will get the information for you by tomorrow."

Altaf smiled broadly. "Oh! Also, just see if you can tell me the relation between this General Wahid Khan and a Major Zubair Ahmed." He shook Junaid Saleem's hand and walked out.

*   *   *

Prakash Rohatgi's Residence,

New Delhi, India

Prakash Rohatgi stood calmly in the lounge when Aman entered. The sadness visible in the morning was still there in Prakash's eyes.

"You asked for me?" Aman asked trying his best to keep a blank expression.

Prakash nodded and handed an envelope to Aman. Aman opened the envelope to find his and Rukhsar's passports with visa extension for two weeks. Aman found another envelope inside. He flipped it open and saw tickets and papers. He checked the papers and looked at Prakash with broad smile.

"I had promised you in Dacca," Prakash said sincerely.

Aman was overwhelmed at the gesture. "This is... amazing. Fantastic!" Aman exclaimed. He checked the destination and asked his host, "I have heard Shimla is a beautiful place. Where are the other places? I have never heard of these."

"They are in the same state of Himachal Pradesh of which Shimla is the capital. These are wonderful places in the Kangra valley. You will love it there." Prakash said with a big smile, "Dharamshala, Mr. Cultural Attaché, I reckon you will love it too. It is a beautiful place with natural beauty, and also for spirituality if that is one of the things you yearn for. It's the official residence of the Tibetan leader, His Holiness, the Dalai Lama."

"We leave tomorrow?" Aman asked trying his best to hide his excitement. Did Prakash read his inner wish. "What is this other place?"

"That is 'the valley of flowers'. You can call it the world's largest natural garden. You are here at the right time. In a few weeks it will be closed for tourists. I am sure you will love it."

"I am sure I will." Aman laughed loudly, and then, suddenly he asked, "Why have you extended our visas?"

"Your visa would have expired tomorrow. Remember, you were on a medical visit. This visa extension allows you to tour the country as well. Moreover, I think Rukhsar would like to spend some more time with her father."

Aman nodded and shook Prakash's hand with warmth and turned around when he heard Rukhsar's voice.

"What's the celebration about?" she asked.

Aman handed over the envelope to his wife. She grabbed and read the content and her eyes lit up. "This is..." she said and choked, "Prakash...!" She said and hugged him.

"You haven't had time to spend time with each other so I thought this would be a good idea."

They didn't know the honeymoon trip would be truncated to less than a day.

*　　*　　*

Islamabad

Pakistan

Junaid Saleem's blood pressure mounted slowly as he saw the information he had in front of him. *'What had Altaf Khos unearthed here?'* he thought to himself. If the contents of this report were true then they had a villain amongst them; a man who could potentially destroy the army, and the country with it. A mad man had drafted an insane plan but wasn't known yet; it was a secret only few Generals knew. Junaid had begun by seeking Wahid Khan's postings at the time of Kargil war. Wahid Khan was posted on two important positions at the time and in both cases there were unusually high casualties. Junaid's inquisitiveness led him to dig deeper. He was amazed to discover that Wahid Khan had a mercurial rise through the ranks despite poor decisions (though some seniors thought that his audacious, though rash decisions in the face of fierce shelling had the potential of a great future commander). He dug deeper into the actions of the current four-star General. He learnt that some army men, coming from every branch, were reporting to him at odd hours. These were dedicated soldiers openly propagated war against the enemies; India and Israel. When the data was complete, Saleem called Altaf demanding to meet.

Altaf sat eagerly opposite Junaid, "What did you get?"

Junaid updated Altaf on the information he had and paused for a while, "this frightened the hairs out of my scalp. Wahid Khan is planning something big. What, I don't know. But I can confirm that your General is provided secret information from every branch of the army," Junaid bore into Altaf's eyes, "This General is being fed information also from your own department," he said and pulled out a folder with six sheets in them, and pushed it towards Altaf.

With unknown fear gripping him, Altaf read the content of the folder and looked at Junaid with panic in his eyes, "How is this possible?"

"You tell me, Altaf." Junaid countered.

Altaf looked at the sheets again and saw the names of the informers in Wahid Khan's ranks. The sheets contained a list of supporters of Wahid Khan. Among these were a Lieutenant General, who was Wahid Khan's first cousin, bureaucrats stationed in New Delhi, Dhaka, Washington DC, and some important capitals of the world, an important functionary at the Head Quarters of ISI. Another person frequently visited Wahid Khan - an extremist militant leader who had terrorist training camps in Northern Punjab few kilometres away from Muzzafarabad, and most frighteningly, a man who was quite friendly and provided inside informations was one of the most respected nuclear physicists of the country, and he was also a high ranking officer of the Pakistan Atomic Energy Commission, who had all the necessary knowledge of Pakistan's nuclear arsenal.

Altaf suspected something. "I asked about the post of Wahid Khan and Major Ahmed, and their relations why the two men should be in confronting mood. What about that?"

Junaid looked at Altaf Khos in disbelief. "I couldn't get the complete story but from what I gather is that the Major took two men from his battalion and ventured out to extract his ten men from the heights because they were being pounded by the Indians. It was an important post so it had to be defended but the Major knew that even at best the men could have probably held out for a day or two - supply lines were cut off and the men on the hill had run out of ammunition and beginning to starve. So the major dared to go, though he wasn't in command of that post. When Lieutenant General Wahid Khan learnt of it, he ordered nearby posts to attack that post. He declared that the Indian soldiers had taken the post and they were camouflaged as Pakistani soldiers. That post was bombed on Lieutenant General's orders, and as far as I have learnt twelve men died on that Hill... all Pakistanis."

"What was the name of that Major, Junaid?" Altaf asked but instinctively he knew the answer.

"Zubair Ahmed." Junaid replied.

All pieces fell into place. It made sense why Wahid Khan wanted Zubair Ahmed killed. Wahid Khan wanted to know if Zubair knew who had ordered the shelling of that post. If Zubair Ahmed knew, he could destroy Wahid Khan's plans. Wahid Khan wasn't willing to take chances. If Rukhsar or Aman Bux learn of this, they too had to be killed, Altaf knew. Saleem looked worriedly at Altaf. Both men knew what was in front of them. The sheets in the folder laid a lot of things thread bare but there were things they did not know. Who were the other three men who were the core of the plan of this planned misadventure? Altaf had an idea about one.

"What made you dig all these up?" Altaf asked.

"They are planning something big and we don't know what. Is that why your agency is keen on Wahid Khan?"

Altaf nodded, "We feared something like this but we didn't know it was this big. Thank you, Junaid. I assure you, you will be honoured for this." Altaf replied calmly but shook within. Accidently, Junaid has stumbled upon a plan which could probably lead to a coup. "How did you manage to get these confidential details?" Altaf asked.

Junaid Saleem smiled through his rimmed glasses, "It was too exciting when I learnt of the plan to 'fix' India. It whetted my appetite. I hinted some questions to three men I found on the list, and I offered to join the group. This morning I was offered to join," Junaid Saleem smiled.

Altaf was silent. Junaid did not know that his life could be in danger if anyone got smart on him. Then a word from his earlier sentence struck him. Coup! Wahid Khan was planning a coup? The thought suddenly frightened Altaf even further.

Altaf put the papers in his bag, thanked Junaid and walked out. He was in dilemma. He had respected Wahid Khan as a General until an hour ago, though not as a human being. Now, Wahid Khan was an enemy who shouldn't be allowed to get away. Altaf decided to give himself time to think of his next move. He thought through the day and arrived at the boldest decision he had ever made. Since he couldn't trust anyone here, he had to trust two men who he knew he could trust: Zubair Ahmed and Aman Khan Bux.

-   -   -

Altaf called Wahid Khan, took an appointment and was at the doors of the General four hours later. "I am off to India. I need new identity papers because the Indian immigration and New Delhi cops already know my previous identity. I will need cash and help from a local I can trust." Altaf Khos tried to be as convincing as he probably could.

Wahid Khan asked Altaf to return in two hours. When Altaf returned, he walked out with a new name and identity papers and surprisingly, with a debit card to withdraw funds from any major bank. Altaf Khos sighed in relief.

- - -

Altaf had a plan and only one person could help him. He wanted details of Wahid Khan's plans. He reached the house of the crippled General but didn't meet him. He met Mariam in her room and told her about his fears. He told Mariam he wanted to see the General's files to be sure the information he had was accurate. Mariam thought of ways to help Altaf. She couldn't do it while Imtiaz was in the house. She asked Altaf to wait for some time and went out her room and asked Imtiaz to quickly fetch some medicines she had run out of, 'urgently'. She told the house attendant that these medicines were rare so he will have to get it from a hospital about seven kilometres away.

By the time the attendant returned she will have done her job. Mariam returned five minutes later and asked Altaf to wait for few minutes to be sure. When asked why, Mariam put her hands around his neck, brought him closer and told him that she had injected a little doze which would let the General sleep until morning in near unconscious state. Altaf Khos smiled and kissed her.

Ten minutes later Mariam checked her patient. He slept like a log. She returned to her room and asked Altaf to follow her. Altaf followed Mariam. Using a torch light Altaf cautiously stepped into the General's room followed by Mariam. She lifted the mattress near the General's head, drew out a bunch of keys and handed it to Altaf. She picked the right key to the safe where the General kept his confidential files. Altaf Khos opened the safe and drew out the files. He sifted through the bunch of files and found the one he wanted. He placed the file on table, and took photographs of all pages with his cell phone. In a minute he was done. He put the files back and locked the safe. Mariam put the keys back under the mattress and they left the room. Back in her room, Altaf checked the pictures he had taken and enlarged them. Seven minutes later, after he had read the content, his face was ashen. This was a disaster. If things didn't go exactly to plan, Pakistan would be destroyed in weeks; if things went as planned, Pakistan would be destroyed eventually but not before millions die - on both sides of the border.

Mariam saw Altaf's white face and asked fearfully, "What is it?"

Altaf waived the cell in front of her, "This is a disaster plan. Chances of its success are less than one in a million. These crazy Generals don't realize that India will get a whiff of this, and when it does, it will strike with all its might and that will destroy Pakistan. We will never recover from it," Altaf said.

Altaf was frightened by the prospect of his country going to war with a neighbour who was many times mightier in every way. Pakistan had no comparison with India in terms of size of the army, conventional weapons superiority... or, and then it struck him. He searched for something and found it in the sixth snap. His doubts were confirmed. His heart sank as he found mention of two names on the files: 'Ghauri II' and 'Shaheen II'. "Oh God Almighty!" he murmured to himself.

Mariam noticed the breathless, fearful face of her lover. She knew it had to be near disaster if a soldier carried such a dreadful expression.

Altaf panicked. He couldn't tell Mariam that the army was moving these missiles for deployment, ready to launch in a few minutes. Mariam tried speaking to him but Altaf's mind was far away. He picked his bag. Altaf made a bold decision!

* * *

Prakash Rohatgi's Residence,

New Delhi, India

Rukhsar and Aman entered Prakash's room and they were humbled by the simplicity of his room. It had no television or music system. For furniture, it had a simple wardrobe apart from a decent sized single bed. There were no magazines or books and no source of any entertainment. It had a telephone and a small table with three revolving stools around it.

Prakash saw them enter and rose from his stool and invited them to occupy the other two stools. Rukhsar and Aman were still smiling when they sat.

"We have come to thank you," Rukhsar said gratefully.

"You are special people, and my friends so don't thank me. If time comes, I will ask you for help, but I won't want you to commit. If I make a request and you think it's in good faith, accept it. If you don't agree to it, I won't hold it against you. I promise you." Prakash replied simply.

Prakash had said it simply but the intensity and sincerity of it made the couple know how deeply he cared for them.

Aman hesitated before he spoke, "You promised to tell us your story. This morning you performed the rites of your family, and you said you were the only surviving member of the family, on your mother and father's side. If you consider us your friend you must tell us your story." Aman insisted.

Prakash nodded in acceptance. He forced a smile on his lips and both, Aman and Rukhsar saw the efforts that smile took to appear. Prakash rose to his feet, "I don't want to narrate my story and mess up your next few days. You deserve the best and you should only think of that right now. As for my story, I promise to tell you when I am comfortable."

Rukhsar and Aman could feel the depth of pain in the way he had said it, but Prakash stood firmly looking at them.

-   -   -

At six, the following morning, Prakash drove them to Inter-State Bus Terminus - ISBT, where the couple boarded the bus to Shimla. Prakash invited them for a cup of tea before the bus left. Prakash gave them a cell phone each, forbidding them to use their own handsets. They didn't want to be disturbed, Prakash joked, by unwanted elements who could be trying to track them down, especially Aman.

-   -   -

The doorbell shrilled. Purna opened the door and found a submissive Altaf standing there, begging to meet Zubair Ahmed. Purna refused to reply and asked him to leave. Altaf refused to budge unless he met Zubair Ahmed or Aman Bux.

Purna ordered him to wait, shut the door on his face and called Prakash. A minute later Prakash stood at the door with a quizzing look on his face. He stepped out angrily asking the unwanted guest if 'really' wanted to be punished. Altaf stood there adamantly unwilling to move.

"What's your problem? Do you really wish to be messed up this time, Altaf? I didn't expect you to get away. Consider it your good luck that you are still free to walk around." Prakash threatened.

"If you wish I will submit myself to it but it is important for me to meet Aman Bux or Zubair Ahmed because it affects my country, Sir. Please trust me, I have no reason to be here except to help them and Rukhsar save their lives. *I swear by God,* I speak the truth." Altaf pleaded desperately.

Altaf's submission made Prakash think. He knew Altaf was not lying but allowing Altaf to meet Aman wasn't possible. It could put the latter's life at risk. Prakash couldn't afford that.

Altaf tried to convince Prakash for over fifteen minutes but Prakash was unwilling to risk Aman's life. Then he said what he didn't wish to say to Prakash, "Sir, all the three lives are in serious threat. I wasn't sent to tow Aman; I was sent here to kill Major Zubair Ahmed. He knows, or perhaps he knows not a secret which puts his life in danger. I am sent here to track down Zubair and kill him. If Rukhsar and Aman know the secret they too must die. Please help me save their lives."

Prakash stood at the door dumbfounded. "If you speak the truth, you may meet Zubair Ahmed and Aman Bux but you must convince me first."

Altaf decided to come clean with Prakash. He had all to gain and nothing to lose. Meanwhile, Prakash decided to give Altaf some latitude. He turned to Purna and instructed her in *Kharia.* She nodded and walked towards Zubair's room.

Watching her go Prakash turned to his unexpected guest, "Convince me," he said, "of your intentions. If you convince me I will hear your story, and if I believe you, I will let you meet Aman Bux and Zubair Ahmed. It is your choice. Take it or leave it!" Prakash said with finality.

Altaf nodded and took a step forward. Prakash thought Altaf was charging and assumed an aggressive posture. Altaf retreated, raising his hands in surrender, "I am unarmed. I have papers in my pocket which identify me as a Pakistani citizen, Akbar Raza, not as Altaf Khos. Thanks to you people I am already in the books of Delhi police as Altaf Khos. If I lie you can have me arrested with fake identity and this time I won't be able to get out, you know that." Altaf Khos pulled out the papers and handed them to Prakash.

Prakash checked the papers and waived Altaf to follow and led him to the room where he was held captive for three days. Altaf eased himself, ironically on the same chair where he was tied up. He smiled at the irony. Prakash sat opposite Altaf and ordered him to start talking. Altaf saw Purna enter the room holding a tray with two glasses and a jug of fruit juice. Altaf again smiled at another the irony; the last time he was in this chair he was battered by the woman who had brought him fruit juice this time. He looked up at her and joked, "Please don't hit me this time. I come here as a friend."

Purna nodded with a smile. Altaf saw a beautiful smile on a face he hated a few days ago. Purna spoke about something to Prakash in *Kharia* and left. Prakash turned Altaf's attention to two cameras in the room, one in front of him and other to his left. "I am recording every word we speak. If your story is true you will meet Mr. Ahmed today but if your story doesn't match up, you will have a very tough life ahead."

Altaf nodded and narrated all he knew about the Kargil height incident where eleven of Zubair's men were killed and Zubair himself was presumed dead until news arrived that he was alive. They knew he was alive so they kept tabs on calls to his house and cell phones. Though Altaf narrated the entire story he did not mentioned the name of the Lieutenant General who had ordered the shelling on Zubair and his men.

"Who was the Lieutenant General who ordered that shelling of the hill?" Prakash asked the obvious question.

"I will withhold the name for the time being," Altaf replied.

Prakash nodded. The name of that Lieutenant General was for Zubair's ears only. "You said that this man is now a General. Why does he want them dead?" Prakash asked.

Altaf held his breath. He wasn't sure if he could answer this question to a man whose intentions he couldn't trust. "I will not answer that question, Sir. This question and the answer to it are strictly a matter of national security. I won't answer that no matter what you think. I will only tell this to either Mr. Zubair Ahmed or Mr. Aman Khan Bux." Altaf said firmly.

Prakash wanted to slap the young man and applaud at the same time. Altaf was dedicated enough to put his life at stake and brave enough to dare his opponent, for the country's sake, even if it could cost him his life. Prakash waited for a confirmation which came a minute later when Zubair Ahmed barged into the room. Zubair stood two feet away from Altaf Khos, his eyes levelled at the Lieutenant, "Who ordered the shelling? If you don't tell me the truth, I swear by God I will kill you right now," Zubair roared.

Altaf was surprised to see Zubair standing in front of him. He tried to recall from his memory if this was indeed Zubair Ahmed. When he was sure, he said, "Lieutenant General Wahid Khan."

Zubair wasn't surprised. He grabbed a chair and slumped in it. Prakash was quiet. He knew he would only be a spectator to a conversation between the two men now. It would be a Zubair show from here on.

Zubair looked at Altaf and raised three questions, "Why does Wahid Khan want us dead? Second question, why aren't you following orders? Third, why have to come to us?"

Altaf Khos looked at Prakash Rohatgi and turned to Zubair pleadingly, "I want to talk to you in private," He replied and turned to Prakash, "No offence..."

Prakash looked at Altaf blankly.

Zubair told Altaf, "You can tell me whatever you wish to say. Whatever you tell me, I will tell him anyway, so go ahead and say what you have to say. Don't miss out on anything."

Reluctantly, and in sheer desperation, Altaf started slowly and told them about the information he had, and about the potential of a coup which he thought was a real possibility.

"You are joking. Islamabad has a democratically elected government. How can a coup take place?" Zubair asked.

"There was a democratically elected government during the Kargil war. Four months after the war that *democratically elected government* was toppled in military coup, Sir." Altaf retorted. "That's the history, isn't it?" he counter-questioned Zubair.

Zubair nodded his head in agreement and asked Altaf for proof to back his allegations. Altaf asked Prakash to send someone to fetch a folder from a black sedan parked next to the gate and find a folder hid under the passenger seat. Two minutes later Purna placed the folder in Prakash's hands. He gave it to Zubair.

Zubair read the contents. This was inconceivable, but some morons had conceived it. He looked at Altaf, "Good work! I am proud that we still have men like you who are willing to put their life on line for sake of the country without being influenced by rank or grade; without being a zealot."

Since Altaf had learnt how Zubair had countermanded his superior's orders and gone to the hills under heavy shelling to rescue his men, Zubair had become an idol in his eyes; a real hero. To be praised by a hero elated him.

"Why have to come to me? What can I do? I am not even in the field or in the Pakistan Army to be able to do anything about it. I am afraid you have wasted your time and effort coming to me." Zubair said.

"I don't think so," Altaf countered, "What you did for your men on that hill makes you a national hero. If you go to press and media with what I have uncovered, it can stop Wahid Khan. His supporters will desert him. Instead of being considered a hero, he will be treated as a traitor; to army and country. With lack of support, his entire plan will fall flat on its face. He could even be court-martialed."

Zubair laughed loudly with sarcasm, "You are naive, young man. Is it that easy? The moment they get a whiff of me, they will tarnish my reputation so such extent that I will become a national shame. I am alive but I didn't return to Pakistan, and I have abandoned my family. They know I am living in India, and they will prove that I work for Indian intelligence agency, *against Pakistan*. These are power hungry men; they who go to any length to achieve their wishes. Opinions don't matter to them. They don't come to power to enhance civilian ratings. They come to power either with their own agenda or simply to save their skins; like in case with Musharraf. In Pakistan's case, there has never been an agenda for citizens. I will be crucified without a trail, my young soldier. Be rest assured of that." Zubair Ahmed said sarcastically.

Altaf was deflated. He knew Zubair was right. Altaf hadn't thought of it. "You can call on your ex-colleagues who can do something to stop Wahid Khan," he pleaded, "he must be stopped. He has an agenda; an agenda which will destroy Pakistan. I... we have to do something. We just can't sit idle and let it happen. Sir... please help me out. You are a hero. At least, guide me how I can stop Wahid Khan." Altaf begged.

Zubair chuckled at his helplessness, "Altaf, why didn't you approach any of your senior colleagues?"

"Because... I am not sure whom to trust. If these papers fall in wrong hands it could be counter-productive. I am not sure who is involved and who isn't," Altaf Khos justified his decision.

Zubair nodded. He had expected this answer. "If *you* can't be certain, how can I be sure who is or who isn't working with the General? I have been away from Pakistan for over twelve years," Zubair thought as he spoke, "I have a personal stake. If they can convince people of Pakistan that I am a traitor, lives of my wife, my daughter and Aman will be in danger. How can I help?" Zubair Ahmed asked.

Altaf Khos asked desperately, "What should I do, Sir?"

"There is a simpler solution if you have the courage to do it. You have your firearms with you. Use it!" Zubair opined.

"That was the first thought which crossed my mind. I have more than one good reason to do it but it isn't easy. I can't even get close to him with a firearm. Wahid Khan has airtight security."

Zubair thought for a moment, picked up the folder and handed it to Prakash Rohatgi. Altaf almost panicked. He was ready to shout but didn't. He trusted Zubair Ahmed and his decision. Prakash took his time studying the six sheet folder while the two men waited patiently. Prakash was looking at a different scenario, from a totally different perspective than the one which had been presented. What Prakash Rohatgi saw in the scenario scared his wits. If the right ingredients were added to this, it could lead not just to a war between the two nuclear powers, or a regional conflict, it could lead to the most dreadful scenario. Altaf or the planners of this scheme had absolutely no idea of what they were playing with. Either the planners were naive and didn't see the global implications of their action, or, if they did consider it, they were too smart and they had a plan of action ready for that. But that was too complicated and hazardous. Prakash Rohatgi was convinced this scheme to be as impractical as the earlier wars. The entire plan looked half-baked without due consideration given to how the Indian army and the International community would respond. The plan would certainly cause great loss of life and damage to India, but it would inevitably destroy Pakistan and set it back from where it would take decades to stabilize if that was possible... or if it still remained in existence.

Prakash shook his head in disbelief, "This is a disaster in the making," he murmured to himself.

"What?" Zubair asked him. He didn't hear Prakash clearly.

Zubair saw Prakash behaving nervously. He knew Prakash was a self-confident man who knew precisely how to handle any given situation. That Prakash Rohatgi was now confused, and even frightened.

Prakash was still scanning the papers. He was wondering what he could do in the situation. He waived the folder in the air, "Give this the right ingredient and this can blow up into a global scenario which even the super powers wouldn't want to think of."

Prakash's tone scared Zubair and Altaf. They had obviously missed something which Prakash hadn't. "What is that?" Zubair asked.

"In a multi-layered plan, Wahid Khan grabs power through a coup in the first step. Then their plan is to bring all militant, extremist groups under one umbrella and infiltrate these *Jihadi* elements into India through Jammu & Kashmir, Kutch and Rajasthan in the second step. Imagine the scenario if these extremist groups come under a unified command to wage war against India. What will happen? There would be carnage in the streets. India will respond with all its might because this won't be a stray incident of terror; this will be an invasion. India will respond swiftly and I can guarantee, this time the Indian government won't restrict itself to limited warfare like it did during Kargil war. Pakistan military establishment will retaliate and there will be a full-fledged war." Prakash looked at the papers for various informations. "Wahid Khan has planned an ambitious and audacious attack but he is rash and stupid. He doesn't understand the repercussions. India will be like a wounded tiger and it will throw all its might into this war and not a single nation in the world will dare to sympathise with Pakistan. Pakistan's fall will be swift and spectacular."

"Pakistan is a nuclear power, Prakash. You are discounting that." Zubair reminded Prakash.

"Exactly what I mean... Shaheen II and Ghauri II are ballistic missiles capable of carrying nuclear warheads. It is clearly marked where these ISBMs will be deployed. That is why Wahid Khan dares to plan such an attack. With conventional weapons it won't last three weeks. They haven't factored the other important aspects of Indian defence preparedness. Don't they know that India has an air-force base in Farkhor, Tajikistan, a naval base in Muscat, Oman, and most importantly, it has a defence pact with Iran which allows Indians to use those bases during war-time? Then what happens when these countries automatically side with the Indians. Then, what will the Saudis do? They have very good relations with India and Pakistan. Who will they side with? Remember, ideologically Saudis and Iranians are opposed to each other. What will the allies of these countries do?" Prakash paused. He was thinking, "That is a summation of an ex-Army General of Pakistan as he stated to an International news network recently. This time Pakistan will be decimated in no time. It will fall back on its nuclear warheads and that is what I fear will destroy Pakistan from which it won't recover, or even if it does, it will take decades. In modern times any country, irrespective of how powerful or influential it may be, can't use nuclear weapons. Any country which uses it first will become an International pariah. That country will incur the wrath of the world and it will have no sympathisers. This isn't the forties. These are modern times where people determine the course a government must take."

Altaf Khos asked Prakash, "What did you mean by given the right ingredient it could become dangerous?"

Prakash shook his head with worry, "Desperate situations lead desperate people to desperate actions. This will be such a situation. Look at the plan in detail. They don't like the west and they hate Israel. What if some zealots, in frenzy blow up an embassy, or take hostages from any western country... or bring down an airliner and that country decides to hit back... and its friends come along with them. Or... what if one of the extremist groups drop a few bombs in Israel at the same time and Israel retaliates like it always does, and the Arabs decide to hit back at Israel and Israel's friends come to its support. It could lead to another world war. Or if there's a US embassy hostage like situation, like it happened in Iran before Islamic revolution? Or... a western diplomat is assassinated? What happens then? I am considering various situations, and every situation looks fragile. Those governments will be forced to take action; and when that happens, it will be a catastrophe. What will the world powers do then? In worst case scenario, a nuclear explosion will be all that will takes to engulf the entire world... and countries around the world will have to take sides. What do US and the NATO alliance do, or what will China and Russia do in this situation? Who will the Arab countries side with? Do the guesswork, gentlemen," Prakash saw frightened faces reflecting his own, "The world is sitting on a mound of gunpowder and it just needs is a tiny spark to blow the world apart. This is the biggest of all flashpoints in the world, and the most dangerous one; India-Pakistan!"

"But there are sane people who will ensure things do not go to that extent." Altaf Khos countered.

Prakash smiled sarcastically, "Remember what happened during Kargil war? If it wasn't for the US President, the joystick Generals may have launched. Had that happened, world wouldn't be what it is today. Mark my words; if there is another world war, Asia will be the battle ground and all the world powers will get themselves involved because the stakes will be too high."

Zubair grabbed the folder from Prakash, and after he read the contents again he had a dreadful feeling in his guts. He had a feeling that if it happened just as Prakash said, it could be far more dangerous than Prakash had stated, "I agree with your deduction but what I fear as a former Pakistani citizen is far grave. Wahid Khan will plunge Pakistan into an abyss from where it may never fully recover. If Pakistan launches nuclear warheads it becomes an International pariah as you rightly said. The scenario I see is beyond that. Pakistan will be in a mess like none before. There will be sanctions and trade embargoes. Even now it faces serious shortages in medicines, food, oil, arms and electricity. When embargo and sanctions are imposed there will be total chaos. There will be no foreign aid and Pakistan will have no assistance from any part of the world. Remember how Bush administration forced Pakistan to be an ally in '*fight against terror*', or else, as it had said to Musharraf regime that it will '*bomb Pakistan back into stone age*'. That will come true now because this time India won't relent and it will bomb Pakistan into stone-age. When India is done with Pakistan, then we will see the worst situation. The few ultra-rich families will flee Pakistan. Institutions will collapse. Without aid, there will be no economy to speak of, and the sub-nationalists will splinter the country into smaller nations and there will be no power to stop them. There will be never ending civil war and without law and order, it will become the breeding ground for extremists… another Somalia - a failed state. That is the grimmest scenario."

Altaf panicked when he heard Zubair's prediction. He cried in desperation, "Please help me stop this. I will do whatever it takes but I can't do it alone. I don't know how to do it; where to start. You people are influential, so help me," he said, and gazed into the carpet, "If I kill Wahid Khan, others within the core group will take the scenario and play it out."

Prakash was thinking precisely what Zubair had said earlier. He had to make prompt decisions and act immediately lest matters got out of hand. "I have to speak with Zubair Saheb alone. Kindly wait outside for us," he said to Altaf.

Altaf started to pick up his folder. Prakash slammed his palm on it and asked Altaf to wait outside. Altaf nodded and walked out. Prakash spoke to Zubair Ahmed and suggested a course of action. Half hour later, Zubair and Prakash agreed on a refined plan. It was the best way to defuse the situation, from its source.

Prakash Rohatgi saw the edgy Zubair Ahmed walk out of the door and turned to work trying to figure out a puzzle which disturbed him; vital information was missing from the papers. How could Wahid Khan merge the splintered groups of various extremist organizations into a united force? How would he infiltrate thousands of extremists simultaneously into India? Where was the cohesiveness going to come from? Logistics for such a grand operation had to be precise. The more Prakash thought about it the more he was puzzled. He closed his eyes for a few minutes to concentrate.

- - -

A sudden fear gripped Aman Bux when he got an 'urgent' text message from Prakash asking him to call 'immediately'. He and Rukhsar had checked into the resort when he saw the text message and two missed calls. He settled Rukhsar in the cottage reserved for them, excused himself and walked out to the garden and called Prakash. Prakash apprised him of the Altaf incident. Aman's fear grew by several degrees with each passing minute. Prakash asked if they would want to return to New Delhi. Aman promised to call him back after speaking to Rukhsar, but they both knew what her response would be.

Few minutes later Aman and Rukhsar were sitting in a car racing towards New Delhi.

Aman called Prakash for an update, and he was told not to discuss the matter while they were travelling. When Rukhsar asked Aman for an update, he provided the same answer as Prakash. Rukhsar was nervous, he knew. She was uneasy but couldn't do anything about it and that hurt her more. She was close to crying when she heard Altaf Khos had returned and just as worried when she learnt that Aman wasn't his main target, it was Zubair. Rukhsar had almost panicked. It had taken some talking and consoling by Aman to calm her.

*   *   *

GHQ, Pakistan Army

Rawalpindi, Pakistan

Wahid Khan smiled broadly. He had received a call from Altaf Khos telling him that Altaf had tracked the whereabouts of Zubair Ahmed to his ancestral home town in Akbarpur, near Lucknow and Altaf was on his way to Akbarpur. He would call back in a day or two when he had Zubair in his custody. Wahid Khan sighed in relief. He revisited the plan in his mind and tried to pick loophole it may have. He couldn't find any and that satisfied him no end.

Right pieces were being set in places. In three months they will be exactly where he wanted them to be. The incumbent government had to run its course until then. He would make his move only when he was ready. Intelligence reports told him that the government was extremely unpopular owing to high inflation, mis-governance and corruption. When nation is sick of the rulers is the time to strike. The civilians would welcome the army's takeover. Wahid Khan smiled. It was all turning in his favour. In two days Altaf will have taken care of the darkest episode of his career; a decision he regretted making at the spur of the moment but he had to impress that devil who was his uncle,

General Moinuddin. Thankfully for him, Moinuddin had not dumped him for it. On the contrary, he was recommended for his 'brave' action in adversity by his uncle, the crippled General. But now he had nothing to worry about. Skeletons in the cupboard made news if discovered. In his case, the skeletons will cease to exist when Zubair was out of the way.

Wahid Khan leaned back in his chair. He had a long list of meetings before starting his tour of the border areas. He was excited to check the border with India in Chamb sector. If he got a chance he would also cross the LOC to see how the preparations can be made for the infiltrators to go in before the regulars went in as *Mujahids*, mix with the real *Mujahids* and begin to wreak havoc in that area. Then it would spread to other areas. His dream of making Pakistan the regional super power by replacing India was going to come true. Then he would dictate terms to the cocky Indians. Wahid Khan smiled as he picked up the call. In twenty seconds his smile disappeared. Who could it be? Who could dare to prepare a secret dossier on him? There were people in the ISI who had asked questions. He had to find out and destroy the dossier along with the one who had prepared it, and the one who had ordered it. Wahid Khan wanted no hiccups in his plans. Anyone coming in the way was going to pay with his life.

*   *   *

Prakash Rohatgi's Residence,

New Delhi, India

When Prakash finished preparing a special dossier, a folder on Wahid Khan's plans, he discussed the draft and contents of it with Zubair. Zubair laughed after reading it. "You are going to punch a big hole in Wahid Khan's plans."

"Let's hope it works," Prakash replied sceptically tough he was sure his plan would work, "I want Aman's suggestion before I send these across to my contacts."

Zubair nodded but was still upset because Prakash had told Aman about the events against Zubair's advice.

"If I didn't tell them, they would have been upset and I want them on my side," Prakash defended his decision. He wondered if should tell Zubair what was on his mind. Then on second thought he spelt it out to Zubair, "I was thinking of asking Rukhsar and Aman to join us. What do you think?" Prakash asked hesitatingly.

"Are you sure it's a good idea? Aman, yes, but Rukhsar? Do you think she can handle the pressure?" Zubair asked.

"Give her more credit, Saheb. She is more courageous than I earlier thought and quite intelligent, certainly."

Zubair raised his head to look at Prakash with keen interest. "First you lure them to India and now you want them to join us? Aren't you expecting too much?"

There was a little smile on Prakash's face when he replied, "I don't think you are complaining."

A laugh escaped Zubair's lips, "No, I am not complaining. It would have been better though, if I had met them in situation where I wouldn't risk their lives."

"No one will harm them, Zubair Saheb. You have my word." Prakash said sincerely.

Zubair nodded his head. "I know."

"So? What do you think?"

"Ask Rukhsar."

- - -

It was late evening when they reached. Rukhsar dumped her bag in the hall and ran to her father's room. Zubair heard the door open and saw Rukhsar standing at the door staring at him with strange expression; a mixture of relief and anger.

Zubair rose and put his arms around her shoulder, "Don't be frightened, my dear. I am fine."

Rukhsar sank her head in his chest and sobbed. Zubair patted her back to comfort her but her sobs grew louder.

"*Abbu* is fine, Rukhsar," Aman said, standing behind her.

Rukhsar pulled her head back and looked at her father. "I am afraid for you and Aman, *Abbu*. Haven't you paid enough for your good deeds? Now they want you to die for it?"

"Death doesn't come at their wish, Rukhsar. It will come when God wishes it." Zubair said firmly.

"Whoever is responsible for this, I want him to pay with his life for this," She promised calmly, firmly.

"They will pay I promise you." Zubair said and escorted the couple to the hall.

Zubair made his daughter sit next to him. Rukhsar wanted to know the sequence of events and its reasons. Zubair asked her to relax and rest for a while. Rukhsar didn't budge. Zubair asked her to wait because Prakash had gone out and expected to return in an hour. Until then they had to wait because the room with Prakash's work station was locked. Rukhsar asked him to tell her anyway.

Purna came to the hall with snacks, tea and a jar of fruit juice for them. She greeted the guests and smiled at Rukhsar.

"Where is Altaf?" Aman asked Purna.

Purna pointed in the direction of a room. "I will send him down" she said and left. While they talked casually about the day's events and the journey to and from Shimla, they sensed emptiness in the house. Each could feel there was something missing but didn't know why. A few minutes later they saw Altaf Khos climbing down the stairs cautiously. He walked to the sofa and greeted them. Rukhsar and Aman acknowledged his greeting out of courtesy but without meaning it.

"I understand your resentment but please understand the scenario I was given. Zubair Sir was portrayed as a villain and our over-zealous '*General*' wanted him punished for treason. When I doubted his intentions and checked, I am here to see if we can work together," Altaf defended himself.

Rukhsar appreciated Altaf for his daring effort to follow his instincts and act on his morality but she couldn't overcome the fact that he had earlier come to kill her father. She did not reply to Altaf. Aman asked questions but there was nothing he could learn more than what he had already learnt through his conversations with Prakash.

Prakash rushed into the house with a big frown on his face. He was supposed to return in an hour from the time he had left but it had taken over five.

Prakash greeted Aman and Rukhsar, looking apologetically at them. "Welcome back! Though I wish it was a week later."

"Thank you for everything, Prakash," Rukhsar replied with gratitude. Now she knew what was missing from the house: Prakash's presence.

Prakash shook his head sadly. He turned to Aman and Altaf. "I think you both should be ready for a long night. It is going to be a brain draining night."

"I want to be there too," Rukhsar demanded.

"You must rest," Aman protested, echoing the sentiments of Zubair and Prakash.

Rukhsar was adamant, "You think I can rest? Whether you like it or not, I want to be present when you people make decisions. Pakistan is my country too."

Prakash looked at Aman and Zubair. Both men knew she wouldn't change her mind.

- - -

After dinner, Rukhsar, Aman and Altaf followed Prakash to his workstation. Prakash pressed three switches and screens lit up. Prakash asked Rukhsar sit to his left and Aman to his right, and Altaf sat behind him. Prakash went about his work for ten minutes before he turned to Aman, whispered softly into his ears ensuring others didn't hear him. They spoke for a few minutes before Prakash opened up the conversation with others.

Prakash handed Aman and Rukhsar copies of the folder brought by Altaf and a dossier on General Wahid Khan. Both studied the contents. In between, Aman kept glancing at Altaf appreciating what the man had done. It needed lot of courage to go against the orders of a man as powerful as Wahid Khan, and Altaf had exhibited courage. Aman waited for Rukhsar to finish before he spoke. "Prakash has certain ideas how we can stop the General from taking control."

"What's his plan?" Rukhsar asked.

"The General's plan is under wraps. It is a secret plan so he thinks no one can stop him. If we expose this he will be forced to quit, or at least he will back off for the time being," Aman said.

"If he is exposed, the General may speed up... pre-pone his plan and bring the date forward. He has huge support in the armed forces, we mustn't forget," Altaf opined.

"There is a chance that could happen but if this is exposed he won't have time to coordinate attacks. He isn't ready for it. He can't take on Indian might without extensive preparation. If he tries to launch without it, his plan will be a spectacular failure - he knows that. Even in such a scenario, he will need at least two months to get ready. However, by then, India will have reinforced its defences which will scare the hell out of him. The General will be aware of modern Indian Interceptor Missiles. Once these are strategically placed, the General's plan will be neutralized." Aman clarified.

"We are forgetting one thing. Wahid Khan must seize power before he can even think of any plan," Altaf reminded.

"He can easily manage a bloodless coup." Prakash declared.

Rukhsar was surprised how casually Prakash had said it, "How?" she asked.

"Do you know what bloodless coup is?"

Rukhsar shook her head, "No".

"You see the thousands of security personnel who guard the gates of the politicians and top bureaucrats? Their guns face the roads to prevent external threat. When the faces of the security personnel and their guns turn one eighty degrees, it's a bloodless coup. The protected become prisoner and the army takes control." Aman explained in brief, "A coup is meticulously planned and executed, especially the timing."

The simplicity with which Aman Khan had explained made the coup sound lot easier than it was, but the effect was massive. The idea of it being so simple scared Rukhsar. She nodded while

Altaf looked at Aman blankly. He was numbed with the thought that if there was a coup, the insane general could take any step he deems fit to execute his plans. Aman spread a chart on the table and explained what Prakash had planned. While explaining, an idea occurred to him and he told Prakash. Prakash appreciated the suggestion and they got to work on it. A few minutes later all agreed how it was to be executed.

"I will have to use some of my contacts for this, which I am afraid I am not at liberty to tell any of you, except Aman. I ask you two to please go to your rooms while we get on with what we have agreed," Prakash requested Altaf and Rukhsar.

The two felt it was an order which they could not override. Altaf rose and left the room. Rukhsar sat stoically refusing to move. Aman Khan tried persuading her but to no avail.

Prakash stared at Rukhsar coldly. "Rukhsar, understand this clearly. Aman doesn't know my contacts. I want a person to be present to observe if I make an error and so I chose him. People I am contacting are a clique which doesn't wish to be known. You must trust me. We are going to create so much heat; Wahid Khan's feet will begin to scorch. He will be shot into oblivion, or in the least, he will recede." Prakash's eyes looked merciless, but his affection for her was clearly visible. He patted her hand and requested her to go to and rest.

Rukhsar looked at Aman for support but found none. She rose and stormed out of the room. She was hurt and both men knew that. When Rukhsar left Prakash sat upright. "In six hours we have to create enough mess for this General to make his coming days the most difficult in his life."

Aman Khan Bux nodded.

"There is one thing though; you know that we are working in the interest of both our countries. I trust you, so I will ask you to swear to me about one thing," Prakash said.

"What is it, Prakash?"

"This is an emergency. I asked you to be here though your presence is not required here, you understand that too. The reason I asked you to be present here is to let you see what I am doing. But you will have to swear to me that you will not, under any circumstance reveal the names or designations of people with whom you hear me converse. It is imperative that these names remain between us and you will never ever contact or mention them in any way."

Aman Khan Bux, the ex-diplomat, or still in that position, he didn't know, clasped Prakash's hand, looked solemnly at him and nodded. Prakash held the hand firmly knowing that this bond won't be broken at any cost. He smiled broadly, "Also, name two people you know, who are potent enough to help us? They must be extremely trustworthy."

Aman grabbed a note pad and wrote down two names and passed it. Prakash looked at the names and beamed. Unable to control himself, he roared in laughter. Aman was confused. He gazed at Prakash with stupefied a look. Prakash bowed his head and controlled his laughter. "Who is the second man in your list?" he asked Aman.

"He is my boss, the Ambassador posted in Tehran."

Prakash told Aman to write the Ambassador's cell number. Aman Khan wrote it under the name and slipped it back to Prakash. "You don't want the number of the first person? He is a decent man who is General in the Pakistan army."

"I have his contact details," Prakash said with a mysterious smile.

"How?" a bemused Aman asked Prakash.

"Later," Prakash said and dismissed the question.

Prakash rose and walked to the opposite end of the room, asking Aman to follow. Aman's jaws dropped at the sight of a communication system he had never seen in his life. He saw a complex system open up when Prakash slid the doors aside. He saw Prakash flick a switch and punch password to operate the system. The system was over six feet wide and twenty inches high. It had audio-visual facility to communicate with six people at a time. It had some special features. Whenever a call was made from this system, if the receiver was known, it will flash a code name, if not, it would display a remote telephone number; that remote phone will relay automatically, if the receiver calls back on that number, Prakash explained. "Let's start with a beloved General Imran Saddiq Pathan. I have known him for over eight years," Prakash smiled and clicked on a button.

Prakash handed Aman a set of headphones. Aman heard the General's phone ring with an unusual humming ringtone. General Pathan's voice boomed, "How are you, '*Satya*' Prakash? I haven't heard from you in long time."

"Good evening, General. I was busy with something. You received my gift on your birthday, Sir?"

"Yes. Thank you. How is lovely Mehjabeen? Any news on that front?" General Pathan asked humorously.

There was a sudden, brief silence, Aman noticed. He didn't have to guess what the General meant by '*lovely Mehjabeen*'. He was surprised at the lack of information he had about his friend who had gone out of his way for his and Rukhsar's sake. Aman felt anger and empathy at Prakash, and he had to resolve this matter with him. True friends don't hold secrets!

"There is an important issue at hand, General." Prakash cut off the topic and switched to the matter at hand. "What do you know about General Wahid Khan?"

A chilled silence greeted Aman and Prakash. Finally, the revered General of the Pakistan Army asked softly. "Why do you ask about him, Prakash? Is this related to him and Zubair where an order was issued during the Kargil war?"

Prakash and Aman were shocked to learn that Pathan knew of the incident. They had an additional, external confirmation that Wahid Khan had issued the orders.

"That is an issue, but for later. Right now, we have a graver situation, Sir. Apparently, this... General Wahid Khan is planning something big and nasty."

They both heard a deep breath taken by the General. It was clear to them that General Pathan had information about this too. For a moment their minds were struck with fear. Could the General also be involved in Wahid Khan's scheme?

"For two days I have tried to find out if the rumours were true; things I heard from the junior ranks. I hope to get some leads by tomorrow. If this wasn't so serious and unless you were sure you wouldn't have called me at this hour. What I learnt has disturbed me. This General is highly ambitious and brutal. If there is any information you can provide, I will be obliged," General Pathan said nervously.

Prakash and Aman heard desperate, decent old army man literally begging for information. Prakash looked at Aman and wondered if he should let the General know what they had learnt. Would it be wise, they thought.

General Pathan understood the reason for hesitancy from Prakash's end, "Prakash, I alerted you about the man Wahid Khan had sent," he said to infuse momentarily lost confidence.

Prakash trusted the old General but the doubt was there. "I want you to speak to a man we both trust immensely, Sir. Kindly speak to Aman Khan Bux."

There was a sudden change in the tone of General Pathan. It seemed like he was speaking to his son, when he greeted Aman in response to Aman's voice. "How are you, son?"

"I am good, *Chacha*." Aman looked at Prakash and decided to trust his instinct about General's integrity. After all, Aman was a protégé of General Pathan. For seventeen minutes he provided and got information on General Wahid Khan.

When Aman was finished, Prakash spoke into the phone. "I am sending you a folder on our usual channel, Sir. Please revert at the earliest. I need your feedback on this."

After the call, Prakash opened two drawers and scanned the sheets and prepared a soft copy folder and sent it to General Pathan.

- - -

Prakash and Aman looked at each other for different reasons. Prakash wondered if he should tell Aman Bux about his kind of work and invite Aman to join the group. Aman wondered if should intrude into Prakash's personal life which Prakash had been guarding zealously. There were questions in his mind and he wanted the answers. Prakash's work was still a mystery and it went deeper as he found out more about the contacts Prakash had. And, who was *Mehjabeen*?

"*Satya*, in Hindi means 'truth'. Why did you and the General say it?" Aman asked.

"Later. We have work to do. It is your..."

Aman cut him off curtly, "Your '*later*' never comes. You said that earlier about yourself. It hasn't come."

Prakash ignored Aman's tone. He heard a friend's complain in the tone; a friend who cared and wanted to share. There was nothing Aman could do. Prakash tried to speak but again he was cut off, "Who is Mehjabeen?" Aman asked.

Aman felt he had touched Prakash's soft chord when he saw Prakash suddenly smile widely. "We have work to do. I will tell you about Mehjabeen 'later'. I promise you again."

Aman was frustrated. He was unable to reach into the man's heart. He also knew Prakash had his priorities. At the moment, Wahid Khan's devious plan was more important than personal matters. They heard the door open violently. Rukhsar barged into the room and stood between the two men. "I can't sleep. How can I sleep when we are in this situation?"

She looked at the faces of the two men and she was fearful. A dreadful feeling overcame her. Aman stared at Prakash and

Prakash was staring at a screen without emotion. She thought Prakash was seeing nothing or perhaps a scene from the past.

"What happened?" She asked them both.

Neither man replied. Aman was still looking at Prakash while Prakash was staring at him with raised his eyebrows daring him to ask again.

"Who is Mehjabeen, Prakash? You have to tell me... us. No *'later'* business this time." Aman asked him again.

Prakash's looked straight at Aman coldly, *"later"*.

Aman looked at Prakash in frustration and threw his arms in disgust. "You don't really treat us as your friends, do you?"

"Aman!" Rukhsar shouted at Aman and turned to Prakash, sitting next to him, "What is Aman talking about? Who is Mehjabeen?" She waited for him to reply. When no reply came, she urged him, "We are your friends. You can confide in us. If there is anything we can do for you, we will do it, I swear. Please tell me... us, Prakash. Who is this Mehjabeen? Is she your sweetheart?"

"Shut up you two," Prakash roared angrily. A moment later, he closed his eyes, "Mehjabeen is eleven years old. She is my daughter," Prakash whispered softly, sadly.

Rukhsar and Aman were silent. They looked guiltily at each other. Aman tried to speak but he choked. He tried to look at Prakash but Prakash and Rukhsar were staring at each other. Rukhsar felt the self-control Prakash had in him to stop the moisture from appearing in his eyes and yet he cried within. Aman was lost for words, "Prakash, I am sorry."

Prakash Rohatgi was quiet. His eyes were fixed on Rukhsar. She clasped his hands, gripping it firmly, providing him moral support, and offering her hand in friendship. She couldn't take her eyes off Prakash. She knew he was fond of her and her fondness for him was a little more than that. She liked him immensely; even loved him. Again, she felt his sadness, and his loneliness.

There was a well of sadness in Prakash which she felt was wishing to overflow but Prakash kept it away intentionally.

Prakash was moved by Rukhsar's concern and affection for him. He pulled his hand out of hers and patted her head with affection. "Thank you... both of you. I told you I will tell you my story, and I will. That is a promise," he said and spun his chair around to talk to Aman. "We have a schedule to keep. Personal problems can wait. Let's get to work."

Prakash offered Rukhsar a set of headphones. "I have only two pairs of headphones but this will do as nicely," he said and plugged an ear piece from his mobile handset. He turned to Aman, "Your turn. Talk to your boss. Make sure he talks about this to as many people as he can. Let's create a storm."

For the next twelve minutes, Aman spoke to Jaffer Sharif, the Ambassador of Pakistan stationed in Tehran, Iran. When the conversation was over, Prakash put the keyboard in front of Aman. Aman typed the address and sent an email and attached the folder to his boss.

Next on the list was a man of immense influence in the External Affairs Ministry in Islamabad. Prakash called '*Tiger*' Chowdhary Dastagir and briefed him in Urdu. Dastagir was petrified when he heard what Prakash said. He was unwilling to accept the story. When Prakash said he was sending a mail with irrefutable proof, Dastagir moaned softly. Prakash sent him the mail and got a call from Dastagir within ten minute. Dastagir promised to revert by following afternoon.

'Three gone and many to go', Prakash thought, checking his watch and calculated. It was three in the afternoon according to EST, Washington DC, USA. He dialled the number. This was going to be the most important call of all. If this contact collaborated Wahid Khan would become history. The bell kept ringing but the contact, Senator Gordon Shelley did not respond. Prakash waited for a few minutes and called again. There was no reply. Prakash hung up and sent a text message and waited. Gordon Shelley was an enigma to many. A second generation immigrant from Ireland, Shelley had worked hard from humble beginnings to where he was today. He was a man of principals and high moral values, and highly temperamental. He could blow hot and cold in less than a minute, especially when he knew he was right and if anyone dared to oppose him. After 9/11 he became a central figure around whom most sub-committees sanctioned or held back fund allocations for Pakistan and other nations whom Shelley considered *'rogue states'*. On every occasion he had justified his stance. In last eight years he had become an Indian lobbyist.

Aman asked about the importance of this particular Senator and Prakash told him why Gordon Shelley, the sixty-two old Senator was on his list. The man had the power to put severe conditions on US supplies to Pakistan, especially military supplies. He could influence an embargo on military supplies almost single-handed. A minute later Gordon Shelley called and spoke with affinity, "Hello, *'Satya'*, my friend, how are you?"

"I am good, *Grizzly*. I need your immediate attention on a matter or extreme emergency. I have sent you an email. Please check promptly and revert immediately, I request."

"It's that urgent, ha? Kay, my friend, I will call you back in ten minutes." Gordon Shelley said and disconnected the call.

While they waited for the Senator to call back, Prakash made another internet call to the Trade Commissioner in the Indian Embassy in Washington DC.,

Rakesh Baruah saw the name *'Satya'* flash on his cell phone. "Yes *'Satya'*. Tell me!"

Prakash repeated the information he had provided others and asked Baruah to check his email and revert promptly.

As he disconnected the call with the Trade Commissioner, he received a call from the Senator. "*'Satya'*, this is a tragedy.

This Wahid Khan must be crazy. Wait till tomorrow morning and see what happens. Lay back, '*Satya*', and watch the show. Let the '*Grizzly*' arrange a spectacle for you," the Senator said and disconnected the phone.

In the next two hours, Prakash called some more contacts in his list: two each in Paris, Tokyo, Berlin and Moscow, and one each in Rome, Canberra and Ottawa. He made another call to Beijing and spoke to '*Butterfly*' Zhing Jiao Ling and asked Ling to revert after scanning the folder. Zhing Ling, the former Chinese Ambassador to India promised to revert the following afternoon after checking from his end for additional information.

The next person on call was '*Falcon*', a secretary in the House of Lords. John Douglas Bentley cursed him jokingly for calling him when he was 'busy' at a pub, but promised him to revert before Prakash sat for breakfast.

Prakash leaned back in his chair and told Rukhsar to remove her earphones. "Why?" she asked.

"I ask you because you wouldn't like the conversation you will hear with my next two calls. Decency demands it."

"Then... I want to listen," she said with a naughty smile.

Prakash shook his head with controlled laughter. He dialled the next in his list. After three rings, a sleepy voice answered, "I am with my wife playing my favourite sport '*Satya*'. This is no frigging time to call, you lousy bugger. It's midnight here."

"It's five thirty in the morning here, you dumb oaf. I know Christine is in Shropshire. I will call her and tell her you are with '*sherry*'. If you don't want that, get your drooping, over-weight bum out of that stinking bed and get to work as I tell you or else I will start clipping your wings, '*Eagle*'. Tell me what you want." Prakash replied with equal vein of humour.

"There goes my '*sherry*'. I will make you pay for this, you dung beetle. I will call Mehru and tell her you are clipping me. You don't deserve her, old chap. She is..."

"Shut up!" Prakash screamed. "I have sent you a folder. I want you to check and investigate further and revert to me in not more than three hours," Prakash spoke angrily.

Forty-eight year old Christopher John Croydon of MI-6 was suddenly serious. Humour was gone and the field agent was alert. "Are you ok, mate? You are dead bloody serious. What's it about? Tell me, I am wide awake now."

Prakash controlled his sudden foul mood and briefed him.

"Is the General balmy or something? What makes the moron think he can get away with it? Never mind, I will check the files and come back by noon."

"Thank you, '*Eagle*'. I owe you one on this."

"Hey, come off it, will you? We are partners, remember. Your problem is mine. I will revert by noon. You take care of yourself and of Mehrunissa and Mehjabeen. All right?"

"I will. Span the wings and soar high, '*Eagle*'. I want the prey's remains, my friend... and give my regards to Christine. Bye."

Involuntarily Prakash's eyes swept across to his guests as they stared at him. He looked away and dialled a number.

A weird ringtone struck their ears. The call was answered by a soft voice. "My *Satya*! Why do you torture '*Mini*' in her dream? She was dreaming of you but you don't come to meet her. I was..."

Normally, Prakash would have gone along but he was not in a mood for private jokes. He cut her off. "*Mini*', '*Satya*' has serious problem. It is as big as Kargil. You helped us then. Help us again. I sent you files in a folder. Check and ensure your friends also see it... and spread it. If you don't want big trouble in the region get out of bed and check the usual channel. Call me back after you have shared it with members of your Committee and the board members."

Li Ming Lai, one of the senior members of the Communist Party became alert. She heard Prakash speak with zest and she knew how serious it was when he hadn't joked with her as he usually did. The forty-nine year old lady held her breath deep and asked him to wait on the call. Two minutes later she spoke again. "I have received your folder, *'Satya'*. I will see it and call you soonest. Take care, my dear friend."

Prakash disconnected the call and fell back in his chair. Aman and Rukhsar were observing Prakash. They knew a few more facts about him. He was extremely influential and it was made obvious by the very powerful and influential people he had spoken with. They also learnt to their pleasure that Prakash was speaking the truth right from start when he had stressed that he was working for India and Pakistan. They had also learnt that Prakash had personal relations with these people and they knew lot more about his life than them, or even more than Zubair, or so they presumed.

Aman and Rukhsar wondered if Prakash really considered them true friends. How come others knew so much about his personal life while they knew nothing; not even about the work he did or which organization he worked for, or with? It was abundantly clear that he and his organization were very powerful; influential enough to make dramatically influential decisions about nations. Prakash zealously guarded his personal life which made them wonder why. But on the other hand he made it possible for them to do things which they considered virtually impossible. In last six days he had been their host, friend, guide and certainly the best friend they had.

Rukhsar wanted to ask Prakash about another name they had learnt during his conversation with the MI-6 man. They knew who Mehjabeen was. Who was Mehrunissa? Why was

Prakash suddenly angry when she was mentioned? Rukhsar leaned forward, looked at Prakash and smiled. "You look really tired. You should rest," she suggested instead of asking the question she had on her mind.

"I am fine. We have to wait for few hours before we get feedback from these people. We can rest for some time and come back in the morning to see what we get but I doubt if we will get much. By tomorrow evening we should get more due to time zones involved," Prakash and rose.

Aman rose but Rukhsar sat rigidly in her chair. Prakash feared she might ask about Mehrunissa. He didn't wish to talk about it, not yet anyway. He wanted peaceful environment when he spoke about his personal life. They had earned the right to know. He leaned forward and said casually but his tone was pleading, "Let's not talk of matters which are not of immediate importance. When we are finished, or we have lesser pressure on our minds, we will talk about them."

Rukhsar bore into his eyes and knew he was speaking from his heart. She promised herself to let it go for now, but grill him when gets an opportunity next time. She nodded and followed Aman out of the room.

Prakash saw them leave and turned to his desk and got back to work. He had to speak to two most important people off all. He called his mentor, Nitin Tyagi.

*   *   *

THE WARS OF 1965

The war of Rann of Kutch and
The Indo-Pak war

Aman Bux led Rukhsar inside the room. At last, they were alone for few hours. Their honeymoon was truncated by destiny but they were alone now... with each other. Since they had arrived in India they had night long conversations whether they were in Akbarpur, New Delhi, Kolkata or Dacca. There was something weird about it all. But, they were alone now. Rukhsar sat next to Aman on the bed and leaned her head on his shoulders. Aman wrapped his arm around her and saw her staring at nothing in particular; her mind clogged with thoughts of what she had heard in last few hours. "Prakash is the best friend we have, isn't it?" she asked without raising her head.

"Yes, he is," he replied confidently and lay back on the bed, pulling her face over his chest.

"But, does he treat us like we are his best friends?" she raised her suspicion.

"He does. He is quite methodical and goes by his priorities. At the moment his priority is the situation, not his personal life.

I am sure we will see a different side of him once all this is over."
Aman analysed.

"Whenever I see him I see sadness and loneliness. But his
presence gives me a deep sense of safety and security. It is as if he
is protecting me... protecting us from every danger. How can I
feel it unless he has sincere concerns for us and for our safety and
happiness? It is strange. We met six days ago but I feel like we have
known each other for a long time." she said. She had felt it since
the day they had met Prakash in the hospital. Somehow, though
Prakash was good to them, he hadn't opened up to them. He was
holding back, not allowing them to peek into his personal life,
and that hurt her. The more she thought of it, the more it hurt.

"Yes, it's true. Some people take time to open up. Prakash
is one of them. I think he has deep wounds and he is scared to
touch them," Aman replied. He raised her chin to meet her eyes
and looked at the most beautiful face he had known. He pulled
her up and stroked her back. Rukhsar smiled and closed her eyes.
Aman slid her to his left, leaned over and kissed her.

Rukhsar heard the doorbell shrill angrily for the third time
when she opened her heavy eyes and called out at Purna to wait
and looked at the time. It was well past ten. She tried to move
out but couldn't. Aman's legs had pinned her lower body and
his hands held her torso tightly. Rukhsar looked at Aman's face
and smiled. He had a childlike expression; like he was smiling
in his sleep. She bent down and kissed him. Aman wriggled in
sleep and firmed his grip around her. She shook him a little but
he did not budge.

Rukhsar pulled his hair backwards softly, "I must get dressed,
dear. We are being called downstairs."

Aman opened his eyelids for a moment and shut it again, "forget the world. I don't care about it. I want to be with you." He murmured to her in half sleep.

Rukhsar laughed at the innocence of the statement. *"I wish the world was as simple and beautiful as you have made it for me right now."* She thought to herself. She leaned against his body and kissed him again.

When the doorbell shrilled again, Rukhsar shouted loudly. "I will be down in fifteen minutes."

Aman sat up in startle. "What time is it?" he asked, and then he looked at her and his expression spoke about his love for her and her eyes spoke of her love for him, and her soft smile reflected her happiness.

"This the most beautiful place in the world... the most beautiful moments of my life..." He said and kissed her.

Rukhsar surrendered herself to him. He was right; this was the most beautiful place in the world. He was right; these were the most beautiful moments of their lives. He was right; the world can go to hell. The moments of intimacy vanished as reality gripped them. Aman looked at his watch and tried to move. Rukhsar stopped him. "I will take time to get dressed so I go first," she said and ran towards the bathroom.

"Aah... Today I realize I am a married man," he joked as she was about to enter the bath.

Rukhsar turned around and smiled, "You better remember that," she teased him and shot towards the bathroom.

- - -

After breakfast, Rukhsar went to Zubair's room and Aman went to Prakash's workstation.

When Rukhsar entered she saw Zubair and Altaf having a heated discussion on something. She was surprised her father had let Altaf into his room. Altaf greeted her and she greeted him back as decency demanded. Zubair looked at her and he noticed she looked younger and prettier than the previous night. He saw radiance in her smile which wasn't there the previous evening. Stress and tension was gone and she looked relaxed. He smiled, "You look well rested. I understand you were up till six this morning," Zubair asked his daughter.

Rukhsar nodded. "I need to check what is happening." She said and rose to leave.

"When Prakash is free tell him I want to speak to him on a matter, but it's not so urgent," Zubair instructed her, "And tell him to rest. He hasn't had a wink since last night. Tell him it's an order," Zubair said seriously.

Rukhsar was startled. Her father's tone told her how dear Prakash was to him. There was a bond between them; like father and son, which allowed him to issue orders. Rukhsar felt a deep sense of relief. She didn't understand why, but the bond between her father and Prakash pleased her; probably because she knew that Zubair was with a man who would take good care of him always. She smiled happily. She now had a power over Prakash, she reckoned.

Aman entered the room and saw Prakash Rohatgi sitting in his chair leaning backwards with his head resting on his palms and eyes shut. Prakash heard footsteps and opened his eyes. "Did you sleep well?" he asked.

Aman looked at Prakash with concern. The man would break if didn't rest. "Yes, I did," he said "but looks like you haven't slept. You could have slept for some time."

Prakash didn't reply. He rose, went to the bathroom and he returned looking fresh and awake. Aman was sure the man had special gift of nature to endure such physical and mental strain and still look fresh when he wanted.

"I was about to leave this morning when my *'Tiger'* called. I mean Chowdhary Dastagir. He found out how Wahid Khan plans to infiltrate the *'Jihadi'* elements. That was the missing piece of the puzzle I was trying to find. Here, take a look," Prakash said and asked him to see the political map of India.

"How did *'Tiger'* find out so quickly?" Aman asked.

'Tiger' spoke to a Brigadier who had dropped a hint to join the 'team' which would lead to a 'glorious future of Pakistan'. Dastagir had taken it lightly and said that he would consider it. Last night, after his conversation with Prakash, Dastagir had called the Brigadier to see if the plan had any merit in it. The Brigadier had met Dastagir at the latter's residence early this morning and presented the plan which was prepared by their leader. Dastagir saw the plan and admitted that it was a good plan so far as the Indians didn't know of it. The only advantage the plan had was the element of surprise with the quantum of aggression General had planned. If they lost that element the plan would fail and there would be a downslide which the army won't be able to stop. The Brigadier assured him that the plan was top secret and only men within the inner circle, a total of ten including the four planners knew of it. After an hour of discussion, the Brigadier was able to convince his retired father's friend to join in.

Dastagir had accepted the offer with a motive. He wanted to get into the inner circle. *'Tiger'* Chowdhary Dastagir asked him for 'urgent' and 'vital' information to check if there were flaws. The Brigadier had obliged, and *'Tiger'* had sent it to Prakash.

"Let me show you," Prakash said and led Aman to the table where Prakash could operate the system. He took a large geo-political map of India, Pakistan and neighbouring countries bordering Pakistan and spread it on the table.

They saw Rukhsar enter the room with a beaming smile. Rukhsar started with fake anger and stern look on her face, *"Abbu* has ordered you to rest," she said and spoke to Aman, "he has been working all night."

Aman replied with equal concern, "I know. I saw how he looked when I entered." Aman said and turned to Prakash. "You really ought to rest, my friend."

Prakash laughed, "I will go on a vacation for a few days once we sort out this mess."

"Where to?" Rukhsar asked with a mysterious smile.

"Somewhere..." Prakash said as the word lingered in the air.

"Can't you tell us?" Rukhsar asked.

"How can I tell you when I am not sure?" he replied but not honestly. He knew exactly what he had planned.

Rukhsar and Aman looked at Prakash silently trying to read his mind. Prakash looked back at them with a lingering smile suspended on his lips which neither could read. Moments of silence passed without anyone speaking. Aman and Rukhsar had a clue about his plans, or at least they presumed they did. The silence was broken by a melodious tune of a flute playing an Indian classical *raga*.

Prakash dashed to his communication system and punched a button. "Close the door," he instructed Rukhsar.

Rukhsar shut the door and occupied the chair she had the previous night. Prakash handed them a pair of headphones and asked them to be quiet during the conversation. Prakash punched another button and they heard a voice speaking in accented Urdu. *"Tiger'* Chowdhary Dastagir explained how Wahid Khan was planning to push his army through the *'Rann of Kutch'* after the *'Mujahedeen Jihadists'* had played their role. They saw a map with arrows demarcating thrust areas from where the attacks would come. Preparations were well under way for the launch of *Jihadi* attacks in these areas - timespan was three months.

Prakash thanked *'Tiger'* and disconnected call. He took out a large print of the map Dastagir had sent and spread it on the table. Aman and Rukhsar followed him. Prakash laid the earlier map beside the one sent by Dastagir and compared the two. A gasp escaped his mouth.

"What?" Aman asked with worry.

"This is like revisiting the first war of 1965." Prakash Rohatgi said with obvious tension on his mind.

"You mean the Indo-Pak war of 1965?" Rukhsar corrected Prakash.

"No, I mean the first war of 1965. The later Indo-Pak war of 1965 was a short war. The first war fought in 1965 went on for several weeks. When it stopped, the actual war of nineteen sixty-five war broke out," Prakash stated.

Aman and Rukhsar were confused. They had never heard of this war. "What about that war?" Aman asked.

"That was an invasion by Pak forces in the *'Rann of Kutch'* and they achieved limited success. Pakistani establishment under General Ayub Khan launched *'Operation Desert Hawk*, in January '65," Prakash said and lifted the maps to a board on the wall and pinned them side by side. He put his finger on the *'Rann of Kutch'* area circling the area bordering Pakistan. "This entire region is inundated with sea water for months during monsoon. It is several metres under sea water in most places. Most of the area is marshy land. In '64 Pakistan forces had acquired the ultra-modern state of the art 'Patton' tanks from US, along with fighter aircrafts which were inducted the same year. These inductions gave Pak armed forces a much needed military superiority over the Indians who were still smarting after losing the China war less than two years earlier," Prakash explained.

"What provoked the war?" Rukhsar asked.

"There was no reason for it. I think it was a trial run to test Indian resilience and also test the military preparedness of the Indian army." Prakash clarified.

"What excuse could there have been for this war?" Rukhsar asked.

"The '*Rann of Kutch*', bordering Sindh province, is the Kutch region in Gujarat. Pakistan claimed that it was their territory and it had a right to the entire body of water which divides the two countries." Prakash said and put his finger across the area on the map. "As you can see here, Indian forces are at distinct geographical and strategic disadvantage here. Solid ground ends a few kilometres along the borders of Pakistan. To the south of it starts the area of the 'Rann of Kutch'. The 'Rann of Kutch' has severe disadvantages. Firstly, the entire '*Rann*' is virtually a swamp when it is not inundated with sea water from the Arabian Sea. To its north is Pakistan and to its east and North-East are the deserts of Rajasthan. So, for huge stretch of this area it is difficult to constantly patrol border posts. I am not sure why Ayub Khan Regime ventured into this war except to test their new weapons, tanks and aircrafts and test the Indian armed forces at the same time. Anyway, these tanks rolled into the Indian Territory and occupied a large area close to Kanjar Kot Fort. It took several weeks to flush out the Pak army from that area and the war ceased when British Prime Minister Harold Wilson intervened and brokered a peace around end April '65. Barely a month later, in mid-May '65 war broke out when '*Operation Gibraltar*' was launched in the Jammu and Kashmir. After the..."

Aman intervened, "What inspired the second war?"

"There was a combination of reasons. First, in December of '63 a sacred relic mysteriously disappeared from the shrine of '*Hazratbal*'. As the name suggests, this is a hair from the Prophet's head which was kept in the shrine. Kashmiris came to the streets in agitation. Within a week, the relic mysteriously reappeared on January third, '64."

"You mean the actual hair of The Prophet?" Rukhsar asked in awe and astonishment.

"Yes, the actual hair from Hazrat Prophet Mohammed's head is in '*Hazratbal*'," Prakash reconfirmed.

"The replacement was the real?" she asked sceptically.

"It is the original. The Government under Pandit Nehru set up a committee which comprised of clergies, politicians and local leaders. This committee confirmed in February, 1964 that the hair was the real relic. Kashmir became peaceful once again but probably, and I am guessing here, this incident gave false perception to some people in Pakistan establishment that Kashmiris had revolted against the Indian rule. President Ayub Khan, some Generals and Foreign Minister Zulfiqar Ali Bhutto hatched a plan to use it to their advantage. *'Operation Gibraltar'* was launched. Regular army was sent into Jammu and Kashmir with a vicious plan. About thirty thousand men were trained for guerrilla warfare and sabotage, with a military officer at the helm of ten companies of around one hundred soldiers. Many such companies were infiltrated across the border." He stopped suddenly, and then laughed.

"What?" Rukhsar asked.

Prakash laughed heartily. "I am sorry. I shouldn't laugh," he said seriously, "I was laughing at the irony. Do you know that the groups had been given names? All were 'invaders' of India. The groups were called *Tariq-bin-Jihad Force, 'Mohammed-Bin-Qasim Force, Mohammed Ghaznavi Force, Salahuddin Force* and so on. Each man in this group, dressed in civilian clothes, carried at least two guns each with loads of ammunitions. They were instructed to find local civilians and instigate them to take up arms against the local and central government. This failed miserably because instead of using the guns, the locals caught and handed them over to the authorities. When the local government got sense what was happening it asked for central assistance. When military arrived, most of these armed men who weren't caught left their arms and ran across to the other side of the border. *'Operation Gibraltar'* flopped."

Prakash stopped when he heard the door open and turned to see Zubair walk in. Prakash returned to his discussion, "After this failure, Ayub Khan Regime launched its third offensive, *'Operation*

Grand Slam." This was open aggression. This time, Pakistan army launched an attack in the *Chamb* and *Akhnur* sector of Jammu and Kashmir. They wanted to cut off Jammu and Kashmir with rest of India, north of Jammu city with surgical strike on Akhnur Bridge which was the only land route between rest of India and Kashmir. By cutting off Srinagar-Jammu highway, they could gain strategic control over Kashmir region. Pakistan army was well entrenched and well prepared for this assault. With superior arms and early advantage, apart from terrain advantage, it was difficult for Indian army to take back the posts. The Indian government, and Prime Minister Lal Bahadur Shastri, decided to give Pakistan a befitting reply, and he broadcast on the radio saying, *'arms will be replied with arms'*. The Gandhi-Jawaharlal Nehru policy of 'peace with thy neighbour' failed, so Shastri*ji* ordered the Indian army to cross the International border and go into Pakistan. Within ten days the Indian army was standing on the outskirts of Lahore and Sialkot."

Rukhsar interrupted Prakash and asked her father, "Why do we celebrate 1965 war as our victory?"

Zubair laughed, "Probably because they succeeded in stopping the Indian army from taking Lahore and Sialkot."

"So, contrary to what we are being taught in history books, actually India won that war, not us?" Rukhsar asked.

"Not really!" Zubair replied, "War stopped when Russians intervened. India tilted towards Russians because they were supplying arms to India after the Sino-Indo war. India heeded to USSR premier's invitation to sit and sort out the matters. Ayub Khan, Bhutto and Prime Minister Shastri sat over the negotiations for six days and in the end, on January 10, '66 they signed the 'Tashkent' peace agreement."

"So, who won the war eventually?" Rukhsar asked Prakash.

"No one won that war! It was a stalemate. Had it gone on for another week probably India would have won it hands down." Prakash replied.

"I don't believe that. India asked its foreign friends to broker peace." Rukhsar said and suddenly lowered her voice as she whispered to Aman, "We are told India *'begged'* its friends in the International community to help them out."

Zubair Ahmed chuckled, "I will give you a book by General Musa Khan of Pakistan army who participated in this war. In his book he gives details of how Pakistan army had run out of ammunitions in a fortnight. The 'superior' *'Patton'* tanks were destroyed and Air Force rendered useless ten days into the war. He tells how Pakistan Government at the time requested *'its'* friends to broker peace with India." Zubair replied with anger. "The bastards just don't stop lying and the result is this," he said, pointing to the maps. "This is the nett result of all lies we were told all these years. There is no accountability so it keeps happening over and over again. They commit blunders and cover them with outrageous lies. The moron who dreams of becoming a *'great regional power'* has no idea how close he is to destroying Pakistan. These idiots, power drunk people lose their mental equilibrium when they come in power. This will be his graveyard..." Zubair Ahmed silently looked at the map and then turned to Rukhsar and Aman. "I can't forgive him for killing my eleven men." Zubair turned to Prakash. In a mellowed tone, he ordered Prakash, "If you care for me, I want you to destroy this man. Do whatever is in your powers. I want you to..." Zubair paused, and then he said calmly, "I want you to kill him, Prakash. If I treat you as my son, you have a duty towards me. *'Kill this man'*, he is evil." Zubair said to Prakash and looked at him with pleading eyes. He wanted to add something but he choked. He looked at his daughter and son-in-law, trying to control the tears but felt helpless. Zubair stormed out of the room leaving its occupants wondering why he had cried.

They were stunned at Zubair's orders. Rukhsar had many thoughts but the one she held on to, was the one where her father had called Prakash his son. She looked at Prakash who was staring at the door. Involuntarily, an emotion escaped his mouth, "So much love for his country and the man is condemned to live in exile," he said and looked at Aman.

Aman Bux was also staring at the door. He understood two things: Zubair loved Pakistan, and second, he loved Prakash as much as he loved his own daughter.

"He is right. Wahid Khan is evil. He must be destroyed but I don't want him dead. I wish he lives a life of indignity. That is apt punishment for a traitor," Prakash spoke softly.

Rukhsar looked at Aman and returned to the question she wanted to ask, "Did you know the truth about the '65 wars?"

"I knew about the war being a stalemate but the war in the *Rann of Kutch* is news to me," Aman replied honestly.

Rukhsar was silent. She was sad. Prakash and Aman looked at her, "What's the matter?" Prakash asked worriedly.

Rukhsar spun her chair and looked at the maps on the board. "Again I have the sad feeling and it's getting worse. It seems I have been living a life of lies. I am supposed to be an intelligent woman, a lecturer at that, in a renowned University and my own system teaches lies. Generations have passed living the lies. We have poisoned those innocent minds which should have been told the truth. Now we learn that they are on the verge to making another mistake," she cried out.

"This time however," Aman Khan said seriously, worriedly, "If these people make that mistake, Pakistan will cease to exist. We have to stop them," he said firmly.

"Why was the war fought in the first place? Bhutto was an intelligent man. Why didn't he stop Ayub Khan?"

Prakash chuckled, "Bhutto went along with Ayub Khan's plans. I wonder if you know... at the time Bhutto was gaining in popularity while Ayub Khan was losing it rapidly."

Rukhsar looked at Prakash Rohatgi blankly. "Why would he go along if Ayub Khan was losing his popularity? He would rather oppose Ayub Khan."

"True. But you forget that Bhutto was a great politician. In an interview with one of the most renowned journalists, he had candidly admitted that if Pakistan was to win Kashmir, Bhutto would become a hero and if Pakistan lost the war, Ayub Khan would take the fall. As it happened, Ayub Khan had to go."

"Ayub Khan's regime was not great but Pakistan saw some progress in his tenure. Why was he losing his popularity?" Rukhsar asked innocently.

"To give legitimacy to his rule, he wanted to be 'elected', so an election was 'organized' rather than 'held' where he won the election but only after it was heavily rigged. The problem was that he contested against the sister of a legend; a legend in her own right: Fatima Jinnah! When elections were rigged, there were street protests throughout Pakistan. That was one of the first reasons. It was compounded by abusive language Ayub Khan had used for Fatima Jinnah. In a British press, in an interview he went so far as to call her an Indian agent. Secondly, all democratic rights of states and provinces were forfeited and people of these regions rioted. There were many casualties in the brutal clampdown on protestors. Then there was an appalling incident for which he was personally held responsible; his sons were accused of abducting an Inspector General's daughter. There were issues like non-development, civil unrest, poverty, and misrule in the country. He wrote a political autobiography in 1967 'Friends, not Masters' which many thought as American appeasement and he was criticized for it. Given such a scenario Ayub Khan needed a redeeming factor. He had nowhere to look so he planned *'Operation Gibraltar'* and after the collapse of this attempt, he launched *'Operation Grand Slam'*."

"Why did he relinquish power?" Rukhsar asked.

"Inflation!" Aman replied, "What Prakash said is true but the important factor was large scale inflation, especially wheat flour and sugar. This affected all classes of society and this was one failure which people couldn't digest. He appointed Yahya Khan as he successor and went into oblivion."

Rukhsar was forming an idea in her mind which neither man would know for the moment. She wanted to tell them when she had made up her mind; a decision when she would pronounce, would shock them all.

Prakash turned to the maps on the board. He knew he had to get help. He had to involve a man who he did not want to call unless it was an emergency. This was an emergency. He slid his chair to his communication system and sat for a while before he dialled.

"Karun Verma here!" Prakash heard a deep throated voice of the man he feared calling.

"Prakash Rohatgi!"

"Hello, Prakash. I haven't heard from you in weeks. All must not be well if you have to call me. Tell me what it is." The man at the other end asked politely.

"I have a situation in hand which could be of great interest to you," Prakash said and briefed him on the situation.

Karun Verma asked candidly, "This is a matter for RAW and MI. Why are you calling me?"

Prakash laughed softly, "There is just one man I know who is on the payroll of one but works for more than three: Karun is working for the 'Central Bureau of Investigation', whereas he, as Vilas Deshpande he works for 'Military Intelligence' and I know, he as Jagdish Prasad works for the 'Research & Analysis Wing'. With one call I make to you I am able to reach all three. Cut the crap and listen carefully." Prakash said and provided detailed information.

They spoke for over thirty minutes and this time Prakash was being interrogated. He gave all the information he had and asked Verma to revert promptly. Karun Verma promised he would revert before the evening was out. Prakash kept his headphone aside, disconnecting the call and sighed in relief.

Aman was confused. "How can one man work for so many organizations?"

"He volunteers for any organization which has a problem with Pakistan. Karun Verma is one of those men who can volunteer to go into a war zone and promise you that he will return in one piece, that too after succeeding in his mission. He has created a reputation which is incomparable with any. Karun has a valid reason for it," Prakash paused thoughtfully and spoke again, "after the second Simla agreement between Mrs. Gandhi and Mr. Bhutto, prisoners of war were exchanged. India sent over ninety-three thousand POWs and got about two thousand in return. However, there were at least fifty-two POWs whom Pakistan denied holding because they were tortured and they were physically incapable of moving on their own but they were kept alive. Few others lost their mental balance. Karun Verma's father, a Colonel was held for twenty years without being acknowledged as a POW. When Karun Verma joined the Intelligence network he sought information about his father. After a year or so he learnt that his father was held in a prison near Peshawar. God knows what identity he used or how he reached or what contacts he used, but Karun met his father in jail. He saw his father's condition and he couldn't bear it. His father was mentally unstable to recognise or even remember his son and physically incapable of moving a step on his own. Karun thought of forcibly getting him out of the prison but that was impossible. Karun knew his father could never be physically or mentally fit again. He pulled out a capsule from shirt collar and put it in his father's mouth and asked him to chew it. The large dose of potassium cyanide took its effect promptly. His father died in a minute. Karun left and returned to the prison later that night with two men. He blew up half the prison compound. Many people were dead including six policemen who guarded the prison. He put his father's body in a jeep and drove it to a forest nearby where he cremated his father and performed the last rites. From that day, Karun Verma volunteers if there is any Pakistan problem. The irony is, though we know him by many names, no one knows his real name."

"You make him sound like John Rambo," Aman joked.

Prakash Rohatgi stared at Aman without commenting on the poor sense of humour.

Aman realized what he had said and apologised, "I didn't mean it the way it came out. What I meant was that he seems to be quite a potent force."

"Bare handed he is good enough for three like me. And his contacts are remarkable. His problem is that he goes into overkill. That's why he is rarely called up. I had one chance of working with him and trust me when I say that he is excellent in what he does, I am still grossly understating it."

Their conversation was interrupted by music of a guitar played violently in sync with heavy metal drums.

Prakash grabbed the headphones. The three listened to the information the caller had.

"Thank you, for reverting so soon, '*Eagle*'."

"When '*Satya*' threatens to call my wife and tell her about my activities, '*Eagle*' must soar. Listen now! I have confirmed news about Wahid Khan. He will be visiting the border along your LOC in Skardu region. My Rawalpindi colleague tells me he is planning to cross the LOC to your side for personal inspection. My advice is, get this bugger there because he had brought forward the date of his takeover. He is planning to topple the government in a month and take over."

"Christopher, you know we don't do that unless it is the last resort. Moreover, we want to neutralize him… I mean, stop him from taking over. We can't allow another dictator to take over a civilian government."

"Rohatgi, my mate, listen carefully. Get Wahid Khan on the hills. It is better than risking the lives of thousands of soldiers, or… two million civilian deaths. I say because I have solid information that he has three men in his inner core who within them, are capable of launching nuclear warheads. This is too close for call, mate. I wish I could do it. This frigging General isn't worth our morality or principals. Eliminate the evil from the source. Let me know what you want to do and whichever way you decide, I will help you out. I have pushed the file to many corners. The papers will be flying all over the place."

Prakash Rohatgi thanked the efficient genial giant from MI-6 and promised to call him back.

- - -

Prakash turned to Aman to talk when another call came through with a whistling tune.

"Good Afternoon, *'Mini'*."

"I visited the Defence Ministry. They know the reputation of this General and they don't like him here, *baby*. Our man in Islamabad has informed the Defence Ministry in Rawalpindi that we will stop supply of essential material if this General comes to power, or if he is appointed Commander in Chief. That is the good news. There's bad news too. This General is going to your LOC. We know that he is going to Chamb. He is in your area so take him out. We support you. Pakistan cannot say anything if he is on Indian Territory."

"Thank you, Li. Your good news is very good. It will make the General think again. I will call you back."

"Uh... you say that again? I don't get a call from you for one year? Come to Beijing, dear." Li teased him as she usually did.

Prakash laughed loudly and thanked her after promising her to call back as soon as he can. He terminated the call.

"She has real the hots for you. Be careful with her," Aman said as he laughed.

"That is furthest from truth. She is nearly fifty and lonely. We are quite friendly. Three years ago she told me of her one sided love story. I told her that she will be fine when she finds love of her life. Jokingly I had added that if she didn't find anyone, she can count on me. Ever since, it is our private joke. But don't be fooled by her sweet talk. She is tough as steel and supremely efficient in her job."

Aman nodded, though he was still smiling. Rukhsar looked at Prakash suspiciously, though she too believed his story.

Prakash looked seriously at Aman. "In few minutes we have received two confirmations that Wahid Khan is on tour of the border posts which are going to be his launching pads for the assault I presume. The suggestions are, take him out... meaning, *kill him*. That is a solution. But I have a problem. We, in principle don't believe in that solution. It is only in the extreme case when it should be resorted to, and so far, to our good luck, we never had a situation where we had to use it."

"You let go of Altaf. He could have been quite dangerous," Rukhsar reminded him.

"That was as a calculated risk. I had gambled. I thought he would either be detained in New Delhi and stay in captivity for some time or else he will be deported to Pakistan and he won't return in near future. I was wrong." He thought for a few seconds and asked her, "Didn't my gamble turn out to be a blessing in disguise?"

She had to accept that it was a lucky break.

"I didn't expect him to get away. If he hadn't turned up at the door, I would have learnt of his whereabouts. Then I would have done something." Prakash explained. "Anyway, I have to speak to someone who is quite experienced in such matters. That will help me in arriving at a decision."

"You don't have to do it yourself. You can ask Karun Verma to do it." Aman suggested, and endorsed what others had suggested. Wahid Khan was large enough threat to be killed without being given a second thought.

"Yes, I can do that. I will take a decision when I am sure it is the only option left," he said thoughtfully, "I met my mentor this morning and on his suggestion I called Karun. I did not call Karun Verma to avail his services. As I said, he is highly resourceful and with excellent contacts. When I fed him informations, the idea was to spread it out to the Indian Military and important people in the government. I would ideally like to see this being handled by the bureaucrats and politicians. They don't look at war as an option. They use these informations to scare the adversaries. Believe me; this must be spreading like wild fire throughout the bureaucratic circles in every important country. That was the reason I sent it out to as many countries as I could possibly send, without overplaying it. It will work like a magic wand. One swoop and all is gone. By next week we may have dramatic news coming in on this. You will see."

Aman nodded. He was a diplomat and he knew how such informations were traded and bargained with.

Prakash smiled suddenly, "have you noticed? This General isn't really good at choosing his men. Obviously, there can't just be one person who gave information to three sources. First information came to us from Mr. Dastgir. He told us that he got the information from a Brigadier about areas from where they plan to launch their assault, in '*Rann of Kutch*'. Next came from MI-6 and the third from a Communist party member in Beijing. The General's close quarters are riddled with informants. The Indian Intelligence networks must be on to it. This General, unless he is something special is destined to go down, Aman."

"Is there anything else we can do?" Rukhsar asked Prakash.

"There is only so much we can do. We provide information for the benefit of all concerned. We can't make decisions like intelligence agencies or Governments. We give information to various sources and we know they will act promptly. That is all we can do."

Rukhsar and Aman had the same question on their minds. It was time they knew the answer. Aman Bux asked Prakash first,

"What is your organization all about? Who do you work for, or on whose behalf?"

Prakash pondered for some time and started to answer. Just then Purna asked them to come to the hall where Zubair was waiting for them at the table for lunch. As the three rose Prakash stopped when he saw a green light turn on. He checked the short message. Wahid Khan's plans came up in detail. He was going to Skardu as scheduled.

* * *

The Records Office,

Islamabad, Pakistan

Junaid Saleem stepped out of his office a happy man. He had the information UAE Embassy had asked for. Junaid was glad he was doing his country remarkable service though he was working in a non-descript government department with well-paid but unenviable job. He checked his bag to ensure he had the papers. He slapped it shut, stepped out of the elevator and rushed to the basement car park.

Saleem fidgeted with the keys of his beaten old car which had already clocked over one hundred thousand kilometres. He saw the guard approach and greeted him as usual. The guard saluted him and came closer. He asked Junaid if he was having trouble with the keys. Junaid joked saying it was nothing compared to what his wife was going to do when he reached home and they laughed at the crude joke. Saleem squatted in his seat and he froze; he saw the end of a silencer attached to a gun aimed at his face. The guard fired twice at the head. He looked around and pulled out the three page document from Saleem's bag. He put the bag back in the car and returned to his cabin. He called the number he had been asked to memorize, and told the receiver that he had the papers. The guard was thanked for the good job and told to deliver it as instructed.

The guard notified his superior that he had found Junaid Saleem dead in his car; he had been shot. When asked, he said he had no idea who shot him or when it happened because his cabin was seventy feet away in the other direction.

*　　*　　*

Prakash Rohatgi's Residence

New Delhi, India

Zubair looked at Prakash, "Without rest it is impossible to make right decisions. If your brain is rested it performs better you told me two years ago, remember? The world has seen two world wars and countless wars but nothing has changed. We keep waging wars without thinking of a solution which could end it once and for all. Forget the Wahid Khans of the world and rest for a while," he ordered again.

Prakash pointed at Rukhsar and Aman, "I told them I will take a vacation after we sort out this mess."

Zubair smiled broadly, "Pahalgam, I am sure."

A frown replaced Prakash's smile. He didn't expect Zubair to mention Pahalgam openly. "I am not sure," he lied.

"You are a poor liar." Zubair said with disappointment.

Prakash didn't reply.

"Why Pahalgam, *Abbu*?" Rukhsar asked. She was able to put two things together; a name and a place.

Her father did not reply. He was staring at Prakash.

Prakash rose from his chair, "excuse me, I have a lot of work to do," he said and walked towards his workstation.

Rukhsar and Zubair looked at each other while Aman stared at Prakash's back. Prakash had confirmed by his action that Pahalgam was his destination. Why was he hiding it from them? Aman rose from his chair and followed Prakash.

Rukhsar asked Altaf and Purna to leave them alone. When the two left Rukhsar turned to Zubair, "*Abbu*, Pahalgam and Mehrunissa... are the two connected?"

Zubair was surprised, "How do you know that name?"

"I heard it from someone I don't know. Who is she?"

— - - -

"I am not willing to work with you anymore, Prakash. I feel insulted that you can talk to others about your love life but not us. You said we are your friends. You must prove it now or else I leave with Rukhsar right away. I am not threatening, I mean it." Aman threatened Prakash with an ultimatum.

"Don't use emotional blackmail. It doesn't suit a decent man like you," Prakash replied with a smile.

"Think what you wish. I mean what I said. Either you tell me or we walk out, I swear." Aman persisted.

Prakash took a deep breath, "Let Rukhsar come."

"I will tell her. You tell me about Mehrunissa and Mehjabeen, and tell me in detail."

Prakash had a delightful smile when he began, "Mehjabeen is Mehrunissa's daughter..."

— - - -

"Prakash was an intelligence officer with MI, the Indian 'Military Intelligence'. Seven years ago when he was stationed in Srinagar he received information that *Jihadi extremists* were planning to attack the Holy Hazratbal Shrine. Prakash was at..." Zubair was answering Rukhsar.

'That's the shrine with The Prophet's hair?"

"*Yes!* That is the one." Zubair replied in obvious anger.

"How can *Jihadis* do that? Didn't they know about the relic?" Rukhsar asked with a confused look on her face.

"Oh, they knew! The idea was to blow up the shrine and let Kashmiri people and Muslim world blame *Hindu* India for not protecting their Holy relic," Zubair replied sarcastically.

"How can *Jihadis* think of attacking or destroying a relic of such reverence? This is sacrilege of the highest order. Were they real Muslims?"

"All were Muslims; trained and armed by Muslims; sent to attack by people of an '*Islamic*' Republic, in the name of *Holy Jihad*. The irony is that the security personnel guarding the relic were all Hindus of the 'National Security Guard'. Many security men died defending the shrine," Zubair said, "One of the most sacred relics of the Islamic world was violated by a sacrilegious act, at a sacrosanct place - the shrine where God destined the hair of *Hazrat Prophet* be kept. What could be a greater sin than this? Who are '*Kaafirs*', the attackers, or the defenders of that relic? Isn't that a point to be discussed?"

"Was the shrine damaged?"

"Not on this occasion. Before it could be attacked, the nine militants were killed."

"You mean that it was attacked earlier too?"

"Yes."

"What happened to the relic?"

"It is safe."

Rukhsar was stunned. She had learnt the truth about many things, especially the war and the lies which were propagated in Pakistan. Off all, this was the most stunning revelation. She wanted to cry. Her own country was lying to her. She started to realize and understand why Zubair was against Pakistan's military and civilian establishment. He knew the truth about these incidents and acts of sacrilege perpetrated by a nation which prided itself in being an *'Islamic'* Republic.

"The *Islamic Republic* of Pakistan," she murmured to herself.

Zubair understood what she meant and felt. "What is *Islamic* about Pakistan, *Beta*?" he called her fondly, "This *Islamic* nation has violated every tenet of *Islam*. The holy word of *'Jihad'* where a man fights the evils within is turned into an external war. The country lives a lie whereas 'Truth' is the cornerstone of Islam. Peace is the message of Islam and we keep training, arming and sending misguided youths to their deaths in the name of *'Jihad'*. Is that a tenet? *Sacrilege!*" Zubair moaned in agony, "They have turned Pakistan into a 'Terror Sponsoring State'. A terrorist attack in any part of the world and involuntarily world turns to Pakistan and its involvement somehow," Zubair was fuming and breathing heavily.

Rukhsar tried to stop him from speaking but Zubair was in a raging mood again. "Our country is called 'Islamic *Republic*'. Strange, isn't it? Since independence, for major part it was ruled by dictators. What's *'Republic'* about Pakistan? We fight amongst ourselves. The Sunnis and Shiites hate each other; the *Qadiyanis* are not considered Muslims vide a document signed by Bhutto. The Baloch, the Sindhis, the Punjabis, the Pashtuns, the Hazaras and the rest dislike and hate each other. Where is the *'Republic'*? Elections are rigged and we call ourselves democratic. Are we?" Zubair said it more as a statement than as a query.

Rukhsar's eyes were fixed on the table. She was listening, analysing and understanding what her father was saying. She knew he was right. After uncovering of so many lies, she had come to a stage where if anyone said lies about her country, she won't doubt it very much. She had to maintain her sanity. She was now trying to analyse every word that was said to her and reason with it. In this instance too she knew she couldn't defend the indefensible. She had a sinking feeling in her heart. She shrugged off the thoughts and tried to think of something else. "You were telling me about Mehrunissa."

"Yes..." Zubair replied softly. He had intentionally diverted the topic to avoid infringing into Prakash's personal life. He wanted Prakash to tell her what he wanted to say.

"*Abbu*..." Rukhsar persisted.

"Prakash will tell you his story. I don't want to intrude into his personal life," Zubair told her honestly.

"He is like your son, you said. Is it fair that I don't know about him, especially after what he done for me... for us?"

Zubair was silent. He was wondering if he should tell her but she was right. They were both equally dear to him.

"Without Prakash we wouldn't have met. We wouldn't have met *Dadaji* or his family. We could have never visited Dacca without Prakash. We owe him. If there is anyway, I want to help him," Rukhsar persisted.

A faint smile appeared on Zubair's face. He had a right to be a little selfish. He wanted to see Prakash happy and if that meant interfering with Prakash's personal life, he didn't care. Hadn't Prakash taken liberty to bring Rukhsar and Aman to India and then got them married? Now it was his turn. Zubair suddenly had childlike exuberance. He turned to Rukhsar. "Prakash received news of the attack and dashed to Srinagar. *Jihadis* were already engaged in a gun battle with security force defending the shrine. The shrine's walls were damaged from grenade attacks. There were casualties, on both sides. All attackers were killed and some security men died... nine I believe. Among the dead *Jihadis* was a man from the outskirts of Muzzafarabad in Pakistan held Kashmir. His name was Rasool Pervez. After gun battle was over and the shrine was secured, the process of identifying of militants began. These attackers traced back to their home towns. Rasool Pervez was different from others, in many ways. He was married to his first cousin; his father and his wife's mother were real brother and sister. Prakash followed this lead. He went to

Gulmarg to meet Rasool's wife and see if she was involved in this attack in any manner. When he reached he was surprised. A group of *Jihadis* had forcibly entered her house asking her to serve them food and... whatever they wished. The group of four men withdrew when they learnt that she was Rasool's wife. This incident had made Mehrunissa very angry.

Mehrunissa, Rasool's wife upon learning that her husband was involved in the attack on the Shrine refused to accept her husband's body; she despised what he had done. To her knowledge Pervez was a farmer in 'Pak Occupied Kashmir'. Attacking the Shrine was sacrilegious. She considered it an attack on her country and religion. She offered all help she could provide to Prakash. Initially, Prakash would contact her for information. Mehrunissa agreed to act as informant for him. She would call him if she suspected anti-India activity. A few days after Rasool's death his family disowned Mehrunissa and her daughter, Mehjabeen. Mehrunissa was forced to return to her mother who had no source of earning. So, Prakash took the responsibility of educating Mehjabeen. He brought her to New Delhi and admitted her in the best school nearby. Then, over the years Mehrunissa and Prakash started liking each other."

"Then why is there a problem?" Rukhsar asked.

"Isn't it obvious?"

"Religion?"

"Yes."

Rukhsar was happy to know he was as honest in his beliefs as he was advocating. *'Love was above religion. Love helped religions grow.'*

- - -

"Is there any chance that you two could get married?" Aman asked Prakash.

"There is every chance if Mehrunissa's mother and relatives agree. It may take years, or eternity or it may never happen," Prakash replied thoughtfully.

"What about Mehjabeen? Does she approve of you?"

"I am not sure... she won't have any issues I think. She knows about Mehrunissa and me. Her mother is honest with her, and Mehjabeen likes me, I know. Whether she will accept me as her step-father is an altogether a different matter."

"Do you meet her often?"

"Who? Mehrunissa?"

"Yes."

"Mehrunissa comes once a month to meet her daughter. During longer vacations I take Mehjabeen to Pahalgam."

"So, another vacation is coming up?" Aman asked with humour in his eyes and tone.

Prakash understood the connection Aman had made. He laughed, "Yes... She has ten days of vacations coming up for Christmas. I will take her to Pahalgam. Then there will be a long gap before her summer vacations in March. when Mehrunissa will come to New Delhi."

Aman looked at Prakash with surprise. He had never seen his friend laugh as gaily as he did now. Prakash laughed like a little child, with all its innocence.

- - -

Rukhsar barged into the room dragging Zubair behind her, "We are going to Pahalgam with him and his angel, to meet Mehrunissa," she declared.

"With the angel, Mehjabeen, you mean?" Aman asked her.

"Yes!" Rukhsar replied and stopped, "He told you?"

"Yes, he did," Aman replied with a mischievous smile.

Rukhsar mocked a punch at Prakash. "That's wicked of you. You didn't consider telling me, did you?"

Prakash pointed at Aman, "He blackmailed me emotionally. He threatened to take you away if I didn't tell him. I didn't want to lose you so I told him," he said and laughed.

Once again Aman noticed the innocence in Prakash. This time Rukhsar noticed it too. She took a step towards Prakash. "I want to meet them ASAP."

"Mehjabeen usually spends her weekends with us. If I get a chance, I can bring her here this evening but I doubt it very much. I won't get a chance to move out of here before tomorrow afternoon."

- - -

Rukhsar realized it was last Friday when she had first met Prakash. Since then her journey had been one of discoveries of truths and revelations, and erasures of misconceptions. In this period she had met her father who she had feared dead, she met her grandfather and his family whom she didn't know existed. She and Aman had travelled across the sub-continent with genuine and false identities. She met a man who she knew would be a lifelong friend and who would take care of her father even if he didn't return to Pakistan.

Rukhsar was wondering which of the things she had done or she had been through could match what Prakash had done for them. In a way she was a reason for uncovering a deceitful plan by an insane General and his co-conspirators. She looked at Aman and Prakash and she was confident that the two men who were playing jokes with her now would be able to thwart the sinister plan. The atmosphere helped in lightening the moods after a rowdy week. Rukhsar held Prakash's hand and made him promise them to allow them to meet Mehjabeen. Prakash relented when Rukhsar said that he should arrange for their meeting with Mehjabeen if *'he cared for her.'*

The happy atmosphere did not last long. A phone rang and Prakash checked the unknown caller. He checked if he had called the number. He had. He waived at Aman to take the call. Aman rushed forward, put the headphones and spoke hurriedly, "Hello, Sir," he spoke to his boss in Tehran.

"Are you ok? Are you safe?" Ambassador Jaffer Sharif asked him in desperation.

"Yes Sir. Why do you ask?" he asked his superior.

"After studying the files you sent me last evening, I sent out some feelers to probe deeper. I got a call from my source that the man he had sent the enquiries to, was found dead in his bathroom. What's going on?" Ambassador was demanding an explanation.

Aman was shell-shocked. He spoke when Prakash poked him, "Sir, I have no idea. I sent you the folder. That's what we know, I assure you." Aman said confidently.

"Wherever you are, are you safe?" Jaffer Sharif asked.

"I am absolutely safe, Sir. Why do you ask?"

"Just a fear."

After the call, Aman Bux looked at Prakash. "Could that be a murder or just an accident?" he asked.

"If they didn't suspect foul play your boss wouldn't have called you," Prakash said it plainly.

* * *

Military GHQ

Rawalpindi, Pakistan

Captain Nazir whom General Pathan had picked to probe the Wahid Khan matter sat confidently smiling at his mentor. "You said you have some information about General Wahid planning something. What is it?" General Pathan asked.

Nazir pulled an envelope and put it in front of the General.

"What is this?" Pathan asked, picking the envelope.

"I want you to see a picture. It will explain many things," he said, pulling out a small photograph from the envelope. "May I?" he asked, seeking the General's permission to approach him. Nazir walked around and stood next to the General and bowed to show the photograph. The General saw the photograph and looked up at Nazir in fear.

"That is me with my uncle, Wahid Khan, you old bag," the Captain said and thumped the General's head with the butt of his gun. General Pathan slipped to the floor, unconscious.

Nazir pulled out the General's gun and put it in General's hand, put the barrel of the gun in General's mouth and pressed the trigger. The General's skull burst into shreds. The silencer ensured the sound of gunfire didn't go beyond the room. Nazir opened the General's computer, removed the hard disk and put it in his bag. He grabbed the cell phone and searched for another phone which General Pathan had used to speak to a stranger in India. He searched for ten minutes but couldn't find. He paced hurriedly out of the building and reported to the man who had arranged the appointment.

* * *

Prakash Rohatgi's Residence,

New Delhi, India

Rukhsar opened her eyes. She looked at her watch. It was five in the evening. Aman was sleeping soundly. She laughed mildly as she thought of the term 'sleeping soundly'. Aman snored while sleeping, though slightly. She laughed and tried to return to sleep but couldn't. She got dressed and climbed down to Zubair's room. She heard an animated discussion between two men. One was her father and she tried to guess the other. The accent told her the other man was Altaf.

Rukhsar entered and sat next to Zubair. "That was quite an animated conversation you two were having. What was it?"

"Nothing serious. It was just about little matters which are of daily relevance."

"Hmm..." Rukhsar said. She was sure it couldn't have been just casual conversation. That doesn't get so animated. She spoke to her father on general issues. Abruptly she asked, "*Abbu*, we got freedom a day before India but there is a feeling that democracy was never there in Pakistan. Why is there such disparity between the two nations? What did they do right and where did we go wrong?" Rukhsar asked.

"Firstly, it is a fallacy that we got independence a day before India. Both countries gained independence at the stroke of midnight between August fourteen and fifteen. So, the date of independence is fifteen, not fourteen. On fourteenth 'All India Radio' was airing the broadcasts till midnight. Pakistani flag was hoisted on fifteenth and Jinnah Saheb took oath on the fifteenth. So, our actual date of independence is fifteenth August, just as India's."

"Could the time zone have affected the decision?"

"India had one time zone till much later. Pakistan adjusted the time zone years later."

"What else?"

"There are many reason which came together to determine our history. The important ingredient missing in Pakistan and abundantly clear in India was leadership. India had leaders like Nehru, Sardar Patel, and Maulana Azad etc. while Pakistan did not have visionary leaders, as you rightly pointed out in Dacca. Jinnah Saheb died within a year, like Gandhiji but the likes of Nehru, Patel and Shastri had a vision. Democracy was missing from the start in Pakistan. Till East Pakistan broke away it did not seen a single day of an elected, civilian government whereas, right through, India had a democratic government from the day the first elections were held, immediately after it adopted the Constitution in '51. Pakistan has no democratic history till '72. Compare that with India. Until '71, we did not have a constitution... Oh, there were two constitutions but both were abolished until Zulfiqar Ali Bhutto gave Pakistan the present constitution. He was the first elected Prime Minister, but Bhutto was an autocratic ruler. Though he gave us the constitution he did not give freedom to judiciary and media. *Khair*, Bhutto was overthrown by Zia-Ul Haq and hanged. Then we had ten years of the worst dictatorship. After Zia died in an air crash, we had a few years of '*handicapped democracy*' which managed to survive somehow, despite external pressures. Then Pervez Musharraf comes along, overthrows a democratically elected government of Nawaz Sharif and we have dictatorship once again till he declared elections and we have a democratic set up once again. But, do you still feel the air of democracy? It's a *'handicapped democracy'* which is crawling its way to what I hope, will be a matured democracy. I pray it does. On the other hand, India kept at it despite adversities. The strength of democracy doesn't come from constitution alone; it comes with confidence of its people in its legal system and the setup of a government. Democracy isn't a dress you wear to be democratic; it's an attitude, an idea, a thought process, it's a mentality free from bias, and laden with responsibility of the citizens and its rulers. Right through, India faced severe economic and natural challenges but it kept going. There was a little phase, a blip on democracy when Mrs. Gandhi asked President Fakhruddin Ali Ahmed to sign a document to declare a state of *'emergency'* in India. When emergency was imposed, Indians revolted and took the fight to the streets. It lasted for roughly a year and a half but it was a lesson Indians learnt quickly. Every citizen and politician now knows that it doesn't want an 'unconstitutional' regime in place of an elected government."

"Why did Mrs. Gandhi impose *emergency*?" Rukhsar asked with curiosity. She hadn't heard of it.

"In the preceding elections, Mrs. Gandhi had won her constituency seat with thumping majority. Remember, she was the darling of Indian people after the '71 Indo-Pak war. However, the man who had contested elections against Mrs. Gandhi, Raj Narain, brought a legal suit against her in Allahabad High Court for election malpractice. The court ruled against Mrs. Gandhi and she would have had to resign, so India had 'emergency' because it kept her in power. But public and media pressure was too much to handle. She declared elections after about a year and a half of *'emergency'* and lost her own seat from where she had won earlier. Then comes another fantastic example of people's choice and their faith in democracy. The government headed by Morarji Desai was in a mess because of infighting which resulted in collapse of his government. In mid-term elections, Mrs. Gandhi was back in power. That power of democracy comes by empowering people, Rukhsar. This also tells us two things; one, the freedom of judiciary; Mrs. Gandhi was all powerful but the Judge had the courage to give a ruling against her. And second, people's faith in democracy. They kept at it and they are reaping the benefits. It isn't the best democracy in the world but with a population of over half a billion going to polls it is a massive stamp of approval." Zubair said and looked at his daughter. "I will give you astounding examples of genuine democracy and its real benefits. Benazir Bhutto as the PM represented Pakistan on Kashmir issue at the United Nations. India had a Congress Government led by PV Narsimha Rao. The Indian PM doesn't go to represent India nor does he send any minister from his cabinet or any of his bureaucrats; he chooses the leader of the Opposition. That speech by Atal Bihari Vajpayee is a lesson in oration; it is also a great lesson in nationalism and democracy. Can you name any politician with the conviction, audacity or courage in Pakistan to take such bold decision? Narsimha Rao overrode disgruntled voices from his own party and asked Vajpayee to do the duty country demanded of him. That victory is a feather in PM's cap brought by his opposite number in the Parliament. India won that debate hands down. International community including large number of Muslim countries overwhelming voted in favour of India. Nation first, politics later! This is how nations are built." Zubair had tears in his eyes. "I am a Pakistani living in exile, in a country against which I fired bullets; whose soldiers I killed. I am exasperated when I see the situation in Pakistan. I look at the kind of politicians and I wish I could kill them instead of the enemy."

Rukhsar and Altaf were silent. They were witnessing a tough man pour out his heart and cry for his country. Rukhsar nodded and involuntarily her eyes moved to Altaf. He was staring at her.

She didn't like the way Altaf looked at her, "What are you looking at?" she asked Altaf rudely.

Altaf lowered his gaze. He couldn't tell her that he liked looking at her because she reminded him of Mariam Zaheer. He shook his head and replied politely, "I was looking at you but I was thinking of someone else. Sorry!" Altaf said softly.

Rukhsar didn't trust his words but she ignored it.

*   *   *

Indian Deputy High Commission,

Karachi, Pakistan

Sixty-one year old Pratima Vaidya held the print-outs of the files in her hand. Having read the first page, she asked the staff members to leave her alone for some time, and not to be disturbed, and she studied the contents of the file carefully. When she was finished, she was angry. Was it true? She cancelled out her doubt because the source of information was most trusted. Retired bureaucrat, ex-Home Office secretary, Nitin Tyagi had sent the folder. He had received this file from Prakash Rohatgi, whom she knew only through her mentor. How did Prakash get hold of such sensitive information which had to be highly secretive and inaccessible to outsiders? If this was true, and she had no doubt it was, then India and Pakistan were headed for a war where only the destruction of the enemy will satisfy the other. She was instructed to help in averting this calamity, and failing was not an option.

Nitin Tyagi's instructions to her were direct: *Create a storm! Blow this up! Scare the hell out of the Pakistanis by providing some sensitive information and add some more from her side as well. Let Pakistanis know that we have this information down to the last detail. Add to it, that we are already speaking to major world powers. This was a full scale war in planning and we want Pakistan isolated from International community. Let it be known that Indian Interceptor Missiles were deployed. Our preparation is well under way and we will be war-ready in two weeks. Even if a bullet is fired, it will be considered as an act of aggression. Inform the authorities that India will respond with all its might. If Pakistanis defend, go on the offensive to ensure they understand what India means when it says; it will retaliate with all it has. India is prepared and ready to strike at any time if they see the plan of an insane General is seen to be implemented. The Pakistan army must be told by the Civilian Government that the plan of one of their Generals would be their waterloo. This time there won't be a mediator whom India will entertain. And, we are willing to break Pakistan into small pieces if this happens.*

Nitin Tyagi had sent this file through Government channel because the Home Office, Foreign Office and the Defence Ministry had given their consent to this ultimatum. It is up to Pakistan to either accept or reject it. Whatever the result, if this wasn't taken care of immediately, we will take action.

Pratima Vaidya was glued to her chair. The original folder by Prakash Rohatgi which consisted of nine pages had been blown to sixteen with additional sensitive informations gathered by the intelligence sources in India, and inducted into this folder. She had to add more information from the Indian Intelligence sources in Pakistan and send a copy across to Nitin Tyagi and a copy to the foreign Ministry in New Delhi.

*   *   *

Prakash Rohatgi's Residence

New Delhi, India

"Where have you been?" Zubair asked Prakash as the latter entered his house.

"I had to meet Nitin Tyagi. I wanted his guidance. He has taken a copy of the folder and sent it to the Foreign office. They already have some information on this and they have 'obliged' me by sharing it with me. Mr. Tyagi has also sent it across to his contacts who could help." Prakash explained, sat on the sofa and asked Purna for his 'special' tea.

"What's the 'special' tea?" Rukhsar asked curiously.

It was a rare occasion when Purna spoke, "Very strong, less sugar, little milk, and it is harmful to him," she complained.

Prakash threw his head back and laughed, "She always says that whenever I ask for my special tea."

Rukhsar and Zubair had regular tea while Prakash had his 'special' tea. They heard a little beep and saw Prakash pull out a small gadget. They had seen him use it often when he was speaking to people within his 'group'. He spoke without hearing a word, "I will call you back, 'Tiger'." He disconnected the call and asked Rukhsar, "Where is Aman?"

"Upstairs... sleeping," Rukhsar replied coyly.

"You should give him time to rest," Prakash said casually.

Rukhsar looked at Zubair in embarrassment. She ran to her room upstairs. Prakash realized his mistake. His joke was in presence of Zubair. Zubair controlled his smile, rose and went to his room.

— — —

Rukhsar was embarrassed but she had a smile. She opened the door and found Aman still sleeping 'soundly'. She leaned over him and hugged him. Aman's hand grabbed her fingers and went back to sleep. They heard continuous rap on the door and a loud call by Prakash. Rukhsar and Aman leaped out of the bed. They instinctively knew this was desperate. "I will be down in a minute," Aman shouted and asked Rukhsar to go with Prakash.

Rukhsar opened the door and her heart sank when she saw Prakash's white face. "What happened?" she asked.

Prakash dismissed her question, "Come with me. Ask Aman to fetch Altaf with him."

Rukhsar returned to her room and came back a few seconds later. She tried to keep pace with Prakash as he leaped three steps at a time.

— — —

Altaf had kept himself quiet and uninvolved with matters of the house as he was told by Prakash. Altaf felt insulted but complied with his host's wish, only interacting when he was asked. It left a good impression on Prakash. At Prakash's workstation, he felt there was something seriously wrong.

Prakash asked Altaf, "Who was the man who provided you with the details of Wahid Khan's background, Altaf?"

"You know it is confidential. I can't tell you my source."

"God damn you. Tell me!" Prakash shouted angrily.

The door flew open and a tensed looking Aman barged into the room. "What happened?"

"Sit and wait..." Prakash replied angrily and turned to Altaf. "I am in no mood to play patience with you. I want the name of the man who prepared the dossier on the General."

Rukhsar and Aman looked at Prakash in fear. Prakash was raging like a wild elephant. He wanted answer from Altaf and if Altaf didn't give it Prakash would punish him. Both knew that Altaf Khos' life, or at least his health hung in the balance.

Altaf stared at Prakash nervously. Prakash gripped Altaf's right hand in a swift move and twisted is anti-clockwise. Altaf Khos screamed in pain.

"Prakash... calm down. What happened?" Rukhsar asked.

Prakash ignored her question and bore into Altaf's eyes with blood shot eyes. He suddenly loosened his grip on Altaf and shut his eyes for a few seconds, opened them slowly and asked Altaf, "Was his name Junaid?"

Altaf's eyes were stuck on Prakash with utter fear of the news he was to hear. "Yes... yes... that is... his first name."

Prakash fell back in his chair. His eyes were still bloodshot but it had sympathy for Altaf. "Junaid Saleem?" he asked.

Altaf knew what he was to hear next. The animal instinct in man always played its part. Altaf nodded.

"From the Records Office in Islamabad?" Prakash completed the identity.

In shock, Altaf did not reply. He stared fearfully at Prakash.

Prakash gazed at Altaf and abruptly he shut his eyes and sat erect. For two minutes he maintained that posture. Rukhsar wondered what was happening. She tried to speak but Aman stopped her. He knew what Prakash was doing. He had seen Prakash meditate in Dacca. Finally, Prakash opened his eyes. There was a remarkable change, a transformation in him. The redness in his eyes had receded. He was calm and in total control of his emotions.

"What happened, Prakash?" Aman asked softly.

"How close were you two?" Prakash asked Altaf.

Altaf noticed that Prakash had used past tense. Altaf choked. What had he done to his friend, he asked himself. Prakash repeated his question.

"He was my best college mate from army training school. He was the superintendent in the 'Records Office'... What happened?" Altaf Khos pleaded.

"He was found dead with two bullet holes in his head. Whoever shot him ensured he was dead. I am sorry," Prakash tried being sympathetic but he was cold and bland.

"How do you know? Who...?" Altaf asked in a whisper.

"I have my sources." Prakash said and turned to Aman, "I have bad news for us too," Prakash said and again remained quiet for a few seconds.

"What happened?" It was Aman's turn to fret.

"General Pathan is dead. He apparently 'shot himself' in his office. I have sketchy details. A visitor wearing an army man's clothes visited him an hour before he was found dead."

Aman put his head back and remained silent for some time. He had just lost the man he probably loved and respected most in all of Pakistan; more than the Ambassador. General Pathan had virtually guided Aman through the career. Rukhsar had heard about General Pathan from Aman a few times. He was present at the party the evening she met Aman for the first time. She personally didn't know the General but she empathised with Aman. And... anger was brewing inside her. Neither knew that Prakash had great respect for General Pathan because he was one of three men who had initially set up this group.

"I will kill that bastard General," Altaf shouted suddenly.

"Mind your language. There is a woman present in the room," Prakash warned him.

"We all want him dead," Aman said coldly.

Prakash nodded sadly.

"Ask *'Eagle'* to give us the details. We will get Wahid Khan on this side of the border, Prakash," Aman said coldly.

Rukhsar looked at her husband. He was a kind hearted man who hated hurting any living being. Here he was, ready to kill the General. She feared for him. "You are not going to meet him. We can arrange something else," she suggested.

"Abbu wants him dead, Altaf wants him dead, and I want him dead. That man has to die. *Abbu* was right. He is evil," Aman said angrily.

"I want him dead too but I have to act above my emotions. I have to ensure we defuse the situation first," Prakash stated.

"Why wait? We know where to get him. He won't expect us. We can ambush him, kill him there," Aman said angrily.

"You don't get it, do you? By now he may know that his plan could fail. He will take any action which he deems fit to ensure his own survival and keeps his plans intact. He has brought forward his plan by two months and now, if his plans are threatened he may go into action right away; military coup is a real possibility. If he thinks he is ready he will take over," Prakash explained calmly, presenting factual situation.

"I am going back to Peshawar." Altaf declared.

"Good. You can't choose a better place to get yourself killed, you idiot," Prakash said sarcastically.

"What do you mean?" Altaf asked. He was confused.

"Junaid Saleem was killed because he had gathered sensitive information on General. Don't you think men who killed him would like to know why your friend would prepare a dossier on a General when he had no reason? They will eventually find out if they haven't already. When they know who ordered it, what they will do to you?"

Altaf realized, "What do I do now?"

"You must speak to General Wahid Khan," Prakash said.

All were surprised at Prakash's suggestion.

"You know his life is in danger and you want him to talk to that General?" Aman was as confused as Rukhsar and Altaf.

"Yes!"

"Why?" Rukhsar asked.

"We will learn if he knows that Altaf asked Junaid to gather the information or not. You must remember Jaffer Sharif said about the man he had sent feelers to. That man was found dead in his bathroom. These three killings are tied to your ambitious General. We will know what he is up to. Either he will react in anger or with patience. We shall create a situation where he will have to respond," Prakash said confidently.

Altaf was nervous. It took some persuasion by Prakash to convince him to speak to the General. Prakash led Altaf to his communication system and asked him for the General's cell phone number and pressed the digits on his system.

* * *

Pakistan Military Camp,

Skardu, Pakistan Occupied Kashmir near Indo-Pak Border (LOC)

General Wahid Khan was at a military camp in Skardu, ten miles from LOC, the 'Line of Control' on Pakistan side. He had surveyed the area on a chopper two hours earlier. Captain Nazir had called to tell him that General Pathan was 'promoted' for his excellent service. The General's laptop and cell phone were 'recovered' but the other phone which the dead General had used to speak to someone in India wasn't found. The ambitious General smiled within. The narcissist loved seeing himself in the mirror and admire his personality. He asked his attendant soldier to fetch him something to eat. The soldier disappeared. Wahid Khan saw the soldier close the door and pulled out his second phone to call his most trusted colleague, a General, his senior by ten years and one of the group of four.

"Good evening, Sir. How was your day?" Wahid Khan asked the venerable General.

"Good! All is well I hope?" The old man asked.

"No, Sir! There was hiccup where a man in the records office made enquiries about me, including the Kargil incident. He was 'blessed'. An hour ago, your colleague, who was a pain for you, has also been 'promoted' as you desired. I am in Skardu. I have surveyed the area and it looks perfect. We can take over the Indian posts in two months when they descend during winter. We can move a regiment across and take *ZajuLa Pass* in eight to ten days if troops move fast, and take the Jammu-Srinagar highway in fortnight. With no resistance it should be easy. With no road link to Srinagar, we can force the Indians to talk on Kashmir, Siachen and even on the Sir Creek issues."

The old General listened patiently. He put two questions and got the right answers. Wahid Khan wished his uncle continuing good luck and God's mercy on him always and ended the call.

- - -

The sub-zero temperature was taking its toll. The men were wrapped in layers of thermals and still the chill reached the body. Wahid Khan felt the chill to his bones. He was irritated. He hated extreme weathers. His irritation had a reason. He had called that moron Altaf but hadn't connected.

If Zubair was alive and he learnt the truth, he knew Zubair would avenge the death of those eleven soldiers on the hills in Kargil. *What could I do? That was the most important post which helped in protecting Tiger Hill where the main battle was being fought. I knew Tiger Hill would fall the moment this post was taken. But that over-righteous Major was too eager to save his men from death. If the war had stretched for another fifteen days we could have persuaded the Air Force to come to our rescue and we could have retained Tiger Hill. With Tiger Hill in our control we would have controlled the Jammu-Srinagar highway, and have control over Kashmir north of Jammu, and Siachen. I did the right thing. Your analysis about the situation may have been right at the time but I was right with the plan we had. You destroyed our plan and now you are a threat to my other major plan. I can't let that happen, Zubair Ahmed... Where are you, Altaf Khos?*

At dusk the surrounding snow-capped mountain tops looked grey and ugly. In few minutes the temperature would dip to ten degree Celsius below freezing and within a week it could plunge to below thirty-five. He hated it. He looked at his watch and cursed himself for choosing this time of the year for this trip; he could have planned it either a mother earlier or four months later. He could have chosen to go to the Punjab section where the real battle would be fought. *In this area the Indians would be putting all their effort to regain the areas occupied by Pakistani forces in Kashmir. When they concentrate in this area, two simultaneous attacks will be launched in Punjab and Kutch taking the Indians by surprise. Before they can recover from that shock three simultaneous attacks on Mumbai, New Delhi and the western state of Gujarat, which were within the striking range of the PAF would be hit. There would be mayhem. The Indians will have to defend their cities first and that is when the Kashmir area could be heavily reinforced and taken. The old adage is true, 'kabza sachcha, daawa jhootha'; 'Possession is true, claims are false'. We will occupy Kashmir, they won't. Then they can shout all they want on the International stage. Kashmir will come to Pakistan. It would be perfect if the Bangladesh Commander in Chief had agreed to be a part of this plan but that coward did not have the courage to take on the Indians in the east. If he had agreed Indians would have had to split their forces throughout the country from east of Bangladesh in Tripura and Assam to West Bengal on Bangladesh's west; from Kashmir in the North to Punjab in the North-west, to Gujarat and Maharashtra in the west. That would be a true nightmare. With the Bangladeshis on my side, even with limited striking power could be a logistical nightmare with over two-thousand kilometre boundary with India. Damn those week-kneed Bangladeshis. How stupid! Why would India waste itself on Bangladesh when it had a real power like Pakistan to handle? Bangladesh should have been there ideally, only for its nuisance value. Pakistan will have to go alone in this war and win it convincingly. Wait till the Jihadis wreak havoc before we finish the job, you Indians.*

Wahid Khan summoned his deputy, Khaled Usmani. The General's trusted advisor scrambled to meet his boss in a hurry. Khaled Usmani knocked, heard the command to enter and he rushed in, "Yes, General?" Usmani asked obediently.

Wahid Khan gestured him to the sofa and asked, "Can we get some rum here?"

"Yes, General. I will have it sent to you."

"Not now! I want to talk to you. Can we ask the Chinese to show some aggression during our operation?"

Usmani looked at Wahid Khan thoughtfully, "I doubt if they will get involved, Sir."

"They are our 'all-weather' friends. If they don't come to our aid at a crucial juncture when should we expect them to help us? When we have an upper hand who wants them?"

"I had a detailed discussion with your political advisor, Yakub Lahori. He told me the reasons why China won't help us even if we are in serious trouble."

The General looked at his deputy doubtfully, "We provided them with best conditions for investments; we gave them everything they wanted. They are obliged to help us."

"Mr. Lahori said that Chinese won't even give us verbal support because it's meaningless. They definitely won't give us logistical support because Indians will consider that as an act of war. It will..."

"Why should Chinese bother about India? It makes no sense. We are their best friends, and they ours."

"Sir, Lahori is right. China is an export oriented economy. Their local purchasing power can't support their industries and India is one of their major trading partners, with mutual trade exceeding eighty billion dollars. Chinese won't spoil that. They may not believe in God but they believe in currencies. China doesn't have good relations with any of its neighbours. With every country it has border disputes; from Japan to India. If they get involved directly, it could bring other players who would like to show their disgust at China. Most of these countries have excellent relations with India; Russia, Japan, South Korea, Philippines, Vietnam et al. No, Sir, China won't get involved directly. In worst case scenario, if China sends one soldier to help us, it could probably lead to disaster."

Wahid Khan nodded slowly. He had not counted on China to help but the way Usmani had put it, China may go with India. Indians were good in their foreign relations with every country. Even Yasser Arafat, Saddam Hussein and Colonel Gaddafi at the peak, had good relations with India, as did the present governments.

Wahid Khan planned to improve Pakistan's foreign relations with all the important countries in two years after he takes over. Yakub Lahori's strategy was simple and effective; ensure that various Taliban factions are brought under control by giving limited sops and drying up their supply of arms. It will force the various factions to sit on the table and accept what was being offered: amnesty... and a new mission to fight. Taming of Taliban and stopping attacks on western interests will help remove the trust deficit of decades. With better relations, he can avail ultra-modern arms.

- - -

Wahid Khan was on his second tipple when the call came. "Where are you?" he shouted into his phone at Altaf.

"I have traced Zubair Ahmed, Sir." Altaf spoke calmly. "I went after him to learn that he was on his way back to Delhi. I am standing a hundred yards away from where he is."

"Where is that '*Qadiyani*'?" General shouted angrily again.

In New Delhi, Altaf looked at Prakash and wondered if it was the right plan. Prakash prodded him. "He is in the house of an agent, Prakash Rohatgi, Sir." Altaf replied.

"Do you know who Rohatgi is?" General asked curiously.

"I think he is a double agent." Altaf lied.

"Where is this Prakash Rohatgi? And, where are Rukhsar Ahmed and Aman Bux?"

"They are in the house, Sir. Can you arrange for a gun with a silencer, Sir? I did not carry any gun with me for obvious reasons. I didn't wish to take any chances at the airport."

"You will get a call in a few minutes. He will arrange it for you. If you need assistance inside the house, he will help you out," General said proudly, taking a swig from his glass.

"Ok, Sir. I will get to Zubair in an hour once I have a gun. I should interrogate him, Sir?"

"Ask Zubair what happened on the hill where he was injured. If you hear my name, kill him, his daughter and her boyfriend along with him," Wahid Khan ordered.

In New Delhi there was a deafening silence in the house. The occupants at the workstation were angry. They had just heard the orders of their death pronounced in a chillingly casual manner.

Altaf tapped on his headphone to create a disturbance in sound, "Are you there, Sir?" he spoke politely into the phone.

The General replied twice in a 'yes', but Altaf didn't reply. He disconnected the call and looked at Prakash Rohatgi.

"Call him back." Prakash ordered and Altaf dialled again.

Wahid Khan took another swig and poured again. He heard his cell phone ring and shouted, "Yes?"

"The line is quite poor, Sir. Can you please repeat what you said earlier? The sound was inaudible," Altaf said softly.

"I can't hear you clearly. Speak louder," General ordered.

"I can't speak louder, Sir. I am sorry. If Zubair doesn't mention your name then what do I do, Sir?"

The General replied instantly, "Doesn't matter! Kill him anyway. The *Qadiyani* doesn't deserve to live."

"And what about his daughter, Sir? What do I do with her?" Altaf asked hesitantly; somehow, he knew what the answer would be.

"Kill the bitch and her boyfriend." General Wahid Khan said without compunction.

"She is innocent, beautiful woman," Altaf said involuntarily.

Wahid Khan laughed loudly, "Is she? Wish you were able to bring her as a trophy for me," he said, and added, "You have fun with her... but before you leave make sure she is dead."

The group at the workstation in New Delhi were fuming but silent. A moment passed before Prakash poked Altaf to speak again. Altaf calmly replied. "Ok, Sir."

"You want to know why, Altaf?" The General asked.

"No, Sir. You must have good reason. And, your order is my command," Altaf replied as convincingly as he could.

Wahid Khan heard the right answer, "You beware of that tribal woman. Make sure you kill her first just to be sure she doesn't beat you up again," General said and laughed again.

Altaf gulped down his hatred for the General, "I will be careful, Sir."

"*Good man.*" The General thought '*That takes care of Zubair and my cupboard skeleton*' General thought and sipped again.

* * *

Prakash Rohatgi's Residence,

New Delhi, India

"He is dead," Prakash Rohatgi said as calmly and coldly as General Wahid Khan had ordered.

Altaf gazed at the marble flooring angrily. Aman and he shared the same feelings. Both tried to speak at the same time but stopped. The anger was palpable; hatred for Wahid Khan was many notches higher. They noticed Rukhsar was silently thinking with glassy eyes on a face red with rage. She was in a daze but her trance like eyes reflected her ferocity. She was thinking of something too vicious, the men knew. She asked Prakash, "You care for me?"

Prakash was baffled. He didn't know how to respond but he looked at her solemnly when he replied, "Yes, Rukhsar."

"Then I want you to do me a favour. Give me a chance. Get me Wahid Khan. I want to kill him, Prakash." Rukhsar begged, "If you care for me... make it possible for me."

Prakash was stumped. He wondered how to respond. He couldn't promise her what he may not be able to deliver. He held her hands firmly, "You trust me?" he asked.

Rukhsar nodded.

"You have my word that no one will get even close to you or Aman, or even Zubair Saheb," Prakash promised her.

"I am not worried about myself," Rukhsar said with fear, "I am worried about him," she looked at Aman, "and *Abbu*".

"I said... no one will even get close to you or them. You have my word." He promised her again.

Rukhsar nodded vigorously to retain her self-confidence and her belief in the three men she cared for. "I want to kill him," Rukhsar was determined. Her eyes were flaring. Her gritted teeth confirmed her resolve. "He is the real '*kaafir*'. He has no right to live."

"He won't live beyond a fortnight, I assure you. He has to die because if he lives millions will die," Prakash said while caressing her head, thinking hard about the options he had. He too wanted that man dead but it wasn't going to be easy.

Rukhsar felt a surge of energy in her. She held Prakash's hand and held it firmly, looking at him with fear.

Prakash looked down at her and pressed her scalp against his chest. "Don't fret... don't waste your tears."

Aman was looking at Prakash and Rukhsar, observing their conversation keenly. He felt their affection for each other to be so genuine, so innocent... they were blessed with so much compassion, and piety of their souls. Prakash found Aman smiling while he was thinking about something deeply. His smile had that rare quality of inner peace which wasn't seen among common men. Prakash waived at him and receded to a corner. Aman followed him. "I want to give her something nice for this day. Instead of the sad memory, let it be a day of fond memories," he said and asked him to go for his Friday evening '*Namaaz*' while he would finish his work and leave to return in an hour.

Prakash took Altaf to another room and instructed him to do exactly as told. Prakash returned to his workstation and asked Rukhsar to go to her room and rest while he was out.

― ― ―

When Aman and Zubair returned after their 'Namaaz' the angry, vengeful Rukhsar was gone and there was a different Rukhsar who was talking to a stunningly beautiful young girl. Aman knew instinctively. Zubair was rejuvenated when he saw the young girl. He lunged ahead to grab her as she ran to him. Prakash was sitting next to Rukhsar with a beaming smile. He brought the girl to face Aman. "Aman Khan Bux, meet my darling angel, Mehjabeen, my daughter."

Aman was admiring the beautiful young lady. Unsure how to respond, he kneeled on one knee put his arms around her and kissed her forehead. "It is a pleasure to meet you, dear."

The girl bowed and captivated him with her ravishing smile. Aman smiled back and offered her to sit next to him.

"For God's sake, please stop behaving like a diplomat; talk like a normal person, will you?" Rukhsar said tauntingly.

"How come you brought her here today? You said we will be meeting her tomorrow," Aman asked Prakash.

"She spends the weekends here. She was upset she couldn't come here last weekend... So, I requested the Dean of the school to grant her extra week as holidays. She is an excellent student and quite a favourite of the teachers... and she never misses a school day. So the Dean granted her a week off. I was planning to take her home next weekend but," Prakash stood behind Rukhsar and ruffled her hair, "this little child," he said playfully, "was upset, so I thought of giving her a doll to play. So... Mehjabeen is here."

Rukhsar and Aman found Mehjabeen to be a chatter box. At times she had to be stopped to give her mouth some rest. For them, especially Rukhsar, she was an angel who filled her heart with joy. Neither Aman nor Rukhsar had the any young child in their family or relatives so Mehjabeen was truly special. Even in Dacca, Rukhsar had younger brothers and sisters as distant relatives with whom she knew she would probably never bond either due to lack of communication or due to disparity in ages. For Aman and Rukhsar, Mehjabeen was like a child they had of their own. Both found it strange how easily they were able to bond with her, and she with them. For next hour the house was filled with celebrations till Altaf called Prakash on his cell phone and tension filled the house.

Prakash Rohatgi hastily issued instructions to all in the house and asked them to do exactly as told.

-   -   -

Altaf ordered Qasim to stop the car fifty feet from the gates.

"This is a big farmhouse, Altaf."

"It is. Call your contact and tell him we are on schedule. I will call the principal after completing the job."

"What are we waiting for?" Qasim asked after completing the call. "What difference does it make if there is an extra man in the house? Let's finish the job," Qasim suggested.

"Sit tight and be patient," Altaf ordered. He was enjoying ordering someone, an experience he never had. Qasim sulked and sank in his seat.

"Let's check what's happening," Altaf said and dialled. He heard the ring at the other end without response. Altaf put the phone back in his jacket pocket and waited.

Prakash heard his cell phone ringing. He put the call on mute without replying and asked Rukhsar to take Mehjabeen to her room and stay there till asked to come down. Mehjabeen was upset but Rukhsar led her to her room.

-   -   -

Prakash approached the grey hatchback and looked around as he neared. The street was empty. He walked to the driver's window and tapped. Qasim waived him away. Qasim saw the man tap on the glass and it bugged him. He slid down the glass and showed a fist, and asked him again to go away. Prakash knocked again. An irritated Qasim rolled down the glass and flashed a punch at Prakash again. "Get lost!" he said. Prakash grabbed Qasim's fist with his left hand and smashed Qasim's mouth with his right. Qasim shouted in pain. He tried to reach for his gun. He felt a hammer blow at the back of his head where Altaf smashed the butt of his gun. Altaf struck again but ensured Qasim didn't pass out. Qasim screamed again. Prakash held his victim's fingers and twisted them clockwise, put them against the car's door frame and jammed the doors on his knuckles. This time Qasim's couldn't scream. The intensity of the pain choked him.

Altaf reached into Qasim's jacket pocket and pulled out a gun with silencer attached to it. He put the gun in his pocket and pushed Qasim into the rear seat. Prakash opened the rear door and smashed his boot on Qasim's knee and pushed him down between the front and rear seats. He climbed into the car and drove it into his compound.

'This is the true irony... and there are many here,' Altaf thought to himself. Six days ago he was tied to the chair where Qasim was sitting and he was occupying the chair now which Aman had used when he had interrogated Altaf. Altaf had wondered why Aman Khan, a Pakistani national, a diplomat at that, was helping and working for the Indians. He had called Aman Khan a traitor then; he realized his folly and now as he stood in Aman's place, he was being pronounced a 'traitor' by his captive. *Irony!*

If working with Indians for Pakistan's benefit meant being a traitor, then so be it. Altaf knew that men like himself and Qasim were used and discarded as and when required. A citizen of India was leading an operation which would save its arch enemy from utter destruction by the enemy's own army General. Though Altaf was the one to have brought it to the attention of Prakash Rohatgi, it was Prakash who was working hard to avert that destruction. *Irony!*

When he wanted to trust a man to save Pakistan, he didn't trust any colleague or countrymen; instead, now he trusted the men he had called traitors. Off the three men he trusted, two were Pakistanis, off whom one was living in exile; and the third, the important man now, was an Indian! *Irony!*

In enemy's capital he was sitting in the house of '*possibly an Indian agent*', working to save Pakistan. *Irony!*

He was in a house which had more Pakistanis living in it than Indians and they were living happily and freely while a General from their country had issued orders that these three beautiful, decent people be killed. *Irony!*

Altaf saw Qasim wriggle in his seat and open his eyes. Altaf slapped his face to check if the captive was fully conscious. He knew it would take time for Qasim to be normal. He was asking Purna to treat Qasim. *Irony!*

Purna injected a dose of medicine into Qasim, applied an ointment like medicine and bandaged the areas to prevent any infection. Prakash dumped Qasim in his chair and stepped out of the room for 'important work', leaving Qasim in 'safe hands' of Aman and Altaf.

In ten minutes Prakash returned to the room hurriedly. "How is he doing?" he asked Aman.

"His speech isn't audible... I hear mumbles," Aman replied without taking his eyes off Qasim.

Prakash nodded. He yanked his prisoner's ear and turned it clockwise. Qasim screamed. "Now he is awake," Prakash said and asked Aman to move to another chair and he occupied the chair opposite his prey. He asked, "Who are you?"

Altaf and Aman looked at Prakash curiously. It was an odd question to ask. Qasim did not reply. Prakash leaned forward and swung his fist, landing it on the nose of his prey. Qasim's nose bled profusely. "Who are you?" Prakash asked again.

The captive struggled in vain. He spat the blood dripping from his mouth and nostrils and looked at Prakash with hatred. Prakash stood up and looked down at his victim's bare feet and slammed the heel of his boot on his victim's left digits. Qasim screamed again.

"You came here to kill three people who are very dear to me. Your people have already killed two men very dear to two of us. Until I get the right answers you are going to bear punishment which may cripple you for rest of your pitiful life. I promise you I won't kill you, but you will wish you were dead. I ask you again. Who are you?" Prakash asked.

Qasim didn't reply. Prakash cursed without letting anyone see the abhorrence he felt at his actions. Prakash steeled his nerves, sat in front of his captive and looked at him without mercy or compassion. He rammed his right fist on his prey's face catching his left jaw. They heard a loud thud as Qasim's jaw cracked. Aman looked at the victim and then at Prakash's fist which had generated such force. He saw the boxer like fist of Prakash turn blue at the knuckles. He knew it must have hurt Prakash too but the man didn't show it.

"Every ten seconds you will have to bear this punishment unless you speak. You may be able to take lot of punishment but make no mistake; I can give you more pain than you can endure. For the last time I ask, who are you?"

"Anwar Shiraz," the victim spoke; his voice barely audible.

"What do you do?"

"I am a Mechanical Engineer working in an automobile spare parts manufacturing unit in Delhi."

"Who gave you the orders to call Altaf?"

"A man from Bannu, a small town in North-West Pakistan. You must have never heard of the place," Anwar replied.

"That's three hundred kilometres from Kuhat," Aman told Prakash. Aman was perplexed. Bannu in North Waziristan was an area where the Government had no control in the region. It was totally controlled by the extremists who were at war with Pak army. If Pakistani establishment launched an operation in the area it had to retreat because it found no local support in the region. Something didn't add up. It made no sense. How did a General from Punjab have access to an extremist from that area? Anwar was lying. "You are lying. Waziristan hates the guts of the *'Punjabi Military establishment'*. They won't take orders from the military," Aman shouted.

Anwar shook his head. "You think what you like, but it is the truth." He said arrogantly.

Aman looked at the bleeding man. He believed the man was speaking the truth.

To his surprise even Prakash agreed to Anwar's version.

Aman didn't agree, "That area is a mess. Thirty per cent of the area is not accessible to the Government authorities. A third of the area is Taliban infested and a third is inhabitable. A tiny portion is left where Pak agencies do as they like. Various Taliban factions fight with each other while Pak, NATO and US forces keep striking the area with drones. And the locals suffer because the Jihadi elements apart from Taliban are raking in money from terror and blackmail. We know that the terrorists responsible for the recent bombings of the Indian Embassy in Kabul are in Miran Shah and they aren't hiding; they roam freely with other set of people who are responsible for the terror attacks on the US missions in Pakistan. This area is the breeding ground for new terrorists, who train and arm local militias. The entire area - from either side of Afghan border, from Peshawar, Miran Shah, Mir Ali or Swat to the north, are havens for these elements. If I want to find the most sophisticated guns I can buy them if can produce hard currencies. They deal in the most profitable business in the world after drugs; arms! It is a mad..."

"That's a lie. We are fight for Islam. We fight *'Kaafirs'* like you. You don't know the meaning of *Jihad*," Anwar shouted.

Prakash looked at Qasim with pity... and hatred.

"You fight for *Jihad*?" Aman exploded, "Can you tell me how many innocent people have died in your *'Jihadi'* attacks? Without exaggerating, I safely say a few hundred thousand. How many real *'Kaafirs'* have you killed? I can exaggerate and say a handful, maybe a hundred at the most? Can you justify bombing a mosque with hundreds of *'Namaazis'* inside? That is your *Jihad*? How do you justify killing innocent people who do honest day's work and you detonate bombs amidst them, in market places? *'Holy Quran'* prohibits death of innocent person. Do you think of it before detonating bombs in buses? Women are held in esteem but do you or your leaders believe in it? Can you tell me where is it written that a woman should be ordered to be raped by men of her own tribe for being in love with a man from a different tribe? That is your version of Islam. It is not in mine. My *'Aaka'*, His Divine self, The Prophet has asked us to ensure that women and children are protected. *'You Kaafirs'* treat them like commodity and use them to satisfy your physical needs. That is your distorted version of Islam, not of 'my' Prophet! The holy month of *Ramzan* is a month of introspection for every man to make him a better person but you don't spare the holy month. You claim to be a Muslim you *Kaafir?* In this holy month men are supposed to keep away from women but you visit brothels, you bastard." Aman said with raging eyes fixed on Anwar. He paused and kneeled in front of the tied man and suddenly stung a vicious blow on the nose of his victim. "You bastards pull down men from buses and spray them with bullets based on their caste or sect or the colour of the skin. *You bastards killed my father,*" Aman Khan Bux's voice boomed and his fist rammed into Anwar's chin again... and again... and again.

Prakash stared at Aman in disbelief. He saw Aman Bux hitting his victim. For Aman, that tied man was his father's killer. Prakash put his hands on Aman's shoulder. "Aman, *my friend*. This man didn't kill your father." Prakash said and pulled Aman to his chair and forced him down.

Aman brushed Prakash aside and slumped in the chair. "These bastards killed my father," Aman Bux said, and cried.

When Aman was calmer, Prakash asked Qasim, "Who is this man in Bannu?" Prakash asked firmly.

Anwar Shiraz was silent. He tried to speak twice but his voice was inaudible. His broken nose and punishment he had taken from Aman didn't let him speak with clarity.

"We want to know, Anwar," Altaf asked, trying to persuade the man he had connived into a trap.

"You shut up. You are a *traitor*. I can answer them, not you," Anwar said with a disgusted look.

When Prakash repeated the question, Anwar Shiraz looked at him with terrified eyes. He didn't have the courage to speak of about it. When 'persuaded', Anwar spoke and when he did, it was his captors' turn to be terrified. "The order was issued by second in command of the *'Badruddin'* group". Anwar replied and leaned back. He wanted to see the terrified looks on the faces of these so called 'decent' people.

"Taliban," Aman murmured, wondering how that could be. *Badruddin* group, a breakaway faction of Pakistani Taliban; the most dreaded off the splinter groups with its own army of dedicated *'Fedayeen'* fighters willing to die and kill without remorse of respect for human life. If it was true, it gave a totally new dimension to what they were up against. These *'fidayeens'* consisted of men from sixteen year olds to men in thirties. These men, mostly uneducated, jobless and poor men had nothing to lose except their lives, had been motivated to fight *'Jihad'* against the forces of the 'infidels', and for the sake of Islam. For Prakash and Aman, a riddle was solved. They had wondered how Wahid

Khan would muster manpower in large numbers to infiltrate Indian borders. These were men who will be sent to infiltrate; to create anarchy before the Pak army went on the offensive. Anwar Shiraz further informed that 'Badruddin' group was promised amnesty if they fought the *'Jihad'* with India. With amnesty and promise of power sharing, the leader, Badruddin Rabbani had committed himself and his men to the General.

The missing piece! Now the plan made absolute sense! Wahid Khan was not an idiot, he knew. The deviousness of the plan was evident from the pieces which had been fitted just right. It was clear that Wahid Khan had more than just casual links with the Taliban and the terrorist outfits. "The missing link now fits perfectly," Prakash murmured.

"Yes," Aman Khan Bux endorsed.

"I have been wondering from where he would be getting thousands of armed and trained men... the non-state actors to infiltrate India before Pakistan regulars come. This is as sinister as the devil would have planned himself. This is pure evil. It..." Prakash stopped and looked around him. "Wahid Khan has to be stopped, and he will be stopped."

When asked about his role in Delhi, Anwar informed that he was one of the recruiters in India to fight from within, when required. Prakash rammed his fist under Anwar's nose, "*You* are the traitor. I swear I am going to make you pay for this for the rest of your Godforsaken life." Prakash kicked his boot in Anwar's abdomen. It sent the chair crashing into the wall and tumbled over. Anwar's head started to bleed. He heard Prakash shout at him, "That is for treason."

Prakash dumped Anwar in his car trunk and informed his mentor. Anwar Shiraz would be kept in captivity till he lived; without trial.

"Where is he?" Aman asked when Prakash returned. He was hoping for an answer which would not destroy his faith in Prakash.

As if he was reading Aman's mind, Prakash stood in the middle of the room and bore down at Aman. "We don't kill people, Aman. I can bet you though, that Anwar would wish he was dead. He is in the custody of the Intelligence services. The information he can provide can be extremely useful."

"Then he might as well then wish you had killed him." Aman replied in retrospect.

"I have no sympathy. Treason and rape should have capital punishment," Prakash said and turned to Altaf, "You have a call to make. A lot hinges on this call. Don't start staring between the calls like you did the last time. You have to be convincing." Prakash said and told him what to say.

Prakash suddenly turned to his friend, "I have to talk to you, Aman, and don't you dare avoid it." He was shaken from the moment Aman had said that his father was killed by militants.

*   *   *

Pakistan Army Camp,

Skardu, near LOC, Pakistan Occupied Kashmir

Wahid Khan waited impatiently for the call from New Delhi. He hoped they hadn't killed Zubair Ahmed. He wanted more information on the mysterious Prakash Rohatgi. The name had cropped up a few times but no information was available on this character - either from Indian or Pak Intelligence. Mystery men like he could be trouble. He was dangerous if his name appeared in a diary, and two private calls were made to him by General Pathan. The rum was taking its effect slowly although he had poured a quarter of it down his throat. He still felt chilly despite two heat blowers working at full capacity. Wahid Khan poured another drink. *'Call me soon. Give me the good news,'* he instructed Altaf and Qasim in his mind. Two hours behind schedule, he saw the name flash on his cell phone. "Yes Altaf. Tell me!?"

Altaf started cautiously, "We got Rukhsar and Aman Bux and also the tribal woman but we are unable to find Zubair Ahmed, Sir. He wasn't in the house when we came in. We interrogated Rukhsar, and she told us that he had gone to the mosque for his

Friday '*Namaaz*'. We checked the house to see if she was lying. Zubair is gone, Sir."

"What? He was the main target, you idiot," General Wahid Khan shouted, "How can you miss him? I don't care how you do it; just get Zubair and do as instructed."

"I am sorry, Sir. We were sure he was in the house when we entered. This is a large estate. He could have walked out from any gate. How we missed him we don't know, Sir, but I know where he is headed. After '*Namaaz*', he is going to Gulmarg near Srinagar to meet someone," Altaf said convincingly.

Wahid Khan was angry but he didn't want to discourage or reprimand Altaf yet. Altaf was on track and doing his job. General was sure Altaf would eventually execute the order. "Go after him. Take him, and I want detailed information on Prakash Rohatgi. His name seems to have appeared from two different sources apart from you. Get to him and let me know when you do."

"Sir, I have some bad news. Qasim is mortally injured. The tribal woman is responsible."

Wahid Khan drew a deep breath. "Kill him! Make sure he doesn't land in the hands of the authorities, and track that '*Qadiyani*', and find out more about this Rohatgi chap. ok?"

"Yes, Sir." Altaf said and took his time, and continued, "Sir, I must alert you about something I learnt by chance when I interrogated the tribal woman, Sir." Altaf paused intentionally to let the information have its desired effect.

"What?" Wahid Khan knew there was real bad news.

"I found a dossier that says you have a plan to overthrow the government in a coup. It also has details of how you plan to tackle India. It has names and designations of people in your 'core' group. I have the dossier in my possession. When I asked Rukhsar about it she said Zubair Ahmed has a copy of it too. Sir, I believe Prakash is investigating you for some reason. The dossier has inputs from agencies in the UK, US, China, France and Australia, Sir. The Chinese, I believe, are holding shipment of arms to us." Altaf enticed the General, as planned, "Zubair Ahmed knows about Tiger Hill orders. He holds you responsible for the death of eleven men."

With each word he heard General Wahid Khan's heart kept sinking. When Altaf finished speaking Wahid Khan was silent. His face was pale. *'How was it possible? How could anyone get the dossier? Who was the traitor?'*

"What do you want me to do, Sir?" Altaf asked obediently.

Wahid Khan was thinking. All information was coming too rapidly for him. Altaf repeated his question but got no reply. The General spoke hesitantly, and coldly, "I want them dead; him and Prakash Rohatgi. Go to Gulmarg. I will send someone to help you."

"Yes Sir." Altaf gave a verbal salute. "What do I do with the bodies of these three people, Sir?"

"Dump them!" General ordered.

"What about the dossier? It might fall in wrong hands," Altaf asked adding to the pressure Wahid Khan may have felt.

"Dispose of it quickly. Burn it! Fetch the copies from Zubair and Prakash. Let me know at the earliest."

"Yes, Sir."

*　　*　　*

Prakash Rohatgi's Residence,

New Delhi, India

Altaf Khos was sweating despite the chill. He shook his head in relief as he took off the headphones. "That went well?" he asked nervously.

"Excellent!" Prakash complimented genuinely.

"Why did you stress on the dossier? He will be alert now."

"There are multiple reasons for it. Firstly, now he will be sure you didn't ask Junaid to prepare a dossier on him. Since you are breaking the news to him that there is a dossier, he will trust you. It will become common knowledge in International community within a day or two that the dossier exists. There's a strong possibility that he will learn of it even earlier... no point in holding back, and lastly, he will want the dossier which he thinks that Zubair Saheb has. He will send you an assistant to help you. We will use that man to get Wahid 'bloody' Khan to come after us and take him," Prakash replied.

Aman Khan and Altaf nodded in agreement.

"What now?" Aman asked.

A faint smile appeared on Prakash's face, "let's have dinner. I don't want tensions in the house when my daughter is here. The pressure will be on the other side," Prakash said.

"What do I do?" Altaf asked.

Prakash smiled, "Have you ever been to Gulmarg?"

Altaf Khos shook his head in negative.

"You go to Gulmarg via Srinagar and Jammu. Tomorrow morning you leave for Jammu. When you get there, call me and I will let you know what to do next."

"Thank you," Altaf nodded with gratitude.

"For what?" Prakash asked.

"For helping me... my country," Altaf said with obligation.

Prakash nodded and slapped the Lieutenant's back. "It's true! My actions will help Pakistan, but know this," Prakash spoke in honesty, "I am doing it more for my country. A war, no matter how inconsequential, always sets warring countries back. It hurts the economies. India has taken off and any setback will harm its economy. We will win the war; off that there is no doubt, but what then? My friend, my obligation and loyalty are to India." Prakash replied with equal gratitude, "I thank you for your courage and integrity. And, I thank you for trusting me."

Altaf Khos' moist eyes said it all. He acknowledged it with a nod and left the room. Prakash looked at the room with sadness.

Aman noticed it and asked for the reason.

"When people can co-exist happily why do they have to fight? God created this beautiful Earth for all human beings, for all living beings," Prakash said looking at the blood stains on the floor. He led Aman out of the room and closed the large room behind him.

* * *

347

Hotel Pakistan International,

Islamabad, Pakistan

Faisal Sheikh, a Junior Secretary in External Affairs Ministry in Islamabad was having a fantastic day, looking forward to a three day break in the mountains with his wife and his eight month old daughter when a call from Pratima Vaidya ruined his plans. Her late evening call and her tone made him nervous. She ordered him to meet her. That convinced him of the seriousness of the situation because she had asked him to meet him in hotel lobby in Islamabad, far from her domain of Karachi. She considered it important but told her to keep it confidential. She had influenced his career to a great extent because she considered him a practical man who saw things as they were - without bias or preconceived notions, and he was efficient. She brought him on board whenever she saw an opportunity. It was this silent affection for him that had helped him in a tight situation.

Eight months ago his wife was pregnant for the first time in seven years of marriage. Faisal's mother, who hailed from Ajmer, Rajasthan, had great faith in *'Sufi Saint Moinuddin Chisti'* whose mausoleum, or *'Dargah'* as it is called, is in Ajmer Sharif, in India. When Faisal told her about his plans to visit Agra to see the Taj

Mahal with his wife, his mother insisted he postpone the trip owing to Zoya's pregnancy. When he said he had planned the trip on her wish, his mother had instructed him to take his wife to 'Ajmer Sharif *Dargah*'. She wanted Zoya and Faisal to pay a visit to offer linen, a '*Chaddar*' on the *Dargah* of the Sufi saint's shrine. Faisal tried his best to persuade her, telling her that they did not have permission to visit Ajmer. His mother wouldn't hear of it. He reluctantly agreed, though Zoya was seven months pregnant.

After his trip to Agra, he had taken Zoya to the '*Dargah*' and offered a '*chaddar*' at the shrine late in the evening. They were glad they had heeded to his mother's advice. It was a uniquely spiritual experience for both because of what they saw there; they thought it was incomprehensible. They found people from all walks of life, all religions coming to pay their respects, seeking blessings of the revered *Sufi* saint. Then he made an error. Instead of returning to Delhi Faisal decided to give Zoya much needed rest and they lodged into a hotel in Ajmer. The three hundred and fifty kilometre travel by road from Agra to Ajmer was tiring for pregnant Zoya. Travelling another four hundred kilometres to New Delhi was not advisable. The next morning brought a weird, sad and yet the most beautiful day of his life.

A crude bomb ripped the periphery of the '*Dargah*'. A local fundamentalist Islamic organization was suspected and authorities went into action. Faisal heard a rap on the door of his hotel room early in the morning. Faisal until then, had no idea about the explosion at the spot they were twelve hours earlier. Faisal opened the door to find two men at the door. He was arrested. When asked, he couldn't explain why he was in the city without prior permission. His visa restricted him to travel to Agra, via New Delhi. The couple were hundreds of kilometres adrift from either place. Faisal tried explaining but it was to no use. He thought of calling his High Commission in New Delhi but he knew he would be reprimanded for violating his travel restrictions. In a moment of inspiration, he had called Pratima

Vaidya. She had heard his story patiently and asked him to remain positive and hand the phone to the cop in charge. The cop had taken the call but swore he couldn't help because the matter was being investigated by an intelligence officer. Pratima spoke to the investigating officer and convinced him that Faisal was caught in a situation. The officer in charge respected her wish but said he could only act if Faisal's story checked out, and asked her to wait for a few hours. In a separate room, Zoya was in real trouble. She was worried about Faisal. The lack of information about where he was, had taken its toll. She went into labour.

When Faisal learnt of Zoya's condition, he had panicked. He had begged the officer to call Pratima. The officer had looked at him strangely, and for some reason he had offered his phone to Faisal. When the Deputy High Commissioner heard about Zoya, she spoke to the officer and promised she would stake her career on line because she knew Faisal was an honest, decent man without any criminal involvement. Two hours later, the intelligence officer escorted Faisal to a hospital where he was reunited with Zoya. When enquired by the officer, they were told that Zoya was in labour room. As the two men waited, a female doctor appeared with a broad smile. Zoya had delivered seven and a half pound healthy baby girl ten minutes earlier she said and led them to Zoya's room.

The officer saw the baby girl and congratulated the parents. "You ought to call up that lady in Karachi. She arranged it. If it wasn't for her, you two could have been in real trouble," he said, congratulated them once again and left.

From that day Faisal was indebted to Pratima. He called her *'Amma'*, 'mother' in respect, and some in jest, at times when he sought favour. Though she had never demanded a favour in return, Faisal knew he had to pay back the favour someday.

He rose to greet her when he saw Pratima Vaidya come out of the elevator and instinctively knew the situation was quite serious. The usually pleasant woman, who would never fluster in any situation, looked angry. Pratima Vaidya led him to a table in a corner and came to the point directly, "I asked you to bring a trustworthy colleague. Where is he?"

"I don't know the situation, *'Amma'*, so I didn't know whom to call. I thought I will see what the situation was and decide whom I can involve, if I must," he replied, using *'Amma'* as a reference to keep the atmosphere cordial.

"When I said it was a serious situation, did you think it was casual?" She asked without emotion. His *'Amma'* reference was not taken well at this instance.

Faisal nodded, "I don't take anything you say lightly. Please tell me what this is all about. You have flown to Islamabad so it must be very sensitive; whatever it is."

Pratima Vaidya opened her bag and pulled out a thick bunch of sheets and placed it in front of him. For the next thirty-five minutes Faisal read the contents of the folder with disbelief. He put the folder back on the table and leaned back with his eyes shut. He knew this was far above him. His position in the Ministry was many rungs below the authority required to handle this sort of thing. "Why do you show this to me?" he asked seriously.

"I have worked with at least twenty men in your ministry and I can vouch that each one of them has a price tag. I had to speak to someone I can trust; whose integrity I could trust, and someone who makes sincere efforts to improve relations without creating diplomatic hurdles. You are pragmatic. If you can work this out, you have an even greater future. I want you to give me a name of one man who is practical and honest in appreciating a situation without going overboard with India-phobia."

"I can't think of anyone in the ministry... but I can refer you to one man who can help us. He has excellent connections and he is practical. My question to you is, why hasn't this already gone to the media?"

Pratima Vaidya's face cracked into a wry smile. "It will come to media attention either, when Wahid Khan disappears from the scene abruptly, or when he takes over."

"If this happens we will be pushed back by forty years. He must be stopped," Faisal said softly. He stared at the folder and asked again. "You have feeds from six international agencies. Why haven't the respective governments spoken to the Government here?"

"You have lots to learn. As we speak, your Prime Minister and three cabinet ministers are in a huddle. They are fully aware of what's happening. Many governments must have made statements but not to the media or in public domain. Do you reckon any foreign government cares what happens to Wahid Khan or Pakistan? If he assumes power, these Governments will issue press statements condemning Wahid Khan and his junta for a while before they start making deals with them; that is if he doesn't execute his plan to go to war with India. Right now those foreign governments will find ways to 'save' the incumbent government by extracting their pound of flesh and taking credit for saving 'democracy'. Your Ministers must have received calls from '*friendly*' governments who wish to see this government tide over, I bet. Options and pre-conditions will have been set and '*offers*' made. If this government survives, get contracts which have been stuck for long time and... Miraculously many hurdles disappear. This is the time to negotiate, don't you think? Multi-billion dollar defence contracts and infrastructure projects will be cleared promptly without a wink. To answer your query, Wahid Khan won't survive if he doesn't take over right now. If he does, we have a war coming and Pakistan's very existence will hang in the balance. If not, then those Governments get what they want. It's all a matter of a few days. Your politicians will have to choose between economic threats, military sanctions, and political exile, or accept the 'Terms and Conditions' offered. That is how the world moves."

"Our government isn't planning any attack on India then why should it face sanctions?" Faisal asked.

"Remove the initial pages where it proves that Wahid Khan is planning a takeover and leave the rest as it is. What do you get?" Pratima Vaidya looked at the thirty-seven year old Faisal with intelligent eyes, "you get scenario where government endorses the General's plan to wage war against India. This is unwarranted aggression. Pure and simple! Your government is implicated. What do you think will happen? Do you think your government can absolve itself from the responsibility of what is happening within its own army? It's happened once before; it will not be tolerated the second time."

"Do you want to meet this man? He has been campaigning for better relations with India." Faisal offered.

"Let him know the situation and ask him to call me tomorrow." Pratima rose, "Faisal, don't make copies of this. I trust you so I gave it to you. It's your responsibility now," she said and picked her bag, "If media plays it, God help us all."

"Your media is good at Pakistan bashing. It is powerful and quite free. Why hasn't it picked up the story? Why hasn't it been broken to them?" Faisal asked as he rose to bid her bye.

"You know what public opinion is? If media hammers it for a day, there will be protests in the streets. Public opinion can't be ignored. Opposition and war mongers will demand pre-emptive strike if only to neutralize a threat. A democratic government can't ignore public opinion. War is a political tool - the most powerful one, used mostly for economic and political gains. So, as far as possible, there will be a lid on this. Such situations have to be handled sensitively either through political solutions, or 'covertly'." Pratima Vaidya said calmly.

Faisal stared at his *'Amma'* and realized she was giving him a vital role to play; a role which could elevate him to higher position if he handles it well. A thought hit him. He looked at her with fearful eyes. "If General comes to power, we have a war. If it's a conventional war, Pakistan will be ruined. If not, Pakistan will be annihilated..."

Pratima replied coldly, "Pakistan will be wiped out if there's a war - conventional or nuclear. It won't survive the war," she said.

Faisal knew this was a warning for Pakistan she had stated clearly that India won't hold back. This was the message was for his government through him... through the 'soft channel'.

"For last few months your government has been talking of *'existential threat'* from various forces within. Add a name to it which is *'the most'* dangerous one you have at the moment... Wahid Khan!"

Faisal picked up the folder, "Who is Prakash Rohatgi?"

"I have no idea," Pratima Vaidya lied.

"How did he get a report like this in his hand?"

"I have no idea." This was an honest statement.

"Why would he procure such sensitive information unless he is working for intelligence services?" He asked pointedly.

"I don't know," Pratima replied curtly, "I know this. He has done both countries a great favour by uncovering the plan."

"What's on your mind, *'Amma'*?" He asked her softly. It was obvious to him that the solution was simple.

Pratima Vaidya gazed into his eyes without replying.

Faisal Sheikh gazed back at her. "Is it the..." he started to ask but her cold look unnerved him, "What is the solution to this? Tell me. You have always guided me in such situations."

Pratima remained silent. If he was intelligent he should know what to ask and when. She gazed at him coldly.

Faisal looked at her with astonishment. Was he misreading? Was she serious about what she meant without speaking? He stared at Pratima but she didn't react. Faisal looked away first, unsure what she meant. He knew that ultimate solution was an option but it won't be easy, and he was glad he didn't have to make it. News was out that a General had committed suicide. Death of another General would be a huge embarrassment to the military and the government.

— — —

Faisal Sheikh walked out calmly, but his mind was racing in every direction. If he had displayed deeper emotions it would have exhibited his weakness, and played right in the hands of his Indian 'Godmother'. Faisal asked for his car to be brought and stood under the dim lights, and opened the folder again with shivering hands.

Faisal's car rolled slowly on the empty Islamabad highway towards his residence; his mind was more in the folder than on road. Who could he trust implicitly to send the files with confidence? Think out of the box, he told himself. When he did, a thought struck him. He decided.

He thought about his decision again. Would his action be a mistake or would it bring desired result, he wondered. He was taking a risk; not to his career alone but to his life as well. If his intuition was right, his action could scuttle the plan. If not, at least it would make the General hold his plans. Faisal Sheikh made a few calls, inquiring about the closest men to Wahid Khan and the Director General of the ISI. He got two names. He called the two and spoke to them and sent them soft copies of the folder. Now ball was in Wahid Khan's court. Will the General continue or re-think about his quixotic plan? Faisal was certain DG of ISI would know about the existing scenario. The DG-ISI may be doing his own investigation but he may not have the full picture. Even if the DG-ISI knew the situation it would frighten him that the Indians too know about Wahid Khan's plan. They will be forced to retract because the files had come from the official channel of the Indian Government, with a stern warning. If the General did not step down or forego his plan,

Pratima Vaidya had said categorically that India would go for a 'pre-emptive strike'. The International community was aware of Wahid Khan's plans, so it would support India. This would be a nightmare for Pakistan.

*   *   *

Pakistan Army Camp,

Skardu, near LOC,
Pakistan Occupied Kashmir

Khaled Usmani was frightened. Wahid Khan was careful in preparing and executing his plans. How could there be a leak? Usmani held a copy of a detailed report in his hand, sent by a bureaucrat who was wise to send it to him. Usmani checked the authenticity of the sender; Faisal Sheikh. The young bureaucrat was noted for his wisdom and foresight. Khaled Usmani was surprised at the accuracy of information in the folder. He had to inform Wahid Khan. Wahid Khan may be a maverick but his intent was good. He wanted Pakistan to be a militarily strong country which would stabilize the country by giving it a chance to fight the enemy within, without worrying about the threat of a powerful India attacking it. A strong government with a strong ruler at the helm was needed. The General wanted to become the leader of the Islamic world. His plan to tackle India first and then counter the divisive forces within before taking on Israel to free Palestine was an ambitious and commendable plan but the problem was the first hurdle. India was a regional power and was on its way to becoming a world power. With a strong India no Pakistan ruler could relax. Thus, Wahid Khan had prepared a *'master plan'* to neutralize India before turning attention to domestic issues. Yakub Lahori, the political advisor of General Wahid Khan was a softy. He considered the plan risky. Lahori felt Pakistan shouldn't worry about India. The giant neighbour had never attacked Pakistan unless it was provoked. General Wahid Khan did not heed to his advice though. Wahid Khan considered India his first priority. But now, Indians knew his plan. This changed the equation in India's favour. The only advantage Wahid Khan had was that Indians didn't know about the involvement of the militant groups. This was a minor advantage but if the Indians were to get information of the involvement of the *Jihadi* forces', India will come with full force and International community will take serious view and side with India. That would spell doom for Pakistan.

With trembling hands, Yakub Lahori placed the report on the table. His worst fear had come true. He had alerted the General of such a scenario but the General had waived it off calling it in an unnecessary fear.

"How did you get this?" Yakub Lahori asked Usmani.

"A junior level bureaucrat sent this to me, saying he got it from an Indian diplomat. He refused to name the diplomat."

"The report is a bomb waiting to explode. We don't know who or how many people have it," Lahori said thoughtfully. "Does the bureaucrat know how many copies of this report exist?"

"There are three copies. One is with a former Pak army Major who is presently in India. He has a..." Usmani realized he had missed something of vital importance in the report.

"What's a Pakistani army major doing in India? How did he get this? And why?" Lahori was surprised.

Usmani linked the two facts he had not put together earlier. "That is the ex-major who tried to bring back his men from the post near Tiger Hill during the Kargil war."

Lahori checked the folder again and searched for Zubair Ahmed. Lahori was surprised, "Why does he have it? Is he working for the Indians now?"

Usmani nodded, "Yes, and I fear he may be working for the Indian intelligence services. He couldn't have the contacts to get to CIA or MI-6 or other agencies that would provide sensitive informations which are there in the files. It has to come from the Indian Intelligence agencies."

"How on earth did they get a sniff of this?"

"I have no idea."

"Where are the other two copies of this report?"

"One is with the mystery man, Prakash Rohatgi. The other is with the Indian diplomat. The diplomat couldn't possibly have parted without retaining a copy."

Lahori picked up the folder and reread the reports in it. For an hour he was reading and making mental notes of the vital informations. He put the folder back on the table, "I will take this to the General in the morning. I have to think on this. Then we will know where we stand."

"This could be a disaster for Pakistan, Yakub."

"We have to avoid this... it's a catastrophe! I fear that many of our influential friends around the world know of this now. Indians have always used their diplomatic channels well. If they do it this time, we will stand isolated... again."

Usmani agreed. "If we can't stop this, the Indians will burn us alive and the world won't have any sympathy for us."

Lahori nodded, "We have a hard day tomorrow. If we are good, we must emerge unscathed, with the plan intact."

"There is another angle to this. If our soldiers learn that our General had ordered the shelling of that post they will revolt and the ex-major will become a hero. We haven't considered it yet, have we?"

*   *   *

Prakash Rohatgi's Residence,

New Delhi, India

After dinner, Mehjabeen insisted on watching a movie like every weekend, and others decided to give her company. For Rukhsar, the movie was an escape from the tensions of last few days. Aman wasn't watching the movie; he was admiring his wife and the pretty girl who sat between her and Prakash, while Prakash was thinking of ways to get to Wahid Khan.

Prakash wanted to keep Zubair away from Wahid Khan. If they came face to face one would die. If Zubair died, it would be an irreplaceable loss. If the General died it would turn into an international scandal where India would be blamed of an assassination, circumstances notwithstanding. India would lose its moral high ground; that wasn't acceptable in any condition.

Two hours later when the movie was over, Zubair smiled at the scene. Rukhsar looked happy and whispering in Aman's ears. Prakash was smiling as their eyes met, and both knew why they smiled. Mehjabeen, who was keenest to watch the movie, was fast asleep. She was lying on the sofa with her face tucked into Prakash's abdomen and her feet on Rukhsar's lap. Prakash put Mehjabeen's head on the sofa, rose and shook her. To their surprise she raised her head with a smile, "Is the movie over?"

"I thought you were sleeping," Prakash laughed.

"The last bit was too gory. So I turned around and fell asleep," Mehjabeen giggled.

Prakash ruffled her hair playfully, "Now it's time for you to go to sleep."

Mehjabeen nodded, held Rukhsar's hand and ran to the stairs. Aman asked Rukhsar to return after Mehjabeen slept. Rukhsar nodded and followed Mehjabeen.

She returned a little while later and found the three men still talking about something in hushed voices. She wondered what the three men were talking about when she noticed that they had fallen silent when they saw her. "What happened?" She asked.

"Is she asleep?" Prakash asked.

Rukhsar smiled, "Yes... like a baby."

Prakash beamed. His happiness was visible from his face ever since Mehjabeen had come to the farmhouse. He leaned back in the chair and drummed his fingers on the table. By his actions, the three people knew he was happy, and it also said that he had something on his mind which he liked a lot.

"What is it, Prakash?" Rukhsar asked.

"While you were watching the movie I thought of something. I think Zubair Saheb and I will speak to Wahid Khan in a day or two," Prakash said with a broad smile despite the shocked faces.

"You are surely joking," Rukhsar almost jumped out of her seat, "Why will he talk to us? Or why should we talk to him?"

Prakash's face changed to a ruthless expression. He looked calm but his eyes displayed crude hatred. "He will speak to us because he doesn't want his career to end, and because I don't want him to get away."

"How can we manage to meet him? Do you think it will be easy to even get close to him?" Aman Bux asked.

"He will come to us," Prakash said coldly.

"How?" Aman asked with raised eyebrows.

"Later!" Prakash replied and leaned back in his chair again. He looked at Zubair Ahmed, "Saheb, you will get your chance to kill him."

Rukhsar looked at Prakash with horror, dreading what could happen if her father and Wahid Khan met. She looked at her father and saw him nodding at Prakash, "I need just one chance," he said thoughtfully.

"You didn't tell us how," Aman asked again.

"I said 'Later'," Prakash replied again.

Aman rose from the chair angrily. "Your 'later' never comes." He said with his fingers pointing at Prakash, "You promised me two things but your 'later' hasn't come yet."

Prakash nodded, "I will keep my promises."

"When?" Aman asked without hiding his disappointment.

"Sit," Prakash ordered. "What do you want to know?"

"Tell me about yourself."

"That is the first question asked to an interviewee these days," Prakash made a feeble attempt at joke.

"Your joke doesn't humour me. Who are you? What do you do? What is this organization you work for? And why?" Aman threw a string of questions.

Prakash looked at the three faces, "To tell you about my family I have to go back and start from many centuries ago..."

Aman Bux was taken aback by the statement. "What do you mean? How can centuries be part of anyone's life?"

"Right! Let me correct my statement. I made an error. It isn't centuries; it is 'Millennia'..." Prakash's voice tapered off. He was gazing into nothing. His mind playing a visual from the past and it hurt him deeply. The sadness on his face made Rukhsar feel for him. She could see enormous attempt by him to control his emotions but the curve of his lips and his eyes displayed it.

Rukhsar asked Aman to exchange his seat with her and she sat next to Prakash, "Prakash," she said, taking his palms, "Will you understand it when I say that I love you?"

Prakash Rohatgi's glassy gaze returned to the present and grabbed Rukhsar's hands in his, "Yes, I do! Thank you!"

Aman saw the pure emotion of loving a person without naming a relation. Surprisingly, instead of envy he saw purity in the way Rukhsar spoke to Prakash and how he replied and in that moment he conveyed how much she meant to him.

Zubair felt a sense of ecstasy in the two line conversation and there he saw why he loved Prakash though the idiot had never told his story to him.

"Tell me what's hurting you? I have observed," Rukhsar said with sadness in her tone, "and I see a lonely man who has shut himself to all. I saw you happy only twice in eight days; once at my wedding, and…each time you see Mehjabeen. What makes you so sad? Is it Mehrunissa?"

Prakash smiled wryly, "I will be, as the saying goes, 'over the moon', if Mehrunissa can marry me. But, for me that angel upstairs is my life. She is my daughter who has been put into my lap by God's blessings. But no, they are not even closely responsible for…" he said and abruptly he stopped.

"Talk to me, Prakash," she begged, "if you love me too."

Tears welled up in Prakash's eyes. He put his arm around her shoulder and hugged her to stop from crying. His heart opened for a while to encompass the past and embrace the present to the woman who had become an extension to his family, in spirit.

* * *

Prakash Rohatgi

The Rohatgi family

"**I** am the last custodian of centuries of my families' history and millennia of history of my land," Prakash Rohatgi started reluctantly others felt, about his family history.

"What? How is that possible? Can you please stop talking in riddles? Just tell us clearly, ok?" Rukhsar asked.

"Śāradā-Peeth! Have you heard of it?" Prakash asked.

Rukhsar had never heard of it, "What is Śāradā-Peeth?"

"It's one of the oldest seats of education of ancient times with thousands of years of history. It's mainly renowned for its magnificent temple ruins of Goddess *Sarasvati*, also known as Goddess Śāradā. My ancestry goes back many generations to Śāradā *Peeth*," Prakash said calmly without any expression but to all three present in the hall listening to him, it seemed like a monumental effort to mention about his past.

"Where is Śāradā-*Peeth*?" Rukhsar asked.

"It is twenty-seven kilometres on the other side of the LOC in Pakistan Occupied Kashmir."

Rukhsar retreated back into her chair feeling deflated. The air of expectancy evaporated from her face and there was sadness written over it. She understood the problem and she had a clue, like Zubair, of what was to come. Aman Bux knew what was coming and he could relate to it.

Rukhsar asked sadly, guessing correctly, "The Partition?"

Prakash looked at her with his expressionless eyes, lowered his head and nodded.

"What happened?" Rukhsar asked.

Prakash was quiet for some time. His guests felt he was in a different world, in another era. Prakash shook his head with a wry smile, "My story is like millions who live in exile because of partition." He stopped and looked into Zubair Ahmed's eyes, "For generations my family was the keeper of the records of Śāradā Temple and its educational arm. The Royal families of Kashmir region were the principle funders of the institution. In ancient times, this... small university, which had various colleges for many disciplines, was a seat of education for thousands of students from India, Africa, Europe, Far and Middle-Eastern countries. Śāradā-*Peeth* developed its own script, called '*Takri*', an off shoot of Sanskrit. *Takri* is the mother of many languages, off which Punjabi is the most famous and the '*Gurmukhi*' script of the Punjabis comes from '*Takri*'. There is hardly any living person who can write the original *Takri* script. It is lost forever, I guess. It was the mother tongue of my family for centuries... for millennia..."

Prakash walked to the other end of the wall and pulled out two wooden boxes hidden behind book shelves and placed them gently on the table in front of Zubair and touched it like he was caressing a baby. He looked at Zubair and asked him to open the boxes. Zubair opened the boxes and gasped; he stared at the contents breathlessly. They were stunning. He looked at Prakash in awe. Rukhsar and Aman stood behind Zubair and saw the antiquity, and their reactions were same as Zubair's. Aman asked for Prakash's permission, picked the content from a box and delicately placed it on the table. He knew what it was supposed to be, but not what it exactly was. He looked at Prakash.

"Those are the original manuscripts in '*Takri*' dating back to twelve hundred years. I can't read the language but I know what is written on those leaves. It tells the story of the 'Seat of Śāradā' meaning the Śāradā *Peeth*." Prakash said sadly.

"What is it, Prakash?" Aman asked with empathy.

"Large volumes of original manuscripts mainly written by Sage Shandilya were destroyed when Śāradā *Peeth* was attacked in fourteenth century. After the attack, the invaders burnt the library which contained thousands of scrolls, with hundreds of '*Shlokas*' in each... very few survived. My ancestors, the keepers of the library were also teachers in four disciplines; literature, Astronomy, science and mathematics. When Dogra rulers defeated the invaders in nineteenth century the temple was restored but the old university could never be restored. Some manuscripts were saved from fire because according to my ancestors, when the attack took place these were in our house, and one of my ancestors was doing a translation of these into Sanskrit. So, it has survived with the family. We treasure it with our lives." Prakash stopped and corrected his mistake, "I treasure it with my life," he said, and stopped.

There was silence in the room. They were wondering if they could feel his pain. Prakash delicately picked the scrolls and put the fragile scrolls gently back into the box, closed the box and caressed it again. "In many cases," he said, "mythological events become legends and then they become history through popularity. Here," he said, touching the boxes, "history turned into legend, and legend to myth."

"What do you mean?" Zubair asked.

"Goddess *Sati*, an incarnation of *Shakti* was married to God Shiva. Sati was the daughter of the King of the Himalaya, King Daksha. Sati's father performed a '*Yagnya*', a ceremonial offering, and invited all kings and royal families but not Shiva. Sati knew

Her father had insulted Her husband by ignoring Him. So, She swore that the insult would be avenged by Her husband and saying so, She immolated Herself in the fire which the priests had lit for '*Yagnya*'."

Prakash turned to Aman, "The other day you saw '*Nataraja*' statue in my study and you asked me about the significance of the statue and its posture. '*Nataraja*', the 'King of performing arts'! The posture is the dance of death, '*Tandava*'. The *Nataraja* posture symbolises creation, destruction and recreation of the Universe," Prakash said and turned to others, "When Shiva learns of what Sati had done, He was angry and He performs the '*Tandava*' in a rage to destroy the kingdom of His father-in-law, King Daksha. When God Vishnu pacified Him that Sati will marry Him again in Her next incarnation, Shiva calms and comes to claim the body of Sati and takes it to His abode, Kailash Mountain. On the way, Sati's body parts fell off... each place where the body part fell, became *Shakti-Peeth*s; there are fifty-one in total but Śāradā *Peeth* is of great importance because Sati's right arm fell here. It is among the eighteen 'most important' *Shakti-Peeths*. It is also a '*Sati-Peeth*'." When Shiv was sad, and He cried and with His tears a lake, or pond, if you wish to call it, was created. The Pandavas built a temple at that site; this temple and the lake is called the '*Katas-Raj Temple*' in Chakwal, in west-Punjab."

Rukhsar hesitated but asked a question which was sensitive. But she trusted Prakash's sincerity, "Is the '*Sati*' custom of self-immolation is anyway related to this incident?"

To her surprise Prakash replied casually, "Yes, it was. But *Sati* custom adopted later was for different reasons. *Sati* isn't a part of Hindu custom or culture. When Muslim invaders won wars they took females as trophies and slaves. In Gujarat and Rajasthan, the women preferred to immolate themselves on their husband's pyre from fear of being abducted and raped. That is how '*Sati*' custom was born. It was also called '*Jauhar*', but later it turned ugly when widows were forced to immolate themselves on their husband's pyre. Thankfully, the British ended this barbaric custom."

Aman and Rukhsar waited for Prakash to resume his story but Prakash seemed reluctant. Prakash excused himself and walked away from the table promising to return soon. Zubair had asked Prakash about his past but Prakash avoided talking on the subject. Today, he felt, for some reason Prakash wanted to tell it; not to him but to Rukhsar and Aman. In a way, this hurt him.

Prakash returned looking fresh. He put the boxes back in the receptacle and returned with another book, another antiquity. He put it on the table and sat down, "This book by an eminent archaeologist, has challenged the theory of Aryan migration to Indus Valley and to the Indian sub-continent, as suggested in his theory by the German, Max Mueller, the foremost *'Indologist'* and *'Sanskritist'* of his era. The theory by Max Mueller was that the Indian sub-continent was invaded by Aryans who came through Central Asia and Europe and pushed local Dravidians down south. The theory by Max Mueller is just that - a theory. There is no scientific evidence to back it up. There are nearly twenty-two hundred excavated sites and we can't find a single, not a single evidence to support the theory of Mr. Mueller. Instead, I have some interesting facts here," he said and carefully opened the book, pulling out a single sheet which had hand written notes on it.

Prakash held the sheet in his hand and looked at Aman, "He has already seen it," Prakash said, pointing at Zubair, "I am sure you will find this interesting," he said and went back to the rows of books and returned with another book in his hand. "Modern archaeologists concur with this theory. According to these, Aryans were native Indians. The Aryans were, and are a proud race. Among hundreds of scriptures, with millions of *'Shlokas'*, there isn't a single mention of their origins being any other than India. In scriptures and texts they mention of a river which flowed from present day state of Himachal Pradesh and Uttarakhand to Gujarat. This river is mentioned with reverence. It was the mighty '*Sarasvati*'." Prakash said and opened the marked pages and displayed the photographs in front of Rukhsar and Aman. "These are satellite images of the dried up river bed of '*Sarasvati*' river."

Prakash let the couple flip through the pages. Rukhsar closed the book and nodded. She wondered what this had to do with Prakash's story. Then it struck her. He had earlier mentioned that 'Śāradā' was the name of Goddess *Sarasvati*. She nodded again and looked at Prakash.

Prakash looked at his guests, "We don't find mention of Sanskrit originating anywhere else except in the Indus valley, in Vedic era. Two other important aspects: first, the historical fact with scientific evidence: last ice-age ended around eleven thousand years ago. Is it possible that there could have been mass migration during the last ice age? If the theory which says that Aryans migrated to India is true, then it must have been either before ice age which is over a hundred thousand years, or after the ice age which is within the last eleven thousand years. We know that the latter is definitely not a case, and we don't find any proof of the earlier one either. The second is a conclusive proof that the Aryans were native Indians. DNA tests prove it. Archaeological proofs are available from east of Indus Valley, Harappa and Mohenjo-Daro to western banks of the Ganges. The plains of Ganga, Yamuna and other rivers add credence to this theory. These are scientific facts."

Prakash put the books aside and sat between Zubair and Rukhsar. While others waited for him to connect his story to what he had been talking about in past hour, Prakash tilted the back rest of his chair and slumped lazily, "You wonder why I went off-track to tell you these facts? This is the background and my family is an important part in history," he said proudly, "*Śāradā-Peeth* was one of the great learning places even when the western world was still in the dark ages and other great religions were centuries away from being born. Great scholars and travellers came to visit this place to witness the greatness of Śāradā-Peeth. In seventh century, Chinese monk Xingzuan came to Śāradā-Peeth to learn *Sutras*, which are the primary scriptures of the Buddhist sect. In eleventh century Al-Baruni visited this university and wrote laurels on marvels of excellence of this educational and spiritual institution. *Śāradā-Peeth* had a fantastic mix of two other great universities of the time: *Taksha-Shila* and *Nalanda*. These two were the first two universities of the world, if you didn't know. It was..."

Rukhsar interrupted Prakash's speech, "*Abbu* told us about it yesterday," she said.

Prakash nodded, "Good. Śāradā-Peeth was also an important educational institution for the Buddhists and other sects of the Hinduism. In the..."

"Excuse me for interrupting," Aman asked, "two questions. Buddhism is a religion. How can it be a sect of Hinduism?"

Prakash smiled with a chuckle escaping him, "Buddhists are followers of Gautam Buddha. Buddha was born in a Hindu royal family. Buddha preached self-realization, seeking the divine within. The existence of God outside is not accepted by the Buddhists; they seek Him within. Buddha did not establish a religion; He preached a medium to seek the Divine called *'Kundalini Yoga'*. *'Kudalini Yoga'* practice finds its roots in a spiritual quote from the Vedas, *'Tat-Tvam-Asi'*, which in loose English translation means, *'That Art Thou'* which says that each human being is Divine. This practice of the Hindu sect believes that God is within and we are part of His divine self. So, since He resides in us, we too are divine. That is the basic principle of Buddhist philosophy. Buddhist scriptures are the *'Sutras'*, and *'Sutras'* were originally in Sanskrit. Buddha gained enlightenment in Bodh-Gaya, a place where God Rama when in exile, performed the last rites for His father, King Dashrath.

So, it is also an important pilgrimage for both sects; Vaishnavs and Buddhists. Buddha's first sermon was in Sarnath, Benaras, which is now Varanasi. The other names for this city are Anand Vihar and most famously, 'Kashi'. All these are pilgrim sites for both the sects. Kashi is also known as the city of God Shiva. From here we get another similarity; Buddhists and Hindus use the same 'Rudraksha' for chanting. A Rudraksha rosary is common among chanters of both religions. If you look at the symbol of Buddha, it is *Swastika*. The Swastika along with 'Aum' are symbols of Hindu sects, including Buddhism and Jainism. Lastly, you see the important wheel? It is called the '*Dharma-Chakra*' that is the sign of Hindus since Vedas." Prakash paused, sipped water and continued, "There are many more similarities. And the ultimate aim of the Buddhists and Hindus is same: to achieve '*Moksha*', which means '*Pari-Nirvana*' or freedom from cycle of death and rebirth, and if not, at least '*Nirvana*'... a state of 'absolute bliss'. I hope it answers your first question. What is your second query?"

"You said Śāradā is Sarasvati. If I am not wrong, *Sarasvati* is not Shiva's console. You told us about the legend of Shiva and Sati, then why is this called Śāradā-Peeth?" Aman quizzed.

Prakash nodded, "You forgot a part where I said it is one of the fifty-one *Shakti-Peeths*. All Goddesses are one; They are incarnations... or you can call it manifestation of one Supreme Goddess, '*Shakti*'. *Śāradā*, or *Sarasvati*, or *Laxmi*, or *Sati*, *Durga* or *Kali*, or any other manifestation of the Goddess we think of, are all one - '*Shakti*'."

"If there is just one Supreme Goddess, how come there are many Gods? Which one do you call Supreme among Gods?" Aman asked hesitantly, knowing he was treading on a delicate subject which he was trained to avoid discussing - religion!

Prakash surprised him by speaking casually about it. "There are many misconceptions about Hinduism. Most common is calling Hindus as Hindus. There is no such religion as Hinduism.

It is actually 'Sanatana Dharma', which means the Eternal religion, with no beginning and no end. Second is that we have many Gods. Yes, we have many Gods but one Almighty - Supreme God, who goes by many names: *Eishwar, Parmeshwar,* or *Param-Pita Parmeshwar.* In the Rig-Veda and the *'Srimad-Bhagvatam',* or *'The Gita'* as it is commonly called, the two primary spiritual texts name Him *'Brahman'*... nothing to do with the Brahmin priests, I must add. That *Brahman* is the 'only' Supreme being. He is omnipotent and omnipresent and thus he resides in us as well... in all living and non-living being, though He has no form. Nothing and no living or non-living entity is Godless. That is why if you remember, I greeted you both with a *'Namaste'*, *'Nama'* and *'Aste'*, which means *'I bow to the divine within you, as He also resides in me'.* He manifests Himself into the omnipotent *'Shakti'*, as mother of all mankind and living beings, and as *'Purusha'*, the father. Then come the three manifestations of *Purusha* as Brahma - the Generator... Creator, Vishnu - the Operator, and Shiva - the destroyer... that's why Shiva is also seen in *'Nataraja'* posture. *Shakti* manifests Herself as their consoles in forms of *'Uma'* or *'Pārbati'*, with Shiva. She is the Goddess of strength and fertility. *Shakti's* manifestation as 'Maha*Laxmi'*, Goddess of prosperity, piety and devotion is Vishnu's console, and then *Shakti* manifests as *'Sarasvati'*, the Goddess of 'Knowledge and music' and She is the console of Brahma. So, there is just one God we pray to, through His numerous manifestations. There are many ways which lead to the Supreme Brahman and *'Kudalini Yoga'* is one of those where we pray to Him within us. This also tells us how Yoga is effective."

Rukhsar and Aman looked at each other trying to understand, although enlightening, had any relevance to the story of Prakash's life. Suddenly, Prakash rose from his chair and smiled at Aman and Prakash, "That wasn't a religious sermon. You asked me a question and I explained with a few details which I thought you ought to know."

Rukhsar responded with a jovial smile, "and I was thinking you were trying to convert us," she said and laughed.

"Shut up!" was a loud roar from Prakash, with some anger.

The three people sitting were shocked at his reaction. They wondered what had angered him.

"I was just joking. I didn't mean to offend you in any way," Rukhsar responded apologetically.

Prakash looked at her and regained his seat and bowed his head thoughtfully, "I am sorry. I lost my control," he said and looked at Rukhsar apologetically.

"What irked you so much?" She asked genuinely.

"When people attempt to convert anyone they don't realize a cardinal sin. We countermand God's wisdom when we try to convert someone. If He wanted you to perform an *'Aarti'* or pray the way I pray, He is wise enough to have given birth to you in a Hindu family. If His wish would have been that I pray with *'Namaaz'*, I would have been born a Muslim. When we attempt to convert a person to another religion, we go against His wisdom. Those who try to convert people from other religions are sinners. For me, conversion is the greatest blasphemy," Prakash said with an emotional zest.

Zubair, Aman and Rukhsar had great respect for Prakash but what he had just said elevated him to a higher level. They were staring at him with new found love which transcended a gift of God; which had become the nemesis of mankind: Religion.

"What do you say to people who convert to other religions? Aren't they also guilt of the same sin?" Rukhsar asked.

"God has blessed us with one thing which separates us from other living beings - a free, analytical mind which can derive its own conclusions and make decisions. If a person is comfortable by praying to Him in a particular way, he should feel free to do so because He finds peace that particular way. It's an individual's choice, and God's gift, the mind, which lets the person make his own decision how he wishes to pray. How can that be a sin?" Prakash replied.

Rukhsar sighed in relief. She realized an instant after Prakash finished that if he had said anything different, she would have lost faith in his decency and honesty. She beamed and hugged him tightly. "Thank you, Prakash," she said genuinely.

Aman felt a tinge a jealousy in the way Rukhsar had hugged Prakash. "Careful, lady, he isn't your husband," he jested.

"Shut up, Aman. You may be my husband; he is the kind of friend I never had; the best," she said and hugged Prakash again. She had trusted him when she saw him the first time and God had retained her immense faith. His statement about belief and practice of faith made perfect sense to her. He had spoken her mind, giving words to her own beliefs.

Aman Bux suddenly felt inferior. Momentarily, he was jealous of a friend and wife who were the two best people in his lonely life. For a moment he was overcome by jealousy, a feeling which was forbidden by the tenets of his own religion. He saw them interact and his feeling of letting himself down grew.

Rukhsar knew Prakash was trying hard to stop the moisture in his eyes turning to tear but failed miserably. Prakash closed his eyes and tears rolled down. Rukhsar put her arms around him, and her eyes were moist. He was hurting within but she was unable reach his heart; it frustrated her. "Won't you tell me, Prakash?" Rukhsar leaning against him with her hands holding his firmly, wanting to feel his pain.

Aman rose from his chair, stood behind Prakash and put his hand on his friend's shoulder. "We are your friends. Talk to us. You will feel lot better after sharing it with us," he said and squeezed Prakash's shoulders to support him morally.

Prakash nodded slowly. He rose to his feet, "excuse me. I will be back in a minute," he said and left the hall.

Rukhsar asked her father, "Do you know his story?"

Zubair wondered what happened, "He has always avoided talking about it," he said, "I think, for some reason, he wants to tell you, and Aman and I just happen to be present when he does. Prakash is a very tough man physically, mentally and spiritually. I know his weakness today; he is weak when he faces his loved ones. He cares for us, Rukhsar."

Rukhsar looked in the direction of the door where Prakash had gone and nodded.

Prakash returned fifteen minutes and he was in control, and the attitude was back in his mannerisms, which bordered on arrogance at times. He sat between Rukhsar and Zubair and looked at the three people looking at him patiently, waiting for him to continue his story. Prakash put both hands on the table and started, "I deviated from my story when I talked about *Shri*-Śāradā-Peeth as it's called in reverence because it is relevant. You should know the importance of the institution and the temple. It had a wooden statue of Goddess *Sarasvati*. Before students begin their studies, an ode is sung for Her. It is called *'Sarasvati-Vandana'*. That's how I began my education too. It is still practiced in many schools today," Prakash said and paused before speaking again, slowly, "Śāradā-Peeth is on the banks of Madhumati river, which is now the Neelum river. Along the banks there's a forest that is called Śāradā-van; 'van' meaning forest in Sanskrit and Hindi. After partition Maharaja Hari Singh, the King of Kashmir was undecided whether to join India or Pakistan. Initially he remained independent. At that time J&K didn't have an army, so the Pakistan establishment decided to take Kashmir by force by sending *'Kabailis'*, the tribesmen, and regular armed soldiers into Kashmir. There was a small Indian force in Srinagar for emergency. When the attack began, Śāradā-Peeth was at the forefront. It was among the first to be run over by the invaders. Mine was an affluent family but it had no security. The temple was destroyed and..." Prakash lowered his head and gazed into infinity as his eyes remained glued to the table. He was on the verge of crying again, "My grand-parents, uncles, aunts, and cousins were butchered in the attack, along with nine others which included four Muslims who worked and lived in temple precinct. My father was seven years old at the time. Jaan-Nissar was an aide and friend of the family who worked there. The morning Śāradā *Peeth* was attacked my father was in an orchid with Jaan-Nissar. When he learnt of the attack on the temple he took my father and hid for two nights and two days in Śāradā-van. When the attackers left, Jaan-Nissar sneaked out of the forest with my father and returned to the temple. My father saw the lowest ebb of mankind's brutality." Prakash paused again, and continued without raising his head; his eyes still gazing at the table; he was visualizing the imaginary sight, "All male members were slaughtered. My uncle and grandfather were beheaded. Three uncles were executed by shots in the heads. Females bore the worst... my great-grandmother's throat was slit and my aunt's head was smashed against a rock. My father's fourteen year old cousin was found tied to a post, raped and beaten to death. My grandmother had a knife in her abdomen; she was still holding the knife in her hand when my father saw his *'Mai'*; she had committed suicide." Prakash's eyes welled up again and three other people in the room felt just as sad. Another pair of eyes cried.

Rukhsar heard the sobs. She turned and saw Mehjabeen on top of the stairs. "What are you doing here?" She scolded Mehjabeen loudly fearing Mehjabeen may have heard what Prakash may have hidden from her and her mother.

Mehjabeen ignored Rukhsar and ran to Prakash. *"Baba"*, she cried, wrapping her arms around his waist. She put her head on Prakash's chest and cried. Prakash held Mehjabeen in his arms, patting her, "you shouldn't have come down."

"Baba," Mehjabeen continued to cry.

Prakash made Mehjabeen sit to his left and held her hands, "You should go back up. This isn't good for you."

Mehjabeen wiped her tears and said firmly, "I am your daughter. I have a right to know."

"You will learn from your mother when you grow up." Prakash tried pacifying her.

Mehjabeen's large eyes were fixed on Prakash. She wanted to hear his story. "I want to hear it from you, not '*Ammi*'."

Zubair looked at his daughter and found her eyes locked into his. They were thinking the same. They had missed the tender moments which bind father-daughter relationship; what they saw between Prakash and Mehjabeen in last few moments. When she was young he was mostly on duty outside Lahore and when she grew up he was gone from her life. The sadness was palpable. Rukhsar lowered her head and turned to Mehjabeen. The pretty girl was determined. Despite Prakash's requests she refused to budge. After few minutes of persuasion Prakash threw his hands up in frustration and told his guests, "Let's talk later. My princess is being a naughty girl. She forgets she must respect her elders' wishes."

Zubair patted the eleven year old sitting to his right. "Let it be, Prakash. Some people would give half their life to live a moment like this. She is old enough to know what she wants. It can't be worse than what she has heard."

Prakash looked at Mehjabeen wondering if she was ready to hear the rest. Her mother had asked him not to tell her the gory tails. He shook his head and put his arm around his daughter, "Promise me you will not tell your mother."

"She knows?" Mehjabeen countered.

"Yes. But, you won't tell her that you know. Or else, you can sit all night."

Mehjabeen nodded. Prakash wrapped her in his arms. He was unsure how to resume. He got help by a query from Aman Khan. "How did you land up in New Delhi?"

"We were in Srinagar. *Babu*, my father, was brought to Srinagar by Jaan-Nissar. The temple was supported by the royal family so they knew our family well. Jaan-Nissar took my father to them and told them what happened. My father was given a house and Jaan-Nissar was asked to raise him till he graduated from college. Jaan-Nissar kept his promise and stayed with him till..." Prakash stopped. This was part more difficult to narrate than the earlier story.

Prakash held Mehjabeen tightly, "Members of royal family took good care of my father's needs. When he was mature, at twenty-one, he was given the papers of the family estate but it was useless because the area was under Pakistan's occupation. The royal family took extra effort by asking government of Sheikh Abdullah to assist the family financially. My father was provided a decent job and he joined Jammu and Kashmir unit of the local Security force. Although my father was doing well in his life, he never overcame the psychological trauma of his childhood. As time went by he started to get worse. When I was twelve, '*Babu*' told me about our family's tragedy for the first time and he repeated it every month. He told us about his nightmares but my mother's support that kept him sane. In '92 I was in military college, Dehradun when I heard about a terrorist attack in our area. I called home. I was told that my parents and..." Prakash stopped. He clenched his fists and paused, "I had a sister seven years younger to me. Due to *Babu's* mental state, my mother prohibited him to venture out alone except for work. While I was in training, my sister somehow persuaded my parents to go to Poonch and Rajouri for holidays. During cross border shelling in the area two bombs landed a few metres from their car and exploded. My father and sister died instantly and my mother died on her way to hospital. Jaan-Nissar was seriously injured. The next morning I lit the pyres, and performed the last rites thirteen days later. Jaan-Nissar died a week later. I performed the rites as his son, and returned to Dehradun. These deaths made me more determined to pass out as the best cadet, which I did. An experienced field officer spotted me and brought me to intelligence wing. Then I was given a chance that I couldn't refuse… and here I am."

"You never got married or…" Rukhsar asked. She didn't complete the last part. Cultural etiquette stopped her from asking that question in her father's or young girl's presence.

Prakash looked at Rukhsar and thought if he should reply. Four pairs of eyes were looking at him; none had the courage to ask him to speak. They felt there was more tragedy to come from Prakash's life story.

"*Baba*, please tell me," Mehjabeen begged her foster father.

"My mentor arranged my marriage with his niece eleven years ago. Archana… she was a banker in Mumbai… my only friend. A week before our marriage she was fatally injured in a terrorist attack… Mumbai serial train blasts," Prakash said and drew a deep breath, "She died the day we were supposed to get married."

The occupants of the room were silent. Zubair, Rukhsar and Aman did not know how to react to Prakash's story.

Mehjabeen put her arms around her '*Baba*' and hugged him. "I am your daughter," she said to console Prakash.

Prakash hugged her with a weak smile. "Yes! You are!"

"And I am his sister," Rukhsar told everyone.

Mehjabeen laughed loudly, mocking Rukhsar. "Are you?" she said innocently without knowing the complications, "You never tied '*Rakhi*' to him."

Rukhsar replied seriously, "I wish I could. I can't because it is a Hindu custom and if I did, there would be uproar."

"Who would say anything to you?" Aman protested.

"And, it isn't a Hindu custom," Prakash corrected Rukhsar, "There are instances where Hindu and non-Hindus have tied '*Rakhis*'. The famous one is when the widow of the King of Chittor, Rani Karnavati sent a '*Rakhi*' to Emperor Humayun, the Mughal Emperor, to save her kingdom from Bahadur Shah, the Sultan of Gujarat. Emperor Humayun was overcome by Rani Karnavati's gesture and set out with a large army to save her sister's kingdom. Meanwhile, Bahadur Shah wreaked havoc on Chittor. Chittor women committed *'Jauhar'* in their thousands. The small army of Rajput men of Chittor took an oath and rode out on suicide mission to either return victorious or die on the battle field. Humayun was late by a few days. When he reached Chittor, he witnessed the bravery of the Rajput fighting the way they did, though heavily outnumbered. He launched an assault and defeated Bahadur Shah. When Humayun reached the gates he heard the news that his 'sister', Rani Karnavati had committed *'Jauhar'*. He returned to the capital a sad man, but not before putting Karnavati's son on the throne of Chittor. That is the legend. We have no proves except for sixteenth century texts on this incident." Prakash said and looked at her with a weak smile. It was the only way he could overcome his sadness. "There is another story which is just as profound. King Ambhi of *Taksha-Shila*, an arch enemy of King Puru ruled the region between Chenab and Jhelum. When Alexander invaded India in 326bce, Ambhi and Alexander joined forces to defeat Puru, or Poros, as he was also called. Roshanak or *Roxana* as she was known was Alexander's wife; an Indian. She knew of Poros' might and feared for her husband's life. So, she sent a *'Rakhi'* to Poros requesting him to spare her husband's life. King Poros honoured her. In the first battle Alexander had to retreat but not before an incident that is now a legend. In an attack Alexander fell off his horse, attacked by an intoxicated elephant. Poros could have killed Alexander but he didn't. In the second battle Poros was defeated but Poros continued to rule because Alexander too spared Poros' life, and started his journey back home."

"Is that when Poros gave that famous reply to Alexander?" Aman asked.

Rukhsar looked quizzingly at both men. Prakash nodded, "Yes. When Poros was captured and brought in the presence of Alexander, the captor asked Poros how the captive should be treated. That is when Poros replied, 'like a king'. It further impressed Alexander. He returned the kingdom to Poros and decided to return home, probably because he was mortally wounded but that is a matter of debate."

"We never hear of it in the history books," Rukhsar said.

Aman laughed, "You mean in Pakistani history texts? This is a story of fourth century bce. When our history text doesn't mention historical events before the arrival of Mohammed Bin Qasim how do you expect great stories of the past to be told? According to history texts in schools, India did not exist from eighth to sixteenth century, remember?"

"What?" Zubair Ahmed shouted in disbelief, "Is that true?"

Rukhsar looked at her husband first and then at her father. She embarrassingly nodded her head.

"Ya Allah!" Zubair screamed despondently, clasped his face in his palms, "How many more lies do our children learn? What other lies do they tell? Tell me," he asked Aman.

Aman laughed despite his foul mood, "Let me tell you what they are teaching our children. Firstly, there is no historical mention of any era before eighth century. History texts start with the arrival of Mohammed Bin Qasim, not as an invader, but as a hero…According to the so called 'learned' historians, Qasim laid the foundation of Pakistan in that era near Multan where Qasim first arrived. According to Mr. M. D. Zafar, our writer of the 'compulsory subject' history texts, 'Pakistan' had extended its boundary from Pakistan and Afghanistan to…," Aman Bux laughed hilariously and paused, "here is the most comical part. By thirteenth century 'Pakistan' had extended its boundaries up to Bengal in the east and down to central India and the Deccan plateau in the south. If you were appalled by what I said about India not being in existence; our texts boast that by sixteenth century, 'Pakistan and Islam' were 'safe and consolidated' under Mughal Emperor Aurangzeb and India ceased to exist at the time. It was all 'Pakistan' at the time. This," Aman said in sadness, "is taught to teenage students. That is the mind-set created in tender, susceptible minds of our future generations? That is the next generation."

Rukhsar was confused. For her it made no sense why this was being done although Zubair had spoken the previous afternoon about the lies... LIES! The word kept cropping up always. She looked at her husband and at her father, and she believed what they were talking about but for her something was amiss. "In Pakistan there is a debate on dates on when Pakistan was formed or born. There are dates when Pakistan or the idea of Pakistan was born; first is during the eighth century when Bin Qasim arrived in India. Second is 1906 when 'Muslim League' came into existence and last was in 1930 when Alama Iqbal demanded creation of Pakistan," she asked Zubair and Aman Bux, "Which of this is true?"

Aman Bux laughed. He stopped laughing when he saw his wife's seriousness. He put his hands in the air in apology, "all three are 'wrong'," Aman stressed.

Rukhsar was flabbergasted. It wasn't just that all the three theories doing rounds in her country were wrong that ashamed her, it was the monstrosity of lies that surprised her. "Please explain, Aman," she asked with severe dejection.

"The word 'Pakistan' was first uttered by a Cambridge student, Choudhary Rehmat Ali in 1940. Until then the word 'Pakistan' did not exist. This term was adopted by leaders of the Muslim League. Bin Qasim didn't 'create' Pakistan. He was an invader, nothing more and nothing less. He invaded 'India' and that is that. He is mentioned as creator of Pakistan and as a hero because with him came 'Islam' into India. 1906 is mentioned because people erringly believe that 'Muslim League' was formed in 1906. 'The All India Muslim League' was created to protect Muslim interests. One of the principal objectives was to 'have cordial relations with Hindus'. Muslim League wasn't formed to 'create' Pakistan. That is a lie. Lastly, Alama Iqbal in his inaugural address in Allahabad in '30 proposed an idea whereby Muslim majority areas should have Muslim rulers - with autonomy. He did not talk of separating from India. The word 'Pakistan' was 'not mentioned' in that address. Alama Iqbal wanted Muslims to stay 'within' India but have 'Muslim states'; remember that India had over five hundred princely states during British rule and many of these were ruled by Muslims."

"Then how did Pakistan come into being?"

"In 1946 it was decided that Pakistan would be created because Congress opposed 'proportional representation' and the idea of 'separate electorates' for Muslims, citing that it would divide India on religious lines which was against the spirit of democracy. This, along with Qaid-e-Azam's call for 'direct action' if Muslims did not get a country of their own, made Pakistan possible. Before '46 even Jinnah Saheb wasn't sure if Pakistan would be created. Then again, with the recent disclosure of confidential documents by the British sheds more light and new theories are being formed; one which marks out the reasons why the British wanted Pakistan to be created. But, there are studies being conducted on this, so we can only hazard guesses," Aman replied with a frown.

Rukhsar nodded but she had another doubt, "Didn't North West Frontier Province vote of creation of Pakistan in a referendum?" She asked.

"Rubbish! Nonsense!" Aman exploded angrily, "In '37 and '45 elections Congress won easily. Out of fifty seats Congress won thirty. In reserved Muslim seats, Congress won nineteen and All India Muslim League only seventeen, all in reserved constituencies. In the referendum you talk about, people had no choice in '46. The two most popular parties, Congress and the 'Khudai Khidmatgars' boycotted the elections and yet the referendum was dead close. Among those who practiced their franchise voted fifty-one per cent for, and forty-nine against creation of Pakistan. The supporters of Congress and Khudai Khidmatgars boycotted the polls. What could have been the result if the two had not boycotted the elections, you decide!" Aman Bux said angrily.

The last part of Aman Bux's speech was a telling statement. He was angry and Rukhsar alone knew the reason for it. All eyes were fixed on Rukhsar. She was staring at everyone in disbelief. It was difficult for her to soak all the information she had received in last eight days. She had been lied to; for thirty-two years. Truths were too overbearing on lies and she was squeezed because it was becoming difficult to adjust to the truths. She suddenly dropped her head in Zubair's chest and hid her face. Zubair caressed her head with sad eyes, "Don't worry child, history has its way of getting even. It will catch up eventually. Those who created the rift between the two nations and its people will be condemned for their actions. We should pity them for their myopic visions and poor wisdom. History will hold them responsible for future of Pakistan and its people. Men who have no respect for the creator of Pakistan, how can you expect them to be honest? On Jinnah's request, the first national anthem was written in Urdu by Jagannath Azad. It was unacceptable by the religious leaders that an anthem written by a Hindu would be recited so they decided to change it after Jinnah's death. The current anthem by Hafeez Jallundhuri was adopted though it is in Persian, a language which barely one per cent of the population understands. That is the extent of hypocrisy and deception perpetrated by the religious zealots. It may be sick to hear these but trust history to have its say. Maybe, it is taking its call now."

Mehjabeen was confused by all the talk. She saw sadness in atmosphere and she hated it. She put her hands in Prakash's arm and smiled. Her smiling face and the divine innocence lit up the room once again when she hugged everyone and said, "I love you all."

*   *   *

Aman Khan Bux

New Delhi, India

Mehjabeen held Prakash's hands firmly as he led her to her room. She knew Prakash as the best person in the world but his story had shaken her, and his emotional vulnerability had dented her belief that he was the toughest man in the world.

Prakash returned to the hall and declared that he was going out for a stroll. His guests understood. He had to overcome the emotional setbacks after he had relived his life's tragedies. Aman asked Rukhsar to be with Mehjabeen while he wanted to be with Prakash. When Prakash objected, Aman Bux asked him to shut up. "You aren't the only grown up around here." He patted Prakash's back and led him through the door. "We will be back in a little while," he told his wife and turned to Prakash. "Let's go, Sir" he said mockingly and walked out of the door.

As they walked through the woods behind the farmhouse, Prakash looked at Aman and turned away smiling to himself. Now that Aman had heard his story, he had a right to hear Aman's life story too. Prakash was disturbed when Aman hadn't called a single person from his family to inform about his marriage. It was odd. Aman had knowingly or unknowingly let it be known that his father was also killed. Prakash had a gut feeling that Aman wanted to share his life story as well with Prakash but he was as hesitant as Prakash was.

"I am sorry," Aman said as they walked through the woods.

"Carry on. You want to talk. I have kept my promise. It's your turn now," Prakash urged Aman. It was also an attempt to divert his mind from the last two hours.

In the darkness of the forest Aman searched for a spot to sit. Prakash lit his torchlight and found a fallen tree. The two men tested the strength of the trunk and squatted on it. In the darkness they couldn't see each other clearly but that was probably what both wished. Prakash wanted to ask Aman again but he waited.

A few seconds later Aman spoke abruptly, "We are 'red shirts'," he said softly, hoping Prakash knew of it.

Prakash's eyes lit up in the dark in disbelief, "It is a brilliant name from the past. Does it really exist?" Prakash asked.

"In form or in Spirit?" Aman countered.

"Either would be fantastic, the latter more so," Prakash had a brilliant smile. The depression of a little while ago vanished and the man was brimming with enthusiasm.

"The latter doesn't exist. Just some token, I gather from men who are still in awe of the era and the man who led the group in that time of the British..." Aman said and paused.

"Frontier Gandhi," Prakash completed the sentence.

"...Bacha Khan" Aman said in sync with Prakash; both men naming the same man differently, although neither called him by his real name, Khan Abdul Gaffar Khan, and also referred to as Badshah Khan.

"Do we really have the ideology of Bacha Khan in your area?" Prakash asked with enthusiasm.

"You know I hail from the Border areas of Pakhtunkhwa. To answer you, yes, that ideology still runs deep among some people but they are an extreme minority in comparison with the neo-zealots. Bacha Khan is a greater hero than Jinnah to his people in that area. His good will still fetches votes for his descendants. Awami National Party was created by his son, Khan Abdul Wali Khan, and grandson son, Afsandyar but the spirit is missing. We don't have *Khudai Khidmatgars*." Aman said sadly. "There are some *Khudai Khidmatgars* in India but not in Pakistan though most Afghan Pashtun tribes still hold Bacha Khan in great esteem. He was a true leader who held all tribes together and led them with dignity."

Prakash nodded, and waited for Aman to continue.

"My grandfather was an active *Khudai Khidmatgar*. He admired Bacha Khan and Gandhi, because Bacha Khan was a friend and great follower of the Mahatma," Aman Bux said. "Though Bacha Khan was opposed to the division of India, people in the area accepted the fact that it was Pakistan's part and there was exuberance about freedom. But soon problems began to creep in. When it was called the 'North West Frontier province', it was still good but when the demand of calling it Pashtunistan or Pakhtunkhwa was realized somehow things turned from bad to worse, especially because of the problems with the *Federally Administered Tribal Areas* - FATA. My ancestors were against partition of India and they actually voted for unison of India during elections." Aman Bux thought pensively, "Pashtun tribes were in general, opposed to partition of India because Bacha Khan opposed it and he was trusted. After independence, problems started because Pashtuns were split between Afghans and Pakistan's northern areas. There was a problem of nationalities. Pashtun families had relatives in both countries but were divided by a border. My grandfather had a good job in Lyallpur which was later renamed Faisalabad. He was taunted and heckled each day so he resigned and returned to Multan where he stayed for twenty years but he was continuously targeted there too by pro-Pakistan groups. Then he migrated to Afghanistan and died there. My father returned to Quetta where he became a successful lawyer. All was well till an incident occurred few years ago. A Baloch leader - a small timer, was arrested and sent to jail on false charges during Musharraf regime. A few days earlier Nawab Akbar Bugti was killed when the cave he was hiding in was bombed. My father defending a Baloch angered the administration. He received threats from the military but he refused to give in. He was a man with a lot of integrity and he took pride in being a *'Khidmatgar'*. No amount of pressure could force him to stop. Six years ago, his body was found with bullet holes in the Gilgit-Baltistan shoot out where he had gone to meet a client. We don't know who carried out that attack... or why." Aman paused, and added, "My mother died five years ago of loneliness and sadness. My father was her only friend and I was always away after my schooling: first in college, then I was staying outstation for work. You know the rest... Rukhsar, I mean."

Both men were thinking about the past and about the man sitting next to him. It was pitch dark except for dim streaks of moonlight that hit the forest floor intermittently as winds pushed aside the leafy canopy to let moonlight filter through. Both men had questions; answers to which they had to know.

"What is *'Satya'*?" Aman asked.

"That's first part of my real name," Prakash replied without turning his head in Aman's direction.

"What? Then Prakash Rohatgi is not your real name?" Aman was shocked.

"Prakash is the second half of my first name. I was named 'Satya-Prakash' by my grandfather on my mother's side. When I got into intelligence network I dropped the first half and used the second. Many people search for Prakash Rohatgi but it never shows up on computers. Only very select few are aware of it. These are people who I trust with my life. 'Satya' is also my philosophy of life - Truth. I live by it and so I use it as my codename," Prakash said solemnly, looking straight ahead.

"What does your organization do? Why do powerful people work with you? It has been troubling me. General Pathan was a patriot who would bleed to death before he would work for the enemy. Why was he working with you?" Aman quizzed.

"We are not an 'Organization'. We are a group of sane individuals who are in strategically important posts working together in best interest of their country. We are spread in almost every important country of the world. Most are from the Intelligence or Military, and some in politics - excepting me. I am in none of those categories. Our only aim is to avert tragedies such as we faced on that day during the Kargil war. One of your top most intelligence officers, ironically, a man who was a sworn enemy of India contacted the head of our counter-intelligence with information which shook them. He provided the information that Pak army was preparing to deploy its nuclear warheads. Both these men jointly spread the news, leaking information to networks world-wide which helped pressurise a lot of people in powerful places. We were able to avert a long drawn out war which could have hit both countries quite hard - Pakistan more so than India, I agree but still, it would have hurt India as well."

"How did you become a part of it?"

"I was brought in four years ago. A very senior bureaucrat, Nitin Tyagi wanted some information related to intelligence. When I met him after providing him the information he told me that he was retiring so he wanted someone to take over a covert sort of work which was related to working with the Governments around the world, and with their intelligence and military but still stay in the background. I had no clue what he was talking about. Then he took me to his house and I saw his workstation just like mine. I was fascinated initially by all the gizmos I saw but when I saw the kind of work I will be doing, it took me over. I agreed and I was brought into the group. It took me a month to get the hang of it; then it was easy. I have friends in virtually every part of the world. I learnt that it was that Chinese lady who sent the transcripts of the conversation between the two Generals during the Kargil war which confirmed their involvement. She had sent it to my mentor and he sent it across to all the important intelligence agencies. That helped a great deal and the Kargil war came to an end."

"Who funds you people?"

"No one. We work for various organizations. We are paid well by large corporate houses who seek our services before they make investments in those areas. Having said that, each of us in the group is quite well off - through the positions we hold in normal life. When needed, we put our money. We get requests from various governments who seek our assistance and we weigh the requests and work for it if it is within our periphery. This farmhouse was bought by Mr. Tyagi who introduced me into the organization. I sold off my Srinagar property and shifted here. This is a big farmhouse and it is my main source of income. If there is a requirement for extra funds, our sources within the governments help us out."

Aman was silent. His mind was working with high intensity. He had an intuition. He wanted to ask the most important question yet, after hearing what Prakash had already said. That question was important to him but he feared that the answer may be the one which, maybe he wasn't ready for. He was contemplating whether or not he should ask.

"Why am I telling you all these secrets? Is that what you are thinking about?" Prakash asked the question which Aman was wondering about.

"How did you know that?"

"It's natural." Prakash patted Aman's back lightly and put his hand on his shoulders, "Aman, in a mad world which has many whimsical, evil men in high, powerful positions, world needs equal number of sane, reasoning minds to counter that threat. This organization as you call it was brainchild of that Pakistan intelligence officer who cooperated with Mr. Tyagi and averted a disaster. He met Mr. Tyagi in a casual meeting on the side lines of the UN. He feared there are too many warmongers on both sides. A natural calamity strikes their country and they think of war; a stray incident happens and they start talking about nuclear bombs. A real incident was when the Pakistan Occupied Kashmir was hit by earthquake recently and a politician declared that it was a result of India testing nuclear weapons in Jammu and Kashmir region to go parallel with how Pakistan tested its nuclear weapons in the Chagi Mountains. It is insane. Imagine what if one of these insane men in power were to use it? We work to prevent it. It doesn't mean we are less patriotic than the other person. In fact, we are more so." Prakash looked skywards as the dim light which filtered through the leaves. Weather had turned cold and both men were feeling the bite of it.

"You are a diplomat and Rukhsar is an economist. I want you two to join me... us, in our endeavour to make this a safer world. When Zubair Saheb told me that she was studying economics it excited me. I am thinking of expanding our horizons to get people from other fields. With an economist and a diplomat added to the group we can help stop so many incidents or prevent a lot of damage from happening; be it economic or political or even terrorism."

"So, you are trying to recruit me."

"Yes."

"Why me, Prakash? And, why Rukhsar?"

"Both of you fulfil the criteria which is essential to be part of this group. A person must be fair and just by nature. The two of you certainly fit that category. The person should be intelligent and willing to work at all times without expecting to be paid for it. For eight days I have observed and done my best to see if you both can do it, and you have. You were married three days ago and we are sitting here in the middle of the night," Prakash joked. "People inducted into the group must be a 'patriots'. That is very important."

"How can a true patriot work for a set up like yours?"

"A patriot will never compromise on his country's future or reveal secrets he may have gathered while he is working for us. We are not an intelligence agency which wants to harm a nation. We are a group of people who work '*for their country*' in various capacities but we are fair people for whom justice is as important as anything else. Only a patriot will be able to work the way we want them to work. Or else, the person will also sell the secrets of our group to other networks. We can't afford that. So, it's essential that a person has to be a patriot."

Aman nodded. That last sentence appealed to him more. "You said a Pakistani intelligence officer started this entire thing. Who is he?"

"It was his idea but he didn't start this. He was instrumental in sowing the idea of such a group. I have to sadly say that he was killed in an attack in North Waziristan while negotiating with leaders of two tribes there. The leaders didn't survive the attack either," Prakash replied, "Anyway, he proposed setting up this... I call it 'group', to my mentor. When he died, my mentor took a serious look at the proposal and he worked out how it could be done. It took him three years to set up a network of people who could be trusted with their lives."

"Why did the Pakistani intelligence officer think of this?" Aman asked.

"It was proposed a week after the Kargil war. You know the circumstances which led to Kargil war. This man was sure that if he had a clue of what was happening, he could have averted it. He was embarrassed by the incident because he had worked very hard to make the *'Lahore Summit'* a success. Few people know that India and Pakistan had reached a settlement on a whole range of issues, including Kashmir. It would have been worked out within four-five years but then the series of events ruined the whole thing: Kargil war broke out, Nawaz Sharif was overthrown, India, and especially Prime Minister Vajpayee lost faith in Pakistan and then you had a decade of dictatorship which totally destroyed the bonhomie which was created and it was replaced by scepticism, mistrust and lack of goodwill because the man who was responsible for Kargil war was in power. A settlement on issues with that government was out of question because Pakistan is a 'Republic' and any settlement with a military dictator can't be considered viable unless it is backed by a civilian government later."

"That is why the Agra summit failed," Aman said softly.

"Yes. Everyone knew that Musharraf was responsible for Kargil. When he came to Agra, he changed his stance but the rift had been created. And there was a 'blunder' Musharraf committed during his visit. He said that Pakistan wants safety of Muslims in India and he feared for the welfare of Muslims. He got a reproach from a Muslim leader, when the eminently respected, Maulana Madani slapped Musharraf by asking him to mind his own business and not to worry about Indian Muslims. Maulana Saheb went to the extent of telling Musharraf to play his politics in Pakistan and not to interfere in India's internal affairs. He categorically stated that the Muslims in India are safe and enjoy the support of over eighty per cent Hindus, a conservative estimate according to him, who stand with their Muslim brethren when latter are in trouble. Musharraf's statement regarding Indian Muslims was uncalled for, but the Maulana's rebuttal was a statement which stung Musharraf. These incidents made it quite impossible to deal with him."

"But Musharraf did change his stance later. You should credit him for that."

Prakash looked at Aman in dim light, "You contradict yourself. You should remember what you said in Dacca. That was a more accurate statement, not now. Reasons you gave for mistrust during that speech to Gulzar Saheb was spot on. Think about Pakistan's situation in International arena, as you rightly said that day." Prakash said and returned to the topic. "Gulzar

Saheb is right. You two can help in making Pakistan a stable, working democracy. It will benefit both countries."

"We are not politicians. We can only do so much. Bits…"

"Small, but vital. What about Rukhsar. Will she agree?"

"I can speak for myself, not Rukhsar. I am tempted to take this offer, but give me time to think. You will understand that I live in a country where branding people as traitors is easy and without reason."

"Fear of death?" Prakash asked.

"No, but safety for children's future is more important to me. Then again, aren't you afraid of it? Death, I mean."

Prakash laughed, "No, I am not. That is a reality which will eventually come. In our belief, death isn't the end. Our lives are transit points; with death, our soul discards our mortal body and migrates to another; like changing clothes. I am not afraid of death. Death is a companion which will keep me company; life will ditch us eventually. That is the unwavering, eternal truth."

Aman looked at Prakash. The last statement affected Aman; it told him how lonely Prakash was in real life. Prakash looked full of life but that was a perfect garb which hid the lonely man within. Aman made a decision. He rose, pulled Prakash by his arm and led him to the house.

* * *

Pakistan Military Camp,

Skardu, Pakistan Occupied Kashmir

Yakub Lahori, political advisor to General Wahid Khan was nervous. He had been up all night thinking about the news given by Usmani. He had thought a lot to find a solution to the problem. He was certain his decision was the best way to wriggle out, or better, to keep the General's plan afloat: play the game Indians had mastered in last sixty-plus years, and add a lie to make it work. He thought of his decision and worked on it to plug loopholes in his plan. He had to present a plausible, viable solution to his egoist General. Lahori hated the man in person but like most of Wahid Khan's supporters he was working with him because the General's intentions were right. If he can neutralize India, Pakistan will have a chance of becoming a developed country from present status of being considered as a failed state. It still was an hour before the sun rose behind the hills but he couldn't wait anymore. The sooner the General got the news the better.

- - -

Wahid Khan was angry. How dare they disturb him at this unearthly hour? What was so bloody important? He barked at Lahori and asked him to come after breakfast but the advisor persisted. Wahid Khan felt something was seriously wrong otherwise Lahori wouldn't dare to disturb him. When Lahori forced him to meet, he reluctantly agreed to meet in an hour.

Wahid Khan read the folder in disbelief. He wondered how it was possible. He was backbitten. Only two people could have had access to these files. Was it that bitch nurse or Altaf Khos? It must be that angelic nurse he had handpicked to take care of his crippled uncle. But how could she have access to Indian agents, especially this man Prakash Rohatgi? That left Altaf Khos, the man he had trusted implicitly. He had access. The other question which bothered him was that his uncle's safe was broken and sensitive information was in enemy hands. This wasn't possible unless someone from inside was involved. Altaf Khos! Wahid Khan swore to make Altaf pay for this. Then he thought of the conversation with Altaf; he had broken the news to the General that a folder existed and as far as he knew only two other copies existed – one with Zubair Ahmed and other with the mysterious man. He would take care of the careless General as well. He had asked his uncle many times to get an electronic safe but his uncle didn't heed and now he was seeing his dreams fall apart. He couldn't let that happen.

"What do we do now?" Wahid Khan asked nervously.

Lahori was frightened. He wondered if the idea would work. It could rebound if it wasn't executed with precision, and yet success couldn't be guaranteed but it was the only solution he could come up with. The warning had come in no uncertain terms. If the Pakistani authorities didn't handle it the Indians would be forced to go for a pre-emptive strike. "What I recommend is slightly risky but it has to be executed with precision."

"Tell me," Wahid Khan asked in annoyance.

"You should meet the Commander-in-Chief, the President and the Prime Minister, and offer to tender your resignation with immediate effect stating reasons as they are," Yakub tapped the folder, "This is an Indian propaganda to malign your reputation you tell them. It will…" Lahori said nervously, hoping the General had the patience to hear his advice. He was wrong.

"What rubbish! Are you an idiot? It will be a confirmation of my guilt. You are my advisor. I am not paying you to destroy my plans," the General shouted angrily.

The advisor calmly heard the General and requested him to hear out the advice first and take his decision, "I said, 'make an offer' to tender your resignation. Let media know about it and you play the victim. If they revert to these papers, deny any knowledge of it. These reports are based on documents these people got from two sources: the 'Records Office' and your uncle's safe. Originals from your uncle's safe are not in their custody, perhaps. These are photographs; it tells me that they don't have the originals. Those documents were used as reference to prepare the report. This report has no substance if we can retrieve and destroy the originals. This entire report will prove baseless," Lahori explained. He saw the door open and a *Hawaldar* enter with tea for them.

General waited for the *Hawaldar* to leave and asked Yakub to continue. Yakub's advice had merit and it appealed to the General's ego. It would be nice to embarrass the Indians.

Yakub saw keen interest in General's eyes and resumed, "If you convince the media that you are a victim of a malicious Indian plan you will become a hero. The general perception is that the civilian government is corrupt. Some people wish that army takes over and puts things right. The government won't be able to remove a 'popular' general. Though you will have offered to resign, the government won't accept it fearing public backlash. When ready, you assume power."

"What about the Kargil incident?" Wahid Khan asked.

"Ask yourself why you issued that order?" Lahori asked.

"I thought if we retain that post, we could fight for weeks to retain Tiger Hill. It was an important battle because it gave us huge strategic advantage. From that hill we could monitor and cut off supply lines to Srinagar and Siachen. I ordered the men to ensure we retain that post. If peace was brokered at that stage with those hills in our control we could control Kashmir," General Wahid Khan said, realizing what Lahori was telling him. He continued, "I add that Zubair Ahmed was a traitor. Instead of inspiring his men to fight he told them to retreat. While we provided back up to those men, Zubair Ahmed asked his men to fire back at our men and we lost eleven men. That *Qadiyani* is a traitor. Because of him we lost Tiger Hill which led to the loss of Kargil war."

Yakub Lahori looked at his General and smiled, "That's it!"

General laughed. This was simple. He knew Lahori didn't like him but he trusted Lahori. "And?" he asked.

"We must retrieve the originals and destroy them. They shouldn't fall in wrong hands," Lahori suggested.

"We can manage that."

"There is something else… " Yakub stopped half way.

"What?" General asked.

"Your uncle shouldn't speak to anyone except you or your closest, trusted people. If he talks, your story could collapse."

General Wahid Khan shook his head in agreement. *My uncle has played his part. He shouldn't live in pain. It is better he is relieved of his pain. Then I will find and take care of the traitor.*

* * *

Faisal Sheikh's Residence

Islamabad, Pakistan

The bureaucrat was sweating despite chilling weather. The two senior army officers had grilled him for an hour. Faisal was tensed but he knew he had to hold his ground or else his career and possibly, even his life was over. In such situations, as he had been trained, he must believe in his actions if they were right and defend it strenuously.

"Why did she call you? She could have embarrassed us by going to the media. Do you realize that she played you with her sweet talk? Do you realize that you have tarnished the image of a decorated General?" Yusuf Leghari, senior of the two men, a Lieutenant General and a committed member of the inner core of General Wahid Khan asked Faisal rudely.

Faisal calmly put his fingers on the folder, "I received this file from an Indian diplomat, gentlemen. Tell me, should I have ignored it when it implicates one of our Generals who is trying to wage a war with India without considering that a civilian government is not in the know of it?" Faisal defended his stance.

"Did you see the originals to confirm that the plan exists?"

Faisal looked at Leghari and his companion, a Major in the Pakistan army. Both stared at him with bland expressions. He knew the report was correct. The presence of the two men cleared any doubt he had. They had a specific purpose for their visit and he wanted to find out. He leaned back in his sofa and stared back in defiance, "Pratima Vaidya is the most respected foreign diplomat in Karachi. She is renowned for her thoroughness, gentlemen. If you tell me that the report is false or forged to implicate a General no one in India knows or cares about, you are mistaken. Mrs. Vaidya is a thorough professional who doesn't make mistakes, or lies. She speaks the truth even if it's considered improper in Indian circles. I vouch for her. I spoke to my superior before I met her and, after meeting her I spoke to him again. My superior told me to send the report to Mr. Usmani whom I do not know personally. I had never heard of him earlier."

Leghari stared at Faisal coldly. "Your *'mother'* has given you a story which, if the international community is ready to accept, allows Indians a pre-emptive strike. This is their plan and you help her in propagating that the General wants to overthrow the government and wage war against India?"

"Please answer my two questions, gentlemen," Faisal said, boring into the eyes of Leghari. "Why would they pick a General who they don't know? And what is your purpose of visit here?" He asked boldly.

Leghari drew a deep breath. He knew Faisal was smart and bold. He smiled, "General Wahid Khan is going to be the next Commander-in-Chief. Indians want to malign him to have psychological advantage over him and Pakistan army. For your information, he has sought permission to meet the Chief of Army Staff, the Prime Minister and the President to tender his resignation. Doesn't that prove that our General has integrity? To answer your second question, we want to know if you saw any original documents in Pratima Vaidya's possession," Leghari asked bluntly.

Faisal smiled within himself. He understood the purpose of their visit. The General can refute the charges if he could be certain that originals were not available. He could declare that the plan was hatched by the Indians to defame a Pakistani General. He knew that the General will go to any extreme to lay his hands on the original documents. Without it, the Indians had no case and with it, they could blow Pakistan diplomacy into smithereens. Wahid Khan wanted to know if Pratima Vaidya had the originals or copies. If she did, her life could be in danger. "If she had the originals she would have shown it to me. But, she didn't. The originals must be with this man - Prakash Rohatgi."

- - -

Leghari boxed himself in the car, asked the Major to drive, and leaned back in his seat and called Usmani. "The lady has no originals with her, so says our man here. I believe him."

He shut off the phone and frowned. A brilliant young man; if only men like him joined in their mission. Pity, it wasn't the case. He breathed deeply. At least that young man, who he was sure would quickly climb the ladders in his career and be an asset for the country, didn't have to be wasted. It was the least he could do; he had saved the life of a brilliant young man.

- - -

Faisal informed Pratima Vaidya about the meeting because he was sure she had a copy of the originals. He had lied to Leghari. He wondered sadly, *why had it come to a situation where he lied to his own men in uniform while he spoke honestly with representative of an enemy country? It was in the best interest of his beloved country and he knew he had taken a chance by lying to Leghari, but it was worth lying if it benefited the country.*

*   *   *

Indian Deputy High Commission,

Karachi, Pakistan

Pratima Vaidya came to the mission directly from airport. She was certain Faisal would do some spadework. He would dig for information and inform her. It would be in Pakistan's interest to cooperate with her. If not, she would leave this country because Pakistan and India relations will hit nadir. That would be a pity because she really liked the country and its people as much as she liked her own country and people; which were the same anyway. She pitied she couldn't say the same about the politicians on either sides, or about the military establishment in Pakistan. That was the significant difference.

She pulled out the folder from her bag and put it in her safe. Vested interests would want the copies of the original documents to be removed. The report in itself would mean little unless the real copies were there as proofs. Before locking the safe she saw the folder and scanned the contents on the letterheads of Wahid Khan and the General who she knew was a cripple. These were going to be the most valued possession in her safe for some time. She put the folder in the safe, locked it and called Nitin Tyagi.

* * *

Prakash Rohatgi's Residence

New Delhi, India

The cell phone tune woke Prakash from deep slumber. He grabbed the phone, checked the caller's name and replied in a hurry, "Yes, Altaf?"

"Prakash *Bhai*, I have bad news." Altaf said, referring to him as '*bhai*' - brother. "Wahid Khan called Mariam and asked her about visitors other than me. She said that there were no visitors barring regular guests and relatives of the General. I suspect he doubts me. Should I still call him and tell him I have reached Gulmarg?" Altaf was pleading.

Altaf knew he could take Prakash's refuge if situation became desperate but he worried about Mariam. If Wahid Khan learnt that she was helping Altaf her life would be a real nightmare.

Prakash asked Altaf to wait till he called back. Prakash looked at his watch. It was past nine a.m. He had missed his pre-dawn prayers. That was strange.

- - -

Zubair and Mehjabeen were chatting when Prakash came to the hall. He hugged Mehjabeen and greeted Zubair but he got muted response from them.

"What happened?" he asked.

"She is still upset. She says you don't love her as much as she thought," Zubair Ahmed said in humour.

Mehjabeen looked at Zubair and snuggled into Prakash's arm. When Prakash had his breakfast, Purna asked if he was free for some time.

"What is it?" he asked, in *Kharia*.

Purna replied in her native language and told her problem. Prakash started to reply but stopped when he heard footsteps and saw Aman and Rukhsar climbing down the stairs. Purna went to the kitchen and reappeared with breakfast for the couple. She served, sat opposite Prakash and asked him again in *Kharia,* in a tentative tone. Prakash replied and fell silent. Aman asked if something was wrong. Prakash heard a beep on his electronic pad. He saw the message and asked Aman to join him after breakfast. Rukhsar sensed Purna was not normal. Something was bothering her. She asked her. Purna replied that she was having a problem with a system Prakash had helped set up in Chattisgarh. She explained the problem the natives faced and how she was trying to sort it out.

Rukhsar Ahmed-Bux, as she had decided her name would be since the day of marriage, nodded and patted Purna's hand and asked if she can visit her native place. Purna nodded with a broad smiled. Rukhsar realized that Purna had an exquisite smile with perfect dentures, and combined with her large black smiling eyes, made her really beautiful when she smiled. "You will love that place in the lush green hills and see the ruins of a temple which is over twelve hundred years old."

"Really? That old?"

"Yes. It is devoted to *Shakti,*" Purna replied proudly and promised her to take her there if she wanted to come.

Rukhsar promised her a visit.

When Rukhsar finished eating her breakfast, Aman left to join Prakash at his workstation.

Before leaving, Aman whispered into Rukhsar's ear, "Talk to Mehjabeen. Convince her, dear."

— — —

When Aman Khan entered the room Prakash Rohatgi turned and smiled asking him to occupy the adjacent chair.

"So, all is going according to plan?" Aman asked.

"Just a little hiccup..." He said and informed about the call he had received from Altaf Khos.

"So you think Altaf's life could be in danger?" Aman asked.

"Yes," Prakash replied without looking away from the screen. He had numerous messages.

Prakash read the messages and smiled. Pressure was being put on Pakistan government and military. US had threatened to suspend military supplies including hardware and spare parts for the Air Force and military. It was also holding back an economic aid of eight hundred and fifty million dollars for the time being. Chinese Government had suddenly stated that it couldn't fulfil its commitment in near future. Australians and British were coming down hard on their aid and so was the case with all major donor nations.

'Tiger' Chowdhary Dastgir informed that throughout the previous day, Pakistan Prime Minister and cabinet ministers were in meetings with various foreign missions persuading them to cooperate but without success. The government was vehemently denying the charges. Foreign Governments had put their decisions on hold until they got a confirmation from either side. When Prakash finished reading the report from Dastgir Chowdhary, he got a call.

Chowdhary Dastgir greeted Prakash on a good job so far. "I have a request, *'Satya'*. If there are sanctions, Pakistan will be set back by a decade. We must stop sanctions from being imposed," a true patriot was pleading for his country; Aman knew when he heard Chowdhary Dastgir.

"It will be all over within this week, *'Tiger'*, I promise you."

"If this works out, we will know that setting up of this group was worth the trouble. Work fast, my friend."

"I will. I will revert to you within the day with better news I hope. Take care, Sir," Prakash said and disconnected the call.

He knew the fear in Dastgir's tone was real. Prakash had to act quickly lest the very basic purpose of creating this group fails. This group was formed to prevent harm to any country, economic threat included. It was an important aspect. But first, he wanted Wahid Khan to trust Altaf without a shade of doubt. Prakash's entire plan was based on it. While Prakash prepared papers to convince General Wahid Khan of Altaf's commitment, he told Aman to read the other messages. An hour later Prakash was ready. He put the documents in front of Aman.

"Why this? We already have the photos," Aman asked.

"Can you spot the difference? Which one is the original?" Prakash asked Aman to identify.

"This is the one which Altaf brought to us. It is taken from a cell phone while the other is... well it looks like the real one in the crippled General's safe, I suppose," Aman said.

"Correct! I did some work on it on my computer and there it is."

"How will this help Altaf?"

"It's easy to presume that the copies of those emails and hand written documents were either stolen from the safe or shot from a camera. No one can be sure when it was done. The dates on these documents go back three weeks. Within this period it could have happened at any time. I will make sure this reaches Wahid Khan. It will convince him that files were stolen lot earlier.

That I think should let Altaf off the hook. Since Altaf brought it to Wahid Khan's notice that the folder exists, he will have little reason to doubt Altaf."

"Don't you think they will check for originals and find that it is still in the crippled General's safe?" Aman quizzed.

"I will see if we can manage to get it away from the safe. But, wouldn't it add to the mystery how the pictures are available although the original is still in the General's safe?"

"You said yesterday that without the original, the report has no value. We both know how important that is," Aman asked pointing out to his earlier statement.

"I still want the originals but they must have been moved by now. We have actual photographs. It proves that the plan exists. What you said in Dacca will come true. The International community will weigh their experiences of last six decades and the track records, and they will decide which side speaks the truth. Six decades of goodwill can't be overlooked. When I produce these, the International community cannot deny that it is not the original because Pakistani authorities cannot counter it with their originals, because it would prove that we are not lying. Either way, we win."

Aman nodded. Prakash had scraped a deep wound which will never heal: Since early days what he had seen and heard, he had known them to be half lies or total. In eight days, he had learnt that almost all had been total lies. On the other hand, Pakistan's elder brother, the giant from which Pakistan was sliced out, had created its own standing in the world. While Pakistan struggled for its identity, India had created a formidable one, and that was coming to its benefit. India's goodwill will be its asset and Pakistan's lies were going to hurt it when reputations are compared. For a moment, Aman had a longing, '*I wish India was not divided, or... I was an Indian*'. The thought shocked Aman. He shook his head in disbelief at his own thought and sighed deeply.

"What happened?" Prakash asked.

Aman shrugged his shoulders, shaking his head sideways. He rose and tried concentrating on the matter at hand.

"Are you ok?" Prakash asked him.

"Yes, I am just thinking about something," Aman said and he changed the topic, "So, what are you going to do now?"

"Yesterday we decided to speak to Wahid Khan. I think I will wait for a day or two. I will push him to desperation and then I will whet his appetite," Prakash had a mysterious smile. He patted Aman and winked.

"What do you mean? How?"

"Wait and watch!"

"Prakash, we can't take things lightly. Many lives are at stake. Future of peoples of two countries is at stake - millions of lives are involved. How can you be so casual about it?" Aman asked with a disappointed look.

Prakash's expression turned deadly serious. His eyes were hard and cold when he looked at Aman Khan Bux. "I do not take matters lightly, especially when my country or its future is at stake. I honestly believe Wahid Khan will be desperate and when he sees an opportunity to get it all back, he will make the mistake I want him to make. We want Wahid Khan and he will want us just as badly. Trust me!" Prakash said with cold eyes still boring into Aman's.

Aman had noticed a change in Prakash's behaviour in last eight days. For first six days he was like a cold, heartless man who could beat the pulp out of his enemy as he did with Altaf earlier and Anwar later. The very man, even when appearing cold and heartless, provided such warmth that it melted him and Rukhsar. Then, in last two days since returning to New Delhi, he was soft and touchy person who was hurt by little comments. And now, again he saw the cold, heartless man who was focused on his mission and he was ruthless in executing it. Aman believed in what Prakash had said about his plan to get Wahid Khan. With deceitful, ambitious and evil General Wahid Khan on one side and a professional, knowledgeable, determined, brilliant man on the other, would make for a fascinating contest. It would be worth watching the two take on each other in a spectacle; the pity was that two countries were involved. It would determine the future course of two nuclear powered nations. What if Wahid Khan got away with his plans? That was the dreadful part. The government channels would take weeks to do what Prakash and his group of people had done in two days. That was the hope! That was the way it had to be!

- - -

The two men emerged from the workstation smiling. Their plan was well chalked out and execution would be incisive. When Prakash had presented his plan to Aman, the latter had pointed out a small, seemingly inconsequential oversight at the time but as they discussed they realized that it could have been a blunder. Aman Khan suggested a simple change which made the plan perfect. Wahid Khan couldn't escape this trap. Altaf Khos was advised what he had to do, and how. When Prakash asked Altaf if there was any way to retrieve the files from the crippled General's safe, Altaf said he would see if Mariam would do it. He would speak to her and revert soon.

When Prakash and Aman came to the hall, they saw smiles abound. Zubair smiled mildly but kept himself to a sixteen year old magazine. Mehjabeen, Rukhsar and Purna were busy talking about something in a hush-hush manner, trying their best not to let the two men hear what they were talking about. The two men wondered what the secrecy was all about as they parked themselves on the sofa. Then it occurred to Aman that Rukhsar may have spoken to Mehjabeen about what he had in mind. He slid closer to his wife and winked at her, "All good?" he asked

Rukhsar whispered into his ears and Aman's smile widened. Aman spoke to her for a minute and patted Mehjabeen. He bent over and kissed her forehead. Mehjabeen hugged him and the ladies returned to their talks. Aman felt left out. He moved to the sofa. Prakash was half asleep. Aman tried to recollect if he had ever seen Prakash sleep. He couldn't recall. The only time he had a chance was in Dacca but Prakash was up before dawn which meant he had a nap for not more than three hours at best. There was something in that man which kept him going despite lack of rest. He always found Prakash at work, either with problems they faced now or with something else. Aman summoned Rukhsar and Mehjabeen to his room upstairs.

- - -

Rukhsar entered with a wide grin and Mehjabeen followed. Aman asked Mehjabeen, "What you two have been up to?"

Mehjabeen giggled at the question and Rukhsar joined her. Aman felt helpless sitting there without knowing why the two were laughing, "Will you please tell me what's going on?"

"We are going to Pahalgam with Mehjabeen and Prakash. We have ten more days' permission to stay. I want to make full use of it," Rukhsar smiled and winked at Aman.

It struck Aman suddenly. He hesitated for a moment, and then he asked, "Will Mehrunissa agree to it?"

Rukhsar and Mehjabeen were surprised at first, and then they smiled, "We have to convince her. I think, if Mehjabeen speaks to her, she may agree," Rukhsar replied.

Aman caressed Mehjabeen's head, "Thank you my dear."

Mehjabeen smiled happily. "*Baba* loves *Ammi* and she loves him very much, I know. I love the idea. They will be happy."

"What about you, angel? Wouldn't you be happy? Won't the memories of your father come in the way?"

Mehjabeen was upset suddenly, "My father never cared for *Ammi*. After his death his family mistreated us, especially *Ammi*. They blamed *Ammi* for his death and threw us out. I don't like them. I don't want to think of my father. He was a traitor, *Ammi* says. *Baba* is my father; because of him *Ammi* and I are happy. He loves us. He cares for us," Her eyes suddenly lit up. "I miss *Ammi* when I am in hostel and I miss *Baba* when I am in Pahalgam. If they get married we can all stay together?"

Aman and Rukhsar empathised with her sadness. They put their hands on her back and patted her... Aman hugged her and promised to get Prakash and Mehrunissa married.

The little-big girl snuggled into Rukhsar's arms. She didn't cry but her heart was joyous, *'I will have a real family now.'*

*　　*　　*

General's House

Lahore, Pakistan

This was dangerous. If caught, she could be killed and her family would incur the wrath of Wahid Khan. Mariam steeled herself to do as she had promised Altaf Khos. She made tea for herself and waited for the right time to administer a dose into the vulgar, crippled old General. The chime of the clock striking ten made her sit up. She walked to the General's room and closed the door behind her. She was a surprised to see Imtiaz Noorani, the attendant still in the room. She expected him to be in the kitchen, preparing lunch. She asked him to leave so she could attend to the General. Imtiaz left promptly.

"How are you this morning, darling?" The General flirted.

Mariam inhaled a deep breath, "I would be better if my dear boyfriend was here. I get bored doing nothing all day."

The General laughed, "Wait for some time. You will know that your boyfriend is a hero of the nation. When he becomes a hero he will take special care of you, dear."

Mariam laughed. The General thought she was happy Wahid would become so important a man. Mariam thought of the irony. Her boyfriend, Altaf was going to be the hero, not Wahid Khan.

Yes, her boyfriend will take good care of her, she knew. She can't let the evil Wahid Khan be the ruler of this country if she could help it. She would play her part to stop Wahid Khan.

She pulled out two bottles and injected the needle into the vials and prepared the right doze and injected the syringe into the General. It would take ten minutes for the medicine to take effect and the cripple would be unconscious, "I will be back around lunch for your ECG, General."

"Ok, my dear," General said and tried to sit on the bed but he found it difficult. Mariam helped him. She side stepped when the General tried to play, and walked out.

- - -

Back in her room, Mariam felt violated again. The revulsion for the two Generals grew with each day. She bided her time, waiting for the medicine to take its effect. Twenty minutes later she returned to the General's room and checked. The General was unconscious. She pulled out the keys and walked to the safe, sifted through the files and removed the file Altaf had taken photos of, locked the safe and put the keys back under the General's mattress.

At the appointed time, her eighteen year old sister arrived, had a cup of tea, hugged her sister and left the house with a packet. She knew where to deliver it. Altaf had arranged for the pick-up of the 'red-taped' folder to be delivered to a lady in Karachi, just as Prakash had instructed. The Deputy High Commissioner would take care of the rest.

- - -

Mariam saw a distinguished looking man standing at the door. He introduced himself and she opened the door and let him in. Usmani asked about the General. She led him to the General's room. The General was barely out of slumber. He asked Usmani to sit while Mariam wheeled him to the bathroom to freshen up. When the General returned Usmani told Mariam to get out and close the door. Usmani asked the General about the files. General assured him that no one had touched the files in a fortnight. The last time he remembered opening his safe was when his nephew, Wahid Khan had come nearly three weeks earlier. Wahid had opened the safe and locked it after their discussion was over. Usmani opened his leather case and pulled out the report, and placed it in the General's hands.

The General's face turned pale as he saw the first page in the file. How was it possible? No one had been near the safe for three weeks. Usmani asked the General to check if the files were safe and wheeled the General to the safe and stepped aside. General opened the safe and searched. The file was missing.

Usmani asked, "When was the last time you saw the file?"

"Three weeks ago, I said, when Wahid and I discussed a matter and he had locked the file in the safe and put the keys back. No one else has touched it since then."

"Do you have visitors apart from General or his conduit?"

"My son works in Karachi. He and his family come here once in a month or two and they stay with me for a few days, mostly at weekends. I have close relatives who visit me often. Some old army colleagues visit me from time to time. But no one has touched the safe, Khaled," General said nervously. He knew the implications. The plan could be exposed and the dream could collapse. Another fear gripped Moinuddin, the crippled General; Wahid Khan, his nephew, won't spare him. Moinuddin was frightened. Wahid would take his revenge - brutally. He had to find the file and the conspirator if he had to survive - if the plan was to be executed. For an hour he and Usmani talked without concluding when or how the file went missing. It was difficult to suspect anyone. The nurse was the General's girlfriend and she couldn't do it even if she wanted. She had no reason to steal the file because she wasn't a spy nor did she have access to foreign spying agencies. Suspecting her would be a waste of time. Altaf hadn't visited the house in a fortnight, so he was beyond suspicion. That left a few relatives who visited the General, or most probably, the old '*colleagues*' of the General.

- - -

Usmani took General's leave and returned to the lounge. He summoned Mariam and Imtiaz Noorani and grilled them for twenty minutes, trying to find out about the General's guests and relatives and when they had last visited. He tried his best but couldn't pressurise the beautiful nurse, who was also General Wahid Khan's mistress. Their conversation was disrupted by a loud bang that came from General's room. He, Imtiaz and Mariam ran towards the room. Barqatullah Moinuddin, the crippled General who had helped General Wahid Khan climb the success ladder by often over-looking the blunders, was in his wheelchair with blood flowing down from his temple. The ex-General had shot himself.

* * *

Richmond Hill

Toronto, Canada

Mir Jamal was a Canadian citizen born in a small village of Tampi, on the outskirts of Srinagar, Kashmir. His father had migrated to Canada after the 1965 Indo-Pak war. The Jamal family had grown wealthy selling exotic Kashmiri *'Pashmina'* woollens and Kashmiri handicraft items across North America. This family was a lifeline for artisans and weavers of areas near Tampi. Though it had migrated to Canada, Jamal family maintained its ties with their native land and helped the locals. For thousands of people in their area in Kashmir, the family's word was law. The Indian Government saw him as a moderate leader with tilt towards separatists and some pro-Pakistan factions in Jammu and Kashmir. Mir Jamal got an email and he saw his chance for vengeance. He called his confidante in Srinagar and instructed what he wanted.

Mir Jamal wanted to convince Wahid Khan that his plans would succeed if he took into confidence local leaders like him. Jamal could offer two thousand men who were armed and trained, and ready to go into action at his command.

With an unexpected opportunity to use the resources of Mir Jamal was shot in the arm for the General. With Mir Jamal on his side, Wahid Khan could influence other Kashmiri forces.

Now Mir Jamal had the opportunity he had been waiting for. And, he won't miss it. Wahid Khan would gladly accept his sole demand: Post of Prime Minister of an independent Kashmir.

*   *   *

Pakistan Military Camp

Skardu, Pakistan Occupied Kashmir

Wahid Khan tried to sleep but failed twice. He was mentally fatigued. His talks with Lahori in the morning had restored his jolted confidence but he was nervous. He was an optimist but since Usmani had read the scenario to him, he sensed negativity in his mind. Lahori had arranged meetings in the evening with the '*bloody incompetent*' civilian leaders, and his Chief of the Army the following morning. Feedbacks were encouraging. Secretaries of the President and Prime Minister had asked him to wait till the matter was 'investigated'; then he would be called for a meeting to '*sort out the matter*'.

Wahid Khan shot up in his bed and started to rethink about the whole sequence of events. How did the plan leak? It was a secret plan. Three people apart from him knew details of the plan. His crippled uncle who had mastered the plan - it was his brainchild. The second was a pro-Pakistan Kashmiri leader who was on Intelligence services' rosters. Third was a General who created the support base within army ranks. He had reached lower ranks and recruited committed soldiers to work on a 'master plan' to neutralize India. The recruits were thoroughly screened and he had also recruited able men from bureaucracy and judiciary. Wahid Khan was ultra-cautious in executing his plan. General Moinuddin had chosen him as the head. Wahid Khan was rigid on some matters and those were followed stringently. Discussions on the plan must be done in person only; the other medium was through written messages carried by trusted conduits and were to be kept in safes. Then how did anyone get a whiff of the plan? Who had betrayed him? The men in the core group couldn't be doubted. He had handpicked each important person who could have access to vital information. He knew Yakub Lahori didn't like him, but loved his country more than he disliked the General. Altaf had worked for him for two years and he never tread beyond the orders issued. Wahid Khan had selected Altaf from military college where Altaf was undergoing training. Altaf's dedication and intelligence were impressive. He was instantly recruited and became the personal courier for Wahid Khan. Altaf instilled so much confidence in Wahid Khan that the General didn't hesitate to discuss confidential matters in his presence. Altaf wouldn't betray him, or Pakistan, and he had taken lots of punishment but had survived in New Delhi. Wahid Khan had to find the traitor from his midst. Someone had discovered the plot and used it to his own advantage. Could it be the nurse? Not possible! His earlier assessment about Mariam was right. She was a nurse with no knowledge of International affairs. She wouldn't know what to do with the files even if she possessed them. Considering her as a traitor was a waste of time. Who then? The thought drove him mad. He was relieved when a call disturbed his thoughts. "I hope you have some good news for me, Altaf."

"Yes sir. I arrived have in Srinagar. I learn that Zubair and Prakash are coming tomorrow. What do I do, Sir?"

"Ask my colleague in Srinagar to call me at in the evening."

Altaf smiled. Wahid Khan didn't suspect him or Mariam.

Altaf checked the background of Wahid Khan's colleague in Srinagar. He took a cab to meet Salahuddin Ilahi.

* * *

Prakash Rohatgi's Residence,

New Delhi, India

Prakash wondered if real parents tolerated such tantrums as Mehjabeen was up to, but he didn't care; if she wanted anything in the world he would try to give it to her. Because she deserved the best, she got the best. Also, it was probably his love for her which brought him and Mehrunissa close.

"What do you want? You are arguing without telling me what you want, dear," Prakash pleaded.

"I want to go to Pahalgam and return with *Ammi*. I want to stay with her too."

Prakash was confused. Her trip to Pahalgam and her *Ammi* coming to New Delhi; how were the two related? Rukhsar sat next to Mehjabeen.

Rukhsar ruffled Mehjabeen's hair, "Men don't understand the little hints, dear. We will have to tell them openly. They are all half idiots when it comes to these matters."

Suddenly, Mehjabeen broke into hysterical laughter. At least her 'aunty' knew what she wanted and her '*Baba*' was naïve. Prakash and Aman sat with stupefied looks on their faces. What did Rukhsar mean? Aman started to ask but stopped half way, not wanting to embarrass himself or Prakash any further. The ladies would tell them anyway.

Rukhsar stopped smiling. Her expression turned serious all of a sudden. She sat next to Prakash and whispered in his ears, "You idiot! Your angel wants you to marry and bring her mother here. She won't have to stay in hostel anymore."

Prakash smiled and slapped his forehead with his palm and thrust his hands out at Mehjabeen. His daughter jumped and squatted herself next to him. She was blissfully unaware of Mehrunissa's problem.

"We will do as you wish, dear," Prakash said, "We have to solve a problem here. In few days we will go to Pahalgam and see what destiny has in store for us."

Mehjabeen snuggled into his arms and her face sunk in his chest. She sobbed. He felt her hiccups and looked at her. He turned to Rukhsar helplessly, unsure how to react. Rukhsar cursed him silently. She sat next to Mehjabeen and saw her crying; she was happy. Rukhsar broke into a loud laughter and slapped Prakash's back, "You're a certified nerd. You can think of all the answers to complex situations of this world but you can't understand simple emotions of a girl."

Prakash was confused. He didn't understand what Rukhsar was talking about, "Can you please talk in simple language? You are so used to your coded languages, for God's sake," Rukhsar shouted in irritation, and even a bit of anger, "Do you know that people also cry when they are happy? She is crying because she is happy, you moron!" She shouted and hugged Mehjabeen. "Come with me, my dear. Let's go and talk in our room," she said, dragged the girl and led her upstairs.

Prakash looked at them walking up the stairs and turned to Aman with uncertainty in his eyes. The diplomat put his arm around Prakash's shoulder and smiled, "I agree with her. You are an idiot," he said and suppressed his laughter, "When you marry Mehrunissa Mehjabeen will have a real family. Don't you understand that?"

"I didn't. When you live for over twenty years in solitude intentionally detaching yourself from outside world, you tend to become emotionally less expressive," Prakash replied in a whisper, looked at Aman and withdrew his gaze in an instant when their eyes locked. Prakash rose and left the room.

Aman cursed himself. His mild joke had scraped the scars of a lonely man. He thought about what Prakash had said and realized how loneliness could be a silent killer. Mehjabeen had probably brought the colours of life back into his life. Aman knew that the virtual father-daughter duo was happy and their tears said it all. Another puzzle was solved. He knew why he saw two contrasting shades of Prakash's behaviour in few days. He was used to a lonely life and now, suddenly, he had a few people around him for whom he cared too much. His life of solitude was being eroded and he was adjusting to a life of a normal family, with all its nuances and sensitivities. It was not an easy adjustment, 'for twenty years', Prakash had said and that was a long time to live without a person you care for, or without someone to care for you.

- - -

Altaf called Prakash with a surprising piece of information. He boasted that the impossible had happened, without coming to the crux. When Prakash forced him, Altaf proudly boasted that Mariam had retrieved the file from the General's safe and it had reached Karachi. "Papers in the files include hand written instructions from both Generals, Prakash-*bhai*." Altaf said and paused, "I thank you for your efforts. Please convey my best to Aman Sir and Miss Rukhsar."

Prakash heard sincere gratitude in the tone, "We are doing it in the interest of both the countries, Altaf."

"I know, Sir."

Prakash smiled, "I thank you for the commendable work," he replied.

"Tell Purna I adore her. If I wasn't in love with Mariam I would have married her." Altaf said and laughed.

Prakash smiled, "You would have a tough time handling her. You know what she is capable of," he said and added, "But, if you ever come to India on another mission like your first one, I won't spare your life," Prakash added seriously.

"I won't. I know that if we work together, we will be better off than fighting," Altaf said, "We are not enemies, Sir."

The phone abruptly fell silent.

Prakash held the disconnected phone in his hand and spoke quietly to Altaf, *'Yes, we are not enemies. It is the few elements on both sides that turn human beings into monsters and they feed on the mind sets they create.'*

- - -

Purna found a giant man at the door demanding to meet Prakash. When she asked him to wait, the man ordered her to tell the owner of the house about him. Few seconds later Prakash ran down the stairs asking Aman to join him, and stopped at the door.

"This is a surprise. What brings you here?" Prakash asked.

"The situation demands it," the visitor replied.

Prakash escorted him to the workstation where Aman had already reached. Prakash introduced the giant, "Aman, meet Karun Verma," Prakash said and introduced Aman to Verma.

Instantly, there were apprehensions on Verma and Aman's faces but they sat while Prakash narrated the story from the beginning. When he was finished, Karun thrust his hands at Aman and shook it warmly. Aman found Karun Verma to be a gentle person and wondered if this gentle person was really the man who had gone on a killing spree to evict his father, and get him out of jail only to kill him and then perform the last rites? It was difficult to believe. Verma was ruggedly handsome, with tanned skin and well-toned body, and a presence that defied the perception of a brutal killer which he obviously was. The multi-agency intelligence officer was as polite a man as any person he knew but the mannerisms of Verma contradicted his oral abilities. He heard Karun Verma saying something which he didn't hear. "I am sorry. Can you please repeat? I didn't hear what you said," Aman apologized.

"I am sorry to hear about General Pathan. I knew him. I can vouch that he was a real gentleman. My commiserations!" The man said with genuine sympathy.

"Thank you!" Aman accepted.

"Now, what brings you here?" Prakash asked Verma.

"I was sent here by our mentor."

Prakash was surprised. Why would Nitin Tyagi send Verma to his house when matters were to be handled quietly? The appearance of this man could trigger alarms in intelligence circles. "Why?" he asked.

"To personally deliver... this to you," Verma said and pulled out an envelope and handed it to Prakash. "He trusts no one else so he asked Karachi to send it promptly. It was delivered to an airline employee who delivered it to me an hour ago. The originals! Ensure that it reaches the Foreign Office when you are finished, he says… preferably Monday evening."

Prakash opened the envelope and found a large red striped folder with a file and bunch of papers and documents. He scanned the documents and placed markers on them. A half hour later, he put the folder on the desk and looked at the two men who were waiting for him. In next few minutes, Prakash said what he had found. There were hand-written notes and maps with detailed marks on strategically important places. The locations where the MRBMs were to be deployed were precisely marked. It contained details of which towns and cities were to be struck at what stage, and had exhaustive details about the strength and weaknesses of the Indian army. The planning was extensive. Prakash put them on the table for Verma and Aman to see. The plan may destroy Pakistan eventually when Indians respond, but before that India would endure an attack unparalleled in its history. The sheer scale of loss of lives in the initial attack would be phenomenal. It was a chilling plan with no consideration for loss of life. The men were silent. They imagined the destruction that the plan could bring to India.

"This bastard must die," Aman Bux said softly, "If he lives, millions will die. If this plan is even initiated Pakistan will be wiped out for good."

"We should expose this. Wahid Khan will be on the run. Agencies worldwide will be on the lookout for him. This can rid us of Wahid Khan," Karun Verma opined.

"Don't be childish. Do you understand the implications of it? There could be any of the many possibilities that it could be a disaster. What would happen to the economy of the region?" Prakash retorted.

"How?" Karun Verma asked.

"In desperation Wahid Khan would take control whether he is ready or not. It will be his only escape route. Assuming he is deposed, we are not sure who the other two in the core group are. We know that Wahid Khan and Moinuddin are the two out of four in the group. What about the other two? Any one of those two can take control and continue with the plan. What then? Then, do you know that India is the back office of more than a third of the world's fortune five hundred companies? What happens to regional and world economy if these offices are shut down for even a week? Indian middle-class is bigger than the top five EU countries put together. India and Pakistan together amount to over a sixth of world population. When such a force goes to war, you bet it will take the world economy with it. Major economies rely on countries like India for their growth. News of real threat of a nuclear war pushes the stock markets across the globe. When world's third largest purchasing economy goes to war, world economy takes a huge hit." Prakash said and looked at Aman, "Rukhsar will tell you. In a full-fledged war economy dives through the floor and inflation shoots through the roof. Do you really want the world media to learn about this? I don't think so."

"True," Aman nodded, "world will panic."

"Absolutely!"

"Then what is the solution?" Karun Verma asked.

"Pakistan Government is under tremendous pressure. It is working hard to convince foreign governments that it's an Indian propaganda. It's a matter of trusting Pakistan's word against India's. The Pak government and bureaucracy has had a bit of success in limiting the damage thus far because the International community has no evidence to counter Pakistan's claims," Prakash tapped the folder, "This is the irrefutable evidence which the Pak Authorities can't deny. This is a bomb! Once the International community has this, it will force Pakistan to act promptly or else they face sanctions for starters." Prakash said, "Gentlemen, I have work to do. Within a week the pressure will be too much, and then they will take care of General Wahid Khan."

"Ok, I will take your leave. If there is anything you want, let me know," Karun Verma said and left.

Prakash and Aman looked at each other after Verma left.

"So? What's your plan now?" Aman asked.

"Exactly as I said. I also want that man to be desperate."

"And how will you manage that?" Aman asked suspiciously.

"I have given him a good reason to meet our colleague. He will make an offer to Wahid Khan which the General can't afford to ignore. He will come to us, be sure of that. You wait and watch!" Prakash replied with a mysterious smile again.

"Who is this man?"

"Later," Prakash replied with the mysterious smile lingering on his lips.

- - -

Prakash got down to work and asked Aman to assist him in sending data to various destinations: Australia, Japan, South Korea, China, UK, Germany, US, France, Italy, Canada, Russia and Brazil. Off these, where Prakash did not have contacts like Brazil or Italy; he sought the help of his *'Guru'*, Nitin Tyagi. An hour later Prakash and Aman leaned back in their chairs. They had messed up weekend plans of Pakistan's Ministries and military alike. There would be insurmountable pressure. Wahid Khan and the crippled General were about to be ejected out of their seats.

'Tiger' Chowdhary Dastgir called to inform that the crippled General had committed suicide. General Moinuddin, the real brain behind the plan had shot himself. Pakistani media and military circles were abuzz with conspiracy theories and suspicion; after General Pathan, General Moinuddin had committed suicide. Was it a coincidence? Some media circles suspected Indian hand in the 'murders' of the two Generals. *'Satya'* Prakash Rohatgi thanked *'Tiger'* for informing him and smiled at Aman.

"I am surprised you smile," Aman asked with surprise writ large on his face, "General Moinuddin was the brains behind this sick plan."

"Yes, my friend. With the master planner gone and his files missing, Wahid Khan will have to re-strategize and start all over again. Even if he is able to assume power it will take him months to recompile the stats General Moinuddin had. It gives us time," Prakash looked at the folder again, "there are two other men in the quartet. We must know who they are. Once we know that, we can relax a little."

* * *

Pakistan Military Camp

Skardu, Pakistan Occupied Kashmir

'*This was a nightmare! How could it possibly happen? Why?*' Wahid Khan thought after disconnecting Usmani's call. '*Why did you kill yourself? You have messed up all our plans. How do I get it all back?*' General Wahid Khan moaned softly.

"What's the rush?" Wahid Khan asked when Yakub Lahori came hurriedly to him.

"There is some good news you will like," Lahori said and handed the General printout of an email.

Wahid Khan read eagerly. This was fantastic, he thought. If civilians cooperate, he had a great chance to really hurt India by taking Kashmir. Mir Jamal was a known anti-Indian. He was responsible for many Indian secrets reaching them. If Mir Jamal was to support from within, it could inspire other anti-India leaders in J&K to take up arms; arms supplied by forces loyal to Wahid Khan. He was aware of '*leaders*' who helped any side where they saw monetary advantage, or any other way to enhance their influence among the locals. There were too many of the kind who had chickened out when they were supposed to come to Pakistan's aid, although they were being paid in millions each year.

431

"What do you make of Jamal's proposal?" he asked Lahori.

Lahori shook his head in disagreement, "They take us for a ride whenever they get a chance. We must be cautious and ensure we get what is promised to us. They promise the sky and give us an umbrella; it's been their trait. They let us down during the wars when we relied on them. I am not sure of Mir Jamal either."

Wahid Khan thought and nodded, "we can't ignore their offer at this juncture. Let's see what he wants in return."

"What do you want me to do?"

"Tell Jamal I want to meet him in person and tell him not to play games. If he wants something tell him to spell it out. And warn him; if he doesn't deliver, he better be dead."

The General's advisor nodded and left.

*   *   *

Prakash Rohatgi's Residence

New Delhi, India

Prakash felt lonely every Monday morning after Mehjabeen left for hostel. He would wander around the house keeping himself busy with nothing. After nine days of hectic activity he was mentally fatigued and physically tired. He wanted to sleep but he had to be awake till others returned. He couldn't leave the workstation unattended when each second counted. Prakash would let Aman keep watch while Prakash slept. The next day being a Sunday, he expected no action.

He walked to the panels lined against the wall with large volumes of books and artefacts safely stored in cavities of the walls behind the shelves. This was his favourite pass time in last twenty years. He never made friends and encouraged none to befriend him. Losing loved ones increased loneliness.

When Nitin Tyagi had bought this land in late sixties it was a forest. Tyagi had wished to spend his retirement days here and he had built a cottage which sufficed his needs but when he approached his retirement age, his elder son had migrated to Hyderabad and set up his 'Information Technology' firm, and his younger son was a stock broker in Mumbai. A year before retirement he had come to this farmhouse intending to sell it. He knew his sons won't be able to maintain it. In those days he was training some bright minds in his personal capacity.

During a militant attack in Srinagar he met a brilliant man without a family. Tyagi invited the young man to New Delhi. Prakash Rohatgi came on the orders of a man who had deep influence over him. When he arrived, Tyagi had showed him what he did. Impressed by the potential of work and freedom to do it attracted Prakash. He resigned from the military and became a 'real' intelligence man, working for various agencies on his terms; the only criteria he considered worth discussing were the benefits to India. He worked in the cottage and stayed in the outhouse. A day after his retirement, Nitin Tyagi handed Prakash ownership papers of the farmhouse. When Prakash asked him how he was to pay for the property, Tyagi had placed a set of mortgage papers in front of him and told him to run the farm professionally and pay the bank monthly instalments. Some months later Prakash learnt that Tyagi had sold him the property at two thirds the market price to ensure he did not face repayment problems. Whenever Prakash wanted guidance, Nitin Tyagi, who still commanded immense respect in various ministries, was there, and he helped Prakash in expanding his network base.

After the death of his family members he had lost interest in everything. He had one mission in life; to do whatever was the best he could do for the country. When Nitin Tyagi had brought him to this farmhouse and explained what he did for the country from this place, Prakash was fascinated. When he was offered to join Nitin Tyagi's 'group' and succeed him once Tyagi retired, Prakash grabbed the opportunity and he had been successful.

A young lady stayed in the cottage with Prakash and Nitin Tyagi: Archana Pendharkar was studying banking in New Delhi and assisting them. Prakash enjoyed Archana's company and the two were good friends although romance was not on the horizon. Tyagi spoke to them individually and decided to speak to Archana's parents and they were engaged to be married in three month's on an auspicious day. In the meantime Archana was offered a job in Mumbai and she left for Mumbai.

A week before their marriage, a series of bomb blasts shook Mumbai. There were serial blasts in first class compartments of the local suburban trains. Archana happened to be in one of these. She was mortally injured. Prakash and Tyagi rushed to Mumbai. Archana died on the 'auspicious day' they were to get married.

Prakash was shattered. Archana was the only friend he had in his life. With her death, he lost the last person he loved. Nitin Tyagi tried his best to keep Prakash company but then he found that Prakash had closed himself totally and found solace in the work he was doing. And, Prakash was getting lot better in his mission; he wanted to be the best intelligence man in the field.

Seven years ago Prakash received a call from a lady he had accused of working for the enemies. She proved later that she was a patriot. When she had called, Prakash had rushed to her house in Gulmarg to learn that she had been thrown out of her house by her in-laws and she was forced to live with her widow mother, surviving on meagre sum the old lady earned as a weaver.

Prakash met her that evening and his life changed when he saw a young four year girl trying to study under candle lights. Prakash had taken an instant liking for the girl and offered her mother to take care of her, and her studies. Mehrunissa, girl's mother hesitated initially but when Prakash invited her to New Delhi to see where Mehjabeen would be studying, Mehrunissa had given in to his wishes for Mehjabeen's sake.

Prakash brought Mehjabeen to New Delhi and admitted her in the best school in his area with a comfortable hostel. From the day Mehjabeen came to New Delhi, she became the only family Prakash had in thirteen years. He looked at her as his daughter.

Mehjabeen never complained but she missed her mother. He took care of Mehrunissa's financial needs and arranged for Mehrunissa to come to New Delhi during short vacations. When Mehjabeen had longer vacations, especially Diwali and summer vacations, he took her to Pahalgam. He would drop Mehjabeen to Pahalgam and pick her up from just before the vacations ended.

Though Mehjabeen knew Prakash was not her biological father, she saw Prakash as her real father. Mehrunissa and Prakash gradually started liking each other. During a brief vacation when Mehrunissa came to New Delhi Mehjabeen was on school trip to Agra. That evening Prakash took Mehrunissa out for a movie, just as he did whenever she was in New Delhi. They had dinner, but on this trip Prakash, instead of taking her to fancy restaurants, took her to have street food. They returned to the farmhouse later than usual.

That evening, lonely souls found a willing partner in each other. They spent the night talking on general topics and the conversation gradually turned to personal talks, and to their past, including tragedies in both their lives. They talked about her life first, and then his. As wee hours stretched, the lonely souls found mutual admiration, respect and affection for each other which strengthened into a bond. Both acknowledged it and surrendered themselves to each other that night. When they opened their eyes the next morning, they were in each other's arms. They had found the love of their lives.

- - -

For eleven days he hadn't spoken to Mehrunissa. He dialled her number and it was busy. He dialled again ten minutes later and Mehrunissa picked it immediately. They didn't care how long they spoke; time was of no consequence. After the call was over Prakash smiled at the thought of Mehrunissa and Mehjabeen living with him, though he did not talk about marriage. He couldn't break a promise he had made.

The thought of the loves in his life replenished his energy level. Loneliness was gone and his mind was calm, and soul was like it was blessed by Divinity within.

Prakash pulled a drawer and drew out an album and opened it, sifting the leaves from back frontwards seeking a particular leaf. He opened the leaf and touched the only photograph he had of Mehrunissa, Mehjabeen and himself in a single frame. He looked at it for a while, closed the album and put it back in the drawer, and went to his workstation. He smiled and sat in trance like meditation, concentrating on his plan. Fifteen minutes later he opened his eyes with a bright idea. He sent out severely incriminating and compelling emails to his every contact. The reasons for the murder of General Imran Pathan and suicide by General Moinuddin were made obvious. This was for Mehrunissa and Mehjabeen. He wanted to spend a little time with them in Pahalgam without bothering to attend to calls or return to New Delhi in a hurry. Aman Bux and Rukhsar had insisted on travelling with him to Pahalgam. He smiled. He wanted them to come to his wedding if…! They deserved it; they had earned it. If it wasn't for their initiative, his marriage with Mehrunissa would have remained a dream because he would have never proposed to Mehrunissa - he had promised her mother.

He thought of a particular moment and smiled. He adored the moment when Rukhsar had scolded him angrily for not understanding Mehjabeen's wish. He was dumbfounded at the time but the authority and ownership with which Rukhsar had scolded him had touched his heart. Rukhsar was special. Two months ago when Zubair told him about his family, Prakash had searched for Zubair's family. When he got information about them, for two weeks he was unsure if he should inform them that Zubair was alive. One evening when Zubair was lying on the sofa sadly, Prakash knew Zubair yearned for his family, especially

Rukhsar. Prakash decided to call Rukhsar and tell her about her father. The next day he called her. He spoke to her and five days later they met in an under-construction hospital room. Having met her, he had an idea; she was an ideal candidate to be brought into the group.

When Prakash first saw Aman Khan Bux he liked the man instantly. He felt an inherent honesty in the man who had accompanied his girl-friend to meet a stranger alone in enemy country. A minute later however, he cursed himself for calling Rukhsar. He had no idea she would bring a diplomat as her companion. Then, a few hours later he was able to bond with them and he knew his decision was right. The lovely couple had no idea that he would not have let them meet Zubair if they had been naive or impractical about history of the Kargil war and real incidents as they had happened. To his comfort the two were open minded. Though it had just been nine days since they had first met, yet he knew he had lifelong friend in Aman, and... he smiled happily; he had a sister who would love her brother always.

An hour later he locked the door behind him and headed for the kitchen. He decided to prepare dinner for his guests.

- - -

He loved Indian movies like virtually every Pakistani, and just as they loved Indian film music. Watching a Hindi film in a cinema hall had been a dream for him for years until a few years ago Pakistan Government lifted the ban on screening Hindi movies in Pakistan. But, to watch a Hindi movie in an Indian cinema hall was a different experience. Sadly for him, Mehjabeen had selected a romantic comedy, a 'rom-com' as she called them. He personally liked movies in the extremes; either a movie on a particular subject or a theme, or a pure commercial, entertaining movies. This was neither and he wasn't enjoying it. The only good thing about it was the enthusiasm of the girl next to him, and his lady love. Zubair was wondering what was going on. The only person who seemed to dislike it totally was Purna.

Aman Khan Bux was amazed at the turn of events. He had expected this Indian trip to be short, difficult and a waste of time. From the onset, he was sure Rukhsar couldn't bring back her father no matter how hard she tried. It would be a miracle even if she was able to meet her father. She was the only living person he loved. When she had called to tell him about her trip to India, he had his reservations. Rukhsar was a tough woman; intelligent and smart, a lecturer in economics but her innocence and trusting nature made her gullible. She was naive in many ways because she was raised in a protected environment. He had pled her to wait till he reached Lahore.

When he had reached Rukhsar's house, Shabnam had supported her daughter's decision and that sealed his chances of talking Rukhsar out of her decision. He had come prepared with his bags knowing well that he may have to go with her. Rukhsar initially, although half-heartedly objected, she knew she couldn't change his mind and she was happy.

Aman had heard contradicting stories about India; news of how Indian economy had simply boomed in last two decades to become a model state for development. He had also heard ugly stories, especially how Muslims were treated in India. He had heard about large-hearted Indians, and about extreme poverty in large parts. At the start of his journey he had made a conscious decision that he wouldn't go with pre-conceived notions. When he put his first foot on Indian soil, almost like magic, his earlier fears and inhibitions had evaporated. He felt a sense of belonging; like he was travelling in his country, and he felt lot safer. When locals learnt that he was from Pakistan, to his amazement, instead of hatred he felt like a privileged person, and he, along with Rukhsar were treated like royalty.

Aman's impression about Prakash kept changing every few hours for two days. When he first met Prakash in the hospital he had liked the man who seemed sincere and decent. When few hours later he saw Prakash beat up a human being, Aman had changed his earlier perception and thought of him as a brute. The next day his opinion changed again when Prakash drove them to Agra, and to meet Zubair. From then on it was a pleasure knowing Prakash as a kind hearted man but the same man was heartless when he came across men he didn't like. Prakash's initiative to get them married was an obligation he could never re-pay in any way. Prakash Rohatgi was the one man he would bet his life on and never live to regret it. He wondered if Prakash felt the same way as he did.

He looked out of the window and saw the lights pass by as their vehicle cruised along, but his mind was elsewhere. An idea hit him. It was a crazy but he liked it. He asked Purna to stop at a coffee shop. Rukhsar and Mehjabeen looked at him wondering why he wanted to stop. Purna stopped the vehicle at an eatery. Aman led everyone to the cafeteria and when they were seated, he ordered coffee and snacks for all and pulled Rukhsar aside and spoke to her privately. When he was done, Rukhsar smiled and waved at Mehjabeen to join them. When she stood near them Aman spoke to her. Mehjabeen giggled happily and gave them the cell number of Mehrunissa. For fifteen minutes they kept calling but her cell phone was busy. Instinctively Rukhsar dialled Prakash's number a few times and it was busy too. Prakash was not a man to converse with anyone for long time. Even his urgent calls were brief. She looked at Mehjabeen and Aman and they all smiled. After snacks, Rukhsar called Mehrunissa again. To her pleasant surprise the call went through at the first attempt. She handed the cell phone to Mehjabeen and asked her to speak to her mother before them. Ten minutes later the group was excited and the vehicle was speeding towards the outskirts of New Delhi.

Rukhsar Ahmed-Bux was glad she was doing something for Prakash. The gentile giant had made her India visit a trip of life time; of memories and discoveries. She had never thought that her trip would be so rich in experience. When she met Prakash for the first time, she had felt an affinity towards him automatically; as if a guiding force told her to trust him and she had trusted him blindly. Throughout the trip, her earlier notion of a poverty stricken nation had eroded. She had been biased against India; consistent anti-India propaganda had brainwashed her. If an educated and liberal minded woman like her could be biased against the *enemy*, how she could blame the layman for being against India, she thought. A rift was created between peoples on both sides. Only the few, who crossed the border and experienced richness of life, were people who became '*liberals*' and were labelled '*traitors*' by vested interests. They intentionally wanted people to think of India and Indians as enemies, or else their existence as Muslims and Pakistanis would cease to exist. There was a fear psychosis under which people of her country lived in; created by political and religious leaders. And that was a tragedy.

If it wasn't for that call initiated by Prakash, she would have never met her father, and she would have never known that her grandfather was alive, and that he had a family which was as good as any she knew. It was his initial push which made it possible for her to be married amidst family members instead of a group of four people who would have been present at their wedding, as she and Aman had planned a month ago in Lahore. She would always be indebted to Prakash for what he was doing for both, India and Pakistan. She was sceptical and nervous when he asked them to join him in averting a war. Suddenly, she shivered at the thought of an evil General who had sent mercenaries to kill them all. Prakash was responsible for saving their lives because he was reluctant to kill Altaf. Normally, a man like Altaf wouldn't see the light of the next day, but Prakash hadn't killed him.

That goodness had paid dividends and today that captive had provided information which would save the two countries from a disastrous war.

Rukhsar's eyes were moist as she relived the last nine days. A thought which intrigued her most was Aman's decision to get Prakash and Mehrunissa married. Would he have taken that decision ten days ago without being biased, she doubted. Aman Khan Bux was a gem but he was also a devout Muslim. It must have occurred to him that he was getting a Muslim woman married to an Indian, a Hindu. It was a conscious decision made without bias. She wondered how he had taken a crucial decision with such conviction. She smiled. It had hardly anything to do with what Prakash had done for them, she knew. It was probably the soil of a country that changed mind-sets. She had witnessed in the last nine days that people in this country, were Indians first; religion was next. It was like Lahore of 40's when people of all religions lived together.

Rukhsar was surprised when the previous night Aman told her about Prakash's invitation to him and Rukhsar to join him as part of his group which worked for better relations between countries. Rukhsar was excited to be a part but now she had a priority. She had thought deeply about it and made her decision. She would also do something else. She knew that Prakash, Aman and Zubair would oppose her decision but she had made it and no one was going to stop her now. So what if her life could be at risk? She was willing to do it for Pakistan and its people. Pakistan, as her father had proved was part of India; the greatest nation mankind ever lived in. She wouldn't let the glorious past be buried. That would be a cardinal sin. She would join politics and serve people rather than be a mute spectator and let zealots run the affairs of her country. If people like her don't venture into politics they had no right to criticise the mess the lesser humans had put them in. She was sick of hearing that Pakistan was victim of terror. What do people expect when terrorists are spawned, militants trained and financed in the backyard, sent across borders to kill innocent human beings, and then use them to fight proxy wars, and then dump them? Pakistan was being labelled as 'terror sponsoring state' and the shameful part was that, with the natural wealth it had, and the potential its talented people had, been listed as a 'failing state'. There was something wrong and she had to do her bit to set it right. She was daughter and granddaughter of brave, dedicated soldiers with high moral values who fought for their nation and were abandoned for doing their duty; brandished as traitors, and forced to live in exile in different countries. She owed it to them to see that their country wasn't taken over by zealots. It was time to stop war mongers who had created a mind-set so biased against India that if someone was to tell its people a lie so absurd that India had stolen a hill, people would stage protests and ask its government to wage war with India, without checking if the hill still existed. She was convinced it was the right thing to do. She promised herself to speak to the three men and tell them what she had planned. Opposition notwithstanding, she would go ahead.

— — —

When they reached Prakash's house the excitement was at its peak. Mehjabeen was overexcited. She ran into the house looking for Prakash but didn't find him at his workstation nor in the hall. She ran up the stairs to find his room locked and wondered where her '*Baba*' was. She had seen his car parked in the garage. She turned to Rukhsar with disappointment as she entered. "Baba is not here," she complained.

Prakash emerged from kitchen proudly aping a professional chef, rolling a trolley and asking all to sit and enjoy the food.

"We will do that, Prakash," Rukhsar said in a taunting tone and a naughty smile, "your cell was busy for a long time."

"Oh? When?"

"An hour ago?" She asked with raised her eyebrows.

"Oh, I was speaking to someone."

"For half an hour?" she quizzed.

"Yes, for half an hour. Is there a problem?"

"No! It's just that Mehjabeen couldn't speak to 'someone' because you were busy talking to her," Rukhsar taunted, with the naughty smile still lingering on her lips.

Prakash avoided looking at Rukhsar. "You should have told me if you wanted to talk to her," he told Mehjabeen.

Mehjabeen giggled loudly.

"What's the matter?" Prakash asked.

Aman noticed that Prakash was free of all worries. He had serenity on his face. "You look very fresh," he said.

"And happier..." Rukhsar added.

"And younger..." Mehjabeen said and giggled.

"What's this all about?" Prakash asked suspiciously.

"We are going to Pahalgam tomorrow." Rukhsar declared.

"No!" Prakash shouted, surprising all by the loudness.

Aman Khan stared at Prakash, "What's the matter?"

"Later," Prakash said and looked at Aman, "Rukhsar and you will go to Pahalgam to drop Mehjabeen and meet her mother. I will join you all in a couple of days."

* * *

Pakistan Military Camp

Skardu, Pakistan Occupied Kashmir

Lahori called Mir Jamal all day but he was unable to reach the Kashmiri leader. He sent Wahid Khan's message via email but Jamal hadn't replied to that either and Lahori didn't dare meet the General unless he had news the General wanted to hear. His cell phone shrieked. Lahori jumped to check the caller praying it was Jamal. Lahori saw the name and picked it immediately. "I have been trying to call all day. Where are you?" Lahori said and delivered the General's message.

Mir Jamal smiled at his end, "I am on my way to Delhi. By tomorrow afternoon I will reach Srinagar and coordinate as the General wishes."

"He wants to see the plan through without hurdles, Jamal." Lahori was polite but the hint of threat in his tone wasn't lost.

"Tell him this is going to be the most telling blow ever," Mir Jamal said and disconnected the call.

- - -

"Yes?" Wahid Khan shouted into the phone.

"Altaf here, General. I regret bothering. I met your Srinagar friend. He promises to provide all assistance. He also says he has some plans General Moinuddin had drafted, but not the whole thing. He has asked me to come again tomorrow and collect it if you say, General."

"Get it. Tell him to call me tomorrow morning. I will be on my way to Rawalpindi in the afternoon."

"Yes, General," Altaf said and disconnected the call.

Can he re-stitch the plan General Moinuddin had prepared so meticulously? With his uncle, the mastermind dead, there remained three from the core group: himself, the Kashmiri leader and a General, the cynical man who wished to be the President when Wahid Khan came to power. He was aware that pressure was mounting on the Government, military establishment and the Intelligence networks alike. The plan was out in the open but till the Indians did not have the documents to back up their claims he was safe and the plan could still be executed. But, with files from General Moinuddin's safe missing, he was sure it would find its way into Indian hands and it would force Pakistani leaders to take action against him. Wahid Khan knew he had to take over before he was forced to leave.

Altaf had done a good job. If he could find and take Zubair, one of his tensions would be gone. He would be the best ruler of Pakistan ever. Wahid Khan smiled and closed his eyes.

-   -   -

Prakash Rohatgi's Residence,

New Delhi, India

"You got the email, *bhai*?" Altaf asked with excitement.

"Yes, I have. Well done, my friend." Prakash said as he looked at the monitor. The attachments were scanned copies of papers Altaf got from Wahid Khan's colleague, the Kashmiri Leader.

Altaf was silent for a moment. The term of endearment from Prakash was touching because he knew Prakash meant what he said. Words had special meaning for him and he used them wisely. "I have some news which you can use," he said and spoke for the next five minutes. When finished, he asked how it could be used.

Prakash was amazed at what Altaf had said. He could make Wahid Khan quite vulnerable. "Yes, we can use it quite well but I have to work out a method."

"Is there anything I can do to help?" Altaf Khos asked.

"I will let you know if there is anything. Here is what you can do, however," Prakash said and instructed Altaf on what he wanted. Altaf agreed to do it.

- - -

It was almost midnight but Prakash's elation didn't let him sleep. After he had declined to go to Pahalgam, atmosphere had turned gloomy, but all, barring Mehjabeen understood the delicate situation. Prakash had left them to decide if they wished to go to Pahalgam without him. He had come to his room and to his surprise, he had fallen asleep. Prakash heard a knock on the door and opened the door to find Aman at the door with a serious look on his face. Prakash invited him into his room. "You look upset. Something is bothering you." Prakash said with same seriousness.

Aman shook his head, "Mehjabeen is upset. She is young to understand. She wants you to come with us or she won't go. We have tried persuading her but she won't listen."

"She is an adamant girl," Prakash said and paused, looking at Aman with exasperation, "If you can't persuade her, then I can't. She is also upset because I was away last weekend. She is a doll but she is over-pampered and hard headed like her mother. I will talk to her but I stand no chance. If she wants me to go then I must. A drop in her eyes and the world can go to hell as far as I care."

Aman's face cracked into a smile suddenly, "She means too much to you, doesn't she?"

Prakash shrugged helplessly, "She is my biggest weakness."

"And Mehrunissa?"

"My second weakness," Prakash said and smiled.

Aman nodded in acknowledgement of what Prakash had confessed to him confidently. "So? What do we do now?"

"Let's see… Oh! I got a call from Altaf," Prakash said with a mysterious smile, and told Aman what they had discussed. "I have sent it to Mr. Tyagi and if he tells me that the foreign governments can pressurise Pakistan to 'handle' the situation, I can go to Pahalgam. As it is, we can only do so much. As a group we are powerless to neutralize Wahid Khan on our own. It is for the governments and its agencies to do it."

"You said Wahid Khan will come to us," Aman said. He did not want Wahid Khan to get away.

"That's true. But that was when we were not in possession of the original papers. Now that we have it, our accusations stand vindicated. Wahid Khan won't survive beyond a week. I am not willing to take the extreme step... It is against our philosophy. We consider it immoral and unethical."

"I want Wahid Khan dead. He sent mercenaries to kill us," Aman was upset, "How can you forget that?"

"How can I forget? But there are times when we must use our intellect instead of raw emotions to arrive at solutions. I want him dead too. We must neutralize his plans first and then see if we can get to him," Prakash replied calmly.

"When do our efforts amount to something?"

"By early next week."

"Until then?"

"Until then we must wait."

Aman saw a glint in Prakash's eyes. He knew Prakash was up to something, "You are not telling me everything."

Prakash waived Aman to come closer.

"What?" he asked cautiously.

"A man works for Indian agencies in a deceptive way. With Altaf's message, I got an idea which I had not thought of. Wahid Khan will come to India. If he comes, he is mine."

Aman was surprised but when Prakash explained Aman stared at Prakash in disbelief, "Tell me, you are joking."

Prakash Rohatgi's smile grew wider and more meaningful.

"It will be a tactical coup. But..." Aman did not blink when he saw the risk, "your life could be in danger."

"There is a small chance it could happen. But then, we have to take chances in life some times. When better than now?"

"You aren't going alone. I will come with you."

"No, you are not. I won't let you risk your life. As it is, your presence isn't required. It's my trap and I don't want to share it with you," Prakash said the first part in seriousness, the latter in humour, and laughed.

"This isn't funny. I am coming with you," Aman Khan said it with utmost seriousness.

"Shut up and go to your room," Prakash retorted.

- - - -

Rukhsar was woken for the second time in two hours. Aman got naughty at four in the morning and now when she heard a loud rap on the door. She saw the time. It was six am. Knock on the door? She raised her head and called out, "Who is it?"

"Prakash. Can I talk to you two please? It's important."

"We will be right down. Give us a few minutes."

"Okay. Wake Aman and pack your bags. We must leave in thirty minutes." Prakash said and turned to leave. He heard the door latch click and saw Rukhsar's face peeking through a slight opening, "All okay?" she asked.

"Yes. Please come fast." Prakash said and turned away.

Rukhsar returned to bed with a worry and shook Aman, "Wake up. We have to leave."

Aman was jolted out of sleep. "Why? What happened?" Aman asked hurriedly, searching for his pyjama.

Rukhsar replied as she ran to the bathroom. "I have no idea. Prakash wants us to get ready quickly and go down fast. We are leaving, he said."

"Where are we going?" He asked.

"I have no idea. All I know is that we are leaving. That's all he told me," she said worriedly and ran to the bathroom.

- - -

Rukhsar and Aman climbed down the stairs with their bags. Their worried looks brought laughter from people in the hall. The couple looked at them and at each other with a stupefied look. Prakash, Zubair and Mehjabeen were relaxed.

Aman sat next to Prakash, "Where are we going?"

"Pahalgam... And, from there, I go to Gulmarg in three-four days."

Aman made the connection. Mehjabeen wasn't the only reason for the hasty decision. Prakash was going to Gulmarg. "What happened?" he asked anxiously.

"I told you she is my weakness. She wanted to go today so I agreed," Prakash replied with equal seriousness.

"If that was the case why the rush?"

"I will go to Gulmarg, but when I am ready."

"What's the hurry?" Aman Khan asked.

"Later," Prakash replied and bit into his breakfast.

Zubair, Rukhsar and Aman knew this wasn't a casual trip. They wanted to ask but Prakash had ended the conversation. He probably didn't wish to talk in Mehjabeen's presence, and he didn't want Aman or Rukhsar involved. Their senses told them this wasn't good. They saw Prakash enjoying his meal.

* * *

Pahalgam

Jammu & Kashmir
India

When the flight landed at Srinagar, Prakash excused himself and went to the coffee shop to meet Altaf. They spoke for few minutes. Altaf noted the instructions and gave a rough map of an isolated cottage somewhere in the foothills of the great mountains. Prakash put the map in his pocket, put a wad of currency in Altaf's hands and returned to the group.

Prakash hired an MUV and the group relaxed in their seats to enjoy breath-taking views of the hundred kilometre drive from Srinagar to Pahalgam. Situated in the Anantnag district of J&K, Pahalgam is an extraordinarily beautiful place comparing even with the rest of the state of J&K, Himachal Pradesh and Uttarakhand etc. or even the gorgeous North-eastern states. The driver of the vehicle gladly accepted extra cash Prakash slipped into his hands to drive slowly, to let his passengers enjoy the views. Three hours later when they reached their destination eight kilometres north of the town of Pahalgam, the group was excited. The natural beauty of the area they passed through was like a short trip where heavens had descended, which was probably why the entire belt had been the chosen region of the great Seers of the ancient era.

When the MUV stopped in front of a small cottage sixty feet above Lidder River, the visitors gasped at the wonderful scenery; the serenity, the unadulterated, unpolluted natural beauty of the area, lined with coniferous trees with a little sound of the river flowing below. The area on the edge of a twelve hundred kilometre forest was surrounded by snowy peaks all around.

Hearing the sound of the vehicle, an old lady appeared at the doors, smiled warmly at the guests and welcomed them. Inside the cottage, the introductions were made. The guests were surprised to know find Mehrunissa was missing. The old lady, Zebunissa, Mehrunissa's mother told them that she had gone to the village market and should be back any moment.

Prakash sitting closest to the door saw the door open as he sipped through the strong tea Zebunissa had served. He rose in anticipation and saw Mehrunissa enter. Their eyes met and the two forgot others for a moment. Prakash smiled and nodded his head with a slight bow. She responded in same vein, blushed and looked away quickly. Mehjabeen introduced her to the guests. Mehrunissa impressed Rukhsar the most. Rukhsar was surprised at how young Mehrunissa appeared. If she didn't know she was Mehjabeen's mother, Rukhsar would not have guessed because she looked younger than her age. Her soft-spoken, cultured mannerisms added to her grace. She wasn't beautiful in a conventional way but she had a presence which accentuated her beauty and her eyes and ravishing smile were the killers. The two women met like they had known each other for a long time. When Rukhsar hugged Mehrunissa, she whispered a line to her and both laughed with conspiring winks.

Zebunissa Haider observed how the ladies met. Mehrunissa had confided in her last night after speaking to Mehjabeen and Rukhsar. For her it was an emotional moment. Zebunissa Haider had shifted from the ancestral home of her husband in Pahalgam after neighbours taunted her of being mother-in-law of a terrorist who was responsible for death of three local men. Zebunissa had sold her house and bought this cottage because it was remote and she could afford it. The cottage allowed her and Mehrunissa to live in peace. With Mehjabeen studying in New Delhi under Prakash's guardianship, she was glad to live here, with minimum interaction with outsiders. She was obliged to Prakash for taking care of Mehjabeen and for making their lives comfortable. But she hadn't approved on one occasion. When Mehrunissa was in Delhi two years earlier, Prakash had come to seek her permission to marry Mehrunissa. Zebunissa had mustered her courage to decline. She had been honest with Prakash telling him quite frankly that she liked him but his marriage with her daughter was not possible: her relatives would disown them if not kill them if she let her widowed daughter to remarry. The other reason was obvious; Prakash wasn't a Muslim. Prakash had understood her problem and promised Zebunissa at her insistence that he won't tell Mehrunissa about their discussion. A year later, Mehrunissa had confessed her love for him. It was not a shock for Zebunissa though; she knew the two were in love.

After the initial euphoria subsided, Mehrunissa and Rukhsar were busy talking to each other, Zubair engaged Zebunissa in conversation. Mehjabeen moved about in excitement without letting go of Prakash's hands. Aman and Prakash were quiet. To everyone's surprise Mehrunissa asked Prakash to come with her for a walk. Prakash was surprised when Mehjabeen let go of his hands and giggled.

Mehrunissa and Prakash walked silently through the forest as they descended towards Lidder River. Prakash looked back and couldn't see the cottage. He found an ideal spot and stopped, held Mehrunissa and both sat on a large boulder. She slid her palms in his hand, looked up at him and leaned over his shoulder with her disarming smile, "Rukhsar spoke to mother last night."

"I know." He replied calmly, noticing she was smiling since they had stepped out of the cottage. He pulled her closer and held her face in his palms, "I am no good at romantic words, dear. I don't know what I should say in such situations, so I will be straight forward," Prakash ran the tips of his thumbs along her cheeks and smiled at her.

"You know I am no good at expressing myself either." She said and capped his palms holding them against her face and kissing his palms.

"Mehru, I want to marry you."

Mehrunissa was happy to let the moment pass by without giving her consent. She wanted to absorb the moment and live it. A few moments later she closed her eyes and smiled. That was enough. He laughed happily and bit his lowers lips lightly seeing her eyes twinkle, and he bent and kissed her.

Mehrunissa lay idly on a carpet of dried leaves and her head resting and she breathed heavily on his chest, wanting to cry in happiness but it was difficult for her to emote. She saw him smile at something he was thinking and suddenly he looked down at her and pulled her up; her body half lying on his. He smiled at her suddenly.

"What?" she smiled as she asked him.

"I am thinking. Mehjabeen is at times, wiser than me," he said and told her how she emotionally forced him to come.

Mehrunissa nodded, closed her eyes. Without Mehjabeen neither she nor Prakash would have a life to live even if they had just each other. Mehjabeen was the bond between them. She had often wondered how and when Mehjabeen started to love Prakash a little more than her. She saw his closed eyes and she knew.

Prakash was the best person she had known. Despite the tragedies of life, Prakash had held on to his sanity and retained his decency and character. She knew he loved Mehjabeen and her more than his own life and she loved him as much as she loved her daughter.

She was always hesitant to call him so she always waited for his call. He would call her every other day, and those were the best moments of her day. She had secretly wished to live with him and her daughter. It was abnormal when he didn't call for ten days; it was unlike him. She knew he was a busy man who was working either on his farm or some complex work which she understood very little. When he called the previous night she was surprised to know that her daughter had gone to watch a movie without him. Prakash had explained who Aman and Rukhsar were - Zubair's daughter and son-in-law. Prakash wanted to come to Pahalgam but his 'most important work in his life' was holding him back. He would send Zubair and his guests with Mehjabeen to Pahalgam and he would follow soon when his work was done. Though they were on phone for a long time he hadn't spoken about marriage; he was oblivious to the plans of Mehjabeen and her new 'aunty' as she called Rukhsar. When she spoke to Rukhsar she felt comfortable though Rukhsar was a stranger to her. Rukhsar had opened the discussion about marriage and she persuaded her to get married because their 'daughter' wanted it. The idea of family once again discouraged her. She had a miserable experience once but this time she knew God would do justice by giving her a husband like Prakash to compensate for her first husband's behaviour towards her and Mehjabeen.

Her marriage would give her a sense of freedom like being released from a life of bonded labour. She had agreed for Mehjabeen's, Prakash's and for her sake. She knew Zebunissa would object but her desire to wed Prakash was overbearing, and she had given her consent. If Zebunissa wanted her to be happy she would have to agree.

She felt the chill on her bare back and she shivered. The next moment she found Prakash's hand providing warmth to her. He rolled over, put his jacket on her shoulders and led her back to the cottage.

- - -

Temperature dipped dramatically with little droplets of rain. As drizzle intensified they rushed towards the cottage. When they entered the cottage both were wet; all eyes were smiling at them. "What?" Prakash asked everyone in general.

"You can't see her till we tell you," Zubair ordered and asked Zebunissa to take her daughter away.

Zebunissa led Mehrunissa to another room and Mehjabeen followed them.

"What's going on?" Prakash asked Zubair.

"Have you proposed to Mehrunissa?" Zubair asked.

"I did... an hour ago. She has accepted it," Prakash replied with a quizzing expression on his face. "Why?"

Rukhsar cut the drama out. She pushed Prakash on a chair and sat opposite him. "We want you to do exactly as we say."

"Okay. What is it?"

"You are getting married this evening."

Prakash literally jumped out of his chair. "What?"

Rukhsar pushed Prakash back in the chair, "It's your lucky day. You are getting married at the Marriage Registrar's office of the District Magistrate's court this evening, Mister. You have an appointment. Do you get that?" Rukhsar smiled.

Prakash was stumped. He was elated, but worried. The look on his face was obvious to Aman and Zubair.

Aman knew why Prakash was tensed. "I think we should let the future take its own course. We can't let future determine our present, Prakash."

Prakash nodded. He was thoughtful and silent. They knew he wanted to marry Mehrunissa but something bothered him. Aman pushed his chair next to Prakash and tried reasoning with him, "You don't have to do it. Army or police can take care of the situation."

"If they smell involvement of Indian security my plan will flop," Prakash replied pensively, "We have two men working for us whom Wahid Khan can't suspect. I am banking on it. I don't want to miss the chance."

Rukhsar roared angrily, "Let Wahid Khan go to hell. Don't let him influence the most important decision in your life."

"My priorities are mine. Right now, neutralizing that scum is more important than getting married. I want to marry her but only when I can devote my time to my family without worry. Situations like these are rare. It is unfortunate that it had to happen now." Prakash justified, "when this is over, I can spend weeks without caring what the world does. I want to wait until the end of this week and then, when things are normal I will marry her."

"You can't take chances with your life," Aman shouted.

Rukhsar turned to her husband with a scared look on her face, "What are you talking about?" Rukhsar asked Aman.

Aman didn't reply. He was waiting for Prakash to answer but the stubborn man didn't bother to look at either of them. He was busy with his own thoughts.

"Later," Prakash said, rose from his chair and walked out into the freezing weather.

Zubair was a silent spectator in the conversation. "You know he won't risk anyone's life. If Prakash has decided there isn't a power in the world which can change his mind."

Aman looked at the closed door and said, "Yes, there is."

- - -

When Prakash returned he found a room full of relieved faces. Soft hands of Mehjabeen pulled him. "*Baba*," she said, and that was all she needed to say.

Prakash held her by her waist and sat her on the table next to him. "Listen angel, there are things in life a person must do, or else all his ideals become lies if he renegades on it. Do you want your *Baba* to be that man? I have an important task to perform, and it is my priority, dear. Let's wait for a week, okay?" He tried to persuade Mehjabeen. But it didn't work.

Mehjabeen's eyes were on the verge of shedding tears. His determination trickled down with those tears that started to roll down Mehjabeen's cheeks. Frustrated at not being able to control the young girl, Prakash had to give in. She always had her way with him and this wasn't going to be any different.

Aman smiled but he was sad too. So much love for a girl who wasn't his blood child. He saw purity of human nature which should bind all mankind. He saw a powerful man who overruled anyone he wanted, succumb to a young girl who had no power over him but one: Love!

Prakash pulled her to him and hugged her. "Please... don't cry. Tell your mother to get ready. If we have to reach the Court, we better start in an hour," he said to her.

Mehjabeen wiped her cheeks, slid off the table and ran to her mother's room. Prakash watched the girl disappear and turned to Aman and waived him to step outside.

Aman was surprised, "Now? It's freezing outside."

"Yes, it is," Prakash said and stepped out.

- - -

"Whose idea was it?" he asked Aman.

"Mine! Yesterday I told Rukhsar to talk to your lady love. We decided to convince Mrs. Haider."

"What persuaded her? She wasn't very keen earlier."

"Rukhsar spoke to her and told her about an incident which happened between you and her."

Prakash looked at Aman without commenting, asking him to continue.

"You got angry when Rukhsar joked about conversion. It was that anger in you which convinced her of your character. When Mrs. Haider heard it she softened but what turned it in your favour was Mehjabeen's plea. That little girl has more power stuffed in her than all of us put together."

Prakash smiled with a vigorous nod, "That is true."

The men reached the river and sat on the rock where Prakash sat with Mehrunissa an hour earlier. Aman sat next to him looking at the pristine surroundings which seemed untouched since nature had created it. This was heaven. If only the region was allowed to live its natural life without being sabotaged by bullets. These had turned this heaven into a region polluted by cross- border shelling, bomb explosions and political wrangling. When people of both sides had so much to give, politicians and men with guns should know that there has to be peace because it was the wish and prayer of peoples on both sides. This made Prakash's job so crucial. Aman was disturbed. He shrugged his thoughts to come out of his thought sequence and looked at Prakash sitting on the edge of the rock, probably thinking the same. "What made you get up so early today?" he asked Prakash.

Prakash replied without shifting his gaze, "I had to meet Altaf this morning so I thought I might as well bring all of you here."

"Why suddenly?"

"He wanted to share information which he couldn't do over the phone. He insisted that we meet in person, and he delivered some papers. I had to come."

"What information?"

"Four days from now," Prakash said and disclosed his plan.

Aman held his breath. Prakash's plan was risky, even arrogantly audacious.

"You didn't tell me about it."

"What good would that do?"

"We are partners. I have a right to know what is going on. You have no right to keep me in dark," Aman said angrily.

"Firstly, we are partners, yes; but only in a limited way. Don't forget I brought you in as a 'partner'. I told you my reason," Prakash replied calmly, "You think I will let you or Rukhsar or Zubair Saheb risk your lives if I can handle it? I won't let you interfere with my work either; unless you accept my offer and join us," Prakash said and stared at Aman.

"Why are you taking chances?" Aman asked worriedly. His instincts told him that Prakash was taking a huge risk.

"Yes, it could be... but I am taking a chance because I think it is the best option. In either case; whether I succeed or not, the authorities will have everything they want," Prakash said.

Aman Bux knew Prakash was right; succeed or fail, General Wahid Khan was sure to lose, and both countries would benefit. But the risk was too high! He liked the idea if only if it didn't involve Prakash. Prakash, on the other hand would not take any chances by letting anyone less experienced or less equipped handle this operation. Stakes were too high and benefits were unimaginably good.

Aman suddenly perked up, "You have four days before you can do anything." Aman laughed and rose. "Let's go. You can't miss this auspicious day."

Prakash rose from his seat with a wry smile, *'If only you knew this isn't an auspicious day'.*

Zebunissa didn't ask *Qazi* Saheb of the local mosque to solemnize the wedding knowing he would decline because Prakash wasn't a Muslim and he won't convert. They couldn't get a Pundit because there were none in the area - most were forcefully driven out over the years. Zubair suggested court marriage and when he contacted the court he was told that the wedding formalities would be over in five minutes at the most. Everyone liked that bit.

Zubair Ahmed signed as a witness at the Registrar's office for Prakash Rohatgi and Zebunissa signed for her daughter, while Aman, Rukhsar and a chirpy Mehjabeen stood as mute witnesses. Mehrunissa and Prakash Rohatgi stepped out of the Marriage Registrar's office as husband and wife.

Two vehicles waited for them when they emerged from the office of the Registrar.

"We are returning home while you two are going on a three day trip to Sonemarg," Zubair said, "We didn't get time to book a hotel so find a good one there. But, we do have a taxi waiting for you," Zubair pointed to a grey metallic sedan parked behind their vehicle. He put a wad in Mehrunissa's hands, "This is for you two with our blessings."

Mehrunissa and Prakash were happily surprised and excited, but Prakash Rohatgi looked at Aman Khan and led him ten feet away. "Thank you! But I can't stay beyond two days. I will be back on Wednesday night to prepare for Thursday," Prakash said and wrote a list of instructions and handed it to Aman. "Follow the instructions strictly. If there is any change in the plan or a hiccup, call me. I will call you twice a day and catch up. Don't try to handle it alone. It could be dangerous."

"Don't worry. I will take care, I promise. You two go and enjoy the time."

Prakash led Mehrunissa to the cab. Both smiled when their daughter hugged them. Mehjabeen had tears usually when she was leaving Pahalgam or New Delhi. Today, there was a wide smile on her lips.

Prakash held Mehjabeen and led her to Rukhsar and Aman, "Take care of my angel."

* * *

Islamabad and Rawalpindi

Pakistan

The contacts whom Prakash sent emails at the weekend were able to exert immense pressure on Pakistani authorities. Though Wahid Khan vehemently denied the allegations the Government and Military Hierarchy knew he was lying. The Chairman of Joint Chiefs of Staff of Pakistan Army, General Masood Baig set up an internal inquiry to verify the charges made by world's most influential Governments. General Baig had heard rumours of Wahid Khan's plans but he had taken it lightly. But since previous week he was forced to look at them seriously. General Moinuddin's suicide and General Pathan's murder had alerted his senses. Baig's instructions to the board of enquiry were clear - *'I want a preliminary report in three days and a complete report in a week.'*

Ministry of Home affairs ordered a separate inquiry to look into the allegations of an Indian report that a military coup was planned.

- - -

In Rawalpindi, Wahid Khan learnt of the inquiries against him. When Lahori advised him to withhold his plans, General laughed, "I want to take over next week, by then there will be a storm on both sides of the border in Kashmir. It must go strictly to plan. I am going to Srinagar to set it up."

*   *   *

<u>Srinagar</u>

<u>*Jammu & Kashmir, India*</u>

If Mehrunissa and Prakash were asked if paradise existed, they would have pointed out to their last two, most memorable days of their lives. Even their family members had restricted their calls to one each in the morning and evening. Prakash spent an hour each day ensuring all was ready for Thursday. He kept in touch with five men on the matter. To Prakash's utter surprise, Altaf turned up at the hotel reception bringing a gift for the newlyweds, and news which elated Prakash. Their plan had worked better than anticipated.

- - -

As the taxi sped towards Pahalgam both were sad that the trip was coming to an end. Prakash was back in the real world thinking of the next two days. He went over his strategy in his mind and re-analysed. For his own sake, he wanted no mistakes, and he knew Wahid Khan had no respect for life. When taxi arrived at its destination, Prakash paid the cab driver and asked him to return in three hours.

- - -

The house was in festive mood. Rukhsar, Mehjabeen and Aman had a surprise for the newlyweds. It was a wedding party with select guests. Two hours later, while the party was still on, Prakash asked Mehrunissa, Aman, Zubair and Rukhsar to assemble in Mehrunissa's... their room.

"I must reach Srinagar army camp before dawn and prepare everything. They are waiting for me. A man from Wahid Khan's circle is arriving tomorrow in Srinagar, my sources tell me. The trusted lieutenant of Wahid Khan is a vital cog in his plans. If we nab him and force him to cooperate, we can trap Wahid Khan," Prakash said and looked at the occupants of the room with gratitude. "You all have given me the life's purest joys which I can never repay." Prakash said and turned to his wife, "I should be back in two days... There is a cab waiting for me outside."

"How do you plan to trap Wahid Khan?" Rukhsar asked.

Prakash explained in brief. Rukhsar and Mehrunissa fretted. His plan was dangerous. "There must to be a less risky way to get him," Mehrunissa echoed her and others' thoughts.

"Yes, there is, but we don't have time. With this I am sure Wahid Khan won't get away even if my initial plan fails. If I look at other options, we risk Wahid Khan slipping away. He could get a hint from any of the agents working in the area. We can't risk that."

Mehrunissa was frightened but held her nerves. She didn't want him to go. She knew the risks his plan had from the night they had reached Sonemarg. Prakash had to tell her why he was reluctant to marry her earlier in the day. He told her everything, and why he wanted to wait for a week till the situation was overcome.

Prakash kissed Mehrunissa. They held each other for some time and stepped out of the room. Prakash went to Zebunissa's room to meet his angel. Mehjabeen was upset. She wanted to stay with them till they returned to New Delhi. Prakash told her he would be back in two days and then they will return to New Delhi together. He hugged and kissed his daughter who meant more to him than if he ever had a real daughter.

Aman followed him to the car, helping him with the large number of gadgets and instruments Prakash was to carry with him. Prakash sat in the rear seat and pulled out a gadget, and handed it to Aman. "When you turn it on you will know my location. There will be a blue line on the map which will tell you that I am on schedule, and a red blip will tell you my position. If I get off track without informing you, the gadget will show you a red line and my location. Then you can call Karun Verma and let him know. Give him the coordinates and he will come for me. Okay?"

"Take care, Prakash and good luck. We all love you," Aman said and walked away from the car. For some reason he had a sinking feeling in his heart.

* * *

The Line of Control

- On Indian side -
Jammu & Kashmir, India

Lahori cursed his General for sending him on this perilous mission. If caught, he'd never see his family again; if lucky, he would be dead. He could spend his life in an anonymous prison in an unknown location, in enemy land if caught. He prayed Mir Jamal was efficient like he was in the past. He trusted the General for his sources and the General trusted Mir Jamal. But Lahori didn't trust Jamal as much as he trusted Saifuddin Ilahi. Ilahi was a solid ally of Intelligence agencies and the *Jihadi* forces, especially from FATA region. If he had his way, he would meet Ilahi before Jamal but Wahid Khan insisted he meet Jamal first.

Though Ilahi had always provided as much as he could, he had skinned Pak Military for his support. Mir Jamal however, provided information which was accurate and he never drove hard bargains. There was a time when a man had to negotiate the worth of his support and Lahori knew Jamal was going to put a high tag on his support this time.

He heard the ping and looked out of the window to see the magnificent view of Srinagar from sixteen thousand feet as the aircraft started to descend.

Outside the terminal, Yakub Lahori was greeted by a gust of cold wind. Though it was ten in the morning, temperature was far below what he expected. He was looking for a man who was to drive him to meet Mir Jamal. A young man with a red bag, with logo of J&K Tourism printed on it waived at him, rolled the trolley and manoeuvred it through the crowd to a grey hatchback. He put the luggage in the trunk of the car and introduced himself, "Altaf! Welcome to Srinagar, Sir."

"Thank you, Altaf. All going according to the plan, I hope." Lahori said and smiled. He liked the young man.

"Yes Sir."

"Good. Your services will be well rewarded."

"I swear to you, Sir, my only intention is to work for the sake of my country's future," Altaf replied with sincerity.

Lahori was impressed. He patted Altaf and sat on the passenger seat. Altaf gunned the engine.

- - -

Prakash had re-worked the plan with the Colonel he was referred to. Coordination had to be precise, and with pinpoint accuracy.

The Colonel was waiting for him at his office when Prakash entered, "You rested well, Sir?"

"Yes Colonel. Did Mr. Tyagi call?" Prakash asked. A lot of hard work was about to pay rich dividends.

"Yes Sir, he did. I assured him we are well prepared."

They went over the plan one last time. When finished and satisfied that all was in sync, the Colonel was excited, "We are ready to go now, Sir." The Colonel said and rose to his feet.

Prakash remained seated, "Let's not rush the winds, Colonel. We will go when it is time to go."

The two men were sipping tea when the signal came. The car had crossed the first check-point. Prakash rose and pulled out his gun from one of the two bags he carried, and tucked it behind. He waived at the Colonel and walked out.

- - -

The car cruised along briskly. The man in the back seat called three people and ensured they were in place when the other car reached the intersection. He didn't want to miss this chance. For over sixty years since partition, the Jamal family had been working to exact the revenge. It was a few hours away. He prayed that his men did not make a mistake.

- - -

Barricades along the route made Lahori nervous. Their car was stopped at the fifth barricade by J&K police patrol. A police officer flagged and approached the car. Lahori was glad to see that the General had picked the right man to escort him. Altaf got off the car, spoke to the cop and he was waived off. Altaf got into the car and hit the accelerator. A few minutes later their car got off the main road and rode along an isolated road and stopped two kilometres further in a remote compound of a regal looking house. Lahori and Altaf were led into the house by a heavily armed escort and offered to sit while the host arrived.

A tall, authoritative looking man entered the house a few minutes later, walked to them, shook hands and then sat next to Yakub Lahori, introducing himself, "Mir Jamal."

Lahori's confidence soared after speaking to the Canadian-Kashmiri. The men hit it off immediately. After some light snacks, Jamal advised Lahori to speak to Wahid Khan and update him.

Altaf offered Lahori his cell phone. Lahori thanked Altaf and stepped aside to speak to the General.

Lahori smiled, "I told him that all's as planned. By evening he will let us know when he is coming."

Jamal and Altaf acknowledged and the three men set out on their journey to meet another man as scheduled. Yakub Lahori and Altaf Khos had no idea who they were to meet. Mir Jamal gave Altaf the address of the place of rendezvous, and stepped aside to make a call. He then asked Altaf to join him and speak to the man he was calling. Altaf was surprised. He realised that Prakash had a fantastic ally in Mir Jamal.

The car stopped at an eatery for lunch. Altaf excused himself to go to the loo and called Prakash, informing him of Wahid Khan's arrival in Srinagar the next day, but the time and mode of transport were still unknown.

Prakash thanked Altaf and called Aman confirming the news of Wahid Khan's arrival the next day. He shut off his phone and ran to the Colonel. "I must go... you start when I message you. Tomorrow comes the big fish. Find me a police officer who can arrest him."

* * *

Jammu & Kashmir

India

Altaf, Yakub and Mir Jamal reached the rendezvous point an hour before schedule. They had to wait. A car screeched to a halt and two men jumped out of the car. Prakash lugged a large bag on his back and walked towards the door. Ajmal Loni, head of the local area police station tried to keep pace with the man he was ordered to assist to nab a Pakistani agent. They stood outside the door of the house and rapped on the door.

Lahori heard the raps on the door and saw Altaf jump off the seat and open the door. He returned to the room with two tall men in civilian dress. The older one, Prakash walked to Lahori, stood two feet from him, and introduced Ajmal Loni. "Meet the Circle Officer of the local police station, Ajmal Loni."

Lahori froze; too frightened to react. A sledge hammer like blow smashed into his jaw. The twin shocks, psychological and physical had the desired effect. Wahid Khan's 'political' advisor was still in shock ten minutes after he was hit. He was slumped in his seat staring at the men sitting around him. Mir Jamal sat next to Lahori. He wanted his revenge but he saved it for Wahid Khan and hoped to get a chance to pay back for the atrocities which had been committed on his family by forces of Pakistan army and their proxies.

Jamal family was known for its well-educated, exceptionally talented members, and philanthropy. In 1947 when tribals invaded Kashmir, Jamal family's lives changed forever. The family armed its men to the resist invaders, but their men stood no chance when faced with hundreds of butchers who had orders to create mayhem. Six members of Jamal family died, including a four year old boy and a twenty-one year old female who was brutalized, before, during and after being raped. The family fled to Srinagar. They swore to avenge the death of their family members. After the war Jamal family properties were occupied by invaders, and under Pakistan's control. The family elders decided to stay on the Indian side of Kashmir. Over the years they recreated their wealth and continued their philanthropic activities in the adopted area. A large family house was built sixteen kilometres from Srinagar. As the fortunes grew, the family's resolve grew with it; they wanted revenge. Jamal family was a religious Muslim family which believed in centuries old Kashmiri philosophy of living in harmony with other religious groups. Mir Jamal was eleven years old when history repeated itself. In '65 when another covert *'Operation Gibraltar'* was launched, numerous groups of armed men infiltrated Jammu & Kashmir region to repeat the forty-eight invasion. One of the numerous groups attacked a bus with Hindu pilgrims on their way back from Jammu. The bus had two members of Jamal family who owned it; among them his father, Mir Kasim Jamal. Twenty-one pilgrims died along with Kasim Jamal and the driver. The driver had done his best to keep the bus under control on the treacherous Jammu-Srinagar highway when the gunmen opened fire on the bus but the bus hit the mountain and skidded off the road and plunged into a six hundred feet gorge. Kasim Jamal died instantly but the driver lived for two days to tell the story of the attack to the security forces. When the news reached Jamal family, they solemnly took a blood oath to avenge the death which was taken a generation earlier. Mir Jamal went to Military School, seething with rage and craving for revenge. He out-performed the rest in his batch and joined the army as a commissioned officer. He joined the intelligence services after the '71 Indo-Pak war, trained as a commando and came up trumps again. A senior intelligence officer heard his story and offered him an opportunity to repay Pakistan. Mir Jamal, though working for Indian intelligence, was asked to align with Pak funded regional anti-India leaders who instigated nationalistic sentiment among local Kashmiris. Until '82 Mir Jamal sent 'sensitive' information to Pak intelligence which was provided to him by Indians. These sensitive informations were known to western agents and were certain to reach Pakistan, so Mir Jamal was provided with these, to gain trust of Pakistan Military and Intelligence establishments. To gain absolute trust a plan was hatched on paper. In accordance with the plan, Indian Navy set up strategic observation post off the coast of Kutch within territorial water limits of India, to monitor maritime activities of Pakistan Navy, and merchant vessels that passed through. Mir Jamal sent the information to Pakistani agencies which alarmed the Pakistanis because its Headquarters in Karachi was within the range of this post. The information created a storm in Pakistan. Mir Jamal was treated like a hero by Pak agencies. The plan had succeeded. He had created a blind trust. Now, it was the time for pay back.

Yakub Lahori knew he was trapped. Wahid Khan knew Mir Jamal and Altaf were helping him but once they were sure that Wahid Khan was arriving, they had taken him.

"Look here," Prakash told Lahori pointing towards a video camera mounted on a tripod. "You know Wahid Khan's plan is a non-starter... at least you know now. I want you to tell us about his plans in detail - when and how it was planned, and by whom...all the minute details... miss out nothing."

Yakub Lahori knew that if he spoke he would be killed when he returned to Pakistan. He remained silent.

"Understand the seriousness of your situation here, Lahori. You are a Pakistani bureaucrat travelling in India with fake identity. You will be arrested for espionage and on charges of inciting violence by speaking to the terrorists..." Prakash said and waited for Lahori to reply.

Lahori had lost courage to speak. Prakash warned Lahori, "I don't think you like to be treated like a punching bag; your body won't sustain."

Lahori was scared to his bones but remained quiet. He saw the faces of the four men staring at him and he choked. If he spoke, he would betray his General his country and he could be killed when he returned to Pakistan. If he remained silent he knew he won't survive the questioning by these men.

"I fear for my family," Lahori pleaded.

"That is all the more reason why you should cooperate. But you will talk eventually, no doubt... It is up to you to decide at what stage you will talk," Mir Jamal said without emotion.

Lahori looked at Jamal and knew Mir Jamal wanted to hurt him. He sat upright, "To you I won't speak no matter what you do to me, you traitor!" Lahori made the first mistake.

A powerful fist landed on his jaw. The punch was well-directed, to ensure it stung without breaking the jaw. Lahori's scream was muted because the strike blew the wind out of him; pain reached bearing point. Another blow and Lahori would need medical assistance. Mir Jamal rose and struck his fist into Lahori's abdomen, "I am an Indian," Jamal said and raised his fist to strike again. Prakash tapped Jamal's shoulder and stopped him. Jamal held back his hands. Prakash wanted Lahori to be conscious. He pushed his colleagues aside and sat opposite the General's political advisor; people who were men of reason; chosen because they were smart, pragmatic and intelligent. If he could turn Lahori it would be beneficial because then Lahori won't lie; truth would come voluntarily. Prakash patted Lahori and tried to reason, "If you speak to us and cooperate... and help us nab Wahid Khan he won't be able to harm you or your family. You know your General's plan has failed. We have exerted so much pressure on your Government that it can't manoeuvre unless it submits to the demands of the International community. Inquiries have been set up but we can't wait. If I send all the proofs I have to the world media... some ultra-sensitive which I haven't yet, your country will be hit so hard it won't recover soon. I hold them back because I have my reasons... oh! I forgot! I am Prakash Rohatgi!" he said sarcastically, "You must have heard about me."

Lahori's eyes were wide with fear. He connected with the reports he had seen. This man had gathered all information which had become General's nemesis. He was now absolutely certain that General Wahid Khan's plan was doomed. Lahori was thinking hard.

"If I send these to our Intelligence departments, there will be a pre-emptive strike. What happens to Pakistan? Take your pick and decide quickly," Prakash suggested.

"How can we give up Kashmir?" he asked in a low tone. "It is our right."

Prakash snapped angrily, "You don't have a right to it."

"It should have come to Pakistan," Lahori barked.

Prakash looked at his victim with a sarcastic smile, "Really? Why?" he asked.

"*Qaid-e-Azam* Mohammed Ali Jinnah's '*Two Nation Theory*' is the basis on which Pakistan was created. That is why Pakistan has a right on Kashmir."

Prakash Rohatgi laughed loudly, "Why?"

"Because it has a Muslim majority."

"Do you know how Kashmir got its name?"

Yakub Lahori looked at Prakash blankly.

Prakash leaned to level his eyes with Lahori's, and bore into his eyes from a few inches away, "A great Seer, a *Maha-Rishi,*

Kashyap was born here thousands of years ago and his followers, the saints gave this place its name. It was an era when no other religion existed. He was a Kashmiri... and Kashmir has over six thousand years of history, you ignorant fool. And, even if you say you have a claim, are you going to kill the locals to get it?"

"We will get it through any means. The United Nations will give it to us," Lahori defended his stance.

Prakash chuckled, "You people are so ignorant. You want to go to UN? Have you respected the UN resolution on it?"

"We have always respected UN's wishes," Lahori defended.

"That is the flaw in your plan. You and your despotic rulers don't even know that the UN will never interfere because you did not honour it. Each time you go to the UN with the Kashmir issue, you are sent back because you dishonoured UN Security Council's resolution."

"That is a lie," Lahori yelled.

Prakash slapped Lahori viciously. "That's for incompetence and for not doing your homework." Prakash closed his eyes remembering the UN resolution's exact words, "UN Security Council resolution no. 47, dated April twenty-first, nineteen forty-eight says, and I quote, '*The resolution recommends that in order to ensure the impartiality of the plebiscite Pakistan withdraw all tribesmen and nationals who entered the region for the purpose of fighting and that India leave only the minimum number of troops needed to keep civil order*'. Unquote. India withdrew its forces from Kashmir totally except for a small token in Srinagar to protect it from scums like your General. It honoured the UN resolution. Pakistan didn't. It still occupies a third of Kashmir overriding UN resolution. Tell me why should UN take you seriously? Why do you expect anyone to take you seriously?" Prakash Rohatgi turned to Jamal, "This idiot doesn't even know what he is talking about."

"I don't believe you. It is a lie. Kashmir was..." Lahori made the second mistake.

Prakash slapped him again. "Every word has a meaning. Be careful when and where you use it. When you call someone a liar think about your actions first. You people are obsessed with Kashmir... because it has a Muslim majority? What will you do with it if, God forbid, you ever have it? It will suffer exactly as the people in POK suffer, isn't it? Kill the Shia population and deprive the rest, of education and livelihood? Your army will use it to train terrorists and send them across the globe to kill people, isn't it? It will suffer the same fate as its western part which is overrun by outsiders. Demography is changed under a sustained plan. You deprive the people of their land and give it to foreign powers..."

"That is not true. We haven't departed an inch of Azad Kashmir to anyone." Lahori protested.

Prakash Rohatgi slapped Lahori again, "You should have information on your subject. Vast area including the entire estate of the Royal family of Kashmir, hundreds of acres... was handed over to the Chinese. If you don't know you better learn of it," he retorted with anger. Enraged, Prakash asked the bureaucrat, "East Pakistan was a Muslim majority area, isn't it? Why did it break away from you? Your Qaid-e-Azam's two nation theory bit dust the day your soldiers started to kill their own countrymen. Your leaders will abuse them like they abused the Bengalis; like when Bhutto called the Bengalis, *'sons of swine'... 'suar ke bachche',* and tells them to *'go to hell'* what should the rest of the minorities think about the leaders? You don't want Kashmir because it has a Muslim population; you want it so you can exploit it just as you do it in all other provinces, like in Sindh, KPK and Baluchistan. But, Kashmir is not for sale. It is a land of ancient seers, of great souls but you won't know that because you don't know its history. Your kids don't even know history. Liars and ill-informed people like you write history books, lying to young innocent minds and poisoning them. Kashmir is a land of the greatest spiritual masters. This is where Gods descended on Earth, where Prophet

Mohammed has the *only* relic of his mortal remains. This is the land where according to some reports... Jesus spent most of His missing years. This is where Vedas were written and Shiva has His abode. Pakistan doesn't deserve land so pious because it has no respect for religion, and especially, it has no spiritual respect for Islam."

Yakub Lahori was silent for a brief time. Then he resorted to reasonable dialogue. He spoke, "It was decided that there was to be a plebiscite but India never let it be done."

"Are you serious? The demography changed after the forty-eight war, and again after the sixty-five war, and finally when zealots like your General infiltrated men into Kashmir and drove out Kashmiri Pundits, demography was changed. Sikhs and Hindus were forced into exile. You expect a plebiscite in this scenario? A plebiscite is done in real circumstances, not in artificially created situations as it's now in J&K. More than a fifth of the present J&K population consists of outsiders whose forefathers came here as invaders, killers and rapists; the scums you sent. Moreover, we don't have to do it because people franchise their rights with higher percentage than rest of Indian citizens, and they have voted despite threats which come from across the border. You forget that India and Pakistan signed the '*Simla Agreements*' and accepted that Kashmir is a bilateral issue which is to be settled mutually and peacefully, through talks. Can you deny that? People of Kashmir dare to dare you and participate in the electoral process which is clean and transparent unlike your elections in the POK where you conduct elections." Prakash stared at his captive, "you dumb idiots have been taken for a ride by your rulers since the partition and you people don't learn lessons. You don't use your brains to analyse and you off all people, a political advisor should know. Tell me something, what is the purpose of your Kashmir mission?"

"To provide freedom to the people of Kashmir," Lahori said promptly, confidently.

Prakash walked to a window sill. He looked out to calm his rising anger or else he would probably kill Lahori. A minute and a half later he turned back to look at a frightened Lahori. Prakash sat opposite him and asked, "Do you know the meaning of the words 'liberty', 'democracy', and 'freedom'?"

Lahori was too frightened to answer; and he did not have an answer to it in real sense.

Prakash calmly bore his eyes into Lahori's and stared for a while, "How can you talk of providing freedom to others when your own people are not free? Are the people in your control free? Are the Baloch free? Are the Hazaras free? Are the Christians and Hindus and Sikhs free? Are the Shias free or the Sunnis free? If they are not free in your own country how can you talk about 'liberating' other communities? Zia-Ul-Haq, your worst dictator literally whiplashed the citizen and then he had the gall to tell you that he was venturing into Afghanistan to bring democracy and freedom in that country and to protect Islam. Then he engages the country's army in a war which your country had nothing to do with, to fight the Russians, and in the process create a monster which is now eating into your lives. Successive rulers have used Kashmir as a toy for their people to lure with. If there's a problem they bring out the Kashmir toy and present it to the kids, and each time with the same war cry. Islam! When they couldn't find a problem in Kashmir, they created it and told their people that they want to resolve the Kashmir issue. Each time the talks got somewhere; there is insurgency to de-stabilize it. In the process hundreds of thousands have died in your proxy wars. Men such as you are responsible for the death of my family members, for the ..." Prakash's outburst was halted by a loud rap on the door.

Occupants of the room turned to the door with surprised looks on their faces. They didn't expect anyone. Altaf drew his gun and cautiously moved to the door. He saw through the keyhole and asked Prakash, "What are they doing here?"

"Who?"

"Ahmed Saheb and Aman Sir."

"What?" Prakash said and ran to the door. He saw them standing at the door with Rukhsar behind them. Prakash led them in and asked Aman angrily, "What are you doing here?"

Aman didn't reply; he was upset. Zubair didn't bother to reply. He walked to the man sitting on the chair all beaten up, but not as much as he wanted to hurt him, "You are Yakub Lahori?" He roared at the man.

With the intent he saw in Zubair's eyes, Lahori spooked. He saw Rukhsar and Aman, and he knew how Altaf and his associates had tricked the General. They were alive. He didn't have the courage to reply to Zubair's question. Mir Jamal saw the three people enter and understood their importance by the way Prakash and Altaf stood in their presence. He rose from his chair and invited Zubair to sit. Zubair held Lahori's fingers and twisted it backwards. Lahori cried out in pain.

"Does it hurt? Your filthy General is responsible for death of my men. The two of you sent mercenaries to kill me and my children? Now, either I get answers or else I swear by my child that I will start breaking your bones one by one till you speak up... or die."

Lahori's eyes caught Zubair's and he knew that it was time to speak or prepare for a nasty death. Zubair meant what he said. "What do you want to know?" Lahori asked.

Zubair nodded at Prakash. Prakash sat in Zubair's seat and asked, "How is Wahid Khan arriving?"

Lahori breathed slowly, "I want assurance that my family won't be harmed. If he lives, my family is dead."

"I can't guarantee anything," Prakash replied honestly. "We want Wahid Khan. If we don't get him your family could be in trouble. So, for their sake and yours, you better cooperate."

"When I tell him that all is readiness he will come. I don't know how he is coming. He will let me know."

"How can he pass Indian emigration? He is a known figure to Indian agents. He will be picked up if he tries to cross the border. He isn't stupid enough to use a commercial airline or a Pak military aircraft." Prakash stopped for a while and thought of the other way. He asked Lahori suddenly, "Who is he travelling with?"

Lahori was stumped. This was a question he didn't expect. He stared at Prakash with frightful eyes. "I... I think it could be one of the Kashmiri leaders," he replied softly.

"Which one?"

"I am not sure."

Prakash nodded, "Wahid Khan and General Moinuddin were among the four men who had planned this operation. Who are the other two?"

"I have no idea. They are very secretive about it."

Prakash and Zubair looked at each other and then at Lahori. "What is their purpose of his visit?"

"He is to meet a man who is going to help the General in his plans to arm and train young men to..." Lahori stopped at that, fearing the punishment he would invite.

"Which man has the power to ask a Pak General to risk coming to India?"

Lahori was silent. If he mentioned the name there was not a chance he could go back. It would be a shock to the men interrogating him and it would be certain death for him if either Wahid Khan or that man got away.

"Give us the name, Yakub," Prakash asked curtly.

"Saifuddin Ilahi," Lahori whispered.

Three men in the room gasped in wonder. They had not expected this man to be involved. Zubair, Aman Khan and Rukhsar had no idea who he was. The police officer was stunned. He came forward and slammed his fist into Yakub Lahori's face hurtling him backwards, "You are lying. I don't believe you."

Lahori had taken as much pain as he could bear. His face was bleeding and his eyelids were split badly. He threw his head forward and cried in pain. Everyone was surprised when Rukhsar walked to Lahori and offered him a glass of water. Yakub looked at her and saw compassion. Guilt gripped his heart. Mercenaries were sent to kill this beautiful woman and he was an accomplice to it. He sipped and nodded in gratitude. He saw sympathy in her eyes and in gratitude he spoke to her, "I hate that man as much as any person. I work for him only for the love of my country. Our civilian and military rulers have ruined the country. At least, this man dreams of making Pakistan powerful. Every politician or army General I know only works for himself. Wahid Khan is doing the same but he really wants to see Pakistan gain respect for its military prowess at least."

Aman leant against the wall. He was observing the goings on keenly without interfering. He suddenly jumped forward, "That is not true. General Pathan was a thorough bred army man; an honest, dedicated man who was killed because he was working for the country."

"I am good at what I do, Mr. Bux. I am a political advisor. If I had one good man who could work for Pakistan I would bear all the pain for him or for the country," Lahori replied.

"Will you honestly work for an honest politician, Lahori?" Rukhsar asked a serious question.

"If I find one, yes I will, Miss Ahmed."

Lahori's sincerity filled her with pride. Rukhsar knew this man was for real. "When I return to Lahore, you will get a chance to do that."

All men gasped at her words. Prakash, Zubair and Aman Bux: all knew they will have to talk to her out of it if she really meant what she was saying. But that was for later.

"How is Saifuddin Ilahi involved?" The policeman asked.

"Who is he?" Rukhsar asked before Lahori could reply.

"He is the leader of a political party which is in alliance with the ruling party. His right arm man is the Home Minister, which in fact, makes Ilahi the de facto Home Minister." Prakash replied and knew how well Ilahi was positioned to help Wahid Khan.

Lahori swore he had no idea how or why Ilahi was involved with Wahid Khan. He only knew that Ilahi's grandfather hailed from Gujranwala in Pakistan. After the war of '48 they stayed back in Kashmir and they had amassed huge wealth by playing with Pakistan military establishment.

This was a problem they had not counted upon. Saifuddin was a popular leader among the masses, especially in his area of Rajouri, which bordered the LOC. Arresting him or killing him couldn't be considered as an option. There would be an uprising against the incumbent Government. Saifuddin Ilahi had to be handled in a different, delicate manner.

Lahori was spewing blood from his mouth. Rukhsar asked Prakash to help him and tried her best to ease Lahori's pain. Prakash threw a set of keys to Altaf and asked him to fetch a first aid box from his car trunk. Few minutes later Lahori was shifted to a room at the back where Rukhsar tended to him. When Lahori was able to speak, Rukhsar asked others to leave them alone.

- - -

"Why did you come here?" Prakash scolded Aman.

Aman shrugged helplessly and explained. When Aman got Prakash's message that Wahid Khan was coming, Zubair said he was going to meet Prakash. He wanted to personally punish Wahid Khan so he ordered Aman to take him because he didn't understand GPS technology. When Rukhsar's and his attempts failed to persuade Zubair from going, Rukhsar said she would go too; neither man had the power to stop her.

- - -

"You are not going to be a politician," Zubair ordered.

"I have decided, Abbu. When Lahori spoke of politicians, I felt guilty because I am also one of those who cast their votes and assume that their responsibility is over. We don't take it seriously. I am not going to be a politician. I am going to be a lecturer and activist who will also be in politics to work for the country and its people... and mankind in general," she said the last part as an afterthought.

Aman tried to talk her out of her decision but it was to be a fruitless exercise. Rukhsar was determined.

Rukhsar Ahmed-Bux knew she owed it to the three men in her life. She justified her decision, "Since coming to India, I have seen remarkable similarities among people of both sides. They are great human beings; sensitive, emotional, respectful and extremely talented. I see no animosity for each other except when we talk of religion or country; then passions take over the simpletons of both sides. All of us are sentimental fools. I believe that people on both countries need to come out of the shadows of partition and 1947 syndrome and look forward, look ahead. We are unable to transcend that mental barrier and the end result is illogical and insane animosity in the mind-set of people. Over eighty per cent of population in both countries was born after independence but we are still stuck in that era mentally." Rukhsar looked at the three men with teary eyes, "The past has nothing but graves and pyres. Those who are dead don't give a damn about it. Mankind has bound himself by drawing lines on maps and calling it their country whereas God created Earth for us to live. Sick, insane minds with devil's hearts guide us to paths of wars and force lies upon us. There has to be a paradigm shift in the way that people think, on both sides. I want to start the rethinking and work together rather than working against." Rukhsar looked at the three men who were impressed by her passion.

Prakash wanted to dissuade her from joining the quicksand of politics but she impressed him by her speech. The only thing left to do was to give her a springboard from where she can launch herself and really take off, and make a difference.

Prakash asked Ajmal Loni to leave. When the police officer sought Lahori's custody, Prakash promised him a greater prize next day. The cop promised Prakash to keep the entire operation secret till the General was in their custody.

Prakash asked Altaf to get lunch while he spoke to the others in private... on a personal matter; he lied the last bit. Seeing Altaf leave, Prakash turned to Mir Jamal, "Mr. Jamal, I can't thank you enough for what you have done."

Jamal had a wry smile, "Strange! You spoke the exact words I wanted to say to you."

The two men shook hands again. After a little chat Prakash asked Jamal and others in the room to follow him. Prakash picked the video recorder and took it to the room where Yakub Lahori lay resting. Lahori struggled and sat up when he saw them enter. Prakash asked him to relax, "Take it easy. It hurts if you fight pain. When you are comfortable, I want you to speak into this camera all that you have told us."

- - -

At dusk Yakub Lahori called Wahid Khan from Altaf's cell assuring him that all was in order. Mir Jamal convinced the General that his plan won't fail. General stumped them by informing him about his means of transportation to Srinagar. When the call was over they were tensed. It was too late to try anything. So they had to plan a new strategy.

- - -

Later that evening, Colonel Goswami met Altaf, Mir Jamal and Prakash outside his camp and the four men re-strategized their plan. It was a risk but it was worth it because this would land Ilahi and Wahid Khan in their laps.

Though Prakash Rohatgi had taken all possible precautions, he felt jittery. His sixth sense asked him to be more cautious. He couldn't tell others how he felt. For some reason he was nervous. He had taken too many chances earlier but at that time he didn't care much because he had no responsibilities. Now he had a family and he owed it to them to take care of himself. He smiled to himself. This experience was new to him and it was worth living, dying for; for Mehrunissa and Mehjabeen he could take any risk, but didn't want to take any risks because he wished to live with them. Their lives were too precious for him and his for them. He had taken all possible precautions but a lingering anxiety forced him to rethink about the plan. When he was satisfied that all was in order, he called his backup; Prakash Rohatgi dialled a number and spoke for over fifteen minutes. Prakash Rohatgi disconnected the call after thanking Karun Verma.

*   *   *

Srinagar

Jammu & Kashmir, India

'*I will make those rotten, spineless politicians beg to me for their rotten lives. They are giving me orders? How dare they? What have they done for the country?* General Wahid Khan thought as he sat next to Saifuddin Ilahi in the latter's jet, thinking about the pressure which was put on him to resign by the Chief of the army.

In a private meeting he had requested the Chief of army to give him a week to prove that he was right in his planning. The Chief had granted him three days to prove or else he would dismiss Wahid Khan and recommend a court martial. Wahid Khan was desperate. If Ilahi and Jamal can give him what he wants in the next two days, and stir up the emotions within the state, it will be proof enough for him to take it to his Chief. '*The old man used his influence to become the Commander in-Chief and he was now ordering men like me? Within a week there will be enough news from this side of the border to take the heat off my back. I will be a hero and I will be the Commander in Chief.*'

The General missed his uncle. If Moinuddin was alive, the resourceful man would have garnered ample support for him to take over. Alas! The General shot himself. *'If you were alive, I would have given you the day you had been dreaming for forty years.'*

"Saif, I have three days. If things don't happen in three days I will be out. You know what that means; your dream of being the undisputed leader of Kashmir will remain a dream. You won't get another chance like this in your life time. If we don't manage it now, we will lose their support for ever, and then they will turn against us," Wahid Khan was talking to Saifuddin Ilahi; it was a little short of begging.

Saifuddin was arrogantly confident, "Don't worry. I have tied up all ends. I will deliver what I have promised, General. You will however, have to keep your part of the bargain."

Wahid Khan reiterated his promise, "You will be the Prime Minister of a united Kashmir, I promise you." *'Let's have control over the valley first then we will see what you want or we want.'*

*   *   *

The private plane carrying the General with his four men and Saifuddin with his compliment of six men landed on an airstrip hundred and twelve kilometres north-west of Srinagar on a private land converted into an airstrip for small aircrafts to land. Ilahi's men disembarked and surveyed the area. Satisfied, they waived to the occupants of the plane. Saifuddin Ilahi stepped out and called Mir Jamal. Two hundred metres from the airstrip to the north, Prakash was at the wheels of the first vehicle, Altaf on the second and Mir Jamal sat in the third, with his man at the wheels. Mir Jamal signalled to the others to roll on. A minute later the three vehicles lined up at the footsteps of the plane. Ilahi descended the steps and hugged Mir Jamal. Altaf Khos greeted Wahid Khan with a broad smile. Prakash was observing without being obvious. His eyes monitored the situation, praying that his men were in place. They had estimated a dozen men to accompany the two men and so far he had counted ten. The three

SATYA

vehicles sped away and reached their destination an hour later. The three men went inside the house to talk while Prakash and the men accompanying Wahid Khan and Ilahi stood guard in the compound. Altaf stood next to Prakash without speaking to him. Saifuddin Ilahi, Wahid Khan and Mir Jamal talked for a little while and decided to go to Mir Jamal's reclusive house in the remote forests of Srinagar. As promised, Wahid Khan will be meeting various local leaders from regions of Jammu & Kashmir, where Mir Jamal had asked them to assemble.

An hour later the three vehicles cruised across the lush green outfields away from the capital, Srinagar. Far from their peripheral vision two vehicles of the Indian army and a police van followed at safe distance. They were locked onto to GPS in the vehicles driven by Prakash and Altaf Khos.

At Mir Jamal's 'safe house', Zubair Ahmed, Rukhsar and Aman were earlier told to remain in the outhouse till they were asked to come out.

In the same 'safe house', Wahid Khan and Saifuddin Ilahi were led in by the host. Jamal introduced Prakash as 'Abdul', his assistant from Srinagar, a reliable man for emergencies, so if the General had any requests he could summon Abdul. Wahid Khan nodded and asked 'Abdul' to leave them alone.

Prakash went to his MUV and checked his electronic pad. The camera in the room was recording the conversation. He put the gadget back in the glove compartment and strolled around the vehicle assessing the strength and positioning of the men who had accompanied Ilahi and the General. It all seemed fine; all as expected. During discussions he hoped Wahid Khan would mention the names of the other two men in his core group. If Mir Jamal was going to assist Wahid Khan in his ambition to become Pakistan's ruler Jamal had the right to know. That should not take more than half hour by which time the men in two military jeeps would cordon off the roads and the forest, while the police van led by Loni will ensure that his men covered the riverside and the surrounding areas. An additional police van was already stationed at the spot where it was supposed to be.

A half hour later, 'Abdul', entered the house in a hurry and apologized for intruding. He nodded at Jamal. Mir Jamal leapt to his feet and came to Prakash and heard what Abdul had to say. Jamal turned to Wahid Khan and Saifuddin Ilahi and informed them that Abdul had received a call from the local cop telling him that two army jeeps were heading their way. Wahid Khan looked at Ilahi. Ilahi was confused, "Are the jeeps coming for us or is it just a coincidence?" he asked Mir Jamal.

As planned, Mir Jamal called the police station and spoke to Ajmal Loni. Nervously, Ilahi leaned over to listen in. Jamal put the cell on speaker mode. They heard the cop stress that two jeeps were heading towards Jamal's 'safe house' hut he was not sure if they were going to the house. Jamal switched off the phone and looked at Ilahi. "What should we do?"

Snake like eyes of Wahid Khan held deep fear; under no circumstances should he be caught. If he was, all allegations against him by Indians will automatically be proved. He had to get out. He was thinking of his move when he heard gunshots fired by the soldiers of the army camp, as planned, but a few minutes too soon. It was wrong timing.

The four men ran out of the lounge. One of Ilahi's men was dead. The other nine took cover behind the vehicles. Prakash ran out and ordered the men to stay low and turned to Jamal, "We should leave. Let me ensure that the route is sanitized," he said and turned to the nine men. He split the nine men into three groups of three each and sent them in different directions. The men looked at their leaders; Ilahi and Wahid Khan. The two men were too confused to respond.

"He is my trusted man, Ilahi. He knows best." Jamal said.

Ilahi turned to the guards and nodded. The men dispersed and disappeared quickly into the forest. The men were headed in the directions where police and Colonel's men lay in wait. The trap was set to capture the men without bloodshed if possible. Altaf, in his MUV came out of the vehicle slowly and stood next to Wahid Khan.

Prakash, Mir Jamal and Altaf positioned themselves as planned. Prakash was in the centre with Ilahi on his left and Wahid Khan on his right, and Jamal and Altaf on far sides flanking Ilahi and the General. He saw the men disappear into the forest and turned to Jamal, "We must ensure the enemy is made to pay for this," he said and turned to Ilahi. Altaf and Jamal got the cue when Prakash turned to stand facing Ilahi and rammed his left fist on the jaw. Ilahi doubled over and didn't see Prakash's right fist strike his left jaw. The second blow was punishing; it shattered the jaw. Wahid Khan saw a fist fly in his direction from Jamal. He tried evading but it caught his solar plexus. Before he could recover Jamal hit him on the face, but the punishing hit came when Altaf banged the General's head against the wall.

Saifuddin Ilahi tried to rise but was caught half way by Prakash's shoe on the left temple. Ilahi screamed in pain; he didn't hear the General screaming in pain. Altaf and Jamal searched Ilahi and Wahid Khan, disarmed them and waited for Colonel Goswami and Ajmal Loni's jeeps to arrive.

A kilometre away in different directions, two groups sent out by Prakash found themselves surrounded by army men with no chance to escape. They surrendered without resistance. The third group, of General's elite security commandos spread around to sanitize the area. When the men heard a gunshot they knew it was a trap. The men fired back and spread further. In the ensuing gunfire two men were killed while the third turned around and scrambled back towards the 'safe house' to protect his

General. Fifty feet from the house he saw the physical assault on his General and Ilahi. The commando aimed his gun and fired six rounds rapidly at the moving targets. He reloaded the gun but before he could fire, a bullet struck the back of his neck and he fell. Karun Verma ran to his target and checked if he was dead. The commando was barely alive. Verma aimed and fired at the man's forehead. Then he heard Mir Jamal's panicked voice and ran towards the house.

Jamal heard shots from the distance and saw a bullet hit Altaf's bicep and two bullets hit Prakash Rohatgi's shoulder and chest. Mir Jamal called out for Zubair Ahmed and Aman Khan.

The room was barren except for four wooden chairs and table where Wahid Khan had a meeting just a few minutes ago. Altaf kicked Wahid Khan into the house and threw him in a corner and grimaced in pain. General moved his hands to his back. The same instant he felt a searing pain on his left foot as Altaf's full body weight transferred to his right foot and hit Wahid Khan as it landed on the knee. Wahid Khan cursed Altaf, "God will not forgive you, you bastard... you traitor."

Altaf raised his foot and slammed it again on the same spot. It caught the General's left hand sandwiched between his knee and Altaf's shoe. The index and middle digits were broken. General Wahid Khan screamed. Altaf Khos' boot landed once again on the injured knee, breaking it. Wahid Khan screamed loudly; his shriek subduing the sound of breaking bones.

"You are the traitor, you lousy bastard..." Altaf shouted into Wahid Khan's ears. He spread Wahid Khan, pulled a rope from the curtains and tied the General's legs and hands together behind his back in a single knot and pulled it tight. Wahid Khan's groans turned louder as the rope tightened behind him. "You like using helpless women like Mariam, and hurting them, isn't it, you bastard? But you are not so brave when you are up against real men, are you? You don't have the courage to bear it though.

The pain you will endure is Mariam's wish and I," Altaf pulled General's hair yanking it backwards to make eye contact with him, taunted him, "I, her lover, am going to make you pay for raping her. If I..."

"What? You traitor! You... touched my girl?" Wahid Khan was shocked. Suddenly, the mystery was solved. How the files disappeared was clear to him now. "You stole those papers..."

"Wrong! I didn't. I just took pictures. Mariam stole it and sent it to us. Not I, you are the traitor. Your acts bring shame to Pakistan, not mine. I am a soldier who works for his country, not for petty reasons like you. You are the traitor, you hissing snake," Altaf said coldly. His arm was hurting.

Altaf raised he right hand to smack again and stopped as the door flew open violently. Prakash was soaked in blood. He was hanging on Aman's shoulder. Rukhsar and her father followed. Altaf helped Prakash sit on the floor. He brought out a carpet and laid Prakash on the carpet. He was bleeding profusely from his chest. Rukhsar leaned over Prakash and held her *dupatta* against his bleeding chest and shoulder. "Please get a doctor. Please..." She pleaded to Mir Jamal.

Altaf rose to leave and stopped again when he saw a rugged looking man holding Ilahi at gun point and forcing him in the house. He was followed by the owner of the house, Mir Jamal.

Altaf shouted at Mir Jamal, "Get an ambulance... a doctor."

Verma slammed the butt of his gun on Ilahi's head rending him unconscious and ran to Prakash. Jamal rushed to another room and returned a minute later. A doctor was on his way with an ambulance and a medical team. The doctor had asked them to prevent blood loss. Prakash tried to move but the bullet in his shoulder limited his movement. Rukhsar was panicking while Zubair desperately tried to console her, and prayed silently for Prakash. Rukhsar pressed the cloth harder against Prakash's chest to prevent bleeding but the blood continued to flow despite her best efforts.

Karun Verma laid Ilahi next to Wahid Khan and looked at Prakash. Jamal and Verma propped Prakash up and made him sit hoping it would help slow blood flow. It worked partially. Prakash was sitting upright but his back was hurting. Rukhsar saw a gun tucked behind Prakash's back which was hurting him. She drew it out and kept it aside. Prakash opened his eyes, saw Rukhsar's face and smiled at her weakly. He waived at her and Aman with his blood soaked fingers to come closer. When they brought their ears to him, Prakash pleaded, "If I die... take care of Mehjabeen... and her mother." Prakash's breathing had become irregular.

Rukhsar shouted at Prakash in desperation, "Will you please shut up? A doctor is on his way. You just stay with me. Okay? You will be fine," she said and held his blood soaked hand to lend moral support and confidence.

Prakash forced a smile and waived at Aman again, "Will you join us?" he whispered.

Aman was surprised at Prakash's question at a delicate time. He felt Prakash was passing the baton, urging him to join the group. When Prakash had asked him earlier he was sure he wanted to join the group but he wasn't ready. Here, and now, he knew how important it was for people like him to put in their efforts if they sought a better future. He held Prakash's hand, "Yes, we will work for the cause, I promise you."

Prakash's faint smile widened despite excruciating pain. With his one hand covering Rukhsar's *dupatta* on his chest, he spoke softly through the pain, "Listen... carefully," he instructed Aman. "My pad... type 'Satya'... see... list of people... in the group... I told Mr. Tyagi... and 'Tiger'... about you..." Prakash stopped for a few seconds and looked at Aman and Rukhsar with his eyes half closed. He mustered all his strength to speak, "They will help you... to know others... in the group," Prakash said and paused. A massive jolt shook Prakash. His body started convulsing. The spasms grew more erratic and breathing became heavier. Despite all efforts, Prakash was losing blood rapidly. Aman held Prakash and laid him on the carpet again. Prakash tried to say something but he was shut up by Rukhsar, "Please, not now. You talk to us later," Rukhsar pleaded.

Prakash's held his hand up asking her to wait. He looked at her and Aman, and turned to Zubair. His voice was barely audible when he spoke to Zubair, "Last custodian... family legacy dies if I die... I want to keep that legacy... hoped... to see a day... I could have... gone to *Sharda-Peeth*." Prakash saw them looking at him with tears in their eyes, "We can live like... brothers... religion... politics... no barrier... I..." he said and his head fell back. Prakash was unconscious.

They heard sounds of laughter from far end of the room. They turned to find Wahid Khan laughing at them. Rukhsar saw two snake like eyes ogling at her and mocking her at Prakash's plight.

The men were staring at Wahid Khan with contempt and anger but Prakash was their first priority. They didn't see Rukhsar pick Prakash's gun and hide it in her *dupatta*. She was angry. She rose and walked to the laughing General. Verma saw the muzzle of the gun and he tried to stop her. Rukhsar brushed Verma aside, folded her blood soaked *dupatta*, and leaned over Wahid Khan. She saw the General's hands and feet tied together behind his back and looked at the man with utter contempt. "You like to see human blood don't you? Taste this," she said and squeezed the *dupatta* into his mouth stuffing it with Prakash's blood. The blood from her *dupatta* choked Wahid Khan. He struggled to spit out the blood but the *dupatta* was choking him. His eyes started to bulge and then there was naked fear in his eyes when he saw muzzle of a gun appearing, aimed at his heart. He held his breath in fear and heard a gunshot and felt scorching heat in his chest. He was lucky. Rukhsar had aimed the gun at his heart but an amateur's gun recoil missed the target and a bullet lodged in his chest. A second shot blew away his left shoulder blades. "Now laugh, you blood sucking leech." She rose and aimed at Wahid

Khan's heart and fired again. The bullet lodged itself into Wahid Khan's stomach. She raised her gun again but stopped when Aman gripped her gun with one hand and put his other arm on her shoulder. "Let it be, Dear."

Wahid Khan doubled over. He tried his best to wriggle but Altaf's knot was too tight and a broken knee and broken fingers were hurting him just as much. Ilahi moved a little as he started regaining consciousness. He shuffled in his semi-conscious state and struggled to move. Altaf Khos was guarding the two injured men lying under him. Mir Jamal asked Altaf to tie up Saifuddin Ilahi.

A doctor arrived fifteen minutes later. He was asked to tend to Prakash first. The doctor checked Prakash and looked at Mir Jamal with sadness and shook his head indicating that the patient's condition was poor. The two nurses accompanying the doctor tended to Altaf, Wahid Khan and Saifuddin.

The nurse tending to Saifuddin informed them that the self-claimed leader was fine except for minor concussions. The doctor asked her to help him to save Prakash Rohatgi.

The nurse, on doctor's instructions administered a strong dose of injection to Prakash and Wahid Khan. As the syringes plunged into them, their pains eased.

The two men were put in the ambulances and driven away.

* * *

All India Institute of Medical Sciences ## -AIIMS-

New Delhi, India

In Srinagar, the SKIMS hospital's first floor, and especially the area with the two 'VVIPs' was cordoned off. Two senior most surgeons were in two Operation Rooms operating on Wahid Khan and Prakash Rohatgi. The Surgeon operating on the General came out with a smile on his face. The bullets were removed and the patient was stable. It would take a few hours before he could confidently say if Wahid Khan was out of danger but the left shoulder was permanently damaged and his intestine would require a surgery by a specialist soon.

In the other Operation Room, the senior surgeon operating on Prakash Rohatgi found serious complications. There were bullet fragments in Prakash's chest which had punctured his aorta and left pulmonary arteries. Though the bullets were removed, bleeding could not be contained. After six hours of surgery when the surgeon came out of the OR his expression was glum, "He needs a heart specialist to perform surgery on his heart. He must be taken to AIIMS immediately," the surgeon said, and wrote recommendations.

Aman Bux assumed control. He called Tyagi updating him of the successful but tragic Srinagar operation. Tyagi issued instructions and asked Aman to follow them strictly.

A special aircraft was flown into Srinagar by the Home Ministry. Saifuddin Ilahi, Wahid Khan and Prakash Rohatgi were transported to New Delhi's Safdarjung airport, and from there they were taken to the AIIMS - 'All India Institute of Medical Sciences'. Aman Khan Bux, Rukhsar Ahmed-Bux, Zubair Ahmed, Altaf Khos, Karun Verma and Mir Jamal accompanied the patients in the aircraft. The aircraft was given special clearance by the Ministry of Civil Aviation and the Home Ministry ensured it flew in utmost secrecy. None except the most important persons were informed of the importance of the passengers in the aircraft. Surgeons to operate on Prakash Rohatgi and Wahid Khan were provided faxed copies of the medical conditions of the two men, and told to be on standby when the patients were brought in.

*   *   *

The patients were rushed to one of the world's premier medical institutions. Prakash Rohatgi and General Wahid Khan were sent to the ORs promptly while Ilahi was given a check-up. The entire section was sealed for outsiders; only people with special clearance were allowed to get through the first of three levels of security.

Aman Bux, with a heavy heart called Mehrunissa to inform her about Prakash's condition. While he spoke to a petrified Mehrunissa, an imperious man in early seventies entered the visitor's area. He greeted Aman and introduced himself as Nitin

Tyagi and updated himself on Prakash's condition and spoke to the surgeon.

He was nervous about Prakash but he had to get things done. He told Aman about the arrangements he had made to transport Mehrunissa, her mother and Mehjabeen by the end of the day. They would fly into New Delhi by the first flight.

The surgeon operating on Wahid Khan informed that the operation was successful but the General's intestine would need another surgery.

"When can we talk to him?" Nitin Tyagi asked.

"Tomorrow, maybe," the surgeon replied and left.

All waited for the news from the other OR where Prakash's surgeons were struggling to save his life.

Karun Verma led Tyagi and Aman to a corner and spoke to them for a while; an unfinished task had to be completed. He didn't want Prakash Rohatgi's efforts to be wasted. Though Aman was reluctant, Verma persuaded him.

A few minutes later, two intelligence officers accompanied by three men came to the hospital and took possession of Saifuddin and escorted him to a farmhouse outside New Delhi where they were to guard him till Aman Khan Bux came to the house. Yakub Lahori was to be kept at the same place but away from Saifuddin Ilahi.

- - -

Rukhsar was angry at Aman for leaving when Prakash was critical. Aman defended his decision but Rukhsar won't listen. Zubair took Rukhsar aside and scolded her for being impractical, "let them complete what Prakash risked his life for. We owe it to him," he said and asked Aman and Karun Verma to leave.

Altaf Khos came to Zubair and pointed at his bicep wound. It would take time to heal. He insisted on going with Verma and Aman. They could use a man who can take care of two captives. Altaf wanted to 'take care' of Wahid Khan but that was out of question.

*   *   *

Prakash Rohatgi's Residence

New Delhi, India

A surgeon operated on Prakash's wounds but heart surgery had to wait till his condition stabilized. Prakash's body lay in a private ward adjacent to Wahid Khan's. The entire section on this floor of the hospital was sealed by two intelligence men sent by the home ministry.

Zubair and Rukhsar sat by Prakash's side silently praying for his health. Prakash's eyes started roving behind the lids, and his body was convulsing severely and sporadically. The nurse requested them to leave the room when the surgeon arrived. While they waited outside, the surgeon tried desperately to save his patient. After fifteen minutes he came out of the room with the nurse tagging him, looked at Zubair and Rukhsar apologetically and patted Zubair's shoulder. He said 'sorry', and left. Prakash had died seven minutes earlier.

Zubair blankly stared at the door behind which Prakash's lifeless body lay unattended. He thought of a son he had for a while, and now he was dead. Zubair's eyes welled up as he looked at Rukhsar... and thought of Mehjabeen again... and Mehrunissa... and he cried. He held Rukhsar's hand, pulled her closer, hugged her and cried some more. Zubair Ahmed realized that he had cried his heart out but Rukhsar was frigid - emotionless. He cupped her face and looked at her. She was staring at the closed door, thinking of the man who lay dead in that room. She turned to look at him, and stared at him in shock, or was it in anger? Rukhsar forced her father's hands aside and looked at the closed door or Prakash's room. She sat motionless for several minutes. Her father's hand was holding her but she didn't notice it. Rukhsar saw the nurses moving in and out of the wards of Prakash Rohatgi and Wahid Khan. She looked around and saw the two Intelligence officers idling outside the glass doors which cordoned off the wards.

Rukhsar saw the nurses in Wahid Khan's room leave and rose calmly. She walked into Wahid Khan's room and looked inside. The General was fast asleep. His cobra like eyes deep in sockets was unaware that his nemesis had died just a few minutes ago. Rukhsar Ahmed-Bux walked purposefully and stood next to Wahid Khan and saw the plastic tubes and various attachments sticking out of his body. She looked around and found a pair of latex gloves in a drawer. She put on the gloves and returned to Wahid Khan and squeezed the oxygen pipe gently. She saw him convulse. He struggled and opened his eyes; they looked terrified. He tried moving his hands but they didn't go far. His hands were cuffed to the posts. He looked at Rukhsar with pleading eyes. Rukhsar saw his eyes and her anger turned to rage. She eased the pressure on the pipe. Wahid Khan's snaky eyes closed as he breathed deeply.

"You bastard," she swore, "You are scared at the thought of your death, you Godless creature! It is God's wish that the man you sent to kill my father and me is working with us and he is responsible for your death," she said and leaned over Wahid Khan's face as she squeezed the tube softly, "You don't deserve to live," she said and increased the pressure on the tube till Wahid Khan's eyes began to pop out of his sockets and his body convulsed for over a minute and then it went limp. She saw the monitor ticks levelled at zero and released her pressure on the tube. Wahid Khan was dead. She walked out of the room.

Zubair Ahmed watched her carefully. He instinctively knew what Rukhsar had done. This was cold blooded murder. He held her wrist and dragged her hurriedly to Prakash's room.

Rukhsar sat on a tripod next to Prakash's life-less body and stared at his face with too many emotion; so many that her face had no expression. It was strange, she thought. Prakash seemed to be alive. His face looked calm and serene and she felt he had a little smile on his face. She held Prakash's hand and rested her forehead on his chest where his heart had stopped beating a few minutes ago. She felt the cold body and suddenly she looked up at him and tried speaking to him. She had a lot to say to him but he couldn't hear. Her eyes welled up as she brought his hand to her heart, "I have avenged your death, Prakash,"… she said and looked at his face again, "I love you…" she said and a loud moan escaped her mouth… and she cried… and wailed… She leaned on Prakash's lifeless body and moaned, and cried... and wailed...

Zubair was exasperated. He hadn't overcome the loss of his 'son'. He never said it so in words but he had always treated Prakash as one. Another fear gripped his mind. How was he going to console Mehjabeen and Mehrunissa? The marriage had lasted four days. Mehrunissa was a strong woman; she may survive the loss, but Mehjabeen? She was more attached to Prakash than to her mother. How would they handle her, he thought and he wanted to cry for his son, daughter and for the losses of Mehrunissa and Mehjabeen. He accepted that this was his greatest personal loss.

Zubair called Aman and delivered the sad news and pleaded him to personally pick up Mehrunissa and Mehjabeen from the airport. He walked up to the two intelligence officers stationed outside the ward and instructed them to arrange for Prakash's body to be taken to his house.

- - -

Aman asked Purna to get him and Verma some coffee, and walked into Prakash's workstation. The two men went to work. They saw the thirty minute video-audio recording of talks between Saifuddin Ilahi, Mir Jamal and Wahid Khan at Jamal's safe house, and they looked at each other in disbelief. They found the two co-conspirators with General Wahid and Moinuddin: Saifuddin Ilahi and General Basheer Qureishi, senior colleague of General Imran Saddiq Pathan. The two men then studied the statement made on camera by Yakub Lahori and all missing pieces of the puzzle were found, and the picture was clear.

When they finished, they saw Purna waiting for them at the door. They put their headphones down and looked at her with dismay. Purna was carrying a bunch of folders. She put it in front of them, "When I heard the news from Mr. Tyagi, I took these away. I will unlock the communication system and you can work at the station," Purna said and kept the files and a set of electronic gadgets.

"I don't know how to use many of these," Aman said and looked at Verma. Verma didn't know that either.

Purna explained how the gadgets worked. Then Aman's cell phone rang. He listened to Zubair and his face turned white. Purna and Verma knew something wasn't right and feared the worst. "What happened?" Karun Verma asked fearfully.

Aman bowed his head sadly, "He died fifteen minutes ago," Aman said as tears rolled down.

Purna slumped in the chair. The only person in the world she really loved was gone. She did not cry; she was in too much of a shock to cry. Karun Verma consoled the two but who would know what he had lost? For four years he and Prakash had helped and looked after each other without meeting. It was a relationship which few friends shared.

- - -

Prakash's mortal remains were brought to his farmhouse an hour after his death. The intelligence officers also announced the death of Wahid Khan due to respiratory failure.

Aman felt guilty. He and Rukhsar were responsible of an injudicious decision; of probably ruining a life to which they had no right. He held himself guilty of forcing Prakash to marry Mehrunissa though Prakash had asked them to wait for a few days. If they had listened to him, Mehrunissa wouldn't be a widow again... and Mehjabeen? He thought of the beautiful girl and his sadness grew many folds.

Rukhsar put her hands on the table and cried, "I don't have the courage to face them."

"We have a responsibility, Rukhsar. We have to pick them up," Aman said putting his arms around her, comforting her.

Rukhsar summoned her strengths and rose from her chair to go to her room upstairs. She held Aman's hand and led him to the room, and told him how Wahid Khan had died. Aman was silent. He couldn't believe his angel-like wife was capable of ruthless murder. A few moments of silence passed. Then he held her face in his palms and kissed her forehead, "Thank you my dearest. I wouldn't have the courage to do it. But thank you for doing it. I know you are a lot stronger than me; it's not a confession, it's a fact."

He had an unpleasant, difficult task to perform. He asked Rukhsar to wait and summoned Altaf.

- - -

Altaf Khos and Aman Bux entered the room where the two captives were being held. Saifuddin Ilahi and Yakub Lahori were seated on the floor with their hands tied behind their backs. Altaf pulled out a gun and without a warning, fired a shot aiming a few inches over Ilahi's head. The act rattled the two captives. Aman pushed Altaf aside and kneeled on the floor in front of them and gave an ultimatum. "Your General, Wahid Khan is dead. I don't care a damn, but I do care about a man who died along with him - Prakash Rohatgi. Now," Aman Bux said with fiery eyes, "I want right answers from you two or you will be the next on the list of dead and no one will ever know what happened to you two. You both know that Altaf and I are Pakistani nationals. If I kill you both and return home no one can punish us. So, your lives are in our hands. If I get my answers you can live."

"I told your wife all I know," Yakub Lahori pleaded. "She has it on a video recorder. What else do you want to know?"

"I will talk to you later," Aman said and looked at Saifuddin Ilahi, the self-styled Kashmiri leader. "You, Mr. two bit leader of fourteen people. I want names of people who are working with you, on both sides of the border."

Ilahi looked at Aman in disgust but he didn't reply.

Aman felt the electronic pad in his breast pocket and he was inspired by the strength of the owner of the pad, and his values. Aman rose to his feet and swung his boot, catching Ilahi's face. They heard a faint sound of a cracking bone. A fraction of a moment later Saifuddin Ilahi's nose and mouth were bleeding. "Talk," he ordered the Kashmiri leader again. A minute passed but Aman got no response. His next kick hit the back of Saifuddin's neck. Ilahi groaned in pain. "I won't stop until I get the 'right' answers, Ilahi. And, God help you if you lie to me. You see, we already know all we need to know including the names of the four men who hatched this plan. Off the four, Wahid Khan is dead and Moinuddin shot himself. The third is you and fourth is General Qureishi. We have the details but I want to hear it from you."

Ilahi laughed. "You can't explain my disappearance to my people. There will be riots in the streets of Rajouri, and it will reach every town and village of Kashmir... You lose!"

Aman Bux rammed his fist onto Ilahi's face under the nose where he had struck earlier. Aman was consumed with hatred for the despicable man. Another blow broke two upper teeth. Ilahi tried to spit out blood oozing from the break in gums but Aman followed his punch with another punch right under the chin. Saifuddin shook violently.

"Please stop... Please..." Lahori begged.

Aman laughed sarcastically, "and you scums were planning to kill millions?" Aman turned to Altaf, "take him to another room. I will deal with him later."

Altaf picked Lahori and dumped him in the bathroom. "If I hear a word from you, I will kill you," Altaf said and returned to the room where Saifuddin was still receiving punishment from a vengeful Aman Khan Bux.

"Your disappearance, like Wahid 'bloody' Khan's, will be a mystery for years. Your people will learn in two-three days that a traitor flew to Rawalpindi in a private aeroplane which had landed today on a private, secret airstrip and crash landed a mile from the airstrip with the traitor and Wahid Khan died in the air crash along with their ten men. Their bodies will be found and identified." Aman Bux said, "Covertly, a video will be released to press, social and electronic media, of a secret meeting in a 'safe house' between a traitor and a General from across the border. You are going to be very unpopular, dead or alive."

Saifuddin Ilahi was shaken to his spine. He had nothing to bargain with; Aman held all the aces. It's never easy to trade if one didn't have a value to offer, "I am a trader. What can I offer you? You have all the answers to your questions."

"You have the most valuable commodity to trade 'for', not 'with'. Your life! If your story corroborates with ours, you go free. I don't have time to waste on you. I want your recorded statement, uninterrupted and un-diluted truth in it."

Saifuddin Ilahi explained the modus operandi and how the plan was to be executed. He laid bare the evil plans conceived by Generals Moinuddin, executed by Generals Wahid Khan and Basheer Qureishi, and why he, Saifuddin Ilahi was a party to it; he wanted to be the ruler of united Kashmir.

When Saifuddin Ilahi was finished, Aman asked Purna to summon two men in plain clothes standing outside the gate of the farmhouse, waiting for his signal. The two men were led in by Purna. The officers took Saifuddin Ilahi in custody. Ilahi shouted at Aman, "You told me I could go free. I hoped you would support me because I am working for Pakistan."

Aman struck Ilahi viciously, breaking his jaw, "Traitors like you expecting a deal to be honest, is sick… I am a Pakistani and a proud one at that. We don't need scums like you to sort our problems. When people of reason and justice sit together they will sort out problems which will be in the interest to both countries and its people."

After Ilahi was whisked away, Aman patted Altaf, thanking him, "You can return and have a happy life with Mariam. You have played the most important part by bringing this whole Godforsaken plan to us. Thank you."

Altaf was sad, "I wish to thank one man and he is no more. I will return after his last rites. I owe it to him," he said, then shook his head in sadness, and asked, "What about Lahori?"

"Guard him! We will decide later if Rukhsar is in mood to make a decision. Right now she may decide to kill him."

- - -

Rukhsar and Aman were surprised how Mehjabeen and her mother looked; calm and remarkably well in control of their emotions. There wasn't a hint of sadness in the eyes, nor any change in mannerisms. When Rukhsar saw them from close, she realized there was too much pain. The eyes were drained of tears and hearts vacant. Aman pitied Mehjabeen. She was just eleven. He didn't see the chirpy girl who threw tantrums for little things and got what she wished. Instead, he saw a girl who had matured far beyond her years within a day.

Mehrunissa and Mehjabeen saw Prakash's body laid on a bier being readied for the funeral. They sat next to it staring at Prakash's lifeless body. Aman and Zubair tried their best to help Mehjabeen emote but she didn't move. She kept staring at Prakash. Mehrunissa sat near Prakash's head with a stoned expression. Mehjabeen ensured the clay lamp did not run out of ghee; cupping the light of the lamp when she felt breeze blowing, and kept the lamp alit. She would touch the cold body of her '*Baba*' at times. There were many people in the hall with Zubair, Purna, Verma, Tyagi, Rukhsar, Aman Khan, Mehrunissa and Zebunissa but they were all concerned about Mehjabeen, but the young girl was calmer than most. Then, suddenly, she wrapped her arms around Prakash and wailed. Her moans made the rest cry with her.

- - -

Purna asked priest, the 'pundit', whom Prakash consulted when he needed, how the funeral and last rites were to be performed. The pundit checked his '*panchang*' and declared that the pyre should be lit later in the evening and the rituals for the last rites should be performed on the third day. And he asked who was to light the pyre and perform the rituals.

Nitin Tyagi nominated Karun Verma because Prakash had no male child, nor a male relative.

The hall echoed with Mehjabeen's shriek. All turned to look at her. She was kneeling at her *Baba's* feet with fiery eyes. "I am his daughter," she shouted, "It is my right to light the pyre. No one takes away that right from me," she cried, "He was my father... he was my father..." she moaned softly and cried, and she broke down again.

Mehrunissa wrapped her daughter in her bosom to console her. Mehjabeen put her head on her lap and cried. Though others tried to comfort her, Mehjabeen wouldn't stop crying. Mehrunissa looked at others for help but it was useless.

"You can't do it. It is the right of the eldest male child or a male member from the family," Mehrunissa tried to explain to her daughter.

"He has no son, or male relative. I am the only child he has," Mehjabeen argued through her tears.

Nitin Tyagi slid close to Mehjabeen and caressed her head, "Your mother is ill informed. If a man has no male child and no male relative, a girl can light the pyre. So, you actually have the first right to do it."

"Then, why can't she?" Zubair asked angrily.

"It is not a pleasant sight, Zubair," Tyagi replied. While he defended his decision he also wanted to spare Mehjabeen the sight of utmost sadness, "It is a heart wrenching sight to see one's loved one going up in flames. One has to wait till the fire consumes the body and turns it into ashes, leaving behind only fragments of bones; these bone fragments have to be collected. Rituals are performed and those fragments, the *asthi* has to be submerged into a flowing river. It is an emotionally crucifying experience, Mr. Ahmed." Tyagi narrated the ritual process in graphic detail to save Mehjabeen from undergoing that experience.

Everyone's eyes were fixed on Mehjabeen. She raised her head from her mother's lap and wiped her tears, "I am his only child. I will do it." She was determined.

Mehrunissa did not wish to bring an issue her daughter was not aware of. She did not wish to involve her daughter in a religious tangle. When Mehjabeen did not relent, Mehrunissa told her the reason. She was a Muslim and the rituals had to be performed according to Hindu customs which included acts which her religion forbids. Mehjabeen was quiet all of a sudden, looking at her mother and others in despair.

Karun Verma wiped the tears from the girl's eyes, "She is wrong again. A mortal remain is not a religious commodity; a soul has no religion. Religion is a creation of man, not God's. So, yes, you can do it if you wish, my dear. I will be happy if you do it because it is your right. Every year on a particular day, however, you will have to perform a ritual for your father, and his ancestors. You will have to do it till you live, and that includes some aspects which is against the religion you follow, dear. That is the real reason why I agreed to perform his last rites."

"He was my father. I will perform all the rights till I live." Mehjabeen replied unflinchingly, honestly and without crying.

Karun Verma looked at others in the room and no one had the courage to oppose her wish. Karun brought Mehjabeen closer and hugged her. "Yes, my dear, Prakash Rohatgi was your father. He will be happy if you did it."

* * *

~Humans~

INDIA
- The Cradle of Humanity -

"India is the Land of religions, cradle of human race,
Birthplace of human speech, Grandmother of legend,
And Great grandmother of tradition;
The land that all men desire to see
And having seen once even by a glimpse,
Would not give that glimpse for the shows
of the rest of the globe combined."
~Mark Twain~

The day after Prakash's death, Mehjabeen performed the rituals with precision as the priest instructed her. She led the men to the funeral site, lending her tender shoulders to the bier when she could. At the crematorium Mehjabeen stressed on electric crematory instead of the traditional wooden pyre. Prakash was always concerned about environment and often he gave her lectures on conservation. This was her homage to him. She was in remarkable control of her emotions when the time arrived; when she had to light the pyre. Since it was an electric

514

funeral, she pushed the bier into the electric furnace and ignited the pyre by turning an electric switch. A little glass window on the side gave her a chance to see her father for the last time as his body embraced fire and gradually turned to ashes. None of the adults, who stood by her side, saw her heart and soul cry when she cupped her face around the glass window to see the fire engulf her father's body. She wanted to see her father for the last time.

On the third day Mehjabeen performed the rituals, guided by the pundit. She performed it with dedication, devotion and perfection.

On the thirteenth day after Prakash's death, the final ritual was performed by Mehjabeen. Barring her, all others gathered in the large hall were adults. As the ritual was performed on the last day of the rights, Zubair Ahmed, Shahida Ahmed and Shadab Ahmed, Aman Khan Bux and Rukhsar Ahmed-Bux, Karun Verma and Nitin Tyagi, Altaf Khos and Purna and the hundreds who had thronged from Chattisgarh and Jharkhand to pay their last respects, were gathered around the little girl who was performing the rights. Those adults, matured people were spiritually moved, and philosophically taught lessons in Humanity by an eleven year old Mehjabeen. She, with the purity of her soul, combined with uncorrupted human nature she was born with, performed the rituals which many adults found difficult to adhere to.

That evening, when Zubair and Aman saw Mehjabeen offer 'Namaaz', they felt enlightened. When she was performing the 'Puja' earlier in the day though, they didn't quite approve of it but they had remained quiet. Now when they saw her praying in her own religious tradition, they saw the beauty of humans in that act of piety which symbolized the piousness of human nature which was as divine as God had created it. They learnt a lesson from that young girl that their purity was polluted by their thoughts of bias.

A conversation from the past and a statement in particular made by Prakash Rohatgi struck Zubair Ahmed's mind instantly. '*Sir,*' Prakash had said, '*God created humans out of love; man created religions out of love of God, and for reason that it will bind humans; now religions divide people and creates hatred. Humans have failed God.*' Zubair understood one thing; Mehjabeen may not be Prakash Rohatgi's biological child but she was his daughter in true spirit. She was born to be his daughter.

- - -

The dramatic change in Mehjabeen was noticed by all. The innocent, chirpy girl was replaced by a girl who preferred to stay by herself but she was never depressed. She was devoted to her studies and to books for study on various subjects, especially history and political sciences. In a fortnight she had turned from being the baby of the house to guardian of her mother, grandmother and Zubair. Aman Bux and Rukhsar treated her like a child but they knew the child in her was gone. Mehjabeen did not speak to anyone about her future plans but the signs were there for all to see quite clearly. Purna was her support in every respect. Zubair and Rukhsar were on a walk quite early one morning when they saw the first signs of things to come. Mehjabeen was training herself with martial arts; being trained by Purna.

- - -

After her '*Namaaz*' one morning Mehjabeen called Verma and asked if he would oblige her by helping her. Verma was surprised. He arrived within an hour and wondered what she wanted. When he entered he saw her sifting through library books in the hall. She saw him and climbed down from the top shelf. Mehjabeen touched Karun Verma's feet in respect and politely asked him and Aman to come with her. They went to Purna's room and told her to open the workstation. Purna looked at Karun Verma and Aman and then at the girl. She led them to the doors and opened the workstation, and handed a set of keys, "This is your '*Baba's* set of keys. Keep it. If you need any help, call me," she said and left.

Verma asked Zubair to join them. A minute later the three men came to the workstation and sat with Mehjabeen.

"We were packing, Mehjabeen. What is it, darling?" Aman asked Mehjabeen.

"Please tell me how *Baba* operated from here. How does this thing work?" Mehjabeen asked with utmost seriousness.

The men looked at the young girl sitting in Prakash's chair. "You are too young for this, Mehjabeen," Zubair said.

"I will learn quickly and grow up soon, *Dadaji*."

Verma patted her hand, "I will teach you but promise me you won't use it till I tell you. Is that clear?"

"I promise."

Karun Verma told her what Prakash Rohatgi did from his workstation. Mehjabeen didn't grasp the complexities which could demand such actions but she promised to teach herself. "Is this why *Baba* had to die, *Dadaji*?" Mehjabeen asked with tears threatening to roll down her cheeks. The men were quiet.

- - -

Rukhsar and Aman went to see Zubair. Rukhsar was sure Zubair had no reason not to return. "Now you are free to stay in Lahore. There are no threats anymore. Why don't you come with us tomorrow?"

"I will come with you but I will return with Shabnam. I will stay here," Zubair said and looked at his study room and his eyes focused somewhere in the distance, "I owe everything to a man. He has left me with a responsibility," Zubair Ahmed said and shrugged sadly, "You are a married woman now. Even if I return I will be staying in Lahore and you will be living in Islamabad or some foreign capital. No, this is where I wish to live. My responsibility is to see Mehjabeen grow up into a fine woman... no doubt she will be, anyway, but I have to see it through."

Rukhsar had tried to convince him thrice in last two days but his reply had been the same. She knew the futility of going over it again. At least he had agreed to return to Lahore with her. It would be nice to see her *Ammi* and *Abba* live together.

* * *

- <u>WAGAH</u> -

Indo-Pak Border
Punjab, India

Karun Verma and Nitin Tyagi met Rukhsar, Zubair and Aman Khan Bux at Wagah border to say goodbyes to the lovely couple who were returning to Pakistan, and to the man they had come to respect immensely.

"Thank you for coming, Sir," Aman thanked Tyagi. "You have been very helpful, especially with our visas."

"It was my duty because you were on our side," Tyagi said and asked, "I hope you will keep your promise to Prakash."

"I will," Aman replied, "As a diplomat I will be able to contribute more."

Tyagi nodded and turned to the lovely lady he was fond of, "I am sure you too will contribute to our group, dear."

"Yes Sir, I will. I am a lecturer. I want to educate people and tell the truth about our history and our past; recent and ancient. And, I am going to contest in the next elections. Both are important for me. I don't want to be like preachers who don't practice," Rukhsar replied.

"I agree," Nitin Tyagi replied.

The couple and Zubair turned to leave. Verma tapped Aman's shoulder. Aman turned around.

"I have some good news for you," Karun smiled.

Aman realized that he had never seen Verma smile. The man had innocence in his smile which accentuated his rugged good looks. Aman looked at him in surprise.

"The fourth man... General Basheer Qureishi? Well, he was forced to resign last night. He will be court-martialed. Khaled Usmani was also arrested. Three commissioned officers in the ranks who were in cahoots with Wahid Khan are absconding but they will be in custody soon I have been assured," Karun Verma smiled joyously.

"What happened to Lahori and Saifuddin?"

"Saifuddin Ilahi, as you know, has been branded a traitor by the Jammu and Kashmir Assembly. The general population believes he died in an air crash with Wahid Khan but I believe he is in a cold, dark cell, deep beneath an ancient fort somewhere where the nation's traitors and foreign agents are held. They never see the light of day. That is not a phrase here, it's a fact."

"And Yakub Lahori?"

Verma looked at Rukhsar. He seemed to be in two minds. "I am sure Rukhsar will be able to explain to you why she has requested his release on her personal bond."

Aman knew the reason. If she was venturing into politics she needed an experienced man and Lahori was a good candidate. He would be a great asset in right company.

"What happened to Altaf Khos? He has vanished," Karun Verma asked.

Rukhsar and Aman laughed, "He was too eager to get to his girlfriend. With Wahid Khan out of the way, they have a good life together ahead of them," Aman replied.

"I don't know that part of the story. What is that all about?" Karun asked.

"If it wasn't for the inquisitiveness of Altaf and the courage of Altaf and his girlfriend, Mariam, we wouldn't have learnt about the General's evil plan. It's a long story. Let's talk some other time," Aman said and shook hands with both men.

Zubair hugged the two men and thanked them once again, promising to be back in a week.

"Zubair, it is a pity you had to spend those years in prison," Tyagi said with deep regret.

"If I spent my years in captivity, maybe it was my destiny. I would spend another eight years if it would result in as good an end as this... except for Prakash," Zubair's face had a deep shadow of sadness.

All faces were sad at the mention of the man they loved too much. Tyagi changed the topic, "What code will you use? A member must identify himself with one. I hope you have thought of one," he asked Aman Khan Bux.

"Dove!"

Tyagi nodded. That was the symbol of peace, an apt choice. "When will we see you again?"

"With *Abba* in New Delhi, and *Dadaji* in Dacca, we will be touring at least twice a year, I suppose," Rukhsar replied.

Rukhsar thought of the three weeks she had spent in India. In this period she had seen and experienced a new world. Her journey of discovery of family and nation's history, discovery of truths and uncovering of lies, and a journey of adventures had come to an end. Now she was embarking on another journey, another mission in life. This time it would be for the people of both countries, working from within the country. And, this was going to be a tougher task. She believed in her philosophy: *Truth needs no defence; Lies can't be defended!*

Buoyed by success, and with new optimism Aman, Rukhsar and Zubair Ahmed crossed the Wagah border, into Pakistan.

* * *

Three months later...

Mehrunissa Rohatgi's House

New Delhi, India

Karun Verma and Nitin Tyagi kept their promises. They came to visit each weekend and spent time with Mehjabeen to teach and train her. For Mehjabeen, those were her best times. She would talk to them endlessly, to the extent of wracking their brains.

When her school asked students to enrol their names for an excursion trip to Europe during summer vacations, Nitin Tyagi told Mehjabeen to enrol her name; she refused. Instead, she requested Tyagi to manage a tour of Śāradā Peeth in POK, for her. Tyagi looked at her in surprise. Zubair Ahmed told Tyagi why she wanted to visit Śāradā Peeth.

Mehjabeen's mannerism and style had Prakash's imprints. One evening when Karun Verma asked Mehjabeen what her ambition in life was; Mehjabeen had replied nonchalantly, "Satya-Prakash Rohatgi".

Verma had laughed. "And what would be your code word?" he had asked in humour.

"Satya," she had replied seriously.

It was late evening. Mehrunissa was searching for her, and found her at the workstation, listening to CDs from Prakash's collection. She scolded her daughter for staying up late but Mehjabeen laughed and continued with her pre-occupation.

Mehrunissa sat next to her with adoring eyes, "You are trying to be like him, dear. He was special. Don't be like him; just be yourself," she said in as subtle a way as she could.

Mehjabeen looked at her mother with confidence, "I *am* like him, *Ammi*. I want to be like him."

"Why didn't you put your name for European excursion?"

"*Ammi*, I didn't want to."

"Why?"

"Later," Mehjabeen said and put on her earphones.

- - -

For a week Zubair had observed that the ladies were having hushed conversations regarding Mehrunissa's health. If he tried to ask, he was told nothing. A day earlier Mehjabeen saw her mother unwell and forced her to come with her to the doctor. The doctor suggested some tests and the reports were expected this evening.

Ladies of the house had gone to see Mehrunissa's doctor and Zubair was in his study when he heard the phone ring. He picked it up when he saw Aman's name flashing. Aman was now posted in Islamabad because his boss, Jaffer Sharief had recommended it. Rukhsar continued as Lecturer and she had started assembling a bunch of youths from her college and local area to form a social-working group; her first step towards becoming a politician and she planned to contest as an independent candidate in forthcoming elections, in a few months' time.

During conversations, Zubair felt Aman was pausing at odd times, wanting to say something but he was hesitant... or shy? When forced, he handed the phone to Rukhsar.

When he asked Rukhsar, she laughed, "The traditional and cultural hesitancy will take few generations to go. *Abba*, you are going to be a grandfather," Rukhsar said joyfully; she was a little shy too.

Zubair rose from his chair in joy. He wanted to celebrate the news. He didn't hear what his daughter was saying. It was one of those moments where mind begins to imagine scenes in the future and present becomes a blur. He got off the call and went to the lounge to give his wife the good news.

Just then the door flew open and Zubair saw Mehjabeen enter the house with her old childlike enthusiasm. He hadn't seen the exuberance or the innocence of the girl in over four months, but she was here now, temporarily. She ran into his arms, held his wrists and danced with him.

"What happened?" he asked. He guessed they knew about Rukhsar having a baby.

"*Ammi* is expecting a baby, *Dadaji*. We will have a baby in the house," Mehjabeen shouted excitedly.

Zubair Ahmed's eyes started to well up with tears of joy. He was in no condition to control himself. Two identical news of great joy in span of few minutes was beyond belief. He eased back in his chair and stared at the beautiful face of Mehrunissa. Since Prakash's death that pretty face hadn't smiled. It was divine to see the old radiance back on her face. Zubair stretched his hand out. Mehrunissa stepped forward shyly, and sank her head in his chest and started to cry. Other ladies crowded around Mehrunissa and tried to console her. Zubair waived at them to wait, and he let her cry. Mehrunissa took time to control herself. She sobbed till she could speak.

Zubair heard her speak but she was inaudible. He caressed her head to console her.

Mehrunissa raised her face to him, "*Abba*..." Mehrunissa said touching her stomach, "He's coming back, *Abba*... Prakash is coming back to us," she said and cried again.

Zubair nodded, "Yes," he said and looked skywards, and words in his mind, he hoped, reached the soul he wanted to speak to, *"Your legacy lives, Prakash. I promise you."*

"What will be the baby's name, *Ammi*?" Mehjabeen asked.

"We can't determine a name unless we know if it's a boy or a girl," Mehrunissa replied with a smile.

"If the baby is a girl, she will be 'Śāradā'," she declared in all seriousness. The matured Mehjabeen was back again.

Zubair laughed, "And what if it's a boy?"

Mehjabeen's eyes were suddenly glued to a garlanded photo of Prakash Rohatgi suspended on the wall behind Zubair, with a lamp lit on a rack, "Satya-Veer Satya-Prakash Rohatgi," she replied.

– – –

Zubair kneeled with his legs folded backwards, his ankles tucked under his hips, hands joined in prayer; and bowed to Almighty. He offered his *Namaaz* to the Almighty.

After his *Namaaz*, he continued sitting in that position and offered another prayer, *'You have blessed me with grand-children on either side of the border, Oh Almighty! Ensure they meet as brothers, not enemies; may they be healthy competitors in knowledge and ethics, not in knives or guns; may they converse with pen and words, not bullets and swords; May they be brothers in morality and friends in humanity; may they never be blinded by fibs, and always live in the light of Truth! Amen!'*

*   *   *

525

~ SATYA ~

THE TRUTH

"Where there is righteousness in the heart,
there is harmony at home;

Where there is harmony at home,
there is an order in the nation;

Where there is order in the nation,
there is peace in the world!

~A poet in Tamil~

*Quoted by The President of India, Dr. A. P. J. Abdul Kalam,
during his speech at the European Parliament.*

<u>GLOSSARY</u>

	WORD	LANGUAGE	MEANING	REMARK / INFORMATION
A	***Astitva***	Hindi	Identity / Existence	
	Abbu / Abbā	Urdu	Father	
	Ammā / Ammi	Hindi, Urdu, some Indian languages	Mother	
	Asthi	Sanskrit, Indian language	fragments, remnants (especially bones fragments) of the body which has been cremated by fire	
B	***Bābā***	Hindi, Urdu and some Indian languages	Father, and in some cases, Grand-father	

	WORD	LANGUAGE	MEANING	REMARK / INFORMATION
	Basant	Sanskrit, Hindi and Indian languages	A month in Hindu calendar	Basant is also a festival, especially in Punjab and North India, to celebrate harvesting season
	Bazār	Hindi, Urdu and some other Indian languages	Market	Bazaars are markets. There are week days where sellers/ merchants from surrounding areas arrive on designated days of the week at a village. These are temporary and also called 'bazaar'
	Bhārat	Hindi, Indian Languages	India	India was called 'Bhārat' since ancient times. It was named after king Bharat
C	*Chāchā*	Hindi, Urdu	Paternal uncle	people also use the term to refer to elderly people as a mark of respect
	Chaupāl	Hindi	An open space in the centre	generally reserved for assembly of villagers
	Chaddar	Hindi, Urdu, Indian languages	Linen	
D	*Dādāji*	Hindi, Urdu and some Indian languages	Grandfather, on father's side	Grandfather on mother's side is called, NANAJI
	Divān	Hindi, Urdu, English	A large room with no doors, mostly a sitting hall	A cot with storing facility is also called a Divan

	WORD	LANGUAGE	MEANING	REMARK / INFORMATION
	Dhoti	Hindi	A long, loose cotton dress wrapped around the waist	
	Dāwa	Urdu	Claim	
G	*Gaddār*	Urdu	Traitor	
H	*Haveli*	Hindi	A large house, Manor	
I	*Inshā-Allāh*	Urdu	By the wishes of Allah	
J	*Jhoothā*	Hindi, Urdu	Liar / Lie	
K	*Kāfir*	Urdu	Non-believer	
	Kabzā	Urdu	Custody	
	Kurtā	Hindi, Urdu	A loose cotton vested dress	
M	*Meher*	Urdu	assured alimony	a sum guaranteed in case of a divorce
	Mehmāan	Urdu	Guest	
	Mandi	Hindi and Urdu	Whole-sale Market	
	Mushāyara	Urdu	An assembly of poets	
N	*Namaste*	Hindi	Nama-Aste: I bow to the Divine in you, who exists in me too	used while welcoming or greeting a person
	Namāaz	Arabic, Urdu	Islamic prayer	

	WORD	LANGUAGE	MEANING	REMARK / INFORMATION
	Nav-Rātri	Hindi and Indian Languages	Nine-nights	The festival comes twice a year and the one in September is especially popular. It is dedicated to God Rama (Ram-Leela) and Goddess Shakti, and lasts nine nights
	Nikāhnāma	Urdu	Marriage certficate	
P	*Panchāyat*	Hindi	An assembly elected by villagers	Panchayat elections are held regularly across India, to cater to the needs of the villagers
	Panchānga	Sanskrit, Indian languages	Vedic Almanac	Panchānga is used to determine auspicious time, date etc. for any ritual or ceremony
	Pujā	Indian Languages	Rites performed during worship	
R	*Rajputānā*	Rajasthani, Hindi	Of the Rajput style	Rajputana was also a vast area in Rajasthan during English period. It was known for the Rajput kings and their chivalry

	WORD	LANGUAGE	MEANING	REMARK / INFORMATION
	Rām-Leelā	Hindi	An opera, usually poetic, performed on the challenges and life of God Rama	Is an annual opera last nine nights, culminating with the burning of giant effigies of the villains: Ravana, Kumbh-Karna and Meghnada, on the tenth day, celebrated as Dassera
S	*Salām*	Arabic, Urdu	Respectful greetings	
	Sarpanch	Hindi	Head of the Panchayat, elected by the members of Panchayat	also called the 'Mukhiya' in some areas
	Satyāgrah	Hindi	literal meaning: True Request	Mahatma Gandhi used to sit on 'fast unto death' till his demands or requests were accepted. This was popularly called 'Satyagrah'
	Shāyar	Urdu	Urdu poet	
	Sherbet	Hindi, Urdu, English	Flavoured, scented drink	
	Shloka	Sanskrit	Poetic couplets, quatrains from the scriptures	All come from the Sanskrit Hindu scriptures like the Vedas
T	*Teekā*	Hindi, Sanskrit	A vermillion powder applied on the forehead	applied always before any religious ceremony, and applied for good luck

	WORD	LANGUAGE	MEANING	REMARK / INFORMATION
U	*Ukku*	Telegu	Steel / Iron	
V	*Vikram-Samvat*	Sanskrit, Hindi	Hindu calendar	Vikram-Samvat precedes the Gregorain Calendar by 56.7 years
Y	*Yagnya*	Sanskrit, Hindi and Indian languages	A ceremonial religious offering to Gods/ Goddesses in a sacred fire with chanting of Shlokas	Every auspicious ceremony ends with a Yagnya
Z	*Zamindār*	Hindi, Urdu	A Landlord with vast estates	
	Zari	Urdu	extremely fine threads made from wires of gold or silver	traditionally used for weaving intricate wedding dresses